Chess with
the Doomsday Machine

Bibliotheca Iranica
Persian Fiction in Translation Series, No. 9

Chess with The Doomsday Machine

A NOVEL

Habib Ahmadzadeh

☙❧

Translated from the Persian by
Paul Sprachman

MAZDA PUBLISHERS, Inc. ◆ Costa Mesa, California ◆ 2008

Funding for the publication of this volume
was provided in part by a grant from
The A. K. Jabbari Trust

Mazda Publishers, Inc.
Academic publishers since 1980
P.O. Box 2603
Costa Mesa, California 92628 U.S.A.
www.mazdapub.com
A.K. Jabbari, Publisher

Library of Congress Cataloging-in-Publication Data

Ahmadzadeh, Habib, 1964-
[Shatranj ba mashin-i qiyamat. English]
Chess with the doomsday machine / by Habib Ahmadzadeh ; translated from
the Persian by Paul Sprachman.
p. cm. — (Persian fiction in translation series ; no. 9)

ISBN-13: 978-1-56859-215-2 (alk. paper)
ISBN-10: 1-56859-215-9

I. Sprachman, Paul. II. Title.
PK6562.1.H63S5313 2007
891'.5534—dc22
2007039549

CONTENTS

Translator's Introduction

Chess with the Doomsday Machine takes place some time early in the Iran-Iraq War and is based on the author's experiences as a Basiji (paramilitary volunteer), defending Abadan, the city where he was born. The island of Abadan is located in Khuzestan, an oil- and gas-rich province in southwestern Iran. Abadan, the city, is located high up on the neck of the electric guitar-shaped island (see map). The island, with its long riverine coastlines and its port on the Gulf, was an important strategic objective for the Iraqis; taking it would have greatly expanded their limited access to one of the world's most important waterways. The city was also a vital economic objective, because, before the Iraqi bombardment, it had been the site of the largest petrochemical complex in the world. Had Saddam Hussein been successful in capturing the Abadan complex and Khuzestan, he would have gained control over a great deal of the world's oil and natural gas reserves. On 22 September 1980, Iraqi forces attacked.

Mr. Ahmadzadeh's novel provides glimpses of life and death in a city under siege. Unlike the few works in English that treat the history of the Iran-Iraq War in detail (see Further Reading, below), it does not deal directly with the historical, geopolitical, or military consequences of the conflict. Rather, it is about three days in the life of a sixteen-year-old Basiji, who is a spotter for Iranian artillery and investigates the places where enemy shells land. We never learn the young man's name, but his code-name, Musa (Moses), accords with his role as the leader of a band of refugees from the fighting. Precocious and insatiably curious, the Basiji's military and street smarts are enough to make him a successful warrior; but his experience of life and understanding of human nature are, given his youth, understandably limited.

Two circumstances add to the young man's military burdens. First, after the driver of a food van is badly wounded, he is forced to swallow a great deal of juvenile pride and accept a demotion from artillery spotter to delivery boy. Second, the Iranians learn that the Iraqis have obtained an advanced radar system developed in the West (the Doomsday Machine of the title), which can fix with great precision the source of artillery fire. In addition to spotting for his own artillery, the young man must now find the enemy's radar, which no one on the Iranian side has ever seen. The new duties season the Basiji in several important ways. Not only responsible for supplying his comrades with hot meals, he must also feed—against his better judgment and military regulations—an odd assortment of civilians stranded in the besieged city. The former driver had adopted these poor souls out of the goodness of his heart, an organ that is not overly developed in the Basiji. At first outraged by the unauthorized generosity of his predecessor, the young spotter gradually takes responsibility for the welfare of the group and uses his military cunning to lead them to safety. The hunt for the Doomsday Machine also teaches him a valuable lesson in humility. At the most crucial point in the search, his eyes fail him—probably the worst thing that can happen to a spotter. As a result, he must rely on people, whom his instincts tell him not to trust, to act as his eyes during an operation designed to fool the radar.

Significance of the Novel

Chess with the Doomsday Machine represents a departure from a great deal of the Literature of Perseverance and the Art of Resistance (*adabiat-e paydari va honar-e moqavemat*), as creative work inspired by the Iran-Iraq War is often termed. Much of the Persian prose arising from the conflict is more biography or autobiography with predictable themes and tropes than fully realized works of fiction. The prevalence of reminiscence in this body of literature has prompted the literary critic Manuchehr Ateshi to write, "it is important for us not to mistake 'memoir writing' about the war years for 'the literature of war'" (Ahmadzadeh 2006: 115). I have read many examples of the memoir-type writing and have translated one of them into English—Ahmad Dehqan's *Journey to Heading 270 Degrees* (Costa Mesa, CA: Mazda Publishers, 2006). Naser, the main character of the book, is a Basiji, who, even before graduating from high school, has served at the front twice. The book chronicles the second time, when he takes part in one of the bloodiest battles of the

War. What lures Naser back to the front a second time, after having been wounded the first time he served, is not patriotism, but the irresistible tug of camaraderie. As many people who have endured basic training and fought together as young adults know, military service often forges lifelong bonds. For Naser and his comrades, war is the definitive communal experience. In effect, they grow up together in war; the eat, sleep, play, and pray together in war, and mourn together for comrades who fall (are "martyred" in the idiom of this literature) in war. War, for many of them, transcends the physical and becomes something akin to a spiritual experience, a metaphysical journey.

Another work that shows a soldier voluntarily returning to the front is *The Beloved War*, which is based on the memoirs of Sa'id Tajik (Tehran: Howzeh-ye Honari, 1999). After participating in a bloody battle for "Hill 1904," Tajik demobilizes. Although he is welcomed back warmly by his family and finds steady work as a house painter, Tajik realizes that life on the home front lacks the meaning and spirituality of life at the front. He breaks his leg in a car accident, and even though he doesn't seem fit for duty, Tajik cannot resist the pull of the front. He tears off his cast prematurely and returns to the fighting.

Much of the Literature of Perseverance reflects official Iranian attitudes toward the Iran-Iraq War. The Persian term for the conflict is "the imposed war" (*jang-e tahmili*). In other words, the War was a plot hatched by the West (US, Britain, former USSR, Israel) and carried out by a proxy, Saddam Hussein, to smother the Islamic Republic in its infancy. But the War was more than a global conspiracy in the Iranian view; it was also a religious cause, a Holy Defense (*Defa'-ye Moqaddas*). As Shiis, a minority in the Islamic world, the Iranians assumed the role that they have often played in history: that of the injured partisans of the first Imam and fourth Caliph Ali, the cousin and son-in-law of the Prophet Mohammad who was assassinated in 661. Many Iranians see themselves as victims with justice and history on their side, but little else. They are the innocents in the eternal battle between Truth and Falsehood (*jang-e haqq va batel*). The fact that the War was imposed on Iranians intensified a shared sense of being buffeted by forces beyond their control. It also strengthened an already negative view of the West, in general, and of the United States, in particular. Anti-Americanism is explicit in *We're the Children of Iran*, Davud Amiriyan (Tehran: Howzeh-ye Honari, 1999). The book draws on the author's own experiences as a recruit to describe the rigors of basic training— the food and the fasting, the endless exercises and drills, the prayers, etc. At one point in the training, the recruits shout of "Death to you, O America," while trampling the American flag (p. 103).

The Literature of Perseverance can become repetitive and cliché'd when referring to the Iraqi enemy. Hasan Rahimpur's *Life was Good* (Tehran: Howzeh-ye Honari, 1999), which is based on the author's service as a blood bank director in an army field hospital near the front. The book portrays Iraqi troops as inhumane and immoral. One of the narrator's informants about the War is Reza, a native of the town of Jahrom in southwest Iran, which the Iraqis occupied for a time. Reza tells him that, after liberating the town, Iranian soldiers discovered mass graves filled with the corpses of young girls, who had been raped by the occupiers (pp. 62, 131). The idea that Iraqi soldiers are corrupt comes to the fore in another soldier's anecdote about "unseemly" (i.e. pornographic) photographs and liquor bottles, which Iranian forces find in bunkers abandoned by their adversaries (p. 105). This bleak view of the enemy makes the contrast between victimized Iran and aggressor Iraq even starker.

Chess with the Doomsday Machine contains no tearful good-byes or happy homecomings. The Iraqis in the novel are not readers of *Playboy*, nor are they drinkers of Johnny Walker. America is not the Great Satan here. The book does dwell on the ravaging of Abadan; but its tour of the carnage, however revolting at times, is not meant to dehumanize the enemy; rather, it is part of the work's overall symbolic structure. While Ahmadzadeh's novel does show the effects of war on helpless civilians, its theme is not victimization. Just the opposite; free will is an article of faith in *Chess with the Doomsday Machine*. Qasem, the commander of the shore base, insists that humans have the freedom to act—they are not, as the Engineer tells the Basiji, pawns in a game they shall never win.

Another element that distinguishes *Chess with the Doomsday Machine* from many memoirs is the complexity of its three main characters. The Basiji, Geety, and the Engineer are complex amalgams of guilt and innocence, naivete and guile, and the sacred and the profane. As the story unfolds, these characters acquire traits that allow one to associate them with figures from the Jewish, Christian, and Muslim faith traditions, which are invoked in the novel's three epigraphs.

As mentioned above, during the second half of the novel, the young paramilitary's task of leading people out of the wilderness is suggested by his code-name. But, at the same time he is playing the role of Moses, he also impersonates another prophet that Christianity and Islam share: Jesus. The Basiji saves a small band of people and gathers them under one ravaged roof for a "simple supper." The Last Supper appears earlier in the book in the form of a painting hanging over the altar of the Armenian church. When the operation to fool the radar enters its most critical phase, the Jesus Basiji is betrayed twice (the book opens with an excerpt from the Gospel of Matthew referring to the betrayal of betrayals; later, Judas appears in the painting of The Last Supper): first by his vision and, second, by the young Armenian priest, who refuses the spotter's desperate plea to take the place of his treacherous eyes.

The main female character in *Chess with the Doomsday Machine*, Geety, is a former prostitute. She lives with her daughter, Mahtob, in a notorious quarter of Abadan that foreign sailors and members of the local gentry had frequented before the Islamic Revolution. As the most profane character in the book, she is Eve, the temptress, who is specifically mentioned in the epigraph from Genesis. A prostitute with a tragic past (a son lost to drugs; abused, robbed, and abandoned by the men in her life), Geety can also elicit readers' sympathy. In this guise, she is the Mary Magdalene whom Jesus healed. Although she clubs the Jesus Basiji's food van to pieces, shreds its upholstery, and curses his mother in the vilest ways, he detects a glimmer of humanity in Geety that is invisible to the Engineer, who has known her far longer. At the end of *Chess with the Doomsday Machine*, the Basiji, without knowing why, calls Geety "mother" instead of the incendiary "madam" that he unwittingly uses when they first meet. In her role as a loving, single parent, Geety now invites comparison to the Mary who mothered Jesus.

The Engineer is the darkest character in *Chess with the Doomsday Machine*. Life has made him a misanthropic recluse. His wife and daughters have left him. The oil refinery that he

"helped build" is turning to slag before his eyes. He lives alone
on the third floor of an abandoned, seven-story building, with a
troop of cats as his only companions. At first the relationship
between the Basiji and the Engineer is hostile. The boy resents
the old man because he must feed him; the unauthorized largesse
means that there will be less food for his comrades at the shore
base. He is outraged when he sees the Engineer give some of the
food to the cats. The Engineer dislikes the young man, because
he invades his home and robs him of his peace and quiet. To
impress the older man with his military resolve, the Basiji shoots
one of the Engineer's cactus plants. The Basiji brings the War to
the Engineer's sanctuary; in carrying out the plan to find and
fool the radar, he draws enemy Katyusha fire down on the
building.

The relationship between the Basiji and the Engineer changes
as they become better acquainted. Hostility and suspicion give
way to tolerance and trust. The older man satisfies the Basiji's
curiosity about several things: the connotations of the word
"madam," chess, Geety's tragic life. The Engineer shares with
the younger man his bitter personal history—how his family
abandoned him; the meager compensation he received for the
decades he spent as an engineer at the refinery. When they are
on the roof of the seven-story building for the last time, their encounter evolves into a seminar on interpreting scripture. The
Engineer asks: "Who was the first in the world to play politics?"
and "Why was Adam expelled from paradise?" The Basiji gives
what he thinks are unassailable answers, but the Engineer rejects
them, arguing that, in both cases, God is ultimately responsible.
This bleak reading of the role of God in human life leads to a
very pessimistic view of the War. He calls the Basiji and his
Iraqi adversaries pawns in a chess game with a predetermined
outcome. The Engineer tells him that his real enemy is not Saddam Hussein, but God Himself. This, in effect, renders the Basiji, his comrades, and the Iraqi enemy *mohareb ba khoda*, or "at
war with God," a high crime in the Islamic Republic. Here the
Engineer becomes the Basiji's evil mentor, nearly convincing
him that he and the Iraqis have no freedom of action, that their
sacrifices are futile. The old man's pessimism is the opposite of
what the Basiji hears from Qasem, his good mentor's. Qasem,
the commander of the shore base, praises the young man's curi-

osity and enthusiasm, and appears at the end of the novel to console him and to make the novel's case for free will.

From what had been said, readers can conclude that a lot takes place in and on the seven-story building. Clearly, it is more than a just a building. Because it towers over the surrounding structures, it is the ideal place for spotting the Doomsday Machine. All the refugees from the War—Geety and her daughter, the two priests, the parents of a comrade, Javad, who was killed before the novel begins, and the Engineer and his cats—gather there for a last supper. "Seven" is not an accident. According to the Qoran (65: 12), there are "seven firmaments and of the earth a similar number." When the Basiji first visits the roof of the building, he notices pieces of rebar jutting out from it and wonders whether the builders had intended to add an eighth story.

The architecture of the building lends itself to a metaphysical hierarchy; the higher one climbs, the closer one gets to perfection. This explains why the nihilistic Engineer lives on the third floor. He does not want to climb higher, to reach the roof and build an eighth story. Lacking the ability to understand the Qoran metaphorically, as the Basiji's good mentor does, the Engineer, despite all his life experience, remains naïve about scripture. He literally believes that the Basiji's comrades want to be martyred so that they can go to the other side and carry out a plan to blow up the Bridge to Eternity.

Further Reading/Viewing

The most useful day-to-day history of the Iran-Iraq War is Edgar O'Ballance's *The Gulf War* (London: Brassey's Defence Publishers, 1988). Though it was published before the War was over, it contains both sides' versions of what happened, as well as information from US intelligence sources. It also provides helpful maps. Another general study of the War is Dilip Hiro's *The Longest War: The Iran-Iraq Military Conflict* (New York: Routledge, 1991). A study of the Iraqi Abadan campaign is Michael E. Hoffpauir's MA thesis *Tactical Evolution in the Iraqi Army: The Abadan Island and Fish Lake Campaigns of the Iran-Iraq War* (US Army Command and General Staff College, 1991). The most comprehensive survey of Abadan in the War is in Persian, and, as far as I know, has yet to be translated: *Abadan dar Jang* [Abadan in the War] (Tehran: Markaz-e Motale'at va Tahqiqat-e Jang-e Sepah-e Pasdaran-e Enqelab-e Islami [Guardians of the Eslamic Revolution's Center for the Study and Research on the War], 2003).

Almost all of the books on the War in European languages I read focus on its strategic implications for the region and for the world powers. A good example is Stephen Pelletiere's *The Iran-Iraq War: Chaos in a Vacuum* (New York: Praeger, 1992). A work that explores the political dynamics of the War in Iran and Iraq is W. Thom Workman's *The Social Origins of the Iran-Iraq War* (Boulder: Lynne Rienner, 1994). Mark Phythian studies the sources of weaponry used in the War in *Arming Iraq: How the U.S. and Britain Secretly Built Saddam's War Machine* (Boston: Northeastern, 1997). Among the few writings in English that use original source materials from the Iranian side is Farideh Farhi's "The Antinomies of Iran's War Generation," which was published in *Iran, Iraq, and the Legacies of War*, ed. Lawrence G. Potter and Gary G. Sick (NewYork: Palgrave Macmillan, 2004, 102-20). In Persian there seem to be countless works of fiction and non-fiction that deal with the War.

To prepare the translation of Habib Ahmadzadeh's book, I have read several interviews with the author that are available in Persian on the web, including:

http://www.hamshahrionline.ir/News/?id=24395
http://kayhannews.ir/860305/9.htm
http://www.motalebe.ir/index.php?action=show_news&news_id=1792
http://www.sharghnewspaper.com/850329/html/litera.htm

I have also read the author's acclaimed collection of short stories "The War Involved City Stories (*Dastan-ha-ye Shahr-e Jangi*, Tehran: Sureh-ye Mehr, 2006). "Thirty-nine and One Prisoners" (*Si-o Noh-o Yak Asir*), a story from that collection, is the basis for the excellent film *Night Bus* (*Autobus-e Shab*; Kiumars-e Pourahmad, 2007). The relationship between the driver of the bus (called *amu* or "uncle") and the young Basiji (called *bachcheh* or "the kid") resembles the relationship between the Engineer and the Basiji in *Chess with the Doomsday Machine*. There are other similarities between the novel and this collection.

First, in "The Wing of the Eagle (*Par-e 'Oqab*, p. 14), the narrator says that his mother is reciting the Throne Verse, in the hope that God will protect her son at the front. Second, in the same story (pp. 20-21), one character says about the Iranian soldiers, "We never learned how to fight anywhere, except during the last several past months, and, if it hadn't been for this War, we'd be in class in this same city, busy studying."

In Iran there have also been seminars and conferences on the growing body of War fiction. These have led to such critical works as Reza Rahgozar's *Nim Negah beh Hasht Sal Qesseh-ye Jang* (["A Partial Look at Eight Years of War Stories], Tehran: Howzeh-ye Honari, 1370/1991).

Finally, there is a curious way—albeit quite accidental—in which *Chess with the Doomsday Machine* echoes the great John Frankenheimer film *The Manchurian Candidate* (the 1962 original). In one memorable scene, Frankenheimer has one character shoot another through a carton of milk, thereby associating murder with one of the most innocent of foods, essential to children's growth. This scene is not in Richard Condon's book (NY: Pocket Star Books, 2004, p. 321). In *Chess with the Doomsday Machine*, Ahmadzadeh associates another blameless food of childhood, ice cream, with death.

Transliteration

Common pronunciation rather than consistency and scholarly rigor has guided how Persian names appear in the translation. So, Parveez rhymes with "car sneeze," Ameer with "a mere," and Geety with "meaty." The Iraqi dictator appears in his conventional form, Saddam Hussein, in the introduction, but the Shiite Imam is Hossein in the text.

A Note on the Text

This translation is based on the spring 1385 (2006) edition. Readers of the original will notice, however, that there are a few differences between it and the translation. This is because the author has subtracted and added to the text in the following ways:

1. two paragraphs added to page 225;

2. one paragraph added and one line subtracted on page 256;

3. one paragraph added to page 257; and

4. "French Cymbeline radar system" has been changed to "Western Cymbeline radar system."

Abadan Island

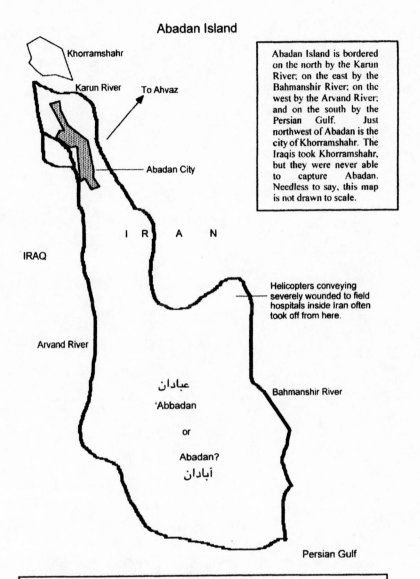

Khorramshahr

Karun River

To Ahvaz

Abadan City

Abadan Island is bordered on the north by the Karun River; on the east by the Bahmanshir River; on the west by the Arvand River; and on the south by the Persian Gulf. Just northwest of Abadan is the city of Khorramshahr. The Iraqis took Khorramshahr, but they were never able to capture Abadan. Needless to say, this map is not drawn to scale.

I R A N

IRAQ

Helicopters conveying severely wounded to field hospitals inside Iran often took off from here.

Arvand River

عبادان

'Abbadan

or

Abadan?

أبادان

Bahmanshir River

Persian Gulf

Iran and Iraq, which share the Arabic alphabet, have also warred over the way Abadan is written. Iraqis sometimes spell it 'Abbadan (with *'ayn* and double *b*), which derives from Arabic *'abbad* or "believer." Most Persian-users, however, favor Abadan (no *'ayn*, single *b*), in which case it derives from Persian *ab* ("water") and *pa* ("watch" or "guard"). See *Encyclopedia Iranica*, s.v. Abadan.

Chess with
the Doomsday Machine

Then she (the woman) took of the tree's fruit and ate.
And she also gave some to her husband, and he ate.
Then the eyes of both were opened, and they knew that they were naked.
Then the Lord God said, "Behold, the man has become like one of us,
knowing good and evil; and now, lest he put forth his hand and take
also of the tree of life, and eat and live for ever."
Therefore the Lord God sent him forth from the Garden of Eden,
to till the ground from which he was taken.
He drove out the man; and at the east of the Garden of Eden he placed
the cherubim, and a flaming sword, which turned every way, to guard
the way to the tree of life.

Torah (Genesis 3:6-22 [passim])

When it was evening
he sat at table with the twelve disciples;
and as they were eating, he said,
"Truly, I say to you, one of you will betray me...
He who has dipped his hand in the dish with me..."
Then Jesus said to them,
"You will all fall away because of me this night;
for it is written, "God will strike the shepherd and the sheep of the flock
will be scattered."
Peter declared to him,
"Though they all fall away because of you, I will never fall away."
Jesus said to him,
"Truly, I say to you, this very night,
before the cock crows,
you will deny me three times."

Matthew (26:20-34 [passim])

When the shining sun darkens.
When the stars fall, losing their luster;
When the mountains vanish;
When the wild beasts are herded together for judgment day;
When the oceans boil over with a swell;
When the female infant buried alive is questioned—
"For what crime have you been killed?"...
When the scrolls of deeds are laid open;

When the Blazing Fire is kindled to fierce heat;
And when the Garden is brought near,
Then shall each soul know what it has prepared for himself.

Holy Qoran 81(The Folding Up:1-14)

TOP SECRET

11-2-1980

To: All units stationed in areas surrounded by enemy forces in Abadan and Khorramshahr.
From: Southern District Central Command.
Re: Radar emplacements.

According to recently received intelligence, the enemy has positioned a unit of the European-made Cymbeline radar system in the above-mentioned operational areas. Therefore any information relative to the location of said system should be reported forthwith to Command so that...

When the army typist was pounding out this directive, filling the page with one black letter after another, he probably never guessed what kind of a storm the message would unleash a few days later—how it would turn our lives and the war upside down!

1

"Okay? ... Okay? ... Only four days!" Parveez said.

The cheerless glare from the refinery blaze fell on the face, making the look in his artificial eye seem even more startled.

This was the second time I couldn't sleep. The first time was when the large storage tank burst into flames, waking me up. They finally found the target, causing a fiery mushroom of a million liters of jet fuel to shoot into the air. As I lay stretched out on the roof of the concrete shelter, I felt the heat of the explosion on my face, and its harsh glare made closing my eyes useless.

It was also the second time I had fallen asleep when I was target spotting. Parveez shook me awake with his hand. Nothing annoyed me more than not sleeping well at night. Qasem, the man in charge of the shore base, knew this and was always careful not to wake me.

"Did you catch anything?"

"Parveeeeeeeeez!...Couldn't you see I was asleep?

I sat up. A low brick wall ran around the roof preventing the enemy from seeing us. Sitting cross-legged behind me, he began to massage my shoulders.

"A seventeen-year-old man should be awake! Look over there. Did you sleep well?"

He was making fun of the time when Qasem said to me, "Bravo! You're becoming a man!"

But I said nothing. Lying up here from nightfall to now, how many of the enemy's artillery positions had I located?

The barrel of one of their guns would rise from the hundreds of earthworks beyond the date groves on the other side of the waterway and fire, and I, in the absolute quiet of the night, would study the horizon for the flash. As soon as my eyes

caught the faintest glint from the shot, I would start the stopwatch with my trigger finger and then train both ears on the
coming sound.

A few seconds later, when the sound came I would press the
stop button, then multiply the difference by 333 meters, the distance sound travels in one second, making its dreadful way from
the rim of the enemy's earthworks, through the date grove, over
the waterway that separated us, and finally reaching the sweep
hand of my stopwatch.

I would record the time in the leather-bound notebook I had
inherited from my father and, in the light of the next day, mark
the position of impact on a map of the city with pins.

"Why don't you answer me? I just caught two more. Bigger
than last time, friend!"

He stopped massaging me.

"Come on, let's look at them. I threw them into the barrel."

"Parveez! I want to sleep. I'll get up as soon as it's morning
and start target spotting again."

"All right then, shush!"

Despite this, he remained sitting right where he was.

What could he be thinking? Two more sharks!

At night when there was a lull in the fighting, he would drag
himself to the bank by crawling along the space between the
jetty and the giant cranes protecting the oil pipes that fanned out
from the refinery. The pipes, which were lower than the jetty but
higher than the surface of the water, offered cover from enemy
fire, a place where Parveez could sit merrily and fish.

In the beginning he would bait the hook with bits of dough
and wait for the fish to bite. But at the start of the war the waterway had filled with hungry sharks that, denied scraps of food
tossed from the ships, did not turn up their noses at the lumps of
bread. This was why he would always return with sharks on the
end of his hook instead of fish. Parveez justified the shark hunts
to himself by saying they helped the balance of nature in the
waterway.

The only problem was finding fishing line strong enough to
withstand the sharks' saw-like teeth. The answer came in the
form of thin cable that he found at the end of a used flare. This
cable was made of many fine wires at least half a meter in
length; he attached these to a special shark hook. The rest of the

line was composed of thick wharf rope, which he unwound and braided into three strands, like girls' pigtails.

So at the start of every evening, when the two sides grew tired of firing at each other, he would slip down into his hiding place and put bits of seasoned dough on the hook, making sure that a short-handled hammer was nearby. When he threw the baited hook into the water, the nearest shark, which had the dubious fortune of avoiding the certain death of the floating mines, and was attracted by the odor of the spicy bait, would bite down onto the hook.

The stragglers he hooked had no choice but to start grinding away on the wire with their teeth. They would begin to twist and turn, instinctively drawing on every ounce of strength to cut the cable, but to no practical effect. This was why they would begin to swim out to sea, not realizing that the fisherman's whole strategy depended on their retreat.

Parveez would allow the shark to play out the slack until it dragged the line to the middle of the waterway. Every once in a while he would yank violently on the line, driving the hook deeper into the creature's jaw, and then he would let it go slack again. After enduring this many times, the exhausted shark became resigned to its fate. Parveez would then pull it in; as soon as the creature's snout emerged from the water, it received several robust blows with the hammer. Then Parveez fished the stunned animal from the water.

What good was the shark to him then?

At first he would slit their bellies open, extract the liver, and rub it over his legs. He had heard that sharks' liver oil was good for muscle pain, even though his own legs never bothered him. Later on, another idea crossed his empty head. He filled a 60-gallon oil drum with seawater and dumped the bulky animals headfirst into it, calling it his "shark aquarium." The poor creatures would remain like that with their tails sticking out until they suffocated.

His sudden silence made me wonder what he was plotting for me. When he put his hand on my binoculars, I firmly planted my fist on it. He didn't cry out in pain, but quickly thrust his hand under his arm and just stared at me.

This was the second puzzling thing! Why didn't he show any reaction? I became more suspicious. Parveez was not the kind to hold back on these occasions, at least not with his mouth. He should have at least taken the binoculars and run away.

To my relief he retreated a bit. Maybe I could use the untimely insomnia to spot a few more of the damned enemy positions. Then, early that morning, I would go about the city looking for places where shells had landed, marking them on the map.

"I would like to go on leave," Parveez said suddenly.

What did his going on leave have to do with me? I looked through my binoculars. Far off, at the temporary division between horizon and sky, darkness had overtaken the date grove.

"Hey, I'm speaking to you! I want to go on leave."

"So, go! Who's stopping you?"

"You have to stay!"

"Where should I stay?"

"Bastard!" he screeched. "Stay here and take my place driving the food van!"

I lowered the binoculars slowly and looked him straight in the eye...so he would know there was no question what I was thinking.

"Okay, no problem. See you later!"

He rose and retreated to the edge of the roof, where he lowered himself down. I looked at him amazed. He didn't even put up a fight. Perhaps without my knowing it, there was an invisible hook in my jaw, and I only imagined that I was twisting and turning on my own. Maybe!

But in any case, I couldn't back down. It was ridiculous...he expected me to go from spotter to driver!

The sharp glare shone in my eyes. I tried to pull the blanket up over them, but it must have been caught on something. I opened my eyes. Qasem's shadow fell on my face.

"You fell asleep up there again, and time for Morning Prayer is over!"

I nodded my head and got halfway up, but he was gone by the time I managed to pry open my eyelids. I crawled to the edge of the roof and jumped down.

Emerging from the dark hallway, I noticed the one-wheeled metal tanker still in its old place, twisted and bent out of shape, its faucet leaking as usual. I turned the spigot. Some time ago pieces of shrapnel had punctured the tire, but Parveez still hadn't gotten around to retrieving it from the repair shop.

The chill of my ablution was beginning to revive me, when I heard the sound of two metal objects grating against each other. This was the kind of sound that made my hair stand on end. It was coming from the cement blocks that several days before had been sent from the shore base to create cover along the pier. The rebar used to thread the blocks together had not yet arrived, so they were stacked uselessly in a heap.

With only my feet and legs washed for prayer, I walked toward the blocks, where Qasem stood by himself, digging rice out of a large cooking pot with a metal skimmer. As soon as he saw me, he turned his back. I should have finished my prayers.

I returned to the shore base and entered the hallway. One side of it had been hit by Katyusha fire, and we were using the undamaged side. In the darkness I made out the ghost of my old dune bike. The blackness of its frame was even blacker than the hallway. After shrapnel had destroyed my brother's personal motorcycle, Ameer had given me this one.

I regretted not having brought the old motorcycle into the shelter...

Inside the room the sandbags were piled so high that, though the lamp was lit, I had to grope around in the dark to find my prayer mat. The green mat was beside a blanket lying under the head of one of the boys—which one, I couldn't tell. I was extremely careful not to step on their legs as they were stretched out one after another, still sound asleep from night duty.

As soon as I stood up in prayer, I sensed someone behind me; afterwards while I was bent down prostrate, I thought I heard footsteps...

When I opened my olive green kit, I found everything there: compass; stopwatch; two ballpoint pens taped together, one blue the other red; wooden ruler; leather-bound notebook; and map of the city in its nylon cover.

I was lacing my boots when again I sensed someone lurking nearby. I raised my head but saw no one. I stood up and put my head through the strap of the bag. The radio set was leaning on its side, as if begging to be brought along. But its battery had run down, and, until a new one could be found, it would have to stay put.

So! What was the order of the day? To locate where the enemy's shells had landed the night before.

One of them, now smoldering, was the shell that started the huge blaze at the refinery, its shrapnel melted by the flames.

I took the motorcycle by the handlebars and hit the kickstand with the back of my foot. The whole weight of the machine was now on me. It was hard to push it, but these were the only moments that my old friend depended on me for support—like some invalid leaning on a comrade.

I went through the gate and entered the compound. To the left, Parveez was loading empty rice cauldrons onto the van. He glanced at me, and then quickly got back to work.

Four days' leave; he must have been dreaming!

I connected the wires dangling from the handlebar and mounted the bike. Parveez got behind the wheel of his van. I brought my foot down hard on the crank. Naturally, the bike wouldn't start on the first try. Nor the second. Nor the third. Not even the fourth. Parveez's van, however, started instantly. We looked at each other again, but this time I was the first to look away.

Once more I tried to start the motorcycle, but I knew it was no use. I felt Parveez's malicious stare on the back of my neck. He never once had brought a square meal to the boys at the base with that grease wagon of his.

People said, "He found some people in town down on their luck and fed them first. He even supplied them with fuel and water, turning the chow truck into a civilian aid cart!"

Qasem once instructed him to tell those people to go to the mosque for food. Parveez told him, "They don't belong to the mosque!"

No one had ever seen these people. We only heard about a "bunch of old men and women" from him.

The wind plastered my hair back on my head and the biting cold made my eyes tear. I was in the back of the van, struggling to keep myself and the bike balanced among the large rice cauldrons. With Parveez driving on a road pockmarked by enemy shells and mortar rounds, it was like running an obstacle course.

Both sides of the road were littered with broken telephone poles and power lines. I could make out the potholes in the road ahead from my vantage point above the mud-smeared cab of the van. "Careful!" I shouted.

But Parveez would perversely aim for the holes, alternately veering right and left, and the van—despite the load of cauldrons, the motorcycle, and me—bucked up and down. I had to swallow my rage and endure the ride.

When the motorcycle wouldn't start, I had no choice but to beg Parveez to bring it to the repair shop with the van. To my amazement he agreed immediately and loaded it onto his so-called food wagon. In the past I'd had to threaten to kill myself before he would agree to do anything like that.

At first, however, he scowled at me like a stern father confronting his sheepish son, who was begging forgiveness for some mischief. I said, "Look, if you don't want to help, don't!" But when I began walking the bike, he quickly agreed, "Come on, get in, don't be a baby!"

He found another crater, which sent the cauldrons flying. Being short, I had to brace myself against the side of the truck with my legs, trying to keep three empty plastic water pails, two ladles and skimmers, the motorcycle, and myself from flying around. I knew Parveez was doing it on purpose; he was grinning from ear to ear. But I had to take it until we reached the repair shop—just wait, I thought, until I get down...

Two alleys down the road was where we lived. If there had been no problem with the bike, I would have gotten out and stopped at our abandoned home.

A smack in the face from a dry branch reminded me of the scorching heat from the night before. I automatically rubbed the place where my cheek burned with my hand. I wished the blackout hadn't forced me to remove the mirror from the bike.

When the truck stopped, I felt like banging Parveez over the head with a ladle, but, just as the driver's door burst open with a few firm blows, there was the sound of shelling, and we both dived for cover. Losing my grip on the bike, I flew through the air, instinctively twisting my body. But my rib cage hit the side of the truck and I fell to the ground so hard that I couldn't even scream.

Parveez had merely dived to the ground. The explosion was a few meters away, in a place in the foundation of a residential building that had cracked open.

I got up feeling an unusual pain in my chest, unable to catch my breath. Though it had been a long time since I was deafened by the sound of an RPG, it was easy to tell that this was not the kind of round that usually went off in these parts. So what possessed me to dive out of the van like that? Perhaps because I was perched up there with the motorcycle and the belief—so strongly held that it had become an instinct—that the closer a person was to the ground, the less the light alloy shrapnel that sprayed into the air would have to do with him.

Parveez also got to his feet and, without thinking, hopped into the van. He pried the wretched motorcycle from the lid of a rice cauldron, and, using the kickstand, stood it up on the bed of the van. I thought that if I'd had a rope, it would have been easy to keep the bike that way, sparing it the wicked bucking up and down.

Parveez was staring at the cauldron with a strange look on his face.

"Look! The handlebar smashed in the lid!"

I looked at it. There was a small dent punctuated by a shiny spot where the two pieces of metal had scraped together. I prayed that the hand clutch was still working. When it rained it poured. That was all I needed: no starter and a bad clutch!

The motorcycle's failure to start was nothing out of the ordinary. From the time the town had been surrounded, Operations had been forced to mix benzene with the gasoline for transport vehicles. This was probably what had killed the motor.

The clutch was fine. My ribs ached, however, and I felt that the place where the branch smacked me had become more swollen.

Parveez was still fretting about the lid, as though it was his own hide that had been hurt.

My heart filled with rage, as I thought: The man is wicked through and through!

This was the third time since morning that he had brought me bad luck. The bike, the branch, and now the pain in my chest! Not to mention the lack of sleep from the night before!

Wasting no time, I got behind the wheel and slammed the door; but it would not close. Another try, this time with more force, and the door stayed shut. I watched the look of surprise and resignation on his face through the rearview mirror. I put my hand on the gearshift, feeling for the billiard ball with which Parveez had replaced the lost knob. From the time he had been given the food van by its original driver, Javad's father, the piece had been missing. Parveez had picked up the ball from one of the bombed billiard tables, bored a hole in it with a bayonet, and grafted it onto the shift.

I put the van in gear and Parveez, without complaining sat on the motorcycle, resting his feet on the bed of the van. His long legs kept the bike balanced easily. I felt like driving into every ditch I saw, but consoled myself with the hope that God would do something to the maniac.

My mind was concentrated on the van. I tried to focus on driving, but the distraction caused me to hit a pothole. The van shot upward and came down quickly. I felt that except for me, everything—the pots, the ladles, the bike and, least of all, Parveez—had flown into the air. He looked at me in the mirror. I told myself that this was payback. With a shrug of my shoulders, I showed my indifference, knowing that he could do nothing about it, and continued on my way.

The road took us through the only half-functioning bazaar in town. How lucky for me to be driving while Parveez was standing in the back where he would be the center of attention. The road was lined with broken-down shops that had been abandoned and now were occupied by local women selling odds and ends. What a racket they made, hawking a few bowls of buffalo milk yoghurt or some packages of greens. These poor creatures set out at the crack of dawn from villages on that same encircled island, to get a little food for the same children who, afraid of enemy shelling, would abandon them among the date groves at sunset when it was time to return. Where were their husbands, anyway?

I couldn't think about it, because there were more important things to think about. After I got the motorcycle fixed, I had to locate where the shell went off the night before and check that against the blast craters; then I had to visit the artillery bunker and see the distinguished, beloved Major, owner of that lovely jeep and coordinate with him the shelling of enemy mortar and artillery positions.

I never asked the Major his name, and he never deigned to offer it. Until our first meeting and that little fracas, I didn't even know his rank; perhaps this was the cause of the frostiness I sensed in the way he usually acted toward me.

I continued down the road until I reached the main crossroads, which before the war had always been packed with of all types of vehicles. On the left side stood a church and the mosque joined at the hip. One side of the white church faced the crossroads.

I slammed on the brakes and went into reverse. Parveez, who had struggled to maintain his balance, waved his arms as if to ask, "What the hell are you doing?" I pointed to the church's metal dome with the cross on top. He now understood why I had stopped. Next to a window on the second floor and far from the roof there were traces of a new blast that had dislodged the window frame. The blast had left soot on the white wall in a weird design that looked just like a flower.

There had always been something odd about that church. Since the time I was a child, I had wondered why the mosque and church were attached to each other like that. Why wasn't there any space between them?

We began to move again.

As we turned the corner, the sound of Parveez's boots scraping against the side of the van interrupted my thoughts. Now he was pointing at something. The front gate was open and inside the church compound you could see a man dressed in black. At first it looked like he was wearing pants and a jacket, but later I realized he was dressed like a priest. Parveez and I looked at one another, stunned. What was a priest doing in the war zone?

But this was none of my business. The important thing was the new shell that hit under the dome of the church. Some time before, a dud mortar round had penetrated the tiles in the compound, and the sappers, directing their prayers to the Prophet and his family, defused it.

If it were not for the motorcycle trouble, I could easily have climbed up there and determined the nature of the blast and the type of enemy ordnance. I floored the accelerator, and the roar of the exhaust got louder the faster we went. The mixture of benzene and gasoline did not agree with the motor at high speeds either, and the exhaust began to fart and fume. Impatience has always been a bad habit of mine; I imagine the day over before it has barely begun. Gunning the engine was a way of compensating for lost time.

But now I paid no attention to the potholes. The van jerked up and down with every bump in the road, and I even ignored the occasional unexploded bomb protruding from the asphalt. The only things on my mind were repairing the bike and getting on with the work I had to do and ridding myself of this vile grease wreck. Trapped in that van, I thought all it would take was just one screeching round for me to die a thousand deaths before escaping from the cab.

But now was not the time for such thoughts; I had to get to the repair shop as soon as possible.

I stopped when we reached the middle of the compound of a school that had been converted to a garage at the start of the war. Ambling toward the van was a young man in a crisp uniform that bore no resemblance to what the other mechanics were wearing. In a quiet voice, which in all the clamor of war was almost spellbinding to us, he said, "Brother! You can't park here. Please, put it under that scaffolding."

He pointed in the direction of some piping that held up a temporary shelter. I nodded and turned the wheel in that direction. We had barely entered the shelter when Parveez dropped down suddenly and flattened himself on the bed of the van. He may have been afraid of hitting his head on the low-hanging scaffold.

I put on the handbrake and jumped from the truck. Sandbags piled up waist-high lined both sides of the row of shelters that formed the garage's small repair area. The height of the bags seemed to be a warning: "Bend down in the event of an explosion to avoid the shrapnel!" So naturally, still clutching their wrenches, the mechanics would double up behind the bags and, when it was all over, go on with their work. The roof of the shelter was covered with metal sheets, but what wouldn't I have given for just a few inches of topsoil over them. The shells, as one would imagine, tended to rain down from high up in the sky.

Seeing me daydreaming, Parveez growled, "Son of a bitch! Come here and help, my back is killing me!"

The back gate was open and half the motorcycle was dangling in midair. After we had quickly wrestled both wheels to the ground, a fairly old mechanic appeared in the distance.

However much I tried, I couldn't recall his name. He nodded hello and then, looking uncertain, stood between Parveez and me.

"What's wrong with it?" he asked.

I wished he hadn't spoken, because it set Parveez off, "How should I know what's wrong? If I knew, I wouldn't have brought it here, would I?"

I wanted to shout at Parveez, "What the hell does it have to do with you? This is my bike!" But I saw the old mechanic slapping Parveez on the back. The bastard had friends everywhere!

I opened the passenger-side door of the van and saw the edge of a black duffel bag hanging from the seat. Parveez's liberty! But that was none of my business.

The return trip took us past the crossroads and the church, until we finally reached the mess tent. The shop, at least according to Parveez, had promised to repair the motorcycle by the next day. As soon as we left the compound, Parveez slapped me on the knee, saying "Four days, man—and you without wheels!"

"Tomorrow it'll be ready. Besides, you clod, I have my own work to do, and you have yours," I said.

"Wait a minute! This job of yours, roaming the streets on your bike from morning to night, forever looking at your compass, your stopwatch! For what? Locating enemy artillery? To hell with that! They're pouring shells on the city all day long like confetti. No one's ever seen you screw up. At least let me introduce you to some cash customers. It'll pep you up, you miserable sap!"

The best answer when this two-legged reptile tried to bite was silence; but he went on so long that the screws in his jaw were starting to loosen.

"One of them is an engineer; as soon as he sees you he'll ask a question. If you know the answer, fine! But if not, he just laughs and makes fun of you..."

Those were the cash customers, all right—meaning a bunch of people Parveez could make fun of. He was always late delivering lunches and dinners to the line, because he was busy mocking these "cash customers." Oddly, the boys were only too happy to give up part of their rations, thinking it was a good deed that would count in heaven. Delivered by Parveez, of all people!

He went on...

"If you agree, I'll let you in on a nice lookout spot."

He waited for the bait to take effect, but I ignored him and continued driving.

"Enough! God! Tell me what I can do for you—say something, at least. It's a perfectly decent place where you can stretch out and relax. I'm telling you, they'll serve you tea. It's different from being up on the roof at the base, where you have to crawl on your belly like a lizard."

Suddenly there were two loud thuds; the Major's artillery unit was firing from somewhere behind us. I put my hand over Parveez's mouth and pointed straight ahead, trying to get him to shut up.

I could never focus on my duties with him around. His entire world consisted of these four cash customers; nothing else mattered. Now I had to do everything and, on top of that, without a motorcycle. Of course, the Major soon would be on the radio beside his artillery, waiting for me to check in.

Okay, no matter. At least I fed a few people. Back to the mess to get a vehicle—go to the waterway. Maybe a launch would move tonight.

Parveez said, "You'd be better off helping the priests! Gathering up their belongings in their church, and taking them to the mouth of the river."

"Drop dead! You think I have nothing better to do than slave for the priests?"

There was a loud whomp coming from the enemy's artillery. I put my hand over Parveez's mouth again. He jammed on the brakes. Though my ears were still ringing with RPG fire, I was listening for the explosion. The sound didn't come. We looked at one another. It didn't go off.

The expected blast finally came, but from far away, in the vicinity of our own batteries. Did it mean that the enemy had already started counter-firing? That fast?

He continued, "You poor guy! Without me where would you've been, with that junky bike of yours?"

I said nothing.

"Okay, turn in the bike! Wait a few days for me to return from leave and I'll tell you what to do."

My silence annoyed him even more.

"I'm talking to you, Goddamn it! Answer me!"

I got a kick out of making him angry.

Near the crossroads I glanced at the open doorway of the church. This time there was a man there dressed in black carrying something under his arm. He was looking around absent-mindedly, apparently searching for an empty corner. Then he lifted his arm and poured the contents of a bucket onto the ground, raising a cloud of dust. He retreated a bit and then started brushing off his clothes with his hands. Then he looked up and saw us staring at him. Without thinking, I waved. He waved back in a peculiar way.

I began searching for my bag, but it was not around. I looked in the back of the van and saw that the green bag lying in the back under a boot. Parveez's boot! If the watch face or compass had been damaged, I would beat all notions of giving food to cash customers or going on leave out of him with a ladle.

"Where are you going? I wanted to..." he said.

I didn't hear the rest. I snatched up the bag and raced toward the church. The sound of the van door closing assured me he was following behind. It was surprising how far he had come with me today. It was definitely because of the food wagon.

I went around the large drainage ditch in front of the church and stared at the electric clock tower near it. The hands on the large white clockface had stopped at exactly five thirty-five, reminding me of the very way soldiers stand at inspection! How many more years would the clock stay stuck at inspection?

The hands of the clock marked the exact time when power went out in the city. I turned around to enter the church and walked to the priest. This was such an unexpected meeting that both of us stood there stunned. Then, we clumsily greeted each other nearly at the same time. After a moment passed in silence, I got down to work.

"Did that shell recently strike the building?" I asked.

"Yes. Last night," he said.

"Excuse me for not introducing myself. I am a Basiji, and my job is to deal with these things. I go around the city locating where enemy shells have landed and recording information about them."

He looked at me in silence, then uneasily fixed his eyes on something going on behind me. Parveez was coming toward us cradling a kalashnikov. Although I had been aware of the weapon he kept behind the driver's seat of the van, I never expected him to take it out at such a time.

I continued speaking to the priest, "Excuse me for asking, but when did you get here?"

"About two days ago, I think. Yes, two days. I came to clean out church property."

I said politely, "With your permission," and, without receiving it from him, I entered the church grounds, which were divided into two parts. On the left side was the small church area. The right side had been converted into a kind of classroom. Separating the two parts was a religious scene made of marble with a metal statue of Mary holding Christ in her hands. The scene was repeated scores of times in the background so that it looked like the infinite reflections in a barbershop mirror. Below the tableau was an inscription in a strange alphabet; the only thing I could make out was the Western date: 1915.

I turned around, and the priest went on sweeping the church compound. There was the sound of broken glass being gathered up. Parveez looked around warily and then walked slowly toward me. "Who's the guy?"

"Look, it's obvious! He's a priest. Why are you armed?"

"How is it obvious?" he asked. "He might be fifth column dressed like a priest to avoid suspicion."

All I could do was laugh. With that blazing intellect...

I said, "Not that this place is teeming with priests, so this one could get lost among them. Unless this is some kind of masquerade party?"

A masquerade is the only place where I could imagine this person—except in a church.

"Look! Look! The Holy Mother's been hit by shrapnel!"

Parveez was right. There was shrapnel exactly where her heart was. It was a familiar scene. Yes, the very one. The statue was just like a canvas painting they put up at our local Hoseyniyeh during Moharram. That one showed Imam Hoseyn cradling the infant Ali Asghar in one hand and pointing at Yazid's army with the other. The only difference was that Ali Asghar was in swaddling clothes, and in the place of faces there were shiny, full moons.

Absentmindedly, I felt the wound with my finger finding the patch where the metal was jagged.

"Can I be of service, gentlemen?" asked another priest, who was older than the first. This one had snow-white features and green eyes. His eyes were bloodshot. I extended my hand and said, "Hi!"

He answered and turned to Parveez, who clumsily juggled the weapon as he shook the priest's hand.

"I came to inspect where the shell hit up there," I said.

"You came to diffuse it? But I am sure that it has exploded."

"When did you arrive, sir?" I asked respectfully.

"Mr. Hovanes and I came by launch yesterday at noon. We wanted to look in on the church and, if possible, transfer the furniture and the books to Esfahan, where the Archbishopric is. I think it was around midnight when we heard the sound of the explosion. We had been sleeping and God was truly merciful. Is every night as terrifying as the last?"

"What's terrifying about it?" Parveez said thoughtlessly.

"The explosions! The blaze at the refinery! Anybody left in the city must be suffering terribly."

I looked down and didn't answer him. The previous night had been one of the quietest of the war. Before going to sleep, I had counted only 30 to 33 shells.

"With your permission, sir, I have work to do over there," I said and, without hesitating, opened my green bag and pulled out the compass, the map and the triangular ruler. Though I was certain that the blast site, owing to the acuteness of the angle, would not indicate the direction of the shell, I still wanted to make sure of a few things.

The first thing was the nature of the shell. I examined the ground. It had been swept clean, but in one corner of the wall I found a piece of shrapnel the size and diameter of a finger joint. This showed that the shell was probably a 120mm mortar round with a range of around six kilometers.

Speaking so that only I could hear him, Parveez said, "You know why they'd gone into the church? They must have been praying constantly and with the rope making the bell go ding dong, begging the Holy Father in heaven to stop the shelling!"

He winked at me. I turned away and rummaged through my bag for the Russian notebook. Paging through it, I found the list of shells recorded last night and ran my finger down it. There had been three shells from artillery positions to the left of the city...one with a heading of 3.220 degrees, a distance of 6,300 meters to the base by the pier. In the column marked "target," I wrote 'church or clock tower crossroads.'

The enemy probably had targeted the crossroads, because on some nights there was a stream of traffic there. This must have been truly terrifying to their own forward lines.

"You haven't found a larger piece of the shell?"

The older priest quickly called out the younger one, "Hovanes! Bring out that large piece for the gentlemen!"

Hovanes returned with the end part of a shell with eight fins attached to the missile body. One of the fins was bent badly. Even before Father Hovanes handed me the piece, I knew that I had been right about it.

"120mm Russian mortar!" said Parveez, always with his nose in everybody's business. One murderous glance from me was enough to convince him to get back into the van....

"So, now what are you going to do?" I didn't respond to the priest's question. Perhaps our friendliness made him expect that at that very moment we would redress the wrong done to his church.

"Nothing for now. All in good time," I said.

I shook hands with both of them and got the sense that they were disappointed that we were leaving. Maybe seeing two people familiar with the state of their city and its problems made them feel easier about being there. In any case, for us to stay longer was a waste of time...

2

The racket in the mess hall took our minds off the war. It was a strange sound made complete by the clatter of large rice cauldrons being dragged across the floor.

Javad's father, Parveez, and I managed to lift the cauldron and put it into the back of the van. Then we loaded the stew pot, which was full of potatoes and eggplant. Steam rose from it when I lifted the lid. I hadn't eaten a thing since the night before. The food made me think of Ameer back at the base.

After a good night's sleep, he had arranged a solitary breakfast, using his briefcase as a table. Now, of course, he would be lounging about, waiting for me to return to the city with the motorcycle.

One edge of the rich, golden-brown, burnt rice on the bottom was peeking out from the white rice. It was so mouth-watering I couldn't resist. I glanced at Javad's father. Reading my thoughts, he extracted a large hunk laced with oil with a skimmer and offered it to me.

I watched his movements as I ate. He was the one who consigned the truck to Parveez after Javad had been martyred. In the past, when the food van reached the shore base, the boys would come to see what was being served. On kabob days the twelve-man base swelled to thirty people; the rest of the time it was merely the normal group. Javad's father would just laugh and amiably dole out enough food for the number the boys told him. But, since he knew the figures, he never fell for Parveez's lies after the mad bastard took over the truck. Parveez even began arriving late: first a half hour, then an hour, and now two hours. On top of that the rations gradually got smaller, so small that one of the boys complained, "Don't tell me you've started selling our food!"

"Bah! We'd better get going. Are you dreaming?"

Parveez drove off again. We entered a narrow road lined with shallow ditches in which tall reeds four to six feet high were growing. Strewn over the ground were jagged pieces of electric poles, along with brick shards and broken branches. For once Parveez tried to maneuver the truck through asphalt, which was rutted in places and dirt-covered.

"Why are you going this way?" I asked.

"Shut up! I want to take you to the lookout spot that I told you about."

"I never said I wanted to!"

But that didn't matter; he was in the driver's seat, and whatever I said meant nothing.

"That's it!"

"Where?"

"Are you blind? Can't you see that tall building?"

I smirked. I had seen it before; it was that same half-built, seven-story building, which loomed above the two- and three-story houses around it. Begun before the revolution, it had remained half-finished. The electric company had been using the ground floor to store spools of cable and other equipment. But one Katyusha shell was enough to turn it into an inferno, and the heat and shock waves that rippled through the building drove it at least a meter into the ground. When Ameer and I had first begun learning the ABCs of target spotting, we thought of using what remained. Ameer went to inspect it, but reported that the stairways on the first two floors were ruined, making it difficult to move around. It was no surprise, then, that we began to use other buildings, which though not as tall, were closer to the water.

Now the great sage of the ration wagon thought he had come up with an original idea. My contempt was very upsetting to him.

He stopped in front of the building. Although it had no door or decoration and although the brickwork was in especially bad taste, compared to the surrounding structures, the building had a certain splendor. The window casings, at least up to the fifth floor, were aluminum; beyond that, there was no sign of window frames at all.

I looked the building up and down, and absentmindedly, started to count the stories. As I did when I was a child, I stopped at three. Had they been there before or not? In the last window on the third floor, were two flower pots with leafy plants—yes, cactus. But what were they doing there?

"You mean somebody's living here?" I asked Parveez.

"No more questions! Stay right there," he said and headed for the entrance, which stood between two burnt-out shops, which, without their doors, looked like two charred craters. I scratched my head, waiting for Parveez to return. The strange part of this business was that I was listening to him. Why?

Just to show him who was boss, I began walking away, but he soon emerged from the dark building with a food pot and a yellow, twenty-liter water jug. Now I just stood there unable to move a muscle. He went by me and in one motion deftly jumped into the back of the van. He lifted the lid from the large cauldron and shoveled rice to the top of the pot with a skimmer. He glanced at me slyly and then picked up a ladle. I couldn't take it any more and asked, "Who's up there? Well?"

Using a bizarre gesture to tell me to be quiet, he put one bent finger and the ladle on his lips and then scooped two heaping portions of stew full of the rich liquid and chunks of meat over the rice. Then he nimbly jumped down from the van.

"You forgot the water bottle!" I shouted.

"Tomorrow you'll fill it up with water and bring it here! Now follow me, fast."

I automatically fell in behind him. Using the light from outside, we negotiated the darkness, but it took several minutes for me to get used to the gloom. The walls were black with soot and instead of stones they had jerry-rigged stairs with loose bricks. As Ameer said, the whole building had settled about a meter. In the center there was a wooden ladder.

"He'll put the washed pots right here, and you will take them to the van, fill them, and place them right here. If he wants to talk, he'll call you from up there. Now I've got to bring you to him. Try not to have too much to do with him. He's one of those harmless cash customers."

"Who the hell are you talking about, you shit?"

"The Engineer, of course!"

I didn't have a chance to ask the next question, because there was an old man staring down at us from the third floor.

Even with a full pot of rice in his hands Parveez had no trouble scrambling up the ladder and reaching the third floor; but for me there was no pleasure in climbing the rickety thing, which shook because the legs were not firmly on the ground. After grabbing the edge of the floor and hoisting myself up, the first thing I saw was a large black-and-white cat and then I made out the shape of an elderly man sitting on a chair and Parveez standing next to him. There was also an old single bed with lead-colored springs and terribly rusted bars for a headboard. In a niche carved into the wall meant for décor or shelving, there was a heap of books and magazines. A kerosene-fueled samovar stood to the right of the bed; it was percolating and water was dripping from its spout into a cup.

Now that I was standing in front of him, I saw he was old but had a full head of hair, most of which was going grey; but what was really surprising was that he was clean-shaven. I absent-mindedly felt along my chin for the few hairs that had sprouted there.

"Well! Who is this now?" There was a commanding tone to his voice.

"Mr. Engineer, this friend of mine is also a cash customer. I won't be around for a couple of days, and I've arranged for him to bring you food."

"Just like that? Without testing him first?"

"No, Mr. Engineer! He will prove himself."

"Don't tell me you've let the cat out of the bag already, have you?"

Parveez was playing vizier to the old man's mad shah, leaving me speechless. Birdbrain Parveez with this feeble friend of his calls me "a cash customer"!

Something stirred in the corner. My God! I had been mistaken; there was not one cat but seven or eight milling around the bed. Lost in thought now, I didn't catch the end of Parveez's sentence. He grabbed my hand and pulled me toward the Engineer's chair. Over the constant droning in my ears, I heard Parveez mutter, "Kiss his hand! Kiss it!"

I smiled in spite of myself. The two of them were putting on quite a show! Parveez released my hand when we reached the chair.

"Well, are you prepared?" he asked.

"Prepared for what?"

Parveez interrupted, "Mr. Engineer, this friend of mine loves to argue. He is always debating with Mr. Qasem. He keeps the lamp on late into the night reading books. Put the question to him, and let's see if he's up to answering it."

"So, young man! I will ask you a fundamental question about life and the world. Give it some thought before you answer. Now sit down."

Parveez pushed down on my shoulder with his hand, and I sat without thinking but soon asked myself: Why should I sit? What kind of charade was this?

"Well, ready?"

"Yes, he's ready, Mr. Engineer, ask him."

It was amazing how well the fiend had synchronized his act with the stranger!

"Well then, what is the meaning of 'what'?"

"What?"

"What does 'what' mean?"

"Do you mean English 'what'?"

"No questions! Answer me! What does 'what' mean?"

"Well, 'what' in English is what we in Persian call _chi_."

"Why do you repeat the question? You only have to answer it!"

"Parveez walked over to the samovar and with a smile on his face poured himself some tea.

"Think! What is the meaning of 'what'?"

"Well, sir, you have my answer. If you mean what does English 'what' mean, then it's _chi_."

"Again he repeats the question! Twenty thousand educators formed a commission, worked day and night for a week, and were not able to answer it."

"You have my answer."

He placed a crooked finger on his lips the same way Parveez had done to silence me half an hour before.

"Quiet! Is this the friend that you praised for his superior qualities?"

Parveez finished his tea. After a second I came to myself and started to move away. The performance of these two lunatics was spellbinding. I thought: The pigeon-keeper should have matured during the time he stayed behind in the city looking after his birds. But it was clear that he hadn't—the shit! It was also clear that, during the several months of our acquaintance, assisting this deranged conjurer was no act. The two of them were serious, not performing for my benefit.

Suddenly I felt something brushing against my leg. A shiny black-and-white cat was licking my boot. Parveez took my hand.

"Mr. Engineer, forgive him. He screwed up! Come on, let's go, boy!" He was now guiding me to the ladder.

I heard whistling sounds and an explosion coming from nearby. The resulting shock wave made the building shudder the way one would expect; but the Engineer continued to lounge in his chair staring coldly at us. I dipped my head as if to say goodbye, and he moved his head in response. With Parveez in the lead we climbed down the ladder. My thoughts turned to revenge—if I were to trip him, the fall would at least break his leg. But he was too quick and had already reached the ladder on the next floor.

Once outside the building, I glanced up at the third floor and the two cactus plants in the window. While we were getting into the van, I noticed that my pigeon-raising friend was still grinning from ear to ear.

"Who was that?"

"Who do you mean? The Engineer? The Engineer!"

"The Engineer, of course, you turd! The madman who's so friendly with your esteemed self. Where did you dig him up? What's he doing living in this god-forsaken place? Answer me!"

"What's eating you? Oh, I see. You're upset because you couldn't answer the question?"

"You monster! Why did you call me a cash customer up there?"

"Okay, *both* of you are cash customers."

The van began to move. At the crossroads there were the signs of a new enemy shell: a charred crater and shrapnel embedded in the green marble of a two-story house. God knows how much the poor owner had spent on it before the war.

The protruding end of the shell marked the center of the still-smoking crater—six black tailfins.

"Stop!" I said. "At least I can take the measurements for this one today."

Without the slightest objection, he stopped the van. I prepared my bag and hung it from my shoulder, but the door handle wouldn't budge.

"Are you blind?" he asked.

I lifted the lock, opened the door, and slammed it shut. When he raised his hand to object, I ignored him. The whole day from morning until now had been a disaster: first the motorcycle problem; then having to be with this soul of refinement and intellect; and finally the what-is-what monster that Parveez called—God knows why—"engineer." Was the title hereditary?

I spread my bag directly over the mouth of the crater. In the distance there was the sound of a passing vehicle. I took out the compass and the notebook. The sound grew louder. I squatted on the ground and closed one eye exactly like a sharpshooter squinting through the crosshairs of a sight. Then I pointed the compass toward the embedded shell. Experience and the daily repetition of the task had taught me the best place to take the measurement. I lined up the compass, the shell and the midpoint of an imaginary upper arc suggested by the blast cavity. Through the glass, the compass read 3.420. I took the map from the bag. Parveez tapped me on the back.

"What the hell's eating you?"

I looked up and saw the Major's camouflaged jeep with the usual driver at the wheel. The Major sported the same metal helmet with the netting and the same mustache, which, time permitting, was either clean-shaven or bushy. I raised my hand but he hesitated before he stepped from the non-existent door of the jeep. Obviously he still had his doubts about how to deal with me. I stood still. After that first day and the whopping mistake I had made, he had been waiting for an excuse. He was at least thirty years older than I, and etiquette dictated that, as his junior, I shouldn't permit things between us to sour again.

"Hi! Please!" I said nodding civilly, which was enough to get him to remove his helmet.

"Hi, something very serious has come up. No matter how many times I radioed you, you didn't answer."

I glanced at Parveez. He stood there like a small boy with his hand on his chest.

"I have to go to the War Room. I will contact you later. Goodbye!"

The arrogance in his tone made me angry. He still thought of me as his own personal soldier. I had to say something to rattle his cage.

"Sir! If you need to get in touch, contact Ameer at the shore base."

He didn't expect this and sat there without saying a thing. The driver wasted no time in starting the jeep—its black, whip antenna began to jerk back and forth and the jeep drove off.

His silence meant that he was still mad about what happened the other day. Screw him!

"What's with him? Such a long face."

As if to spite the Major, I didn't answer. The food van drove off. Parveez began to whistle—the same tune he would hum at night at his post. The Major's jeep was on my mind. What a jeep! It was my dream to own that camouflaged beauty with its back antenna, the extra jerry can of fuel, and the shovel and axe at the driver's foot. But for the time being there was only that junky motorcycle.

Parveez started to turn the wheel, but I grabbed it with both hands. He stepped on the brakes.

"What's the matter with you?" he asked.

"Don't turn! Why are you going there?"

"There's another cash customer here, that's why, you sonova...! Are you going to let me get on with my job or not?"

I was of two minds again. I had been aware of the place since childhood—even passing by the nearby streets made my blood boil. Although after the revolution they had taken down the huge, iron gate and cleared out all the women, I hadn't once been in this district.

Parveez drove right into the compound. There were small, old-fashioned houses lined up, but in no particular order. I had the feeling that these houses and the small neighborhood had been built only for momentary pleasure. The buildings had no architecture—just four walls and large windows. The men who entered the area would stroll down the dead-end street, pick one of the houses and then....

I closed my eyes and unconsciously rubbed my right leg. Why, after all these years, did I remember where the gatekeeper had hit me with his stick? What had happened that summer afternoon still bothered me.

I had been in the park with my head in a book, and children my age were pulling up flowers and catching the goldfish in the reflecting pool with a net. Suddenly there were the shouts and screams of the children running away. I raised my head and saw the attendant coming toward me. Terrified by the look in his eyes, my first instinct was to escape also, but I trailed far behind the others. They raced on, easily clearing the iron fence around the park, while I tried to run with two heavy books under my arm. When I began to climb the fence, the books slipped out, and the muffled sound they made hitting the asphalt shot through my whole being. I stood stock still, and then turned quickly. These were books I had to have for school. The attendant and I stood a few feet apart with the books between us. I dove to the ground to get the books, but, before I could, the attendant had planted his foot on them.

"Hello there, cash customer!" Parveez shouted.

There were two empty pots in his hand. The wooden door of the house opposite us was half open, and a woman without a headscarf was visible in the doorway. I stared with my mouth open and the woman, whose grey hair put her between 45 and 50, ducked back into the house. I could have been wrong—it might be a man with long hair. Parveez was already on the van scooping food into the pots.

"*That* was a woman?" I asked.

He didn't answer. After filling the pots he bent down and took three slabs of bread—doughy from being wrapped too long—out of a red, plastic tablecloth and draped them over the pots.

"That was a woman?" I repeated.

He stopped, looking at me out of the corner of his good eye—or was it the artificial one? I could never tell which was which.

"No, it was a toad. Of course it was a woman!"

So I wasn't wrong—but what was a woman doing here? Especially in this neighborhood, in a city under siege? I racked my brains for an answer, thinking that she obviously has no one outside the city to stay with. But what about inside it—a son maybe? But if that were true, why was she here? In this foul place where, even when I was a boy, I had been able to sense the traces of rot and malice given off by the houses?

Parveez jumped from the van with the pots in his hands. The food was enough for one person, so the woman was definitely alone. The woman's arms emerged from the shadow and took the pots.

"Tonight my friend here will bring you supper—kabob, so there's no need for the stew pots," he said to her.

The door closed, and Parveez looked at me with the half smile that was perpetually on his lips. I said nothing, thinking that it was better not to argue. The end of all this running around the city was in sight. Soon I would be laughing at him and his cash customers, on my motorcycle and gone.

"Lost in thought, again? Let's drive on a bit; I need to feed you like I did these cash customers."

"No, go to the War Room!"

"What about feeding the boys?"

"Nice of you to remember! This is the first time you've mentioned them since we started traipsing all over the city, but let's see what's bothering the Major first."

"Fine, but only for five minutes. No going inside to have tea, or I'm gone, okay?"

A question had been plaguing me for several minutes now, and he was the only one who could answer it. Perhaps one of the only differences between us was that he could accept folks as they were; a person's past or his future meant nothing to him, while my curiosity about them was limitless, which got me into trouble.

"Why don't they get their food from the mosque?" I asked.

3

    . I looked up at the sky, thinking that if it rained, it would probably dampen the blaze at the refinery.

"Why don't they get their food from the mosque?"

"What! At it again? All you have to do is feed these poor creatures for three, four days, tops. Why are you asking so many questions? This is no time for such rubbish. Remember: tomorrow's ice cream day! ICE CREAM!"

He turned the wheel and the van jerked into motion. I should have kept my mouth shut and actually prevented all of today's miseries back at the base. But the sooner I left Parveez and got on with my own work, the sooner he'd be back by himself with his pots and ladles.

I glanced at the godforsaken neighborhood again. There was nothing I wanted more than to reach the end of that stinking alley and erase all memories of our imposed visit.

We reached the end where a large iron frame still stood without its gate, which they had removed after the revolution. Despite all the shrapnel hits—large and small—and the passage of time, I could still make out the dark blue of the frame. This is where the gatekeeper would sit and spring to attention as the well-heeled and familiar customers went by, but, later, would laugh to himself bitterly at their shows of respectability as they entered the lane strong and proud, striding ramrod-straight, and, after a few palpable ticks on the clock, left without a word, backs bowed under the weight of their exertions.

And then there was that railroad spike—so much larger than a regular nail—they used to hang up the sign announcing the business hours of the district. The letters were big enough for me to read the sign whenever I passed by in a bus or car after that first fateful afternoon:

7AM to 2PM—4PM to 10PM

Seven in the morning, exactly the same time that the second blast of the horn signaled the beginning of the workday for the refinery workers. And only two hours' rest for the women...

What would *they* do during those two hours? Naturally they would eat lunch, which would take half an hour. Then what? Would they nap until it was time for the next customer? Or would they think about how they deceived them with their love? Or about the children they would have to raise? They would probably wash for prayer, unroll their mats next to the grimy, floor cushions where they entertained and throw white veils—all with the same floral pattern—over their heads and weep and weep as they bent their heads in prostration—until the creak of the ancient hour hand would sound the stroke of four, telling them it was time to get back to work and the gatekeeper would again be on the lookout for customers.

I thought: Yes, like me, he was just a lookout...!

Suddenly I heard the sound of a shell. The frame of the gate disappeared in a cloud of white smoke and splinters of glass began to dance toward my eyes and, last, the terrifying explosion came without warning.

As I dove to the floor of the cab, I felt a warm liquid on my face, then the sudden weight of a heavy object, which despite having my eyes closed, I knew was Parveez, and then the van may have lurched, causing me to bend even more. There was the strangest ringing sound in my ears, but this meant absolutely nothing. I had to try to pry Parveez off of me somehow, but there was something in the way. I freed my hands and arched my back. He wouldn't budge. "Parveez! Parveez, answer me!"

There was no answer. I couldn't see, so I wiped my eyes with the back of my hand. My face was bathed in blood, and now it was all over my hands. Parveez's body was wedged between the steering wheel and my back, and I tried with all my might to turn it but the body—now twice as heavy—prevented me. I reached up and latched onto the edge of the cab, and tried to move the wheel again.

I managed to pull myself out from under Parveez's body, then quickly turned around to look at him. There was no sign of that crab-like powder burn on his face. I ran my hand over his jaw and felt warm blood on the left side. Shrapnel had smashed through his teeth and emerged from a wound on the right side of his face, which was now spurting the blood that I had mistaken for my own.

His eyes were shut tight and his head seemed wobbly on his neck. Suddenly I noticed the white, creamy foam covering his lips. His teeth had been honed into jagged shards and he didn't seem to be breathing. I forced his jaws open with my fingers, pushing them through the foam to keep the mouth open, and with his newly sharpened front teeth digging deeper and deeper into my knuckles, I felt a feeble rush of air on my fingers. He was still alive!

The next step was to stop the bleeding. How? I looked around for someone to help. But that was futile. With scores of shells—large and small—landing all the time, there was rarely anyone about—no one even paid attention anymore to see which part of the city had been hit. I had to do something about the teeth and the bleeding.

I had an idea. There was a cardboard Basiji ID card laminated in thick plastic in my shirt pocket. I took it out and jabbed it between my fingers and his palate; but that left the problem of the bleeding. I kicked open the door and jumped out of the cab. The van and the ground around it were covered in a layer of dust and debris from the explosion. I circled the vehicle to reach the driver's side, and putting both hands on the handle, yanked it open. This time the battered door offered no resistance. After placing my arms under Parveez's shoulders, I pulled him from the van.

Now I had to lay him out in the back. How heavy he was! Still I managed to get him behind the cab and his body slid onto the bread cloth, which made me worry for a moment about blood seeping onto the bread. I quickly pulled the cloth out from under his ribs, but it was too late, so I threw it over the stew pot.

"Is he dead...? Do you need help?" said a fairly husky voice. I turned around to see a woman standing a few yards away. It was probably the same woman.

"No, just some cloth or a blanket to tie around his waist."

She came nearer and looked inside the van as though to assure herself. Then she retreated a few steps and put her hand on her Arab headcloth and with one quick motion removed it, allowing waves of black and white hair to fall over her shoulders. I stood there gaping.

"Take it. Didn't you say you needed some cloth?" she asked.

Without thinking, I grabbed the veil as it dangled from her hand. She had given me what was, in her view, the best and closest thing she had. I tied it around Parveez's waist and jumped down from the back of the van and got behind the wheel. When I started the van, it automatically jerked forward. It had been in gear when the shell hit. As I tried to put it into neutral I thought about other pieces of shrapnel that may have missed the doors and windows and struck the radiator or even the motor. What if the cooling system was shot? Or even the oil pan? Or the gas tank?

The van climbed up the inner curb and down the other side of the walkway. I knew I had to get out of that place as soon as I could.

The half-shattered rearview mirror showed the woman standing there without her veil, receding farther and farther into the distance. What a weird day!

That was how I went from being a spotter working to wipe out enemy artillery to driving the food van Parveez left behind.

4

Behind the wheel again, I was thinking about the last thing Parveez said to me: "You'll feed them for three or four days, and tomorrow's ice cream day. Ice cream!"

I sighed. This had been an odd day, and I still had not come to terms with my new situation—from determining the angle of ascent and being an artillery spotter to.... I pounded the wheel in frustration.

If only I hadn't gotten into this heap and become friendly with the stubborn ass, who was now lying in an ambulance with several tubes coming out of him, I wouldn't have swallowed his bullshit and....

But it was all over; the change was made and there was nothing I could do about it. Driving a food truck! If Asadollah, with that bushy beard of his, standing behind his artillery could see me now: one of his spotters doling out food. What a horrible picture!

I can just imagine it: I climb to the watchtower and bark out instructions as usual, "Listen! One hundred right, twenty down. Do you read me?"—then, Asadollah rocking with laughter and saying, "Mind your own vegetables, chef! What's for lunch? Stewed eggplant?"

I couldn't take that. I had to find a way of escaping from this pile of junk. How?

Why hadn't I thought of him before? Sure, good old Javad's father! The very person! There had to be a way to maneuver him into thinking it was *his* obligation to start driving the truck again. Of course, since the day Javad had been killed in that curious way, his mind had been elsewhere, but still...

There had to be a solution. Tomorrow I'd definitely pick up the motorcycle from the repair place and then get on with my work.

Screw the cash customers! Why couldn't the Engineer with the cats eat at the mosque just like everybody else? Half the boys' rations had been wasted on them already. Or take that loony woman—I asked her to go find some cloth and she pulls her headscarf off—just like that! As if she were waiting for an excuse. O Parveez, you son of a ...! Serves you right—instead of going on leave, you've got three big slugs in your jaw, so you'll never trap me again. My curses actually worked.

I started driving toward the shore base to deliver the boys their meals, but then I thought: What about the War Room?

I parked on a lane behind the city's main bank, which the military had converted to a War Room. Several barrels full of garbage that no one had bothered emptying—not even the soldiers—blocked the lane, and two stray dogs were warily rutting through them. One, a large black dog, raced away as I pulled up. The other, a grey mutt, merely lifted its head from a trash bag and watched me. After I got out of the van, I fixed my stare on the dog's eyes, but it didn't react—just kept looking at me. I made my eyes wider hoping to scare it away, but it didn't. Ordinarily I would have kept the game up for maybe half an hour.

The noonday sun still reigned over the asphalt. I raised my hand as if to hit the dog, but it wouldn't budge, paying absolutely no attention. As I walked away I turned in its direction, but what was the use.

Standing in the small sentry box was a guard holding a rifle with a bayonet and wearing a steel helmet. Completely surrounding his box, except for a small opening for the entrance, was a wall of sandbags. The bags would only neutralize shrapnel from remote hits; but if a light shell were to land a few meters away, the shrapnel could easily penetrate the box and the walls of the War Room.

Contrary to his usual practice, the guard did not accompany me inside; his stare was my only escort as I entered the building. Bank posters still hung on the walls, and as I walked through the corridor to the lobby, I read: "Open a revolving account and your money will always be in your pocket!" and "Prosperity means looking ahead—guarantee your future with a savings account."

In the lobby, workers stood in pairs around a long counter on which they had placed a huge map of the operations sector. The map was covered with a slab of thick glass inscribed with colored markers—blue for us, red for them. Even at that distance I could see that there was very little white between the two lines and that the red had the city surrounded!

The Major and several other officers were leaning over the map. Lounging in a chair was another officer holding a steaming cup of tea. One of the officers had two plump stars on his shoulder—shiny like Major's. That disagreeable encounter with him had taught me not to call out to low-ranking officers and that the more stars a man had the higher his rank.

I took a deep breath and said, "Major, sir!"

They turned to look at me with odd expressions on their faces. The Major, now seeming irritated, showed them something on the map, then came out from behind the counter and walked to me. When he was a few feet away, he stopped and invited me to sit in one of the metal folding chairs they had for observers.

When we were both seated, I stared into his eyes, but he wasn't looking at my face. Following his gaze, I understood the reason for the odd stares. My clothes were covered in dried blood—Parveez's. I felt I had to explain.

"After you left, that driver, who was with me, was hit by shrapnel."

"So it's obvious that he's lost a lot of blood. I hope to God it isn't serious."

I wanted to say, no, his intestines were only perforated and he's hooked up to two plasma bags and there are four catheters emptying fluid from his stomach..., but all I could say was, "No, the doctor said that now..."

"Major Fahimi," someone from behind the counter (the officer with the extra star) called him.

"Pardon me," the Major said. He stood quickly and walked over to the officer. I looked up at the fluorescent bulbs, which got their power from a generator and bathed the entire area in bright light. Then I remembered the boys, who were still hungry, waiting for Parveez and the food truck. The longer the conversation between the Major and the officer dragged on, the less I wanted to wait around. I thought: Come on, man, get on with it! Did your Excellency have something he wanted to say to me? Get it over with!

Without thinking, I nudged the leg of the low table in front of me with my foot.

The Major returned and sat down again. He said, "It's better that we get right to the matter. My dear brother, during the last several days, when you've been target spotting on that side of the waterway, have you witnessed anything strange?"

"Like what?" I asked.

He didn't answer and remained silent for a while. I was a little curious. On the other side of the waterway for three kilometers there were date groves in which the enemy had hidden their artillery. Also on that side was the Faw-Basra road and, beyond that, a flat stretch of desert that would sometimes mushroom up when hit by shells. Just two months ago, we had presented the Major with an operations report containing a thorough account of the fortifications on the other side. What could we have missed?

"So..." again he stopped and I made a movement with my head indicating I didn't understand. He realized that he needed to be more candid.

"Two days ago our artillery came under fire."

That was not news; our batteries were always taking return fire from the enemy.

"I know what you're thinking," he said, "but this time the matter is much more serious. Early in the morning two days ago, we retaliated after one of their attacks. Not more than a minute passed, however, when an enemy shell hit the very earthwork where our countering artillery was dug in. Luckily the gunners had left the area. I barred them myself from shelling any more. Yesterday around noon, we began responding to their fire...and you can guess the rest."

"Again they hit our guns!"

"Not the guns, but a shell landed, exploding exactly at the foot of the earthwork where the very unit that had responded to

their fire was housed. One serviceman was severely wounded—
it's unclear whether he'll survive."

This was getting interesting. Every artillery unit had at least
six batteries lined up behind one berm. The units were spaced at
odd intervals and placed at various angles. In the past, enemy
fire would come close to our emplacements, land in a date grove,
or hit the odd mud-brick house of a villager, but what the Major
was now describing spoke of a precision and a level of target
acquisition that we had yet to see from the enemy.

"Maybe the flash of your guns gave away the positions. Or
maybe it was fifth column!"

"It's been less than a week since we moved to the new position and have yet to fire a single shell at night. So the enemy
couldn't have seen the flash to get an approximate fix on our
artillery. But a fifth column? Apparently you haven't grasped
what I humbly put to you just now; the gun the enemy hit was
the very one that countered their fire."

Somewhat confused, I asked myself: What could I have done
about it? What had I missed?

He rose again and walked to the counter. He pointed to one
end of it and briefly said something that I couldn't hear. One of
the officers put a letter in his hand. As he returned to where I
was sitting, the Major reread the letter, and I could see that it had
a top-secret seal. He sat facing me and said, "Go ahead, read it!"

I took the letter from him in a state of shock; this was the first
time I ever saw a regular army person let a Basiji have a secret
document. It began with the usual "In the name of Him the Exalted" and the heading "Southern District Central Command"
with the seal of the Armed Forces on top. It said:

According to recently received intelligence, the enemy has
positioned a unit of the Western-made Cymbeline radar system
in the above-mentioned operational areas. Therefore any information relative to the location of said system should be reported
forthwith to Command so that the Air Force can bring about a
way to destroy the system.

I stopped reading and looked up puzzled. What did this radar
have to do with artillery? The letter continued:

Features of the Cymbeline Radar System

Based on received intelligence, the above-mentioned radar is one of the most advanced systems for locating artillery emplacements, mortars, and long-range missile batteries. With an accuracy of plus or minus five meters it can detect our batteries and alert forward enemy positions so that they can fire on them. Unfortunately there is no image of the said system in existence and even its dimensions are not known. Random reports, however, indicate that the system relies on blast signatures to detect artillery positions. In other words, the radar mathematically calculates the precise location of a shell after it has been fired.

Conclusion

The following steps should be taken:

Forward spotters should take steps to locate the said system.

Once the exact positions of enemy anti-artillery are known, commanders should engage in repositioning their own units.

The letter was signed and sealed by the General Commander of the Southern District Operations, and copies were sent to several centers identified only by number.

Ameer and I should have been peering through our binoculars for that radar. But there was still one important problem.

"So, Major, if we don't know the shape and size of this radar, or whether it's on wheels or mounted on a boat or if it's got a dish—like anti-aircraft or even whether it's something completely different—how are we supposed to find it? Or even whether we'll be able to spot it, because they've camouflaged it? They won't put up a sign or anything saying: Dear Mr. Lookout, here it is!"

"Fine, but our job is no less difficult than yours. According to the order, we have to move our positions. But even after we find a suitable place and dig all the necessary earthworks, as soon as we fire the first shell, that radar will pick up our new position. And ..."

"Okay, okay, I'll tell the boys."

"What's the rush? I've ordered tea for you."

"No, I'd better go and get after that radar fast."

I had to do anything to keep him from finding out I was now a messboy with an apron, ladling eggplant stew into pots. That was why I parked the food truck in the alley behind the bank.

After he shook my hand, I waved goodbye. The other men were still ranged around the map, busily conferring. I passed through the corridor and, without giving the sentry a second look, stepped into the alley. I was conscious of the blood on my uniform and how frightening it must have looked to them.

Near the barrels overflowing with garbage, I noticed that the dog was still there; but this time he was lolling in the shade. When I got to the van I saw that the tablecloth with the bread was open and several slabs had been pulled from it. I didn't have to look to know that they were red with Parveez's blood.

I wasted no time climbing into the back and tore open the cloth. There were at least four other slabs edged in red. Although my own clothes were covered with blood, I carefully tried only to touch the unstained parts of the bread. After folding the slabs together, I tossed them toward the trash barrel. They untwisted in mid air, hit the side of the barrel, and landed on the ground next to it.

A gray dog lumbered over to them; his right front paw was bent, where he had taken some shrapnel. He stuck its snout into the partially folded bread and started licking the blood from it. This made me nauseous and I left immediately. I wished I had thrown the bread into the water where the sharks could have claimed it.

Now there were two missions on my mind: first feed the boys, then find the radar. I had no stomach for the first mission, but I had to carry it out—if only this one time. I had a healthy appetite for the second, however, because it involved artillery— though the chances of finding something with no known shape were nearly zero.

I started the van and in this combat zone kept my head low behind the wheel—it was a combat zone because the Major or another officer might see me driving the thing.

God, Parveez, what I would do to you right now!

5

Ameer asked irritably: "So what did Qasem do?"

"When he saw the van coming with its windows blown out
and with me at the wheel, he knew right then that something had
happened. He sent Kazem to bicycle to the hospital. Now eat
your lunch! We've got to take turns doing something about the
radar situation."

Ameer merely toyed with his food. For about half an hour
after learning that someone was hit by shrapnel, the boys always
reacted like this—as if it was our fault that enemy artillery could
still pound the city. We never argued about whose turn it was.
Though he was heavier than I, Ameer scampered up the refinery
scaffolding like a cat. We took turns sitting up in the part facing
the water and measuring the blast signatures from enemy artillery.

"Have you given any thought to who's going to take over the
van?"

"Not really. I'll go and see Javad's father; maybe he'll do it."

"You know it won't make him happy to drive that thing
again."

I shrugged, thinking that this was some way of bolstering his
friend's spirits!

I knew he would be very angry about the loss of the motorcycle. It was his turn to go up there and spot targets, but now with
no motorcycle he would have to walk the whole way—unless he
used Parveez's wreck.

"The Major didn't tell you what it looks like? Not even a
hint...something—there's no limit to the bizarre shapes you
think you see in those date groves and bull rushes."

"The esteemed Major condescended to say only so much.
Forget it, man! We'll take a look and if we find something, we

find something. If not, not; we haven't put our names on the dotted line so they can't come after us if we don't!"

But Ameer, always the sharper one, saw a point that escaped me—what with the hectic day I'd had.

He said forcefully, "If it's found, it's found? You don't understand. There're firing at us from the other side of the waterway with shells and missiles, and we've moved heaven and earth just to rig together some rusty artillery and fire back at them."

"So what?" I asked.

"So what! Look, now they have radar that can find our artillery after we fire it without the slightest error. This means that the minute we fire back, they'll wipe out the battery and kill the boys in the unit. So, tell me, who is going to defend the city from all of the enemy shelling?"

Ameer was right. If even the Major could put aside his self-regard and forget about the slight to his pride, then the issue must be very serious.

"Now you're talking! So long as we don't fire at them, then their radar cannot find us. Right? That's strange—it's just like the frog."

"The frog?"

"What does it have to do with frogs, son?"

"Everything. Several months ago I read in a book that a frog's eyes see in two dimensions—unlike humans who can distinguish three dimensions. For example, if a fly, the frog's favorite food, were to remain motionless in front of it, the frog wouldn't be able to tell it's there—even if it stays that way for hours and the frog starves to death, he'll never shoot out his tongue. But if the fly makes the slightest movement, the frog will swallow it in half a second.

"Great, Mr. frog expert! We are the flies and if we make the slightest move now, we'll wind up luscious morsels for Mr. Froggy. Now will you let me change my clothes? God, it's been like this all day, my whole life..."

He didn't complete the sentence. I began to unbutton my ̄ ̄ ̄ Ameer walked to the food truck. I took off my shirt hirt and the green cloth my mother had tied around s beginning to show. I felt like washing for prayer, ater at the shore base was in short supply, used only for drinking and cooking. I'd have to wait until night when I could go to the shore.

I was very tired, and still hadn't performed my noon and evening prayers. The creature hadn't even let me complete my morning prayer. It served me right—wandering around with a pigeon-keeper like Parveez. I hope to God Javad's father agrees, because if he doesn't then I'll have to drive this rattletrap of a wagon for the next few days.

When I asked the boys, "Anyone want to help out a wounded comrade by delivering the food for a couple of days—it'll count as one of your good deeds," they just sneered, as if to say "no, that's you!" These thoughts made me forget where I was in my ablutions: had I already poured water over my left arm or my right?

First, he lifted my hand from my face, but I didn't wake up. Then he gently shook my feet. He said all of these things when I dropped him off at the shore base and then he stressed, "Look in on Asadollah! Tell him what's happening! Tell him that until the problem is solved, we won't make any requests for shelling. So long!"

Then he put the radio in its case that hung around his waist and began fiddling with the knobs. The battery light went on and he entered the building, confident that it was working. He would spend the whole night stretched out on the roof with his eyes fixed on that side of the waterway, while I crawled under a cozy blanket and until morning...but what about the van? Javad's father....

Javad's father said nothing and kept his head down. As always he was calm. Even when they told him about his son's death...when we went into the kitchen and he and several others were trying to avert their faces from the steam rising from the open pots as they struggled to carry them to the benches. He was about to return when he saw us in the doorway—Qasem and I both looking down. Not a word was said. He merely sat down. It was clear that he had been waiting a long time for the moment when two soldiers would come to give him the news of Javad's death.

The others eased him to his feet. Qasem took him in his arms and whispered something into his ear that I didn't hear. Then he alone spoke, *"Verily we belong to God and to Him do we return,"* and we headed for his home so he could tell Javad's mother about their son's death.

"Fine, but there's only one thing."

All I heard was "fine"— it was unbelievable—now I was rid of Parveez's evil legacy.

"But several days ago I sent Javad's mother to see her daughter. Starting tomorrow, I have to go to the delta and wait for her to come back. It's not clear which launch she'll be on, so I'll have to be there two or three days.

So much for my luck—his "fine" was not a real "fine," and now I had to wait a few days. This was a clear and present threat to my good name. All it took was for some Major to pass by in his chic jeep and see me in an apron holding a ladle!

"You're not going to stop in on Javad's mother? She's been asking after you a lot. I explained to her that you boys have a thousand things to do, but as soon as they have a chance they'll come by."

I was too angry to be polite and asked bluntly, "Now when did you say you'll return, God willing?"

But he only laughed and slapped me on the back. "No telling, but I shall return. You can count on it!"

I realized that had anyone else but me asked him to start driving the food truck again, he would have refused. But I was still exasperated and said goodbye coldly. But then I thought: You're never going to grow up! Do you think the world owes you something? What do your problems have to do with this poor old man?

I looked back to see Javad's father cleaning the blood off the chairs and another old man wiping off bloodstains with a rag. A third worker was lugging rations over to the van—Shami kabob with pickled vegetables and flatbread, which reminded me of what Parveez had told that woman about there being no need for the pots...

"Did you d...d...deliver the food?" moaned Parveez.

He was lying in bed covered by a white sheet and with yellow tubes attached to various part of his belly. He was pale. There was a sign over the bed forbidding food and drink. His intestines had been punctured in several places. The nurse said, "By morning he'll definitely be sent to the delta so they can evacuate him by helicopter." That last word was enough to tell me how grave Parveez's condition was.

Every day a small helicopter executed a million stunts to reach the friendly end of the delta. As it hovered a few meters over the ground they would load only the most serious cases, and the helicopter would return to the base.

In the clinic more than thirty beds were arranged by twos in one long row, making it difficult for anyone, including the nurses, to move in and out of them. There was a drip in both of Parveez's arms—one was a clear liquid, and the other was a plasma bag. I paused for a second to read Parveez's blood type—B positive, the same as mine. What a coincidence!

"Well, you said you wanted to go on leave. Instead of three or four days, now it's one month easy!"

He answered me in a weak voice that came from the base of his throat, "T...morrow, i...t's ice.....c....ream day. Don't....forget!"

That faint malicious grin formed on his face. I stared at him in amazement. His condition was not all that good. The doctor said that he needed an immediate operation. For the time being, they were able to pump enough serum into him to replace the blood he had lost; but it would be difficult to maintain this.

The blood dripped from the reservoir into a smaller holder and then into a narrow tube so that it could enter Parveez's vein.

"I...I...in b..ad...sha...pe, aren't I?"

If I answered him in a kind voice, which was out of the ordinary, he would have known how bad it was.

"You bet!" I said, "You're already on your way out. Don't tell me this was a way for you to palm off that majestic conveyance on me? You can't fool me; you're about to pen your last will and testament? I'll be left with all those cash customers on my hands. Happy now?" I began fiddling with his serum drip. In the first couple of months of the war, Parveez, like me, had seen tens of friends die and recognized the special way we looked at the boys in serious shape. No matter what I did, I had to keep that look out of my eyes.

Remembering the woman who tore off her Arab headscarf and gave it to me, I asked him, "Parveez, before you check out, tell me something! This woman you brought food to—who was she?"

"G...ee..." and he started taking short breaths. "G...ee...t...y."

"Fine. I got it; her name is Geety."

He confirmed this with a movement of his finger. The ward nurse spotted me from across the room and with a firm gesture told me to leave immediately. Though they gave all the wounded sedatives, here and there you could hear the sounds of moaning. I moved my head and hand to tell her that I was just going.

"So, Mr. Parveez, goodbye! As you enter hell and spy us playing football up there in heaven, don't let it get to you, okay? I've got to go. Need anything?"

The rest of what I said was total nonsense; my mind wasn't working right. I didn't know how to keep him from thinking about the danger of infection he faced.

"D...d...n't let m...my fa...mily find ou...out!"

"Don't be an ass, boy. Somebody's going to go there and spill the beans."

The nurse was now nearly on top of me with her arms folded across her chest.

"No...day after t...tomorrow is my si...sister's wed...ding, if they f...find out, it'll b...be ruined."

I nodded my head in agreement. Then I held his right hand in both of mine and squeezed it. But he was too weak to respond. Unable to utter "goodbye," I turned my back on him and walked away. So after all we had been through that day, I finally discovered why he was in such a hurry to go on leave—his sister's wedding! Why didn't he say anything to me? The celebrations now would probably turn into mourning for Parveez, given his condition. But what could I do? They were waiting for me to deliver the Shami kabob that was in the back of the van.

6

Despite the smoke, I could see the sunset was glowing bright red on the baked mud houses when I reached Geety's quarter. I stopped the van. I still had misgivings about entering the area—the same old terror!

I grabbed the olive green kit and parked the van in the middle of the street. I had to take measurements on the blast before the sun went down.

The new blast was so sudden that I didn't have time to jump from the van. The shell hit the wall, making a large hole—a bizarre triangle inscribed in shrapnel. This was of no use; only the type of shell could be determined. I sat on the ground and picked up a piece of shrapnel. It was about the width of two fingers in diameter and as long as my hand. Mortar shrapnel was never this bulky, so it was an artillery shell. In the fading light, I searched for the tail fins; but there was no sign of them. Ordinarily the six fins landed two or three meters from the blast site; therefore they should have been there. In the notebook I wrote:

Shell, probably 122 or 130mm; heading, unknown; time, 18:30

I was about to put the notebook and compass back in the kit, when I heard a loud hissing noise coming from the direction of the van. I turned around and saw the first enemy flare of the night, wobbling on its axis in the sky like a Japanese lantern and making shadows that fell on the lane dance madly.

I stood transfixed by the scene. The light from the flare took me to another world, to the festivals of my childhood and their fireworks.... I looked to the right and, in the unaccustomed quiet of dusk, I saw that a huge cloud of smoke from the refinery fire had somehow transported the metal frame at the head of the lane and its unhinged, absent door and all the little houses in the neighborhood from the present to the past.

The gatekeeper materialized for a moment, chasing me and the other boys. It was here that he napped on his stool in the scant shade of the afternoon. The children were whispering to one another, and I didn't know where I was. "What is this place?" I asked.

"This is that place," said a voice and everyone but me started to laugh. Then one of them put his head near mine and whispered something that for years had remained a mystery: "Before the revolution this was *the* place where foreign sailors, who disembarked at the city's port, would come and, with big grins on their faces, prowl for that thing the locals got clobbered for." My face was crimson.

The next thing I knew, I was still standing there. There was a small door within a much larger one that was just opening. The children had gone. A young woman in a floral print chador emerged from the door. I stared at her, thinking that this must be one of *those* women. The rouge on her cheeks, her green eye shadow, and the gum in her mouth made her look exotic. She did not see me. She walked over to the gatekeeper who had just woken from his nap. He smiled at her and she pretended to rearrange her chador to show what was underneath. She was carrying a cheap purse made of red plastic, and was wearing a white sleeveless dress with the top buttons open.

The gatekeeper lowered his voice and asked, "So soon?"

The woman snickered vulgarly.

He said, "Yeah! You're afraid that Khorshid's going to chew you out."

They both laughed. The woman turned around me and stopped laughing when she saw me. I was still dazed by what I saw; the sight of such a creature with her long eyelashes and eyes the color of honey was unthinkable to me. With a look, the woman drew to gatekeeper's attention toward me. He suddenly jumped from his perch and put his hand on his stick.

He shouted, "Little bastard! Scram!" and then he threw the stick at me. I heard the woman scream, "Don't hit him! It's not right."

The stick hit me in the right thigh, and my screams mixed with hers. It hurt so much my eyes closed. When I opened them I saw the woman standing over me saying, "That was wrong. Look what you did to him."

The gatekeeper grabbed the woman's arm and said, "Get moving. This is none of your business!"

I rose and limped away. As I fled I turned around for a second and saw the woman rubbing her eyes. She might have been crying or adjusting her false eyelashes.

My leg hurt badly. I stopped to roll up my pant leg. There was a black-and-blue mark, and the leg was swollen. I was late for class...

Mother washed my legs. It was already too late for the first class, and without Mother I didn't dare go to school. This was the third time she had asked me about the bruise on my leg and why I was late for school; but I said nothing. After she finally swore not to tell Father, I told her everything that had happened. She said nothing and merely continued to wash my legs, but I was lost in thought pursuing a larger question. Finally it burst from my lips, "Okay...why do the women have to go there...how come?"

Her sharp look was enough to tell me that I had gone too far....

It was dark now. I got into the van and retraced my old tire marks on the pavement, stopping in front of the woman's house.

Four sticks of kabob and two pieces of bread were enough for her. Was she one of those women? I wondered. Or did she have nowhere else to go? If not, what was she doing in this neighborhood?

Balancing the bread and kabob in my arms, I beeped the horn, but the wooden door didn't open. This time I kept my hand on the horn, but the door still remained closed. Maybe a shell had finished her off and her body now lay in a pool of blood on the floor. But maybe what kept me there was that old childhood mixture of stubbornness and fear.

Reluctantly I walked to the door. The dark brown inner door was firmly bolted from inside.

"Who's there?" asked a woman's voice—Geety.

"It's me. I've brought your food."

he door opened a crack and the specter of a woman black headscarf, holding a large club appeared. She looked at me and then hid the club behind the closed half of the door. She reached out and without a word took the food. I stood there unable to move, and perhaps she was taken aback by my hesitation.

"Well?" she asked.

"Nothing! Do you need anything else, Madam?"

All at once she erupted. Her eyes were round with rage and, with the bread and kabob tucked under her arm, she braced her hands on her hips and, using all the might a woman could muster, screeched, "Madam... that's your mother! Your aunt! Your mother's a cunt!"

The two halves of the door made a loud crunch as she slammed them shut. It took a few moments for the shock waves from her eruption to break over me. Then I climbed into the van.

As I drove away I could feel the anger rising in me. She cursed my mother—my mother! A woman who never harmed a soul! What did I say? I treated her with respect. I brought her food. Let her choke on it, stupid cow! What a difference a day makes! Gives me her headscarf in the morning and now she curses me for being polite. She didn't even have sense enough to ask after Parveez. Fine, so be it—see if I ever feed you again! Screw the Engineer, too! I'll be damned if I bring him his food! Am I their flunky? A full day of target spotting and, on top of that, slaving for Madam Geety and the crackpot Engineer armed with only a ladle and wearing an apron around my waist! From now on I'll be delivering food only to the base. To hell with the rest of them! Let them go to the mosque like everybody else. All of this is Parveez's fault, perforated bastard.

The van jerked violently to a halt sending me flying. If there had been glass in the windshield, my forehead would definitely have banged into it. My chest slammed into the steering wheel and a new pain was added to the old woes. I started to rub where it hurt.

Looking beneath the van I saw part of a concrete light post that had been split in two that day and now blocked the road. Finding it an easy target for the day's frustrations, I kicked it hard.

I put the van in reverse and went back to the crossroads. The tall buildings that loomed over it were bathed in blue light. Standing there, I could hear the sounds of several large vehicles growing louder by the minute. I got out of the van and flipped up the seat. I took out Parveez's kalashnikov, put it over my shoulder, and hopped over the fallen post. My first thought was to make sure that if I had to run, there would be nothing in my way but chunks of brick, splintered doors and doorframes, and shards of glass. My body was poised to clear the obstacles in the darkness.

The only thing visible when I reached the crossroads was the faint glow from the vehicles' headlights, which were partially covered with tape because of the blackout. The beams illuminated only part of the trucks, leaving the long gun barrels trailing behind in ominous shadows. The first vehicle went by pulling a 130mm artillery piece. The second also passed with artillery in tow. There were six trucks in all, with the Major's jeep trailing behind. The unit was obviously repositioning.

I ducked behind a wall as the jeep went by with the Major certainly in it. They were moving the artillery because of the radar, but, as Ameer asked, what could we do about it?

I ran back to the van and again noticed the stanchion lying there. If it weren't for that post, the Major would have spotted me in this heap parked in the middle of the crossroads and would definitely have had a good laugh. So no harm was done.

I rolled slowly toward the shore base so as not to attract attention from the other side of the waterway. When I reached the building, I parked the van behind the water reservoir in the shadow of a motorcycle and a van without a roof.

The artillery boys' truck! What were they doing here?

As I got out of the van, Kazem, without saying a word, jumped onto the back and began divvying up the ration of kabobs for the base. He was the only person who could be trusted to take the right number of meals.

"Isn't there a lot more here?"

"What do you care? Grab your share."

"And upon you be peace also, brother rookie food-van-driver! If you had come two hours later, you could have delivered breakfast too!"

I heard a sound behind me—it was the bushy-bearded Asadollah. I made a face—this was all I needed. I remembered the way he would tease me and sing his own praises over the radio.

"Asadollah, sir! You're out, again? I looked everywhere but couldn't find any trace of your marksmanship."

"Try opening your eyes! Don't tell me that when you were up on the roof you didn't have your carrot juice? Remember: you're not perched there anymore, hugging the scaffolding and barking orders at us—a little to the left, pull it back a little! As if you were in charge!"

Once he even cooked up an elaborate joke for the lookouts. He said, "The enemy has sent you a morale-booster. The citation reads: 'We hereby acknowledge our gratitude for the many efforts of the spotters in directing fire toward our fields. This repeated shelling represents an advance in the plowing of our fallow land, and it has also offset a shortage of iron ore in the area. God willing, at the end of the War, which will also mark the conclusion of this remote plowing, the spotter corps will be awarded the Qadisiyyah Victory Medal at a gala to be held in Basra.   Signed, Father Saddam, Minister of Agriculture.'" When he finished reading the "citation," he was the one who roared with laughter.

Asadollah had originally been a spotter. In those days, he would joke around with the gunners, trying to provoke them as much as we did; but now that he was in charge of an artillery unit, he changed his tune and would drive us crazy with his banter. But tonight, I was in no mood for it. That foul-mouthed crone had truly gotten under my skin. All Asadollah had to do was repeat one—just one—of his tired jokes, and I would go off like a rocket packed with TNT, and there was no telling what I would annihilate. Asadollah had apparently read this in my face and stopped his teasing.

"We were waiting for you. Everyone has been ordered to go to the artillery base for a meeting."

I didn't answer him and entered the hallway where the soot-stained kerosene lamp was emitting fumes as always. This lamp had become a source of frustration, even though Qasem had explained to me, "What's the use? Even if you lower the wick, it'll still smoke because of the kerosene!"

Despite this, I lowered the wick, then the specter of Qasem appeared before me. The lamp light made his cheeks and eyes stand out more than usual.

He said, "Ameer took the motorcycle."

"Where?"

"The artillery base. I was waiting for you, too."

It now dawned on me that the motorcycle had been repaired.

"He took my motorcycle?"

Acting as if the question was totally out of line, Qasem answered firmly, "Of course! What did you think? Quick, let's go. Asadollah needs to get back to his base."

Sensing my hesitation, he became more puzzled.

"What's stopping you?"

"Should I bring the van?"

It was another one of those questions. Ordinarily the food truck stayed at the base where it could serve as an ambulance in case we had wounded. At the outset of the war, Qasem's plan was to bring the boys to the end of the jetty to shoot and draw enemy fire toward them.

"There's no need. That was the reason why Asadollah brought the artillery truck."

I was still annoyed by the old woman and the fact that I let her insults stop me from bringing the Engineer his food. The van being there, however, was a reminder that I had to do something for him.

Asadollah kept on teasing me all the way to the base, but I didn't take the bait.

"My mom's apron is still at home. You need it? Don't be shy, let it be my gift to you!" and he laughed. "We don't dare argue with such an august figure on the radio. We know that one contrary word from us would be enough to have our rations cut in half!"

He didn't find this humiliating, not even in front of Qasem who was completely lost in thought. He usually lapsed into silence when there was something serious on his mind.

The first time he explained his weird plan, we thought it over for a minute, then concluded that he'd gone crazy; but when it was put into practice everything fell into place exactly as he had outlined it. Ordinarily the enemy bombarded the city with a fixed number of shells, and Qasem wanted us lookouts to report the number each week so he could calculate the average. His conclusion was surprising. Even on quiet days, when there was little fighting, the enemy showered the city with around 180 shells—give or take ten. This way, we discovered the average daily number of shells the enemy intended to use to destroy the city. Qasem proposed that we fire on the enemy's forward positions early in the morning, forcing them to train their guns on us—on our forward line—rather than the city.

It was a dangerous plan. The boys had less than a minute to fire from the reinforced-concrete positions along the jetty, before the enemy would respond and they had to dash to the only cover behind the line. But this was a way of protecting the city from bombardment during the rest of the day.

Qasem's plan had always seemed to go off without a hitch, except for one time at dawn when Parveez, who was retreating, hesitated and a stray piece of shrapnel deprived him of one of his eyes. Afterwards, Qasem said that Parveez had fallen because of a severe lack of stamina that resulted from not having eaten for 48 hours. Not eating for 48 hours! To this day I have yet to discover how the driver of a food van stayed hungry for that long.

Ameer said, "The motorcycle? There was nothing wrong with it!"

"But it wouldn't start, no matter what I did that morning."

"The mechanic said that one of the spark plugs had been halfway out. Had you unscrewed it?"

Ameer's question made me angry. Why would I do such a thing? I thought.

"How did you know that it had been fixed?" I asked.

"A boy from the repair shop brought it back, saying that the owner had wanted it serviced by evening and delivered." Ameer and Asadollah both started laughing as what had happened slowly dawned on me. When I had gotten up that morning, Parveez was the only person near the motorcycle. He must have done it.

I thought, serves the bastard right that the shrapnel hit him. May he suffer until morning, then he'll know who he's dealing with.

It was a moonless night, and the only light that fell on the artillery base was the fugitive starlight, which had managed to penetrate the smoke. There was just enough light to tell one gray object from a grayer one.

The depression was the picture of a lunar volcano. Piles of earth rimmed the crater. Emerging from it was a long, gun barrel on two legs the height of an average man. The legs stood on a thick metal plate that had three broad supports with sharp ends driven into the ground to absorb the recoil from the gun.

Ameer was perched on the edge of the crater, while Asadollah and I sat on wide planks from the dark munitions boxes we had found scattered about. The base had two 120mm guns that worked in tandem. The number of artillerymen had changed from what it was in the first wave. None of those things were important to me at that moment. I was hungry and out of sorts. The little information Asadollah gave me on the ride to the base hadn't explained much.

Fiddling with a discarded shell casing, Ameer began to speak, "Yesterday artillery lost another gun, and we haven't fired a single shot for three days now. There's no telling what would happen to us if we actually did."

Asadollah joked, "Nothing! Suppose what the Major said about the radar was right. The lookouts would have no complaints if two or three artillerymen were sent to their graves each time they fired!"

No one laughed, and Asadollah thought it better not to interrupt the conversation again. One of the boys emerged from behind a house on the right side, holding a flashlight. Though he tried to keep the beam on the ground, the light reflected off the asphalt illuminating the walls of the structures, which quickly disappeared as if swallowed by the darkness.

"Are you saying that we should pack up the guns and sit twiddling our thumbs?" I asked. I had the feeling that the question depressed everyone.

"It's an interesting strategy," Qasem said.
"What is?"

"Listen! So long as we don't fire at them, there's no danger to our guns. But as soon as we fire one shot it's enough to give away our position, and then..."

We all knew what came next, so no one completed the thought. "It's a weird situation," Qasem continued. "Our inability to fire puts all the initiative in the enemy's hands. This miraculous radar has made firing suicidal."

I thought of Ameer's frog-and-fly analogy, how if the fly doesn't move, the frog can't see it. But as soon as it moves, the frog shoots out its tongue and that's the end of the fly.

For a moment I felt we were flies perched there on the crater, while there was an electronic frog just waiting for us to move on that side of the water.

Qasem said, "Here's a thought, but I don't know whether it'll work or not."

No one spoke.

"If we were to make the footprint of the crater smaller, maybe it would do something."

"Qasem, beg your pardon; but we don't understand what you're talking about."

The light from the flashlight fell on Qasem's face. It was Mohammad, an olive-skinned boy from Arab stock, who had been Asadollah's radio operator for a while.

"Didn't the Major say that the radar was accurate within five meters?"

"The Major didn't say it; it was in the report."

"Whatever. Listen! Either we fold our hands and do nothing and wait for them to scare us to death, or we fire and die."

Ameer said, "Fine, but the first thing is to wait a while to see if we can find that radar."

Qasem laughed in response to this. "Okay. During the two days it'll take to make the crater smaller, you and your friend can try to find the radar. Of course, nobody knows what it looks like."

Qasem was right. We didn't know what it looked like, whether it resembled the other radar and had a rotating dish. We had formed a picture of it: a large antenna camouflaged among the jumble of reeds and date palms on the other side so that we could hunt for it from up high on our perches. *High*? The one-story building at the shore base? No, we had to find another vantage point.

I absentmindedly turned toward the refinery. The northwest wind was still driving thick smoke from the two burning storage tanks toward the waterway. I thought, maybe one of the two refinery towers! But the smoke would get in the way. No, I had to think of another place, a tall building where I could sit for hours scanning the date groves and the endless desert.

"This is my plan. You two will have a maximum of two days to find the radar. If you don't, we'll have no choice but to start shelling again, but this time with a new strategy.

"The Engineer's building!" I blurted out.

All eyes turned to me, and Mohammad shone the flashlight directly in my face. Mohammad, of all people! Normally he didn't say a word when we had these discussions, so I knew nothing about him. Most of the time he sat in a corner, reading the Qoran under his breath. Often there was a faint smile on his lips, which under these circumstances, was a miracle in itself.

The light bothered my eyes. "Put that away, man!" I said, then explained, "It's a possible lookout spot. One of Parveez's screwy friends lives in a burnt-out seven-story building. I'll start at seven tomorrow morning."

Stunned, Asadollah looked around as if to ask: What's going on here? He knew that the boys in his unit would be in the most danger. Qasem rose and took the flashlight from Mohammad, then began digging a small hole in the ground with a sharp piece of wood.

He said, "Here's our artillery!" Then he drew two parallel lines and said, "And this is the waterway between us and our friends over there!"

He made a small mark on the other side of the river representing the radar and two X's close to one another. "This X is their command and control which receives the information and the other is the artillery that acts on it." Then he shone the light in our direction, meaning Ameer and me, saying "Now if you two don't find the radar..."

He shifted the light to Asadollah's face and said, "Mr. Asadollah must find a way of fooling the radar."

"How?" asked Asadollah, whose nervous smile made him seem even more fearful in the light.

"I'll tell you! Up to this point we've been focusing on the strong points of this radar system, which is exactly what they want us to do. But I'm concentrating on its weaknesses—those five meters plus or minus. Let's say it doesn't turn up, then we'll have to find a way of convincing the enemy that the radar's margin of error is greater than five meters. If we can make them doubt the accuracy of their system, that would be enough. Make them think that it's more than 100 meters, meaning the distance that an experienced spotter using his binoculars can measure from a blast site. If this happens then their new radar will no longer be of any use to them.

"Okay, fine, but that's exactly the point. How?"

"By returning to the time when enemy shelling took place in the waters on that side of the jetty."

The he shone the flashlight on the circle of earth around the artillery. "We'll dig the smallest possible hole for the artillery and then fire, praying that the radar is indeed accurate to a distance of five meters. We'll respond to every one of their shells with one of our own.

"But what about the artillerymen?"

"We'll have a dugout and cover it with a reinforced roof, and connect it to the artillery trench so they can take shelter in it after firing."

Qasem sat down again and tossed the piece of wood he was holding away. The white sliver hovered in the air for a moment and landed among the broken boxes.

Complete silence reigned for a few seconds. We had two days to find the radar. If we didn't, then Asadollah and his men would have to hunker down in their shelter waiting for 42 pounds of pure TNT from the enemy's 130mm guns. A direct hit would make gathering even the smallest scraps of their flesh impossible.

"It would be a good idea to find a new place for the artillery."

"I agree. And one other thing: no one is to know the new location except for the boys in the unit. Understand?"

He meant me. There was a prolonged silence. The time for joking was over; now it was all business. This was a dance to the death with a partner already dead, but who, nevertheless, kept watch over the city from the other side of the waterway. All we had to do was take one breath, and it would go into action murdering the lot of us.

"But if they were to lose faith in their radar, then maybe things would go back to square one—the old exchanges of blind artillery. Before anything happens, however, you two must do what you have to!"

Ameer and I looked at each other. If we could discover where they had hidden that system, there would be no need for Qasem's dangerous plan.

I read the resolve in Ameer's eyes. The plan involved far more risk than what we had been taking after the enemy fired, which would be to run as fast as possible from the area where we thought the shells would land. This time, the basic idea was to stay where the shells would be sure to hit. Why? Because there was no time to run to a safe place. This was the issue: standing on the spot where an enemy strike was certain—and inside a depression filled with munitions, at that! This was the most terrifying type of war that until now we had brought upon ourselves.

After a moment, it was pitch black. Qasem had turned off the flashlight. There was only one thing on my mind: the Engineer's tall building—the Engineer, who had eaten nothing since lunch.

7

The van, with its faulty brakes, screeched to a halt in front of the seven-story building, I was trying to think of a way to avoid the embarrassment of having to explain to the Engineer why his dinner was so late.

As usual, the door made a creaking sound when it opened. I pushed the seat back, removed the kalashnikov, and put it over my shoulder. I still didn't trust the Engineer, the half-deranged old man with his strange questions, on this dark night....

As I reached for the kabob and bread that had somehow survived the boys' greedy fingers, I looked up at the window on the third floor. The shadow of a man appeared in the light of a lamp or a candle. There was also the shadow of the flowerpots with cactus plants. A thousand unanswered questions roiled my mind: Why was this man living in the building? Why hadn't he been evacuated with everyone else?

There was enough light from the stars to guide my way to the building, but when I got inside, it was pitch black again. I stopped for a moment to allow my eyes to adjust to the dark. "Come on up."

It was the Engineer's voice, an old man's voice, wavering up and down. The light from his lamp was visible through the shattered steps. I rearranged the weapon on my back, hung the binoculars strap from my neck, and, balancing the bread and kabob in my right hand, dragged myself slowly up the stairs.

When I neared the top so that my head was level with the brick floor, light from the soot-stained lamp flashed directly into my eyes. My eyes closed automatically in reaction to the assault. When I opened them, instead of the lamp I saw the Engineer squatting before me...

Sitting on his spring mattress, I would occasionally watch as he wolfed down the food. He made a sandwich consisting of two sticks of Shami kabob between two half-slabs of flatbread. It was obvious that he hadn't eaten anything since the afternoon.

"Won't you have some?"

Though I hadn't eaten, I didn't feel hungry. I was under an incredible strain. I was also very tired and needed rest as soon as possible. I was only waiting for him to finish.

The whole time he was eating he didn't glance at me once. He didn't even ask why I was late. Perhaps he felt he had no right to ask.

After finishing his homemade sandwich, he poured water into a glass from a jug and drank it down, then wiped his mouth with the back of his hand.

I looked at the books crammed into the unfinished niche in the wall. The Engineer got up, walked over to the bed and sat next to me, making the bedsprings go up and down. I knew that he was surprised to see me. Most likely he hadn't heard about Parveez being wounded, and I didn't feel like telling him. The only thing we had in common was that I was going to spend two full days on the roof of the building he occupied, and I had no idea why I felt I needed his permission. Who was he to deny it?

"Well, where's your friend?"

When I didn't answer him, he got up from the bed and walked a few steps away. Then he stopped and turned and gestured for me to stand up. He said, "Young man! First get up and answer my question! What is the meaning of 'what'?"

Geety's insult came to mind: "Madam... that's your mother!" Now this.

"Answer the question at once! What is the meaning of 'what'?"

With all that had happened that day, I could have done without having the Engineer pull my leg. But it was clear that now, with a full stomach, he was like a cat looking for a mouse to distract him. He would learn that I wasn't a harmless mouse.

I carefully unhooked the kalashnikov strap, switched off the safety, and cocked the weapon. With one eye I aimed it at the window and with the other watched the old man's bewilderment.

"You want to know what the meaning of 'what' is? 'What' means HEARTACHE! Means AGONY!"   Then I pulled the trigger and a shot rang out, and—BAM!—there was the sound of the bullet striking something substantial. The old man ran to the window.

"My cactus pot!"

I turned. One of the flowerpots wasn't there. I remained cool. Maniac! With all of the soil and flowers around, this one kept cactuses.

I shouted, "Back here, NOW!" and he returned immediately, trembling with fear.

"Why did you shoot my cactus?"

"Because of all the nonsense that comes out of your mouth. 'What does what mean?' That's a question? I don't know what made that friend of mine fond of you, but for the next two days I've got to be up on the roof, and I'm in no mood for your clowning."

The gun gave me the upper hand. I was really tired, but there was nothing I wanted more than a chance to think seriously about the radar.

"I'm going to get my blankets and go to sleep up there."

Still shaken by the shooting, he didn't react. So much the better! I needed all the sleep I could get...

I was awakened by rumbling noises in the distance and thought I was dreaming. After a moment I opened my eyes and noticed that the sky was still leaden and the sounds of battle were coming from the shore. Still not conscious of my new sleeping quarters, I immediately felt a chill throughout my entire body. I pulled up the blanket over my head to warm up, but this was no time to sleep; I had to say my Morning Prayer....

"*Peace be upon you and God's mercy and His blessings.*"

The sounds of snoring were still coming from the Engineer's bed. I moved my head twice and finally kissed the rock that I had used as a prayer stone. The old man's snoring was highly irregular; it was the kind of sound that enemy scouts could detect from 500 meters. Good thing he wasn't at the base!

I walked to the window and tossed out the makeshift prayer stone. Ordinarily it might have hit a passerby, but with the war on....

When I got to the window I looked down and saw, near the van, the fragments of the flowerpot spread out like the blast mark made by a mortar. I scratched my head. I needed a good shower.

There was one slab of flatbread from last night left in the bag. I tore off a piece and wolfed it down. I felt rested from a full night's sleep. I remembered shooting the old man's flowerpot and that Parveez was in the hospital—not knowing whether they had evacuated him or perhaps because of the bleeding he had…?

I should have kept these random thoughts out of my mind. There was an important task ahead. Determined to stay focused and find the radar, I swallowed the bread decisively. Having no need to remain downstairs, I left for the roof, planning to be there until noon when it was time for lunch.

The old man was still snoring, making a weird racket. I crept over to him. He was stretched out on his back. If it weren't for his snoring, I could have folded his arms over his chest and put the cactus plant in his hands instead of flowers, making him the perfect corpse! I also noticed something else strange; there was no sign of the cats. What attracted them to this miserable old geezer was a mystery to me. But I had wasted too much time already….

The dawn sky was still overcast when I set foot on the unknown terrain, which Parveez had first discovered. The roof was made of bricks, which at any moment could have acted like a kind of reverse minefield and caved in sending me to the lobby. I was very careful where I stepped. At several points rebar jutted out from the roof, indicating that they had intended to add more stories. Why hadn't they? Once the war and the siege were over, would the damage caused by the fire on the ground floor permit further construction?

I was going to be looking through the binoculars for a long time. To prevent them from shaking and making my eyes tired, I used a piece of wood as a stand. I turned the knob on the right lens from zero to five. The vision in Ameer's right eye was better than mine, and, whenever we traded the binoculars, I had to make this adjustment. Everything was ready now, and I began my vigil.

As usual I had to wait a second for the blurry green shapes to arrange themselves into something recognizable. Then green date palms and tall reeds that hadn't been mowed in ages came into view. I lowered the binoculars slightly and a small part of the waterway between the houses and the cranes at the port disappeared from view.

The sun was now up behind me. The shoreline on the other side of the waterway was walled with sandbags. The wall was occasionally interrupted by perforated projections, which every novice lookout, after a few turns at the binoculars, would recognize as camouflaged bunkers.

I moved the binoculars to the right. The wall of sandbags continued until the shoreline of the island curved away. It was totally silent. The brief outburst of this morning was over, and the two sides seemed like lovers saying goodbye after spending a frightful night together.

I was wasting time scanning the shoreline; no one in his right mind would have positioned the radar on the coast. My eyes should have been first on the date groves and then on the desert beyond them.

As I was moving the binoculars, a black object caught my attention. There was only one—a giant with a halo of frizzy hair and his back to the waterway. Two seconds later he disappeared in the pathway formed by the wall of sandbags and the trenches behind it. If I had had the radio with me and waited a little longer, I would have alerted the artillery. But I had no business stalking enemy soldiers along the shore. The radar was my sole objective.

I decided to scan from right to left beginning with the first palm tree. There were only reeds there. Maybe they covered the radar with them?   I stared as hard as I could, but either their camouflage job was perfect or there was actually no strange object among the reeds.

What did strange thing look like? What were the chances of the two of us finding it, given the little information they had given us—and only in forty-eight hours?

I know that Ameer was perched on one of the refinery towers doing exactly what I was. Had he found anything yet? We were searching from two different angles, but it made no difference who discovered it first. What terrified me was Qasem's plan. Two soldiers in one foxhole would fire; then the radar would find their precise position and.... There was nothing more dangerous!

No one even asked who was going to carry out the mission. It had probably been decided ahead of time. Asadollah would never allow anyone but himself to do it. But who would be the second man, the one who operated the radio?

A feeling at the back of my neck announced his presence and then a slight shadow reduced the warmth of the morning sun slightly. Keeping my eyes glued to the binoculars, I asked bluntly, "What do you want?"

He didn't answer. He was probably nosing around to see what I was up to. After finally ridding myself of Parveez, I now had this halfwit on my hands doing an excellent impression of him. Why didn't he answer?

I pictured him taking revenge for yesterday with a big club in hand like the one Geety hid behind her door... and now creeping up on me and about to...!

I jerked around, fearing he would bash in the back of my head.

The old man was holding a glass of steaming tea. He retreated and the gold-colored liquid lapped against the lip of the glass. I wondered what would happen if it spilled.

"What's wrong with you, sir? You're always spoiling for a fight. I brought you some tea, that's all." Without taking his eyes off me, he bent down and gently placed the glass on the bricks. Now I was convinced that this was no Parveez; but I didn't know how I should act toward him. Last night must have really gotten to him! He just stood there looking around in amazement.

"Sir! I've never had the nerve to come up here before. How incredibly beautiful it is; you can see everything as far as the horizon!"

Today he spoke like a book and in a tone completely different from what it had been the other day. So last night must have had some effect!

I rose slowly. My knees were all pins and needles from sitting cross-legged so long, but I ignored them.

Raising the glass I asked, "How do you make tea?"

"I'm afraid to answer—you might shoot. Dare I say it: with fire!"

I had put the glass to my lips when he made this joke. He was grinning from ear to ear. I drank down the tea and the bitter liquid went through my body.

He said, "Wait! I have some sugar!" He rooted in his pocket and took out a yellow, misshapen lump of loafsugar. I rejected it with a wave of my hand. If I'd put it in my mouth, the flavor would have stayed there and then it would have melted in the hot tea and gone down, only to make me thirstier. It didn't seem worth climbing down seven flights of stairs for a few sips of water.

But the problem of what I was going to do with the Engineer remained. He no doubt had the same problem: What was he going to do with this stranger who had disturbed his tranquility?

"You're very stubborn, young sir!"

I ignored him and sat down at the binoculars and once again the lenses of my eyes fused with the lenses of the binoculars.

"What are you doing?" He asked as he squatted near me and I turned my head. "Are you, sir, from the Department of Transportation?"

I reached into my pocket and pulled out a blank piece of paper and showed it to him. "Take a look! It's my first-class endorsement! Now are you going to let me work or not?"

It was clear he couldn't make head or tail of this nonsense. He pursed his lips. On his left cheek there was a whitish spot where on old wound had healed. The skin on his lean neck was a mass of weird creases and folds. Looking at him made me sick, and I wondered whether my own skin would be as nasty after I got old.

"Am I being too nosy?"

"No, sir, but I have work to do. I'm not up here for my health. I'm looking for something." He folded his arms around his knees as he squatted there, eagerly awaiting the rest of the story.

"Looking for what?"

I had already said too much. How was it any of his business
what I was looking for? I was slowly getting the feeling that he
had gotten the upper hand in this exchange.

"Would you please let me do my work—okay?" I seemed to
be pleading with him—the clock was ticking. I hoped to hell
that Ameer had found something, sitting up there at the refinery.

I jammed my eyes into the eyepieces again. There was the
grove with its tangle of uncut reeds and unpicked dates rotting
on the trees. Would the new fruit be able to break through those
old clusters? I thought. When I had posed this question to
Kazem, he just dismissed it: "You've been in the sun too long.
Why fret about trees? Has the city run out of calamities?" That
night when Kazem repeated my question for the boys' amuse-
ment, everyone laughed except Qasem who said to me, "Bravo!
Bravo! What you observe makes you think. You're slowly becoming a man!"

Now everything—the old man, the radar, the seven-story
building—was forgotten. I got back to work again.

"What did you say you're looking for? Did you lose something?"

In a measured and calm voice I said, "No, I didn't lose anything, but I am trying to find something."

"This is what you do? You find things?"

My attention was no longer focused on the other side of the
waterway, which was the worst part of bantering with the Engineer.

"Yes, that's right!"

"And after you find it...?" He stopped to wait for me to answer.

"Nothing! I'll annihilate it."

I felt an extraordinary sense of power. No doubt his next
question would be: How? With what? And I would say, with
artillery!

"Well, after that, what happens?"

This took me by surprise. He factored in everything, and out
came this, of all questions! I thought: Man, you should be asking about the thing I want to destroy or how I'm going to do it.
What kind of question is: What will happen after that?

I was still mystified by his question, when he asked in the same bookish way, "When you have destroyed whatever it is, then what?" and his features gradually changed from a friendly smile to something more tongue in cheek. It was obvious that he was playing with me, which made alarm bells go off in my mind. He sensed this, and the wry grin vanished from his face.

"No, no, I didn't mean it that way. Look over there!" he said pointing in the direction of the refinery where the large storage tank was still on fire, sending up clouds of smoke and making a terrible hissing. What he was getting at escaped me.

"So?"

"You don't understand?"

"No."

"I made that refinery."

I laughed. So, it wasn't Parveez who dubbed the poor soul "Engineer." First, the idiotic question about "what," and now...

"It looks like you lose your mind every two hours or so, right Hajji?" I was surprised how easily I got back to work and was about to peer through the binoculars again when he said, "No, young sir! I put it the wrong way. For at least forty years I worked on the same rig that is turning to slag before our eyes. I know every inch of it. I know who installed every part of it. How many workers..."

His eyes grew wider in recollection, and he was paying no attention to me now.

"...but now! Forty odd years of slaving away, bowing and scraping before the British foreman, the blast of the siren telling me when to go to work and when to leave for home, and now all of its burning. For God's sake, turn your telescope around! Stop watching those rube Arabs and behold the majestic thing turning to ash. That is everything. If someone had told me when I was young, 'Stop working so damned hard,' I would have laughed in his face, or, like you, I would have become livid, but now..."

His head began to shake, and I sensed that his emotions had gotten the better of him.

"...Young man, my dear young man! It's a good question. What happens next? I don't know which stinking gismo you're searching for out there, but after you—to use your own esteemed verb—annihilate it, then what?"

"You fool! Can't you see that I'm looking for the same artillery pieces that destroyed your Excellency's refinery?"

"To destroy them?"

"Yes."

It was a good thing that I hadn't let the word "radar" slip out. I had said as much as I could.

"Dear Sir, this is exactly what I mean. So what if you hit that piece of enemy artillery? What's going to happen then? They'll just replace it with a brand new one, right? Yes or no?"

I absentmindedly nodded in agreement, and he let out a deep breath as if a great weight had been lifted from his shoulders. I had been completely taken in.

"The world will go on exactly the same way until eternity. They'll supply the artillery and you'll destroy it. Why not stop the madness?" With that he plucked up the empty tea glass and headed directly to the stairway. The squeaking that his tennis shoes made on the half-built stairs slowly faded. I breathed a sigh of relief, then, just to show him I was still as determined as ever, I yelled down, "Hey Uncle, you never said what the meaning of 'what' was!"

8

The sun was directly overhead, which told me I'd been sitting at the binoculars for at least three hours. I scanned every inch of that ground—from the first strands of barbed wire along the shore to the mouth of the irrigation channels. Mud walls popped up here and there among the reeds, and then there were those five soldiers rashly digging out in the open. Each time my scanning reached the roadway and the vast desert beyond the date grove, I started to search all over again, training the binoculars on those five men with their green helmets, khaki uniforms, two shovels, and a pick. Three men dug while the other two sat where they were out of sight. What were they up to? Ordinarily I would have sent a few bullets their way.

The radar—the radar was ice cream and today was ice cream day. Where would Parveez get the ice cream, anyway?

"Eat shit, you good-for-nothing! What do you care where it comes from?" This was his usual reply. The ice cream was a brand that came in cups, which had clearly been in a freezer for ages. But where was Parveez now?

At daybreak, they would transport the wounded in buses with the seats removed to the channel nearest the delta. Waiting there were launches that had taken advantage of the darkness to reach the city. Their cargo consisted of everyone and everything: leftover household furniture, soldiers on leave, the wounded and, today, Parveez with his critical injuries—if he was still alive. What was I thinking? With all those honest and worthy souls to His credit, why would God want to martyr the likes of Parveez?

All these thoughts cycled though my mind, but deep down, in a place all my own, I was afraid, afraid of what horrors were in store for Parveez...

There were only three cats by him. One with thick brown fur scampered under the bed as soon as I entered, but the two smaller black-and-white cats that seemed to be siblings remained, paying no attention to me, and snatching pieces of food from the Engineer's hand.

I thought my eyes were deceiving me. He was feeding them the kabob from last night, the food that I had brought. There was nothing left in the pot. He was giving it to the cats!

I sat down slowly on the bed and put the weapon on the threadbare but clean sheet. I studied the end of the gun and then reached over to detach the magazine. The sound made the cats prick up their ears.

The Engineer didn't move. He sensed he was in danger. I took the magazine in my left hand and began to extract the bullets with my thumb. One by one they fell out and landed on the bed. The cats were fascinated by the clicks made by the first few, but by the time the tenth and eleventh bullets had been ejected, they had gone back to their food.

By unloading the magazine I had hoped to calm the Engineer's fears. I wanted him to answer a question that had been on my mind since morning. But of course the ground had to be prepared first.

"Did you take any bread this morning?"

He meant the bread in the plastic bag.

"A little bit. It was something to tide me over. There's still some in the cloth in the truck. Go and get it!"

"*I* never touch other people's things without permission."

I didn't say anything. Why should I feel ashamed for taking a few pieces of dry bread? Parveez had been giving him our rations for at least three months, and none of the boys ever complained. But, then again, he was right.

"If it bothers you, tell me. I'll go down and get it."

He didn't answer. I had wasted enough time, and decided to go ahead and ask him the thing that was on my mind. "I have to go but before I do, I need to ask you a question, okay?"

He gathered himself and, obviously suspicious, said, "Please!"

There was no hint of friendship in that "please" or in the dry way he said it, but I had no choice. He was the only person I could ask. I didn't want any of the boys in the artillery unit—not even Qasem and Ameer—to get wind of what had happened yesterday.

After a short pause, I asked, "If you call a woman—one of these sluts—'madam,' is it an insult?"

I waited for his expression to change and would have settled for the smirk. Soon a smile broke across his face.

"Did I hear correctly? A slut, if you call her 'madam,' would she be insulted?"

I nodded. He let the pieces of kabob and bread fall to the floor. Out of the corner of my eye I saw the brown cat emerge from under the bed and join the other two.

He put his hand under his chin, appearing to ponder the question. Then, in one rapid motion, he sat down next to me on the bed, making the bullets roll into the depression that formed in the mattress. I was very careful about ammunition.

In a tone of voice that showed his interest, and motioning with his hands to get me to repeat the question, he said, "Again, please! Again! Again!"

I said it once more but this time barking it as a command.

He rose from the bed and nearly shouted, "Quiet!" Then, lowering his voice, he said, "Say it again."

I had no choice. He knew that the weapon was not loaded and that I was in obvious need of an answer from him. He was in complete control and knew it.

"This happened to your Excellency personally?"

"Yes!"

"Fine. Now fill in the details, every last one!" He sat again and I wished I had never asked him. I felt completely trapped.

"It's nothing, really. I said to some woman, 'Do you need anything else, Madam?' After I said that, she put her hands on her hips and cursed, 'Madam, that's your mother!'"

I had said all I could, too ashamed to repeat the other foul things she said.

"Where was this woman?"

"What do you mean, where?"

"This woman, she was someone that you had never encountered before the start of the damned war? This was something that occurred recently, correct?"

I nodded.

"Well, where?"

I was stymied but I was also embarrassed to say the name of the place. I knew what was happening; he was probing like a prosecutor. Finally I pointed vaguely in the direction of the place and said, "That neighborhood...neighborhood..."—repeating the word like a broken record.

"Which neighborhood?"

I took a deep breath. As I let it out, I said, "The neighborhood with all the filthy houses! Happy?"

He erupted and began cackling with such force, his knees buckled and he landed on the floor, startling the cats, each of which fled to a different part of the room. Only the brown one dared to stay by the edge of the stairs, probably knowing the Engineer better than the other two and I. I wondered how many of these alarming eruptions and guffaws they had heard from him.

I reached out and like someone smoothing sand on a beach gathered up the bullets from the bed in my fist and put them next to me. Then I rapidly reloaded the magazine.

With each bullet the magazine became heavier. The old man paid no attention; but, after managing to open his eyes, which were red and teary from laughing so much, he suddenly got quiet. If this crazy old man made the slightest wrong move...

I quickly finished loading the magazine, inserted it back into the weapon, and placed the extra bullets in my side pocket.

"By any chance, did that woman have dark green eyes?" he asked.

He was right; she *did* have dark green eyes.

"How do you know her?"

"That's Geety! At one time, she was a real looker. They used to call her 'Gorgeous Geety.' Well, you know, in those days people had a name for women like that: 'madam.' What about her daughter? Did you see her? You devil!"

The way he said 'devil' gave me a bad feeling. I put the weapon over my shoulder. I had my answer; Geety probably thought that I had called her 'madam' on purpose. But what was this about a daughter?

I got up from the bed and walked to the stairs. But I stopped suddenly at the point where the furry brown cat had been, and asked, "This Geety has a daughter? In that place?"

"Yes, sir."

The radar, the Engineer, the cats and now a daughter...

"Are you coming back?" he asked softly

"Why do you ask?"

"It's obvious, isn't it? This place, young sir, is my home."

I pointed my trigger finger at him threateningly and corrected him, "It *was* your home. For a couple of days, I have to be on the roof. OK?"

"OK."

Just my being there was enough for him to lose his composure, but was there anybody in the whole city who had peace and quiet, what with all the shelling on both sides?

9

"Ice cream! It's ridiculous!"

Javad's father asked in surprise: "You don't know where he got the ice cream?"

I fell in behind the two other vehicles. The blue van in front was much more beaten up than Parveez's. It looked as if it had flipped over two or three times, and naturally each time they would have to get out and right it, restart it, then be on their way. Not one of the lights was working, and there wasn't a part of the van that didn't need bodywork. They had left no spot undented, which itself was an art. I told myself to be careful; otherwise, the same thing would happen to me.

We were leaving the city, traveling a short distance from the date groves on the outskirts. The second vehicle was a white ambulance with red stripes painted on it. Its right front wheel wobbled alarmingly, forcing me to keep my distance. Like us, they must have had only one vehicle; why else would they be using an ambulance to carry food? We stayed on the asphalt road until we reached an intersection where there was a sign with an arrow, and the lead van swerved suddenly to the right. We followed.

The sign over the front gate had been removed, and in its place someone had written in poorly formed black letters "Mehr Ice Cream Factory." The soldier standing guard unhooked the chain across the entrance and we filed in: first the blue van, then the ambulance, and finally Parveez's van. I told myself that I must never—even for a few hours—claim ownership of the van. It was Parveez's van—Parveez's van.

But why did an ice cream factory need a guard?

I jammed on the brakes suddenly to avoid hitting the ambulance, which had stopped in front of a high concrete curb dragging the van along as if the two vehicles were joined by a cable. The blue van parked at the entrance to a large warehouse.

The driver got out. He was wearing khaki. He glanced at me but said nothing. On the loading dock there was a man wearing a white cap and high black boots. They said something to each other that I didn't hear. The white cap turned to me and asked, "You've come for ice cream?"

Half out of the van, I said, "Yes."

He said, "Ice cream is out back!" He smiled and pointed the way. I got behind the wheel again and, turning around, saw two people straining to open a pull-up door. When I got to the back, I heard the deafening roar of a diesel generator, which made me long for the quiet motor of the War Room.

There was another vehicle, a Land Rover with no wheels, a hulk rusting in one corner of the compound. The door of Parveez's van groaned open in its familiar way. After I got out, the driver of the blue van, wearing sunglasses, appeared. In a thick Esfahani accent he asked me, "Where's Parveez at?"

"And peace be upon you too," I said sarcastically.

He explained, "Sorry! But I salaamed as you were opening the door."

Once again, that damned truck had put me on the defensive.

"Parveez, you mean? He took some shrapnel and bought it." This took him by surprise.

"Took shrapnel? Surely you jest, sir?"

"No, I'm seriously sure. Now where do we pick up the ice cream?"

At a loss, he just walked away. The back of the warehouse was just like the front, a small compound surrounded by a concrete wall the height of an average man. It was clear from the looks of the dock, it had been used to load trucks and trailers with ice cream. The warehouse keeper was sprawled out on a felt coverlet. I had noticed him when I jumped up on the dock. He rose.

"Arvand?" he asked.

"Yes."

"Fifteen people?" he asked and pulled on the large door, which slid open easily. Behind it was the smaller door of the freezer with a fluorescent light. When the second door opened,

plumes of frost smoke poured out. The Esfahani finally con-
quered his doubts and asked, "Say, are you really tellin' me he
was martyred?"

"No, Sir! The guy's like a cat—he's got nine lives. Don't
worry!"

"So he's alive? Thank the Lord!"

"You mean you're actually glad that Parveez survived?"

"I don't know why you're sayin' that but Parveez is a saint..."

"Saint, my ass!"

"...he showed us them poor people on his route, tellin' us to
bring 'em grub whenever we delivered."

It seemed that not one food van had been safe from Parveez's
charity. Still, I had to be thankful that there was someone who
understood what I had to go through.

The warehouse keeper, his face hidden behind the cartons,
put them on the dock.

"Two boxes for Arvand: four boxes for Fayazieh."

The Esfahani's truck had come from the Fayazieh front, then.
I picked up my two boxes, which were labeled "Mehr Ice Cream
Cups—Pasteurized and Homogenized," and jumped down from
the dock with them in my arms. The Esfahani walked to the end
and then carefully climbed down from the cement overhang.

I stowed the boxes far from the warm stew pots. I knew that
if I didn't move fast, I'd be delivering a load of sweet milky liquid; but then I remembered I had to look in on Javad's mother.
She had been asking about me a lot, which is what his father had
said in front of all those people loading the food. That was em-
barrassing, so I had no choice. The radar could survive a few
hours without me looking for it.

I honked goodbye to the Esfahani and, as I waited for his
truck, which was in the process of turning around, to get out of
the way I looked around. The diesel generator was constantly
going, supplying the warehouse with power with two thick ca-
bles attached to a metal post on the roof. There were two other
warehouses identical to the first, but they were not connected to
the generator. This meant that their freezers were not working
and that the ice cream was probably leftover from pre-War
times. So why did they spend all that time and energy on keep-

ing it fresh? It meant that the freezers had to work constantly and the diesel...?

The Esfahani was gone. Retracing my path, I reached the front compound. The ambulance was still there. Both men were bent over the table each. A strip of white cloth with nylon chord was stretched out between them. Next to them was a wooden box that may have been...no WAS a coffin. What was a coffin doing in an ice cream freezer?

This aroused my curiosity enough to stop the van and get out. It was a coffin and both of the men, the one wearing the high boots and the ambulance driver, were busy wrapping a body lying there rigidly in a shroud. They were trying to bind the shroud with the nylon cord. The lid of the coffin was lying on the ground.

I was stunned for a moment. The frozen ice cream! It was clear from the taste that it had melted and then had been frozen again several times, which meant that if for any reason the power went off, the ice on the bodies in the next freezer compartment would also begin to thaw slowly. I wondered how long it had been that we feasted on this ice cream.

Mehr Ice Cream Company! Morgue of Martyrs! I looked at the cartons without paying much attention. They had begun to sweat. I looked around and I realized why they never shut the power off in the ice cream freezer. My mind flooded with images: the frosty beads of water on the ice cream cartons, the trap door of the freezer, two frozen enclosures side-by-side: cups, cones, colorful popsicles on one side and the bodies of dead soldiers, Basijis, Guardians of the Revolution, and ordinary people on the other! Both caverns fed by the same refrigeration. Cold sweat on the cartons! Bodies...!

The two men, one holding the corpse by the head and the other by the feet, hoisted it and laid it into the coffin. For a moment the thought of helping them crossed my mind. But that was not me. Never! I was behind the wheel trying to get away as fast as possible.

The van lurched forward. I made a u-turn and drove to the front gate where for the first time I noticed that behind the wall by the entrance there were hundreds of coffins stacked around haphazardly.

As the van left the compound, the sides of the coffins disappeared from view. But there was still one question on my mind: How many of them would be allotted to us once Qasem's risky plan to defeat the radar went into effect.

10

"So where's the ice cream? Isn't today ice cream day?"

"This food is more than you deserve, and I don't feel like arguing about it. Take it or leave it, brother."

"God! What's eating you?"

He lifted the cauldron of food from the lowered gate of the van. He stopped, shrugged in resignation and then went on his way. I opened the cargo belt and sat on the gate watching thick, black smoke as it rose from the refinery toward the gathering clouds in the sky. I wished it would rain. Were they storm clouds? I wondered.

I was dejected. Mehr Ice Cream Cups—Pasteurized and Homogenized, good tasting and fortified, made with real cow's milk. Parveez had been feeding this ice cream to us for weeks.

It was depressing. The refinery with the smoke rising from it seemed even less important after what the Engineer had said. "We build it and they destroy it. They bring up the artillery and you, Sir, annihilate it." Did he say "Sir" or "Excellency"? No, "Excellency"! Stop these idiotic thoughts, I scolded myself. Did it make any difference what some old lunatic called me?

Mahmoud said, "Come, here is the radio. There's an extra battery in the side compartment. Asadollah brought it. Then he took all the boys to help."

With a sweep of his hand he loaded the backpack into the van.

"How's Parveez?" he asked.

"Nothing new. Kazem didn't send any word. He was in bad shape, right?" It was clear that it didn't bother him much. Mahmoud was like this. I tried to answer him without emotion and changed the subject.

"No, not that bad. Besides the radio, did Ameer mention anything else?"

"The radio's more than you deserve. I don't have the patience to talk more. Load up and go!"

He made his voice sound hoarse imitating me. I didn't respond and turned on the radio. It started hissing like a snake, a sound that was very familiar to me having spent hours alone in the field listening to it. It was like the noise made by the monstrous oilrigs fizzling in the flames.

I looked up. Mahmoud had gone. I had to bring Geety and the Engineer their food...

Though it was noon, the thick smoke and the storm clouds neutralized the effect of the sunlight. An eerie anguish began to gnaw away deep inside me and I had no explanation for it. I turned right onto Geety's street and approached her house slowly. I should have brought the old woman her food sooner so that I could be at the Engineer's apartment on time.

I asked myself, why are you being this way? The ice cream! You're letting yourself fall to pieces just because of such a minor thing?

I stopped automatically in front of Geety's place. The club was still in the half-open door. I had absolutely no interest in seeing her face, and wished that she had placed the pot outside the door so I could fill it and leave. I bring this woman food and in return, instead of thanking me, she just stands there, hands on hips, swearing like a sailor—yeah, right!

The pot wasn't there. I hesitated for a moment.

Screw her! There was no contract that said I would wait around in the midst of all the problems with the radar? Was madam at home? Surely she must have heard the van screeching to a halt. Maybe her highness was still in a snit?

But there she was. "Hello, did you bring the food? What are we having today?" She had become very polite, perhaps wanting to make amends? Probably sorry for yesterday, I thought. I shouldn't have been so quick to judge her. In any case, I had to deliver the food and be on my way. As I turned I said, "Bring out your stew pot! I want to..."

I stopped in mid sentence; the woman standing there was not Geety. Not a woman, either, but a smiling girl with black hair down to her shoulders. It was the same girl the Engineer had mentioned, and I had completely forgotten about her. I pulled myself together and asked, "Your mother isn't around to get the food?"

The girl just stared at me blinking furiously. She was wearing a dress that covered her from head to foot was. I couldn't tell what color it was in the darkness.

She said, "My mom's gone" and smiled.

I looked up and down the street doubtfully. When I kicked the passenger door open, it groaned as usual. I stepped out, noticing that the van was in worse shape than before.

The horrible sound of the door opening erased the smile from the girl's face, and she watched nervously to see what I would do next. I sensed something abnormal about her. I asked myself, where was her mother? What should I do now? Why didn't she bring the pot so I could be out of this hole and get on with my work?

"Madam, please bring the stew pot!" and I realized that I had said it again, waiting for a string of curses.

Very deliberately she said, "I can't."

She must have been about fourteen or fifteen, but her voice put her at seven or eight. There was a certain innocence about her.

Why the hell not? I wondered. May God never forgive you, Parveez, for what you've gotten me into!

"Listen, miss! If you want the food, you'd better bring down the stew pot soon! I've got to go."

"My mom's tied my feet. See!" Sitting in the doorway she raised her right leg. There was a white length of ratty hemp rope around her ankle. Stunned, I walked two steps forward and followed the other end of the rope with my eyes until it disappeared in the darkness of the hallway.

"Why has she tied your foot?"

"So I won't go out and play—she says there's a demon outside."

"Demon?"

"You go out and a demon will eat you, won't it?"

I banged my palm against my forehead. The company of cash customers was now complete—all I needed was this one. I looked at her again and asked, "You two live here alone?"

"Sometimes auntie comes in that truck."

"What truck?"

"That one" meaning Parveez's van. Apparently there was another cash customer that the lunatic had on his list but had neglected to tell me about. Suddenly someone started screeching, "Little brat! Get away from him! Get away!"

The woman came running from somewhere outside of the quarter. I stood there stunned as she sprinted toward me. I ran for the van while she veered off toward the house. When the girl didn't budge, the mother shoved her with both hands. "Get inside! The Devil take you! Get in!"

The girl disappeared in the darkness and the woman went behind the door for the club. A moment later she emerged holding it in both hands.

"You're here for my daughter?" she shouted and lunged at me, leaving no chance to get into the van and drive away. Suddenly aware of the danger, I ran toward the back of the van. She raised the club with both hands.

"STOP! If you're a man, stand still!"

I had no choice but to turn around and keep my distance. She raised the club, then, using both hands, proceeded to bash in the hood. After it caved in she pounded it three or four more times.

"Stop that!" I shouted. "Are you out of your mind, woman? I haven't done anything!"

"SHUT UP!" With each blow she let out a string of curses—the roof, the door, the chassis...and, when the club began to splinter, she reached for the door handle and the van creaked open. She climbed into the cab and began to claw at the upholstery and seat cushions. The black leather seat covers flew from the cab.

"What are you doing? DON'T! DON'T!" I shouted.

Now that the club was no longer in her hands, I approached the van. I was a few feet away when she leaned half out of it with something in her hands. It was a weapon...Parveez's gun!

"I'm going to kill you!" she screeched and pointed it at me. I stepped back automatically. The thing was loaded.

"Don't touch it! It'll go off!"

But it was too late; her finger was on the trigger. When the weapon failed to fire, she started to grapple with it. I couldn't think of anything to do. There was only one way—escape from the neighborhood on foot, but what about the van and the weapon? I could just hear the boys taunting me when I returned without them, "Bravo! You go to find the radar and lose Parveez's van, instead!" Especially Asadollah.

I stood frozen in place with my eyes closed. They sprung open when the gun finally went off. I looked myself up and down and found nothing wrong. The weapon dropped from her hands and she fell to her knees. Suddenly the quarter was quiet.

"Mama! Mama! Come! I'm scared."

The woman remained on her knees and I stood there shocked by what had happened. The girl's persistent cries finally caused the lump in the woman's throat to burst, "May God wipe you from the face of the earth! Didn't I have enough misery without you?" Her uncontrollable sobbing became a full-blown cry, but there was nothing I could do about it except get behind the wheel. I cautiously circled the woman, dragging the weapon along with my foot. I wound the strap around my boot and raised the weapon with my foot. The woman didn't react; she was oblivious to everything. Then I heard the girl's voice—now only a whimper—masked by the woman's cries. It came from the base of her throat like the mewing a baby makes her parents fight.

The roof and hood of the van were littered with splinters. The way the grille was bashed in made me worry about damage to the radiator.

I scratched my head. The girl's mewing could be heard occasionally amid the woman's cries. I sat by the curb unable to think of anything, wondering why she had done it. Did she think I had designs on her...? Why was there a rope around the girl's ankle?

I had to leave as quickly as possible. The door of the van was half open, revealing the shredded driver's seat. So be it! It was time for me to go; but I hadn't given them their food yet. I stood up and called out to her, "You've made a mess of things for no good reason. If you want food, fetch a pot!" She didn't even raise her head as her tears continued to fall. Now I was at a total loss.

"Bring your bowl, woman. I need to go!" I said desperately.

Without so much as a glance at me she got up slowly, went to the door of the house, then disappeared into the perpetual darkness of the hallway.

"May God strike you dead! Why are you crying? Shut up!" she screamed at the girl, and the mewing stopped. Then there was the clanging of pots from the darkness. She returned with a bowl in her hand and took a few steps, then put it on the ground and retreated to the house. I heard her bolt the door and prop the club behind it. I picked up the bowl and stood there, thinking that I should have left the miserable place sooner. Everybody was waiting for word about the radar—whether I had found it or not.

The plan would go into effect the morning after they dug the trench around the artillery.

I filled the bowl with more than the usual amount of stew, knowing that there were now two people in the house. I took out a little for the Engineer, which left nothing for me. I put the bowl back on the ground.

I looked up at the sky before getting into the van. It was still overcast, and I wanted nothing more than for it to rain. Perhaps the woman and her miserable daughter had shed enough tears today to make up for the clouds.

Parveez's heap started right up, but now there was a whistling sound coming from under the hood. I ignored it. Whatever happened, happened. If the van broke down along the way, the only thing I could do would be to empty the tank, dowse the wreck in gasoline, and watch it disappear in the flames. What a stupid idea! I thought. How was it the van's fault? How was I to blame? Was it anyone's fault at all?

11

When Parveez's van came to a stop, the old priest turned toward me and smiled. They had loaded a military truck with furniture and the soldier-driver was lounging beside the huge steering wheel. He seemed to be resting.

I put the weapon over my shoulder. After the episode with Geety, I had decided never to be without it. As I left the van I noticed the clock tower again with its marble base, standing as tall as four men. The clock had been silent for some time. Though the power was out, it still could have functioned with a pendulum; but now there was no one around to keep it working. The few people who passed by on their way to the mosque for food could have delegated someone to wind the clock every noon.

In the besieged city there were still a few hundred people that would march like school children to the mosque for their food. It was my luck, though, to have these three on my hands, feeding them with the rations meant for the boys at the front.

I inspected the van. What was I going to tell them? That I went to Geety's—no, Gorgeous Geety's—to bring her food, when I happened to meet her daughter and the woman's pride erupted and she took it out on my van. My van? I was beginning to think that this disgrace was going to be with me like a millstone around my neck until Doomsday.

As I reached the army truck I saw that the driver was indeed resting, smoking as he squatted on the seat. Most likely he had become a smoker thanks to the free cigarettes at the city customs office.

The old priest seemed in a better mood than he was the day before. After I greeted him, he said, "Hello, son! Things have been totally peaceful since the last time I saw you, haven't they?"

Then it hit me; he was right. Except for the sound of firing at dawn yesterday I'd heard no explosions. Why had the daily shelling stopped? Why didn't the other side fire?

"My son, we've loaded up all the furniture and in an hour we'll be gone. If you have a letter or some message for your family, I would be only too happy to deliver it for you."

I thought about it. A letter? If I had known, I probably would have written something. But now? No! I shook my head. The priest nodded sadly and said, "No? You don't want to write one? For your mother! It would make her really happy."

This was the second time I had heard someone refer to my mother.

"Much obliged! But, no! By the way, where's your partner? Sorry, I mean that young priest..."

"Dear Father Hovanes, you mean? The man has really out-done himself in packing up all the books and the furniture." He pointed to inside the church and continued, "He also recited the final prayers to protect the church from harm. Please, come in— be my guest!"

He stepped ahead of me and I followed automatically. We entered the church. The benches were still lined up in two rows. Why hadn't they packed them up? Sitting with his back to us on the front-most pew, before the special wooden enclosure for the altar, was Father Hovanes. There was debris everywhere: dust, dirt, and chunks of brick.

I looked up. Under the white dome below where the shell had hit was a painting of the Last Supper. Though the blast had distorted the image, you could still make out Jesus with all his disciples sitting around a table and the worst thing was the face of that traitor Jew...

"Why didn't you take this painting? It's undamaged." I asked.

"Many things couldn't be taken, son!" said the old priest and opened his pale arms as if to embrace the picture from afar.

"Of course it's not an original, but beautiful just the same. Do you like it, too?"

Jesus sat in the middle of his disciples, but the strange thing was that the shrapnel had missed the picture. As he ate, Jesus, who knew that Judas was going to betray him that night, was looking out of the corner of his eye at him, strangely.

If some shrapnel had gone through the roof and pierced Judas' heart, I thought, the other disciples would certainly have yelled, 'Judas has been hit! Judas has been martyred!' and until the end of time everybody would have known him as a martyr and not a traitor. O dear Judas, suspended there in the Last Supper picture between the shrapnel and the Messiah, instead of Him why hadn't you tasted the Elixir of Martyrdom? Enough of these stupid thoughts! I said to myself.

"I'm sorry! Don't you like the painting?" repeated the priest.

"No! No! I like it."

The old priest put his hand on Hovanes' shoulder, gently distracting him from the book he was reading. I raised my hand in greeting and Hovanes got out of his seat. He closed the book and put it under his arm, then, avoiding the debris on the floor, made his way toward me. Then I thought: What if the young father was hit during the siege? What would his gravestone say?

FATHER HOVANES, MARTYR—GAVE UP THE GHOST IN THE CAUSE OF MOVING ARMENIAN CHURCH BELONGINGS WHILE THE CITY WAS ENCIRCLED

There would be a cross, perhaps white, on his grave.

"How are you? Very nice to see you again," he said extending his hand. I glanced at my palm; it was filthy. I wiped it on my pants and shook his hand.

"Where's your friend?"

Who?...O yes, Parveez? He's been wounded!"

The two priests looked at one another, probably surprised by my tone.

"How is he?"

"I don't know. He's being transferred today, I believe." Trying to change the subject, I asked, "You two, God-willing, are going to the delta in an hour? You know at night over there in the date grove, the swarms of mosquitoes…"

I left it at that, thinking that these two would be traveling by launch through the straits at the same time we were implementing the promised plan. Two people would escape the siege, but I would remain here, and, more importantly, the radar would still be there on the other side of the waterway.

We came to the church door and entered the compound.

"Well, looks like it's time to say goodbye," I said and reached out to shake his hand. The young priest took both of my hands amicably and squeezed them.

"I hope to see you again some day, safe and sound, after the horror of this war."

I shook my head reluctantly, too tired to engage in pleasantries. The old priest repeated the gestures of his colleague. My eyes fell on the statue of Mary and Jesus again. Without thinking, I walked to it and touched the place that had been hit by shrapnel, feeling with my fingertip the jagged metal border of the wound and getting a strange pleasure from this. The relationship between Mary and the date 1915 still puzzled me, so I asked the priests, "This is a statue of Holy Mary, correct?"

The young priest looked at the older one. The expression on their faces told me the question made them uncomfortable.

"So, what does the date mean?" which is something I had wanted to ask when I first saw it.

"No, this is not a statue of Holy Mary."

"No? So, Madam happens to be…?"

That word sprung from my lips again. Good thing Gorgeous Geety was not around.

The young priest was standing almost face to face with the mystery woman cradling the baby. If not Mary, who was she?

"This statue is a memorial found at every Armenian church. It commemorates the massacre of the Armenians by the Ottoman Turks," said the priest, waiting for me to react.

"That's why it's dated 1915?"

Both priests nodded. Arching my eyebrows, I said, "I hope to God when you get to Esfahan you can make one just as lovely for us Iranians!"

The old priest ran his hand through his beard and smiled, but Hovanes, ignoring the humor, remained impassive. The old priest took my hand and said, "Good friend, may such a thing never happen to your people!" We arrived at the front gate. The driver was still resting. The truck, I could tell, had been requisitioned from the War Room.

I said to him, "Hope you choke on those free smokes!" The soldier laughed and brought the cigarette to his lips for another puff. His shirt was half unbuttoned.

"I wouldn't worry about it!"

"Yeah, wouldn't worry, but if a rope happens to come your way free of charge, maybe you'll hang yourself, okay?" I walked on and reached the van. The old priest peeked inside.

"By the way, have the two of you eaten?" I asked.

"Yes, they were very kind to send some over from the mosque."

That would have been something to see: the two priests, pots in hand, standing in the same line with the old men and women receiving their rations from the local Sheikh.

"You also drive the food van?"

I was behind the wheel ready to go. I glanced around and saw the cargo strap, once white but now sallow with food and grease stains, and in the cab the broken windows and doors of the cab. First the shrapnel and then that unbalanced bitch! The one thing that salvaged my dignity in all of this was the radio antenna poking up from the seat!

I wanted to say to them that I was a lookout! You don't believe it? Come and switch on the radio. Contact the base and ask anyone. They'll tell you!

Absurd thoughts, I know, and the justification only made matters worse. I looked at the two priests—perhaps for the last time! I lingered while the Engineer's food got colder. Finally I answered calmly, "Yes. Yes, I also drive the food van." I didn't wait for them to say anything. I thought, whatever happens will happen. I was fully resigned to my fate—driver of the food van, I admitted it.

12

Earth from the shattered cactus pot still littered the sidewalk, forming exactly the pattern of an exploded shell. It was as though after the pot toppled from the third floor and hit the ground it was inscribed in a circle of dirt. But where were the pieces of the broken pot?

I looked up, and there was the Engineer, who having seen me scatter the earth with my foot, glaring at me from the window. I went to get the rest of the food.

"Sir, should I come down?

"Don't shout! No!" I said, but then realized I wasn't right. He had to bring down his pot, because the cauldron was so large that the two of us would not be able to haul it up.

He was still staring down at me. "Should I come down?"

But then I thought of something else. "No, throw your pot down!"

"Catch," he said and the pot landed right in my hands.

After the Engineer had been fed, I had to be a lookout for a few hours and then in the evening look in on the artillery unit and see how far along the plan was.

For a second I thought I felt a drop of water on my right cheek. I touched it with my hand and realized that the clouds, which were veined with black smoke from the refinery fire, had gathered. Was it raining?

I tilted the cauldron so that the remainder of the stew gathered in one place and then struggled to scoop out the last portion for the Engineer.

He took the pot in both hands and look at it bewildered, "That's it? This is all you're giving me?"

I tried to control my anger and tilted the cauldron to show him it was empty. I said, "Do you think I've kept some for myself?" and angrily let the cauldron fall. The clang it made when it hit the bed of the van did not unnerve him.

"You came late, but that's okay. I'm hungry!"

"Fine, eat more bread with it!"

"Why should I?"

"I didn't figure on the extra person. Besides, I didn't withhold anything from your portion."

"Which extra person?" he asked pointedly.

He had become quite bold, demanding his share from me as if it were his rightful inheritance. I ignored him, and, having retrieved the radio form behind the seat, headed for the stairs.

I was tired, more tired than usual. I put my arms through the radio knapsack and climbed the stairs. When I reached the third floor, I noticed the furry cat sitting on the bed. There were several very white chess pieces also on the bed. So the old man also played chess! But with whom? It didn't matter.

I continued on up the stairs and heard the clacking of the old man's shoes behind me. Evidently he was back in his magnificent abode on the third floor.

Ah, the cats! He was probably grumbling about the food because of them. This was reassuring.

I was on the roof now, but the sound of his footsteps did not stop. He emerged from the stairwell panting. I sat down on the bricks also gasping and relieved myself of the weight of the radio. The man was there without his pot. "D—did you want something," I asked in a broken voice.

He didn't answer. Circling me warily, he went to the low stone wall along the roof. He bent over and looked down on the street and then returned. Then he stared at the ever-smoldering fire at the refinery. What was he looking for? He must have seen it a thousand times from his third-floor window. So what was so fascinating about the flames now? I had to get down to work. I searched for the crevice in the wall where I had stashed the binoculars.

"Engineer, did you touch my binoculars?"

Ordinarily I was careful to cover the eyepieces with the plastic caps, but it was clear that someone had tampered with them. All the signs pointed to the Engineer.

"Me? You mean me, sir?" he asked and pointed to himself.

"It's okay, not a problem."

I set up the piece of wood and firmly planted the binoculars on it.

"I beg your pardon! With your permission, I only looked at the refinery with them for a second. Of course, I never thought."

The eyepieces were very dusty. I opened my shirt and cleaned them with my white undershirt.

"Are you still looking for the same thing as before?"

"Huh...yes!"

I stared into the binoculars. Two circles appeared as usual, but his time the right eyepiece was clouded. Why? It was set at "three," though I normally had it at "one." He rested his chin on his hands and stared at the refinery. I only hoped that he would sit still like this until the job was done. I turned the eyepiece setting it to "one." Now everything was clear: the date grove, the waterway, and a small part of the desert—the usual scene repeated countless times. Then a voice said, "Poor pawn!"

I turned around to see him standing there, hands on hips. "Were you speaking to me?"

"Yes, you! You with your head glued to binoculars, come up here robbing an old man of his peace and quiet." He was almost shouting, but that was fine; there was no one around to hear. There was a smirk on my face: Peace and quiet! I mean, _really_!

"I have no patience for this. Let me work."

"My dear sir, you have invaded my home, robbed me of my tranquility, and smashed my cactus pot. You come up here and sit on the roof with these binoculars to look at those poor souls on the other side of the water."

"Wait a second! What did you say, first? 'Poor pawn!' Right?"

"Yes! You're not a pawn?"

He rushed forward nimbly and snatched the binoculars from my hands and put them to his eyes. Then he started walking toward the wall around the roof.

"Get down, old man! They'll see you! There are snipers over there who'll shoot you!"

He retreated quickly. "That's right! Kill or be killed! They're pawns to killing and so is your Excellency. This chess

game is a farce! Two wretched opponents with no choice but to
kill one another."

I tried to stay calm and thought of Parveez. What an assortment he had gathered. Each one more screwed up than the next.
The Engineer's behavior was obviously a relic of his demented
past.

"First, give me back the binoculars. Then you can jump up
and down to your heart's content."

"And why do you want these binoculars, sir?"

"Clearly I have work to do that requires me to be up here and
put up with a crazy person like you. HAND THEM OVER!"

He maintained his distance. Evidently he had been waiting
for his chance, and this was the best time. "First, answer my
question!"

"Of course, what is the meaning of 'what'! Right?"

He exploded with rage. "NO, SIR! For two days I have been
in mortal fear of you and that weapon yours. Now, hasn't there
been enough of this nonsense, sir? Answer my question!"

If he had thrown the binoculars to the ground, it would be like
shattering my life. The thing rose and fell as he gestured with
his hands. The weapon! O MY GOD! I had left it in the van
and was standing there as I went into the building. I hope he
didn't... The best thing was to calm him down. "Stay calm!
Fine. Now, tell me, why are you so upset!"

"Why am *I* upset, sir? This is my home. It's mine. I had
been living in peace and quiet, minding my own business until
you showed up and started camping out on my roof. What are
you looking for that is so secret I can't know about it? I live
here, you stinking ingrate!" The binoculars were still in his
hand.

What a disgrace! I had to calm him down somehow. "Fine,
okay. Fine! Control yourself! Calm down! I'll tell you."

All my senses were trained on the binoculars.

"Well, tell me!"

"There's something out there that I have to find. That's all!"

He looked down at the binoculars and in a tone that suggested
I owed him more than that said, "Give me more details!"

It was a clear case of blackmail. The binoculars had become
his magic lamp and I was his genie.

"Didn't you say you would tell me?"

"I'm looking for something."

"What?"

"A piece of equipment."

"What equipment?

"Never-the-hell-mind what equipment! What's it to you?"

"This is my home. I have a right to ask."

"Who said this is your home? You've just showed up and occupied it. A seven-story building! You should thank God for this war. It saved a tramp like you from going door to door..."

He didn't let me finish. "Me? *I'm* the tramp. You're insulting *me*? I, I..."

"Enough I, I-Iing! I have work to do. Give me the binoculars!"

"For your Excellency's information, I am former refinery staff, retired after thirty years of unbroken service with a occupational rating of "nine." Yes, nine!"

"I don't care if it's a hundred. Now you are delusional!"

"I'm delusional? If you were candid, you would say I am the soul of reason. Look which of us has the problem? Who's going to ask the first question, me or you?"

He had started a dangerous game. I looked up and saw a mass of black clouds. Where, I wondered, was the rain?

"Okay, fine, Mr. Reasonable. But under one condition!"

"What condition?"

"The loser has to shut-the-hell-up! Okay?"

He thought it over for a few seconds. I was waiting for the next act in this farce, but...

"Okay, but since you are the guest, you raise the first question!"

Only a few minutes ago he was insulting me; now I was his guest! Where to start? Looking around, my eyes fell on the uneven stonework of the wall...

"Take this building! Would any rational person make a home in this building, which doesn't have a working door or one unbroken window? The winter's been cold and the summer is definitely going to be hell, right?"

"That's all?" he said emphasizing "all." He was right; that wasn't reason enough. I thought again. Why did I agree to play this idiotic game?

"Yes, the cactus. As far as I know, cactuses bloom once every few years or so. Why would any reasonable man take the trouble to plant barbed-wire when there are all these beautiful flowers he can find outside his window every time he wakes up in the morning?"

"That's it?" he asked, and I thought: Screw it! Yes, that's it. What did he want a formal diagnosis from a psychiatrist? Enough, already!

"That's all?" he repeated.

"Or, what about what is the meaning of 'what,' a question that has stumped thousands of academics...?" I had hit it! Bulls-eye! I stopped there.

"No more?"

"Yes, that's it for now!"

He crossed his arms over his chest. I could feel my beloved binoculars begging for mercy.

"Permit me, Excellency, to ask a few questions?"

"No, you answer mine first!"

"No problem, sir, I'll respond. You raised three issues, or, if I may restate your intent, three incontrovertible proofs that your humble servant is unbalanced!"

"Good! Stop beating around the bush! Answer! See? You can't!"

"Right away, sir, right away! The first question: You asked, why this building? I am truly sorry. Before you raised this question, I took your Excellency at least for a professional soldier, but now I am fully aware of the mistake I made. Young man,..."

Why, I wondered, did I agree to participate in this? Why, for God's sake?

"...thirty-five years ago, your humble servant was a simple worker at the refinery, this very one. Early one morning I awoke without hearing the blast of the horn. I thought I had been dreaming and had not heard the horn and went to work, but for the first time the refinery was closed. An impossibility, and do you know why? No, you don't. It was September 1941, on the eve of the occupation of this installation by Indian and British troops, my friend! The British foreman asked me, 'Why did you come to work? Go home until I tell you to return.' Then I realized why the horn hadn't sounded. I went home. The entire war in the city lasted no more than an hour!"

"Get to the point! What does all this have to do with it?"

"One second! After two days, the foreman promoted me with a small increase in salary, just pocket change—in those days. Yes, thirty-five years ago I experienced war and was not afraid. And now the answer to the first question: A single-story house is safer than a twenty-story building, isn't it?"

"Yes, but not a collapsing seven-story building."

"When the foundation of this broken-down building is able to bear all of this weight, would the addition of one old man like me change things? Now the second question. You made reference to the cactus. Well, a cactus requires almost no water. Could any other plant survive under these conditions, sir?"

These answers were probably sound, but there was no rational answer for the third.

"Now the last question: That gallant comrade of yours with his sterling character—compared to yours—likes to jest, which has caused me some grief. He was merely joking. That's all! And now there's another little matter that I would like to raise. If you believe that I am mad, does it make sense for you to try to reason with me?"

He was right about that. I had never considered this point and now found myself in a very difficult position.

"Now with your Excellency's permission, it is my turn to question you. Ready?"

I said, "Fine, please go ahead!" and reached over to turn on the radio. It came alive hissing like a snake. I wondered how I could convince this man to leave me alone. Nothing seemed to deter him.

"Why are you disturbing my peace and quiet?"

Was there any greater injustice than this? First, I become the food van driver against my will; then, after enduring God knows how many hardships I manage to do my duty as a lookout, and finally I deliver this man's lousy rations—only to be told that I'm the one at fault!

"You've got it all wrong. I had to come here—and don't ask why! Besides, I'll only be up here three days, at most. After that, these palatial ruins are all yours and your cats'."

"Unacceptable."

"Fine, so be it. Next question."

"You said you are looking for some piece of equipment? Why from up here? That equipment…"

I had to cut him off, "I won't answer this question."

"You see, sir? You see? I have a right to know. Besides, I may have seen something that could be of help to you.

As if this man had been able to find the radar when I was not around? How was that possible when he didn't even know what I was looking for? "Did you see something with the binoculars?"

"That depends, but it is not unlikely."

"Did you see something or not?"

"If you give me an honest answer to my question, I will answer yours."

Precious time was being wasted. I had to risk it. "Okay, look over there and listen carefully," I said pointing to the other side of the waterway. "They have a type of machine that is able to locate the precise position of our artillery every time we fire at them, and then…" I suddenly clapped my hand together, causing him to start. I continued, "…don't drop the binoculars. We haven't shelled them for two days now and have been scouring every inch of their territory to find that machine and, God willing, destroy it."

"And if you don't find this equipment, this machine?"

"Nothing! Only, whenever the mood strikes them, they can unleash Armageddon on the city."

"And you?" he asked very thoughtfully.

I said, "Us? We'll have to sit twiddling our thumbs!"

"So your Excellency is looking for a machine that the Iraqis can use to bring Kingdom Come to the city?"

"Right."

"How fascinating! You are in search of a Doomsday Machine, then?"

"Whatever you want to call it is up to you. Just tell me, have you spotted anything suspicious over there or not?"

He didn't answer, but it was clear that he was deep in thought. At least the question kept the old man busy making him less liable to fidget.

"Well, this Doomsday Machine of yours, what does it look like? What are its dimensions? What color is it?"

Very good questions, I thought. What could I tell him?

"Why don't you tell me? Perhaps I can help you, sir!"

"The truth is, I don't know. No one knows. Maybe it doesn't even exist."

The words tumbled from my mouth in spurts and starts and I wasn't sure the Engineer had heard them. But he had. First he looked at me irritably; then his face broke into a broad smile.

Interesting! Very interesting, sir! You shatter a man's peace and quiet—and under what pretext? There is a Doomsday Machine lurking on that side of the river, and you are the one responsible for finding it. But what it looks like, you don't know. What color it is—again, you don't know. Does it even exist? Unknown. So, how are you going to find it? Tell me: If you had heard such a story from another person, it wouldn't have raised any doubts in your mind, sir?"

Now I was in a real bind. I had put everything on the table and in the end he figured me for a fool and that was the reason for all the ambiguities.

"Give me the binoculars. Enough of these games!" I said firmly. At first he didn't make the slightest move. But then he came forward slowly and handed me the binoculars, which I snatched from him.

"But, old man, we agreed not to lie to each other! You said you saw something."

"Yes, I did—something new," he said and it seemed he was still playing games. He took no notice of the suspicion in my voice.

"I'm not lying." He said, "Get up and train your binoculars there," and pointed to some of the buildings in the city, not to the border waterway.

"That's not the border, is it?"

"Yes, I know, but it won't do any harm to take a look anyway, sir! There are several people working over there."

I reluctantly put the binoculars to my eyes and saw that he was right. In a space between two of the buildings, several people were busy laying sandbags.

It was the boys: Asadollah and the rest! I looked more carefully and saw Qasem, Mohammad and then Jafar. What was Jafar doing there? The only things he was good at were lamenting the death of martyrs and playing the fool.

The height of the sandbags indicated that they were almost finished digging the artillery emplacement. So the new site could be seen from this building. This was a lucky coincidence when it came to carrying out the plan. I happily turned to the Engineer and said, "Bless you! This is wonderful!"

"They're Iraqi?"

"No, sir, they're our boys."

I returned to my lookout post and mounted the binoculars on the wood again. "Now I have one small request, Mr. Engineer! You win, I'm crazy, but the only thing I only ask is that you let me do my job."

"No problem, but I'm hungry."

"Didn't I bring you lunch?"

"My dear sir, those few spoonfuls of stew aren't even enough for my cats."

"Why couldn't your Excellency, who has shown such good sense in cultivating cactuses instead of flowers, keep ants or roaches as pets instead of cats? That way, you wouldn't have to give away so much food. What do you want from me?"

I looked him straight in the eye. Now that I had the binoculars, I didn't see any point in arguing with him further. He rose and walked toward the stairs, while I peered through the binoculars. Now I only heard his voice.

"I said you all were nothing more than pawns, just like your colleagues on the other side. It makes no difference whether you're white or black. You both fumble about for the same obscure thing until it's time to die. Really, what a farce."

As he descended his voice grew fainter. Even the way this man could insult a person was extraordinary.

I remembered that day after Parveez was wounded, when Qasem had said that trying to define this war and the bloodshed was a task for fools and madmen. We were not at war; we were merely caught in it. And now the Engineer was saying...

Back to the date grove on that side and the desert...

The sounds of one explosion after another rocked the roof. I was suddenly spread-eagled covering my head with my hands. One after another, Katyushas whined and screeched overhead. The shelling seemed strange after two days of quiet.

Out of habit I counted the rockets: 22, 23, 24, 25..., 30. The Iraqis had launchers that fired thirty rockets at a time, so they had emptied one, which explained the multiple explosions. One after another they landed and, depending on the nature of the terrain where they hit, made a different sound.

The Engineer and I had spent two hours arguing. The shelling was so unexpected that I didn't dare look into the binoculars to see where they hit. 26, 27, 28, 29 and finally, with the thirtieth one, my heart relaxed. Each rocket struck in a different place. I got up and looked around. Great clouds of dust and smoke had risen from several points in the city and now were beginning to merge right over the market.

I could have been mistaken—but were they were testing us, daring us to respond and then, with that radar, destroy us? I couldn't get my mind around the problem.

I quickly picked up the radio and went for the binoculars. There was a small cloud of smoke and dust at the far end of the right flank of the date grove. It didn't make any difference, but I made a mental note of it so that I could record it in my book later. I took a deep breath, thinking that I had to get to the places where the rockets landed as soon as possible to take measurements. But what good would it do? There was no time to put the information to use anyway.

I was passing the fifth floor and shifted the weight of the radio backpack, which was slipping with each step I took. I had to tighten the straps.

The Engineer was standing in his throne room on his own floor, waiting for me. There were seven small stairs between us: six, five, four, three, two, and now we stood face to face. I said, "I don't have any time to talk now!" and continued down the stairs. I was gradually distancing myself from him.

"Where're you going, sir? Are you afraid? Is the Doomsday Machine operational?"

Were those his guffaws that were making the stairs shake? Evidently he was delirious, laughing hysterically and on the verge of tears. But this laughter, coming as it did when God knows how many people had been killed and wounded, was not easy to take...

I reached the ground floor and ran to the van. Even though going down the stairs was not as difficult as going up, I was breathing hard. I opened the door and pulled the shredded seat up. Everything was there: the weapon, the olive bag, etc. I was taking the radio out of the backpack when I heard the Engineer's voice. I looked up to see him pointing to the cactus plant.

"I replanted the cactus you broke next to this one. You think it will live again?

I put the radio down and sat behind the wheel. I had to drive to the market. What would I see there? I sighed.

How could I help now, I asked myself, except to carry the bodies of the dead?

Were we really no more than pawns after all? They could destroy the city whenever they wanted. Now, with their Doomsday Machine—as the Engineer called—in place, they would finish off the rest of us...

I turned the key. The engine started making that strange whistling and jolted into motion. I could still hear the Engineer's voice over the rumblings made by the van, "Ice cream. Where's the ice cream?"

13

"Why are you just standing there staring? Come and help!"
As the man said this, he pushed aside the struts that had come
down when the roof of the bazaar was destroyed. I was not sure
which way to go. In the few minutes since my arrival, the vege-
table bazaar compound had filled with people in shock.

Others used any means to get to the scene to help. One of the
Katyushas had landed on a manhole cover and exploded. This
was the worst kind of hit because, unlike the rockets that bur-
rowed into the ground, none of its shrapnel was neutralized and,
what was worse, pieces of the metal cover had become deadly
projectiles.

I stepped forward with only the olive bag over my shoulder. I
walked toward the soldier who had called out to me. He was
furiously pushing aside the debris from the explosion. Again I
hesitated. What was my role here? I should have measured the
blast cone and returned....

I shifted the bag to my back and began to help, all the while
thinking that behind me along what used to be a file of women
selling yoghurt from cloths spread on the ground, there was a
layer of blood streaming toward the dry ditch beside the road. I
wondered how many people had been hit.

He shouted, "Hurry up and dig! They're going to shell us
again!" and then angrily flung aside a large piece of a concrete
overhang. There was nothing recognizable under the mound of
debris. I quickly began to push it aside. "Are you sure there's
somebody under all of this?" I asked.

"I bought some greens from her not ten minutes ago."

Three well-dressed passersby arrived and without saying a
word began to pitch in. The shortest of the three was wearing
clothing red with blood, and his hands were in even worse shape.

In a few seconds a woman's hand emerged from under the debris; tarnished bracelets circled the pale-white skin.

The soldier instinctively began to tug her by the sleeve causing the bracelets to slide down and disappear in the darkness beneath it. After his sudden reaction, the soldier started to dig again, but the woman's body remained buried. He touched what appeared to be the last chunk of debris covering her. As he rocked it, the woman's hand jerked back and forth.

"She's still alive!"

The soldier shook it harder and the woman's hand jerked even more violently. One of the bystanders warned, "Don't shake it!" and he took the soldier by the hand so that he couldn't move.

"Grab the other side!" I said, "Try to lift her up, not pull her forward—right?"

Then the man positioned himself by the woman's feet and the soldier stood by her head, while the rest of us watched.

"One, two, three, LIFT!"

Both men struggled to raise the large piece of debris. The woman's body rose from the neck with it and then slowly began to tear away from it. The shorter man put his hand over his mouth and ducked into a corner to throw up. A twisted length of grooved rebar had entered the back of the woman's neck and come out the other side. Apparently the force of the explosion had brought the large piece of debris, which was studded with these rods, down onto the poor creature. We could see greens stained with dried blood near the body. The woman's eyes were wide open as was her mouth. She had obviously suffocated to death.

They finally managed to push the large piece of debris aside, completely uncovering the lethal length of rod that pierced her neck (about two feet). The two other passersby tried to lay the woman on her back. After the rod was extracted from her neck a fresh stream of blood began to flow. Then they pulled her by the arms toward the road, while her blood made its way toward a pile of debris.

"Come and help!" they called out to the soldier and me. I came forward and grabbed the woman by one ankle while he took the other. Contact with the woman's naked foot gave me an unfamiliar feeling. Touching a body, especially the body of a woman, was horrible, worse than being wounded by shrapnel.

When they were lifting up the large piece of debris covering the woman, I noticed how the threaded rebar rotated and, acting just like a drill bit in reverse, extracted a milky-pink mixture of flesh and cartilage from inside her neck.

All four of us managed to make our way over the uneven ground, which was littered with stones and pieces of brick, and deposit her body on one of the yoghurt-seller's cloths. The corpse was still quite warm.

"Use the van to take her to the morgue," someone told me. I stared at the broken-down heap. The Arab woman was now alabaster white; getting her to the morgue a couple of minutes sooner or later would make no difference.

"This is a food truck. You can't carry bodies in it."

The soldier nodded as if to say sourly, "you should know." I looked at my hands and clothing, which luckily were not bloody. I shifted the bag from my back to my right side.

"They may hit this place again. Let's wait over there until the ambulance arrives," I said and pointed to one of the stalls whose door had moments before been blown off its hinges. All three of us agreed and without hesitating disappeared into the darkness. The short passerby remained sitting at the entrance to the row of stalls wiping the blood from his palms onto the wall.

I opened the bag and took out the compass. I tried to examine where the shell hit from a distance, which was difficult. The shell had landed on the manhole cover, altering the final shape of the blast. I had no choice but to stand nearer and take measurements. I flipped open the compass; after it stopped rotating and settled on true north, I lined up my body in the direction that the shell had come from. For the sake of greater accuracy I needed to use a rod. Absentmindedly I turned around and looked at the bloody length of threaded rebar lying beside the wall. But I had no desire to have anything to do with the thing—at least not for a few hours. Though it wouldn't be accurate, I took a measurement anyway...

"What are you doing? Come and help us with this poor creature!" It was the short man. I quickly shut the compass and the reading: 5.947 in my notebook. Site of explosion: getable and Greens Market.

"Don't waste your time, sir! They're coming," said someone from inside the shop. Their eyes were on the ambulance—once white but now camouflaged with mud—coming our way. I put everything back in the bag and walked slowly toward them.

"So, are you helping?"

I said, "I have something to do" and, as though guilty of some unforgivable crime, added quickly, "I have to measure the blast cone."

"Didn't you say you drove the food van?"

I preferred not to answer. The ambulance, which was missing its back door, arrived and, after we all pointed to the body, stopped by the cloth where it lay. Two people nimbly jumped out of the ambulance and placed a stretcher by the body. Then, in one turning motion they lifted it up. My eyes flashed as I realized that they were going to take her to the freezer at the Mehr Ice Cream Factory. After it froze, would they put the body into one of those boxes labeled "Mehr, Tastier than Ever," and bring it to the graveyard? There they had a power shovel working all day long piercing the earth, preparing hundreds of graves...

Did she have anyone? Where was her family? Probably outside the region in a town, safe and sound, where they didn't know what had happened to her. She was probably supporting them with the money she earned. What about her husband? ... After she was completely frozen, what I had seen at the factory would be repeated. Those two people would take the body from the freezer and put it into one of those coffins piled up against the wall. How many coffins were there? Scores! No, hundreds! And maybe one was marked for me, tomorrow.

"Daydreaming? Come on! They're going to hit this place!" The soldier said this as he walked away. The passersby had already gone and the ambulance was about to round the bend in the road and disappear.

I looked around, then walked to the van. The yoghurt-sellers market would remain like this for hours—smashed clay pots strewn by the side of the road, their contents spilling into the drainage ditch and, a little beyond that the woman's blood smeared on the ground. The white yoghurt mixed with the red blood—just like the white cartilage and red flesh leaching from her wound.

I opened the door to the van so violently that had Parveez been there he would probably have cursed me for it. As I sat behind the wheel I thought about the whiteness of the yoghurt and the ice cream. Now I realized why I had dumped today's entire ration of dessert into the Shatt al-Arab!

14

"Your tea!"

He was petting the head of the furry cat as it gnawed on a bone. I lifted the tea glass from the bed. It was ice-cold. How long had it been sitting there? How long had I been thinking about the woman selling greens and that bloody rebar?

What was going through her mind when the rocket hit? Had she been arranging her greens? Had she been napping?

I tried to raise the temperature of the tea with the back of my hand but it did no good. That was no way to warm tea!

Several chess pieces were still lying on the bed. White pieces: four pawns, two castles, a knight, the king and a bishop—and black pieces: only the king and three of his pawns. Where was the chessboard? Having dismissed the cat, the old man was fiddling with his rusty samovar.

Taking advantage of this distraction, I looked under the bed. I had guessed right; the board lay there in the darkness. I pulled it out. It was a very worn piece of cardboard torn down the middle. As if holding a mouse by its tail, I gingerly grasped it between two fingers and pulled it out. I looked up and saw the Engineer staring at me instead of the cats. I placed the board on the bed next to the chess pieces. Where were the rest of them?

Everything about the Engineer was so confused.

"Engineer! Who do you play chess with?" I said with a raised voice, and, still at the samovar, he, his voice equally loud, said, "Excuse me?"

I nodded at the chess pieces and he understood.

"With no one, sir! Nobody!"

I gathered the pieces in my hand. The heads of two pawns popped up between my fingers as I forced them into a fist.

"With no one? So how do you play...?"

Not letting me finish, he jumped up, got out a thick black book and sat down beside me. I spilled the pieces onto the board, and they moved back and forth like a pendulum until coming to a stop.

"With this book, young man."

"Why with a book?"

He moved his head in surprise and said, "Well, because there's no one to play with!"

What a stupid question I asked! But how could you play chess with a book? But I thought it better not to distract him again and let him explain.

He sat down beside me and opened the book in front of me. "Take it!"

I took the book without any resistance. On both pages there were drawings of chessboards with the pieces spread out on them and letters and numbers in English written under them. I raised my head from the book. The Engineer had spread out some pieces on the board and was grinning.

"So!" he said, "my splendid young sir! White checkmates black in three moves. That's the problem; please go ahead and solve it!"

I glanced at the board first and then at the book. The pieces were set up like the picture on the right page. So he played single-handedly! It was a book of chess problems.

I looked down at the book again. It was open to page 226; but that was only about one-fourth of the problems in it.

"Well, solve it, sir!"

"Me?"

"Yes. All of the problems in the book are like this—white mates black in three moves. Go ahead, please—produce the three moves!"

"You mean that black never mates white?"

"In this book, never! I haven't seen it. It's always white in three moves. Do not waste time. What's your answer?"

"But I have no idea how to play!"

His face looked like it had been dowsed in cold water. It was true. The only things I knew about chess were the names of the pieces and that white always went first. Nothing else.

He knocked over the pieces with a swipe of his hand. Once again they wobbled drunkenly on the board. I sat there quietly looking at the Engineer.

"So why did you give me a problem from the middle of the book? The book probably gets more difficult the further you go in it."

"No!"

I felt like saying, 'Go to hell, no!' But I controlled myself. My concentration was totally shot. As soon as possible, I had to go to the artillery unit and report what had happened at the greens market to Qasem. No point sitting around doing nothing. The radar had yet to be found and there was no reason to think that the problem would be solved soon.

I had to laugh at what the Engineer was doing. He picked up a chess piece and threw it into the air. Before it hit the board, he picked up another piece and caught the first one. Jacks with chess pieces!

"Onesies or twosies?" I asked him.

He ignored me.

"Now why are you angry? Okay, so I don't know how to play chess. That's no reason to sulk." He dropped the piece onto the board and it bounced and then landed on another piece. I felt sorry for the lifeless pawn. Why should it be a victim of our feud?

"You, sir, are exactly like a pawn. A poor black pawn."

"I'm a black pawn? Okay, agreed." He was upset all right. In a way, he had a right to get it off his chest.

"You think you are not?"

"What's wrong with you? I admitted it! I'm a black pawn! And your Excellency is a ...?"

"I haven't played the silly games that that God of yours has been devising for ages now." He stood up and gathered the board and the pieces. He looked around uncertainly as if not finding what he was looking for. The furry cat snaked in and out of his legs. Finally, the Engineer had no choice but to throw the board under his bed.

I felt like kidding him and said, "From now on your rations are cut in half!"

"Why? What for?"

"Well, that woman's daughter has been added to the group."

"How is that my cats' fault? Your old friend, he gave us our full rations." Then suddenly he became withdrawn and started muttering to himself. "Ever since that Geety and her daughter came back, it has been one disaster after another. That's when the food began coming late. O, Parveez! Dear, sweet man! Why were you late? The cats are famished! He went to take this woman her food and now our share, because of her little one, has to disappear."

To irritate him I produced my best sneer. This was the weak point of all human beings, their most basic need—food! And even the Engineer with all of his clowning was no exception to the rule. But, what did he say? *When they returned...*

"You said Geety and her daughter returned? Where had they been?"

"Why should I answer you? You cut my rations in half."

This was blackmail pure and simple. "I was only kidding! You'd think I'd let your cat food go to the dogs. Let them eat their fill in good health! Don't change the subject!"

"It's been one month."

"Where were they?"

"What am I, an encyclopedia? It's just that your friend had said that they were back."

"You mean that after the start of the war, she got behind the lines with her daughter? Was that possible?"

When the horrid bombardment began, anyone who could get out of the city did. These two people, females at that, with all the towns safe behind enemy lines available to them, took refuge in this risky, run-down, sleazy neighborhood. Why? Why didn't they get their food at the mosque? What about that violent encounter with the woman and her club and the rope tied to her daughter's foot?

"The first time I met them was in the greens market!"

"With her daughter?"

"No without! Afterwards Mr. Parveez said that she was now living with her daughter. I assumed that she had left the daughter with someone.

"Had you known her before that?"

"I knew her first husband. He was an old Kuwaiti with frizzy hair, which had fallen out to about the middle of his head. He had a thoughtful face but only spoke Arabic. He took her back with him to Kuwait, and people said that the Arab had got himself a local girl from one of the cold-weather villages and deposited her in the middle of a Kuwaiti hell devoid of greenery and water. Sir, you were not around during those days. This was the way the Kuwaitis operated. After a while she returned with a child in tow."

"The same girl?"

"No, it was a boy. There was something between the father and..."

"The mother? I understand. But isn't it strange that she would come back to the city at this time? What do you think? She must have had a reason!"

He sat down again beside me, seemingly deep in thought.

"This is ice-cold!" he remarked and in one gulp finished his tea and then wiped his mouth with the back of his hand. It wasn't sweet. Drinking tea without sugar and so cold? How could he stand it?

Discussing Geety's life brought a thousand questions to my mind. There was a son in addition to the daughter?

"What happed to the son?"

He said, "I don't know," then went on with what he was saying before. "The girl is from the second marriage. The second husband was more of a bastard than the first. He spent all of the money he had gotten from selling her Kuwaiti gold on his addiction and then kicked the pregnant Geety out of the house. Then she started to get even in her own way. The second husband threw her out of the house with one swift kick. That's when she started to do those things with other men...and just for a few pieces of bread. I'm letting your Excellency in on other people's secrets.

I took a deep breath and then let it out. He was right. None of this was my business. But who knows where it might lead? "So that was the reason why she returned to that godforsaken place?"

"No! Geety never lived in that neighborhood. After a couple of years she saw the light and stopped doing those things and left the city with her daughter and son. They said that she took up sewing and made a living that way.

"After the revolution?"

"No, before. Several years before."

"What happened to the son?"

"I don't know, sir. I just know that she sold everything. I'm telling you—just for the sake of feeding my cats—things that have nothing to do with either of us! Haven't I said enough?" It was clear that he was very upset; his pride had been hurt. I felt the need to change the subject.

"Mr. Engineer! You didn't say why you gave me the hardest problem in your book."

Sitting hunched over by the wall, he answered indifferently, "It was not my choice. I only had enough pieces for that problem."

"You mean that you don't have a complete chess set?"

He looked away. "No! Is your Excellency's chess set perfect?"

"Mine? I don't play chess."

He rose and put his hands on his hips. The cat's ears pricked up. Its owner was now deep in thought. Then he muttered: "So your Excellency is not looking for a game. Then why do you climb up there on the roof, my dear man? How come?" He looked up and pointed toward the border waterway. "Your adversary is over there!" He exploded, "But where? Have you observed it? Seen it? Waiting for it to move? I am waiting...for it to go into action! Make its move and put all of us out of our misery! End our life sentences!"

His eyes welled with tears. This was the first time I had seen him truly upset. He turned his back on me and stood facing the books.

"Do you think I enjoy being in this seven-story slum waiting for the putt-putt made by the exhaust from that van? When you get old, you'll understand. You may be worse off; I never killed anyone in my life, but you want to. Now you're young and proud and don't think about the future. But the years will go by—that is, if you survive the war. I was worse than you in my day. Much worse! No doubt you will waste the next thirty-five years on some useless pursuit. It doesn't matter; whatever happens, happens. All of it's meaningless! Everything!"

He bowed his head. I didn't feel like defending myself; but since I had gotten this far, I thought I should learn more about him. "Why did your Excellency stay? Why didn't you get out with everyone else?"

"I had been waiting for years for an opportunity like this, to have a quiet corner all to myself, far from the crowd."

"So you're happy the war broke out?"

"Better to put it this way: it makes no difference to me."

"Where is your own family?"

He turned to look at me, "Do I have to answer this just for a piece of bread?"

That was not my intention. "No! Don't answer if you prefer not to—absolutely!"

I rose, uncertain what to do. I had to go to the base. Very evenly I said, "Mr. Engineer." He didn't answer. "I want to make it so you won't be yoked to that van anymore. I mean that if the food comes late, I will owe you."

He looked up and said, "Fine. How?"

"Simple. You go up on the roof and, when I'm not here, scope out the other side of the waterway with the binoculars. Agreed?"

"But I won't know what I'm looking for?"

"That makes two of us! You've heard the story of the guy who once saw a madman peering into a hole. The guy pushes the madman aside to look into the hole himself. Know what he said to the madman? He said, 'I don't see anything!' The madman answered, 'I've been looking into the hole for ten years now and haven't seen anything yet. And now here you are expecting to see something after looking for only a couple of minutes?'"

The Engineer screwed up his face and then slapped me on the back and said, "This makes you the madman?"

"At this point," I said, "I can't tell who is sane and who isn't! Just make a note of anything you see out of the ordinary and when I come, show it to me." Who knows, I thought, maybe the Engineer was the one destined to find the radar.

"That's all," I said and extended my hand. "Okay?"

He took it and said, "Certainly! But in return, I get to choose the kind of food! By the way, dear general, what happened to today's ice cream?"

I looked at him. I was certain that if he were aware of where the ice cream was stored, he wouldn't touch dessert; but, for now, it was better not to say anything.

From this moment our company had one more lookout. There was a strange threesome: me, Ameer, and the Engineer! If Qasem and the boys only knew!

I had no choice—at least the old man would have something to do, and the binoculars, likewise, would be put to good use. Maybe he would even discover the radar. What would I do if he did? Could I tell the boys: I hadn't found it, but the Engineer had?

This was absurd! The thing hadn't been found yet, and I was already arguing with myself about who was going to get the credit!

"I'm going."

"Will you be back for dinner?"

"Obviously!"

"Then bring more food. The cats and I are famished."

Fatigue, hunger, and an acid stomach were making me miserable; that was why I hadn't drunk the tea.

"Okay! Okay. Goodbye, for now!"

I walked to the stairs. The furry cat quickly vaulted onto the bed. The Engineer bent down to pick up the chess book and walked to the book niche.

I was dead tired and wanted nothing more than a good sleep. But that was impossible. First, I had to visit the new artillery base, then the mess hall again. There was no time to rest in the meantime.

I drove to the base, feeling as though I were trapped a whirlpool of a thousand concerns: thoughts about the greens-seller, Mehr ice cream, Geety, the Engineer and, above all, the Doomsday Machine...

15

"What *are* you doing?" asked Asadollah, puzzled by the way I was bobbing up and down. The trench was perfectly visible from between the branches. It was better not to say anything. To answer him would be to set off an avalanche of questions: You did *what*? You gave the binoculars to that old man? You told him about the radar? Why do you insist on making yourself a laughingstock for all the boys?

"You didn't say what you are doing!"

"Nothing. The trench isn't finished?"

I had come to the new base just in time. My back was to the seven-story building. From this angle only the seventh floor and roof could be seen. I was sure that even from that distance I could make out the Engineer's noggin on the roof. A small bump along the roofline, against a field of clear sky.

The size and shape of the trench was what I had expected. They dug down to about one and half times the height of a man, then placed the earth they had removed around it and patted it down. It was just wide enough to hold two people and the artillery piece. There were also two rows of sandbags.

I stood over the trench, thinking that nobody would believe it. The Engineer was still up there spying on me with my own binoculars! What a joke!

"Is Qasem coming?"

"He went to the War Room, maybe to see the Major."

"Why? Didn't he say not to tell anybody about the plan until the last minute?"

Asadollah stood facing me, but then he suddenly jumped into the trench and began pacing it off with his boots.

"The last minute? Well, that's tonight!"

"Do you mean it's happening tonight?"

I didn't feel like tallying Asadollah's paces, but he had gotten about a quarter way around it, patiently placing the toe of one boot to the heel of the next.

"If it doesn't rain!" He pointed to the sky. I looked up and saw the gathering clouds.

"Who decided? Qasem?"

"No. The enemy did—with today's round of shelling!"

I turned around; there was the old man's black dot of a head! I had the feeling he could also hear me. Something had to be done; I jumped into the trench, forcing Asadollah sit down with me.

"So that's the reason why the boys aren't here?"

"Qasem saw that they were tired and told them to get some sleep until tonight."

Tonight, I thought, if there's no rain, the plan goes into effect and I have to rid myself of that lousy food van somehow. But this had nothing to do with Asadollah; I had to wait for Qasem.

"Why did Qasem go to see the Major?"

"If I tell you, lookout boy, you won't believe it."

"Try me, maybe I will."

I got up gradually and gripping the edge of the sandbags slowly poked my head out of the trench. There was no bump on the roofline now. Did this mean that the old man had moved? Why was he looking here? What was so interesting about this trench? We had an agreement! What possessed me to place so much confidence in him that I would tell him everything? With my own binoculars...?

He pulled me down by my shirttails. "If you aren't going to listen, why do you ask? What's with all the games today?"

I crouched down again, seriously worried that I had been played for a fool. Maybe there was no radar after all and this strange man was part of a fifth column plot, standing up on that tall building reporting everything to the enemy.

What the hell had I done? I asked myself. The operation is tonight? What a stupid shit! I had no doubts about the priests; but now I was worried about this old man...? The day after to-morrow, when all this comes out, who'll believe it? Even if they accept that it wasn't my fault, they'll still laugh their heads off—especially Asadollah! Hey, artillerymen, he'll say, do you know about lookout boy's latest fuckup? He told some fifth column geezer about our plan; he even handed him his binoculars, so he could report from the best spot in the city. To top it off, he even served the guy food!

They'll be rocking with laughter.

Asadollah explained, "Last night Qasem said that when the plan goes into effect, the battalion won't provide covering fire. Tonight it's going to be quiet: just us and the radar, that's all! Are you listening?"

"Okay, okay, I understand."

I heard him but I had lost the ability to process it. What must be done? I got up again...he was there! That same bulge, watching again.

"You want to guess what happened, handsome? Qasem said, 'Tonight is the end of all these games.'"

"No!"

He was curious now and stood up. I pulled him down by his belt.

"Down!"

"Why?"

"To hell with why! Just sit!"

Asadollah squatted down in the hole surprised. "Have you gone crazy, son?"

"Shut up! Where're your binoculars?"

"Don't you have a pair?"

I had to do something. The Engineer now had a commanding view of everything with my binoculars. I could picture one of the experienced Iraqi lookouts—radio in hand—any minute now issuing the order to fire and turning this place into a ghastly cloud of smoke and pulverized earth.

"Be still! Follow me and keep your eyes straight ahead!"

I turned and looked at him in way that said this was no joke. I couldn't explain, but artillerymen were used to obeying what lookouts told them to do on the radio. At this point Asadollah, reacting automatically, obeyed, following me but muttering angrily to himself.

"What the hell's up?" he asked.

"Just be quiet!"

I felt that if he could see us, he could somehow hear...! But all he needed to kill us was to see. We went where there were more trees. "Hurry up and bring your binoculars. Not a word!" I said and accompanied him as he went for them. I picked the spot where the trees were densest and I felt we had adequate cover.

The old man with his strange ways! What did I know about him except for a few silly details? During the Second World War, he was a worker at that junk pile of a refinery, which was now turning into slag. On the other hand, he knew everything about me—straight from my own loose lips! And before that from all Parveez's chatter!

Looking through the branches, I tried to spot that seven-storied heaven, which had now turned into the seven circles of hell...

There it was—the Major's jeep appeared in the trees with its sporty antenna. There was someone sitting beside him—Qasem. The jeep got closer and closer. I poked my head out from between the trees. If the area were under enemy surveillance, under normal circumstances I definitely would have warned them. Careful! Get off the road! There's somebody up there—yes, up there—he's watching you! Floor it! Faster...!

But it was worse than that. The Major's jeep had parked by the food van. What I had feared most had now come to pass.

"Here're the binoculars. Just don't forget to return them!"

I took them from him. The Major—dressed in khaki—got out of the jeep before Qasem did. They spoke to one another, but I couldn't hear what they said. Though I had the binoculars in my hand, I preferred not to use them where Asadollah could see me. I had to wait for an opportunity to be alone.

I said hello—naturally, after Qasem—and the Major extended his hand, showing no signs that he still harbored a grudge. Qasem bent down to embrace me and kiss my cheek, a clear indication of the peril of the situation. Qasem was very consistent in the way he acted. He never openly showed affection to anyone, generally preferring to greet the boys at arm's length. This was why I found his hugs so menacing.

"And upon you, peace! I know what you want. It's all solved. Javad's father is waiting for you to hand the van over at the mess hall." Qasem was bringing this up in front of the Major!

What made him do that? The Major was probably still angry! This was why I shrunk to almost nothing whenever he was around. I had tried to speak to him two or three times, but the opportunity never presented itself. The first time I met with him, we discussed coordinating the firing—shelling and the like, and how Ameer and I were doing as lookouts. While all this was going on, I called out to him at least ten times, 'Lieutenant, sir! Lieutenant, sir!' After the meeting, one of the soldiers came out and walked over to the motorcycle to tell me, "His rank is major, at least several pay grades above a lieutenant." That was when it hit me—how a crass young recruit who well after the start of the war still couldn't tell a lieutenant from a major and how my mistake had embarrassed him in front of the men. There was no doubt in my mind that he was the one who sent the soldier out and...

The Major was deep in thought while I was standing beside Qasem. The four of us walked to the trench. Qasem was dressed head to foot in khaki. He gave me an especially enthusiastic slap on the back and said, "Are you ready, son? Tonight you've got to be really on your toes."

I automatically looked in the direction of the Engineer's building. The little black dot was still there, but leaning slightly to the left.

"Let's get out of here!'

I wanted to tell Qasem everything, but not in front of the Major. Without saying a word, he inspected the trench and then stared at two other trenches dug there.

"This one?"

"That's for ammunition—eight to ten shells."

"And that one?"

"That's where our men will take cover between shellings. We searched hard to find a piece of iron to cover the trench; but, as you know, no door can take a direct hit no matter what it's made of."

The Major nodded, then walked slowly away from the trench.

I said, "Mr. Qasem, come over here under the trees. I need you for something."

The three of them gathered with the Major, who was still deep in thought. Before reaching the trees, he stopped in a place exactly in the Engineer's line of sight! He turned to Qasem and said, "Are you certain that you don't want back-up fire from us?"

Qasem said decidedly, "No! I know it's out of the ordinary, but we only need the radar to discover our position." I grabbed Qasem's arm and pulled him aside.

"Could you hurry a little? There's something I have to tell you." After we were under the trees, I felt relieved and stood still.

"Well, what is it?"

Asadollah had lost all patience with me. I was trying to find an explanation for my behavior, but my mind wouldn't work...when all of a sudden I had a flash.

"What about the people? The people in the city!"

Asadollah repeated what I had said, but Qasem answered, "There'll be no problem for them. If this radar actually exists, it will go directly after the trench. Right, Major?"

He merely nodded. I felt like yelling: Even you are saying 'If it exists'!

"If it doesn't exist, what then? Suppose somebody in the city supplies the enemy with all this information? Then what?" I said.

It's been two, three days now that we've been driving ourselves crazy, and we're not certain that the thing is real yet!

Qasem was still staring at me.

"You have a point. If our plan works and they think they've destroyed our artillery, then maybe they'll start bombarding the city. Even in that case the plan says we have no right to fire back. The only way around this would be to fire at night when there's nobody around in the open areas."

He looked at the Major, even though I had raised the question. But what difference did it make? It was only a few hours ago, at noon, when the massacre at the market had taken place and the woman with her greens...

I thought of that threaded length of rebar again, emerging from her neck flecked with bits of red flesh and white marrow and the gushing blood! Where was she now? Most likely in the Mehr ice cream freezer, congealing. Three hours had gone by since she was martyred. Was that enough time for her to freeze or not?

The Major said, "I have to return to the artillery base and plan the shelling for tomorrow. God willing, you'll be successful!"

He moved to shake both of our hands and when he took mine he squeezed it harder.

"I hope to God that you're able to mislead them tonight. Everything depends on it. Goodbye!" And then he walked to the jeep with Qasem. Asadollah gave me a smack on the back and asked, "What the hell's with you? You keep saying things that make no sense. What did you want the binoculars for?" He took them from me.

"Give them back! I need them."

Only a few hours ago I had been playing hide-the-binoculars with the Engineer. Luckily, Asadollah stopped arguing and the binoculars once again were in my hands. I didn't wait but put them to my eyes. First, to cover my tracks, I looked at the trench; the sandbags were so close they seemed glued to my eyes.

I shifted my position like a rifleman crouching behind a wall and trained the binoculars on the roof. There he was—the Engineer! I fixed the crosshairs of the binoculars on his head, thinking that perhaps he had done the same thing to one of us.

I slowly lowered the binoculars and put them in Asadollah's hands. I had to get back to the building as fast as I could. Qasem was calling out to me, "Get going and bring Parveez's friends their supper. At 9:30 turn on the radio!"

"I don't have a watch."

"Come. Take mine! Parasite! Tonight's probably my last one on earth anyway. But I'm going to instruct the boys in my will to get it back from you!" Asadollah removed his so-called alarm watch from his wrist.

"Fine, thank God! Seems like I'll be rid of your Excellency's noxious presence tonight. Who's going to be the second man?"

"Nobody special—nothing to bring to the table. Mohammad—Mohammad Khalafi!"

"So it's just you two: Asadollah and Mohammad—outstanding! The fewer the artillerymen, the happier the lookout!"

"You wish!"

"Yeah, maybe it'll come true, too: a shell's goin' to land right in that trench and rip you guys to shreds and you won't even get to heaven. I don't think there's a single artilleryman in heaven."

"Up yours! If it looks like it's going to be bad, I'll take one of those unexploded shells to the grave with me, and head for the Bridge to the Afterlife. When you guys get there, you'll see that the bridge has been blown up and you'll be forced to camp out on the other side for all eternity!" He started laughing and slapped me on the back again.

Blow up the Bridge to the Afterlife!

Qasem returned carrying seven or eight metal helmets stacked one upon the other, the last of which dropped to the ground.

"Mr. Qasem, why didn't you ask me to help you?" asked Asadollah running to him.

"How many times do I have to tell you not to run?"

Though it made no difference, I also went over to him and picked two of the helmets. Then I walked to the trench.

"What was Jafar doing here today?" I asked.

"Tonight before the show starts, there's a mourning ceremony scheduled. Jafar is going to recite."

Qasem took one of the helmets.

"I think the one that's in your hand will fit. Try it on!"

The helmet went on and I fastened the strap under my chin. Voila! The perfect soldier. The clanging sound of metal against metal echoed in my ears. Asadollah was banging on my helmet from behind with his own.

"By the way, how did you know that Jafar had come here?"

What could I say? I should have said that the Engineer had us under surveillance from up there and had told me.

"Don't bother! What's new with Parveez?"

"Nothing, at least for now. I've got to go now. See you later!"

"Will you be there for the ceremony tonight?"

"Definitely! I just have to show Javad's father two stops. After that, I'll be a totally free man!"

There was nothing more to say, and neither of us had any taste for tearful goodbyes. There was nothing special about tonight; all the nights seemed the same. And this plan was nothing more than previous ones—except there was a greater chance of being hit.

Despite this, during the ceremony I thought I would say a warmer goodbye to Asadollah and Mohammad.   Perhaps...

16

Behind the wheel now with the helmet on my head, I turned the key. I looked up and noticed that the old man was still on the roof. Knowing that the weapon was safely stowed behind the seat was reassuring. A moment ago I had been watching as Asadollah and Mohammad took their posts in the trench, and then I had left.

I wouldn't be out of the Engineer's sight until I rounded the bend. As I approached it, I was surprised not to see his head. No, I wasn't mistaken—he was waving. But to whom? Why? I stopped the van and he started waving again. He had both arms in the air and was rotating.

I had to be sure he was waving at me. I got out of the van and started waving both hands. He noticed me and waved back. I repeated this and he did the same. I put my hands on my hips, wondering what to do.

"Are you nuts, boy? Leave it! Get going! What's this all about?"

I turned. It was Asadollah's voice. He was next to Qasem staring open-mouthed at what I was doing. Embarrassed, I began waving at them and shouted, "My arms had fallen asleep and I wanted to loosen them up a bit."

I got back into the van. After rounding the bend in the road, I was certain he couldn't see me. Which would be worse? I asked myself: that the Engineer was in fact fifth column, in which case what would happen to him would be clear, or would it? If not, his strange antics would continue. This was making me dizzy...

I stopped in front of the entrance and without looking around walked in. I was looking for the only person who could free me forever from the evil of the Engineer—Javad's father!

I lifted the lid of the first cauldron. A dense cloud of steam rose, followed by the fragrance of rice! Without looking inside I replaced the lid. I went to the next pot, which was rimmed in crimson sauce—yes, that must be the eggplant. The lid was greasy, and I tried to lift it with as little of my finger as possible, but the grease did what grease does, and no matter how much I tried—even with three fingers—it wouldn't open.

There was no time; I had to get back to the august Engineer, to his building, as soon as possible. When the Katyushas started to fly, I remembered how the stairs echoed with his laughter.

"Where to? You scared? Has the Doomsday Machine gone into operation?"

What had made him say this? Had he been warned in advance? Don't tell me he had a radio hidden somewhere in that room and was in contact with the enemy? I was on the roof when the firing started. But where was he? Why didn't I think of searching the other floors?

"Roast chicken with potatoes. I know you like it," said Javad's father. He was dressed in a dark, threadbare coat, a white floral print shirt and gray slacks. Up to that point I had never seen him in civilian clothes. He stepped forward holding a singed potholder and lifted the lid. Chicken roasted with tomato paste and surrounded by oven-browned potatoes. Now I realized why I went straight for the cauldrons; I was so hungry my stomach was tied in knots. Without thinking, I scooped out a few potatoes with my hand. They were still warm and I immediately shoveled them into my mouth. Fully cooked, they went down easily. Javad's father looked at me in surprise and replaced the lid.

"Why didn't you say you were so hungry, cousin? I would have served you some. How could you put that hand in the food?" He took my hands and held them up to me. The palms were blazoned with thick black lines. Where did they come from? O yes, the steering wheel. I remembered the Engineer thinking I should have been there by now.

"There's no time, uncle; I have to go."

He turned and took a white handkerchief from his pocket. "Don't fret, my dear! Mr. Qasem came and settled everything. I already told you; I'll do it! You see, today's rations are all set. I hope the boys enjoy them. Mr. Qasem doesn't tell us anything, but he told me to send everything to the concrete bunker. I thought to myself, they're not coming out."

As he spoke I cleaned my hands with the handkerchief, thinking that even he knows something is up!

"Come on! Let's go."

"Fine, but, first, let's go inside. There's somebody in the room waiting to see you there.

Someone to see me?

"Come, now!" He grabbed my hand and dragged me inside. The room was in one corner of the mess.

"Guess who's waiting." He opened the door and there, standing in prayer, was a woman in a floral print chador with her back to me. Who was it? Then I noticed Javad's mother's purse. It was her. I smiled in spite of myself.

"It's Javad's Naneh, son!"

"While she's finishing her prayers, I'll go and prepare the chicken."

He left, closing the door behind him. I didn't want to get the carpeted floor dirty with my boots, so I sat down awkwardly. She lifted her head slowly. I guessed this was her second prostration. So, Javad's mom was back!

How long had it been since I visited her last? At least two months. How could I face her? No, that was her first prostration and now she was doing the second. I looked around the room. There was Imam Khomeini's picture on the wall and below that, pictures of three of the boys who were martyred. Javad was not among them. What times we had! How many times did I kid him about his poor aim? "Too much to the right again? You're not doing those people down there any favors with shots like that!"

He was always laughing. The only child of this old couple. After all those prayers and benedictions and letting his hair grow without cutting it for seven years until he grew up and had that cane and...

But seven or eight months ago it was Javad's fate to be trying to defuse an unexploded bomb in the middle of the road, when it exploded in his hands. The news immediately added at least thirty years to the lives of the old man and woman.

Where was Parveez now? Was the danger over? His sister's marriage must be tomorrow. If Parveez...

Her forehead was still pressed to the prayer stone, and the sound of her prayers filled the room. My hand felt heavier; it was Asadollah's watch with its metal band and its black and white chessboard face with the hands that rotated on an axis of evil. Unlike most watches, the second hand did not pause with each tic, rather it went around with unvarying speed until arriving at where it began and then beginning all over again and again and.... The other hands chased after it, panting and wheezing, but the second hand soon lapped them and, as if running the mile, looked back at them with a sneer.

I wondered how these ideas entered my head. Was I spending too much time talking with the Engineer?

"It's you, child! Bless your heart! How long have you been sitting there? God love you! I'm talking to you. Why don't you say something?"

Was I so lost in thought that Javad's mom had been calling me and I...

The safety pin that normally held her headscarf around her chin was open, which always reminded me of my mother. How many nights had I spent with them? What scrumptious dishes! There were the sugared dates and walnuts and the local eggs with that bread...and his mom spreading the picnic mat under the date palms, devouring Javad and me with her eyes.

"Where did you go, child? Lost in thought? What's wrong? Tired?"

"Hi, Naneh! When did you get here?"

"Bless you! Bless you! After what happened to Javad, you've become more and more of a stranger. You couldn't once ask Javad's father to come see me and do my heart good. Come, child, come here. Let me kiss your head."

Embarrassed, as usual, I crawled to her on my knees. She took my head in her hands and kissed me. I felt like taking her hands and kissing them, but as always shame got in the way.

Her eyes filled with tears and she wiped her face with her headscarf.

"Don't cry, Naneh! Why the tears?"

Sobbing, she said, "Child, whenever I see you I think of Javad."

"So there's only one thing to do; I'll never visit you again!"

"No! Please come around. I want to see you!"

I heard the door open and saw Javad's father wiping his pants with a damp rag.

"Hajj Khanom! If you're ready, get up. The boy has work to do. He's got to hand the van over to me quickly and get on with his work. Up! One, two, three...!"

She got up and draped her cloak over her shoulders. I noticed she was limping, favoring her right leg. I rose and snatched her purse from her.

"Naneh, your leg?"

"I fell on the ground; old age—what can you do? My knee is swollen."

"Why didn't you stay with your daughter?"

Javad's father nodded in agreement. "She doesn't listen. It would have been better to stay a few more days with Soghra—at least till you were all right! Now if they start shelling... You want me to carry you on my back?"

He was right, I thought.

"Tonight you're both going back to the house in the date grove?"

"Of course! Where else can we go? It's our house, after all!"

His answer was like a splash of cold water on my face. After tonight's operation, there was no telling what would happen to the neighborhoods of the city. Why hadn't Qasem explained things to Javad's father?

We walked past the cauldrons—first me, then Javad's father, and finally his mother limping behind. The sound of his voice froze me in place, "Where to? You don't want to bring the cauldron? I filled it myself. Tonight's there's something special..."

The helmet was on his leg. The radio, weapon and the olive kit were all behind the driver's seat. I should have been wearing them when I got out of the van; the helmet on my head, the radio backpack on my waist, the kit by my side, and, least portable of all, the weapon with its strap around my neck...

"Man! You have the van only two days and looked what you've done to it. No windows, no doors, no chassis. Why, by the way, is the hood so bashed in like that?"

"That's just the war!"

If Javad's mother weren't there, I would have told him about Geety's rampage.

"If your friend came back and saw what you did to his van...? May God restore him to health!"

"Parveez has nine lives like a cat!" I said, perhaps trying to reassure myself.

"Parveez?   I hope to God he doesn't come back!"

"Bite your tongue, child! That's no way to talk!" Javad's mother was always complaining about the tone I took.

"Well, Naneh, what should I say? Every bad thing that's happened to me during the last two days has been that bastard's fault! He's such a fraud, he may have planted the charge in a wall himself so that when he went by, it would explode sending him on his precious three-day leave..."

I decided not to continue, what with all the blood he had lost... Why was I speaking like an idiot today?

17

"There it is! That's the building!" I said and showed him. Javad's father laughed.

"So the Engineer's still here? You bring him food?"

I jammed on the brakes, making us lurch forward.

"You know the man?"

Javad's father sat stock still staring at his wife. "What do you mean?"

"Do you know him or not? I want to know."

"Before the war, no; he came a couple of times and got food from the mess. I would drop him off when it was time to go. After I found out how far it was, I would bring him his food myself. That's all! Is there something wrong?"

"So you were the one who told him about Parveez, right?"

"Why do you ask? What's happened, son?"

"Nothing!"

I put the van in neutral again. It had stalled. While I tried to start it, I thought it wasn't so much Parveez's fault. Javad's father was the person who introduced them. Everything will be cleared up today.

Sputtering and gasping, the engine finally started. I put it in gear again, but the van moved in starts and stops.

"Something's wrong with the engine."

I shook my head and began to think about the woman. Did Javad's father know Geety as well? If he did, then my job tonight would be easy. I'd park the wreck in front of the building, hand it over to him, and that would be that...

It stalled again. I tried to restart it, but it didn't turn over.

"I told you, son, there's something wrong with it today."

"The fan's definitely shot!"

I shouldered open the door and jumped down. As I was opening the hood, Javad's father also got out on the driver's side. He clearly didn't want to change places with his wife because of her bad leg. The fan and the belt were fine. What did that mean?

Javad's father put his hand on the gas hose and said, "Try to start it!"

I did, but nothing happened the first time—nor the second, third, fourth, or fifth. The starter motor began to whine.

"Come here, my boy!"

I walked over to him. He was holding the gas hose in his hand. "There's no gas coming through. Did you fill up any time during the past two days?"

Leaning on the van, I passed my hand through my hair. Gas? That was the last thing on my mind.

I looked up at the building, which was about fifty meters away, and found the third floor and the Engineer's cactus pot in the window. He was there looking at us!

"Come down, mother!!"

"You can't fix it, child?"

"I have to radio the boys to bring some gasoline—it's out."

She started to gather herself together and, picking up her cloak, reached for the door handle.

"Wait, the door doesn't open!"

I turned around quickly and yanked with both hands. The door creaked opened slowly and she stepped down. No doubt she was put off Geety's handiwork: the shredded seats. I pushed the seat back and, first, pulled out the radio, then the weapon and the olive bag. The helmet was on the dashboard.

"Take this!" I said and handed the weapon to Javad's father. He balked and shook his head, but took it anyway.

"Give it back!" Without reacting, I took the weapon from him. I unhooked the safety and pumped the bolt, depositing a round in the chamber, and put the safety on again. I had no doubt that the Engineer was watching, which was all I wanted for now.

The radio was lying on the ground. I unpacked the antenna and screwed it into place.

I felt a drop of water on the back of my hand. Black clouds had gathered in the sky. All around, the earth was dotted with drops of water. Then, little by little, it started raining in earnest. I switched on the radio and the receiver crackled and hissed. I turned the dial to find the right frequency: 70_ 70...

The righthand dial showed 70; I began tuning the left one until it showed 70 also. Now all I had to do was press the button on the receiver to send the message. It seemed that there was no end to my bad luck; but if I'd only been more attentive, all this wouldn't have happened.

I pressed the button and put my mouth near the speaker, "Ehsan, Ehsan—Musa!" But there was only hissing.

"Ehsan, Ehsan—Musa! Ehsan—Musa! Ehsan, Ehsan—Musa! Ehsan—Musa!"

There was no answer. The radio at the artillery base was definitely off. I'd have to call the boys at the pier. "Reza, Reza—Musa! Reza, Reza—Musa! Reza, Reza—Musa!"

More rain. Javad's mother sat in the van by the open door. My mind wasn't working. I put the radio on my back.

"We're wasting time."

The Engineer was in the window engaged in his constant vigil. I took the weapon off my neck and strapped it around my shoulder. It rested on my chest. I should have treated the Engineer in a more measured and premeditated way. I raised my right hand and waved to him. He waved back. I cupped my hands around my mouth and shouted, "Come down and help. Come down!"

He nodded and disappeared inside.

"Naneh, get ready. We have to walk a few steps."

Despite the weight of the radio and the weapon, I managed to pull myself up into the back of the van. Two cauldrons of food: one with rice, the other with chicken with all the fixings. How was I supposed to deliver the food for the boys at the new artillery position? First, I pushed the rice toward the back with my foot, and then the second.

The Engineer popped out of the building and walked toward us. He had changed his clothes. The furry cat was walking with him step for step. Before he could get to the van, Javad's father

stepped forward to greet him. Naneh arranged her cloak while
Javad's father kissed the Engineer's cheek.

"Greeeeeetings, my good sir! You haven't come around to
visit this most abject of the abject. I had asked Mr. Parveez
about you."

What a master he was with words! It was almost like he had
never spouted any of that other nonsense—so formal to the old
man with that buttery 'greeeeetings' of his. Well, tonight I'll
show you which one of us 'gents' is the bigger bonehead!

"Come on, Mr. Engineer! You take that side of this pot and
Javad's father will take the other one!"

I grabbed the two inner handles of the cauldrons. The Engineer said nothing and took the other one.

"One, two, heave!" The three of us lifted the two cauldrons
out of the van. I felt a mad burning sensation down my spine.
The weight of the radio, the weapon...

"At least take that hunk of iron off your back, Child!"

I laid the two cauldrons on the ground. In one turning motion, I wriggled my shoulders out of the straps of the radio pack
and walked on. The Engineer was quiet. I reached down and
spun the two tuning knobs. I couldn't take my eyes off him for a
minute.

"Fine, leave that also!" said Javad's mother.

"No, Naneh, we have to have it."

I pulled the weapon tighter to my chest, then crouched down
to grab the two handles again. The three of us limped along, carrying the cauldrons with Naneh shuffling behind us, and the
pressure on my back lessened. The furry cat walked away and
went searching for something among the ruins of a store next to
the building. The rain had stopped, but there were signs of
moisture in the dust that covered the road.

We turned when we got to the entrance of the building and
placed the two cauldrons on the burnt-out remains of the wooden
spools. Everything was going according to my basic plan.

Javad's father asked, "Okay, now what should I do!"

I turned to the Engineer and said, "Mr. Engineer! Do me a
favor and bring those blankets of mine from up there, will you?
Naneh's leg is giving her trouble. She can't go up those stairs."

"Of course! Certainly! Right away!"

He walked away rapidly. I hurried over to Javad's father and in a voice that his wife couldn't hear, said, "Listen! I don't trust this man. Bringing the food was an excuse to get him out of the building. While we're away, go over the whole building, everywhere you can think of."

"To look for what?"

"For a radio, a weapon, anything suspicious! This engineer may be fifth column!"

His eyes widened.

"That old man? I don't think so, son!"

There was no time to argue. I heard the sounds of his footsteps on the stairs. So he was able to get up and down those stairs almost in one breath!

"We'll talk later. If Naneh needs anything, bring it down from the third floor yourself!"

"He may object, no?"

"Let me handle his objections."

The Engineer brought all three blankets. "That corner is the best one. I cleaned it myself. It'll be the safest place in the building when they start shelling us." He spread the blankets there. I winked at Javad's father and he gestured with his head that he agreed.

"Engineer, you don't need to spread the blankets. Come! We have to go somewhere."

Right then, he put his hand on his hip and became deep in thought. I was afraid he had guessed the plan! If he were really fifth column...?

"No, wait? Let me fill my pot first. Then we can go!" He made immediately for the stairs and, without knowing it, got in the way of the plan. Before the van was destroyed, I figured I would somehow contact Ameer on the radio, while the old man was away give the building a good search. But now it was better. Ameer had to stay by the waterway for tonight's plan to work. I should have brought the radio with me so I could get in touch with the boys.

I looked at the watch. It was after six—six twenty to be exact. There was about a half hour before sunset. I would use the pretext of delivering Geety her food to get him away from the building.

He filled the pot halfway with rice, then buried his hand in the pot of chicken.

"Finish it. Let's go!"

"Wait. I want to grab a fat, juicy one!" and he took a chicken by the thigh, but before he could get it into the pot it separated from the rest of the bird and fell back into the cauldron. Then he pulled out another whole one from underneath and threw it in his small pot. Finally he wiped both hands on his pants. Strange man, I thought: What stopped you from taking the one on top?

"Where are we off to now? To bring the van from the side of the road?"

"Pick up the pot! We have a long way to go. It'll take an hour."

"But this container belongs to me!"

"No one's saying it's not yours. We have to bring someone food. Don't you see that the van is dead? Follow me!"

We walked to the van. This time I remembered the radio. It was on my back. The helmet was still on the dashboard. With everything else I had to carry, I couldn't bear to have that heavy thing on my head during the long march ahead of us.

The Engineer followed me, pot in hand. When he saw me with the radio on my back, he seemed troubled—or, at least, he realized that the situation was not ordinary.

"Ready? Let's get a move on! You go first!"

He started walking and we passed the doorless entrance to the building where Naneh and her husband were standing. I waved goodbye to them, but the Engineer, who had the food in his hand, merely nodded. He sensed that our relationship was in the process of change. He probably read it in my expression. I heard Naneh's voice call out to me, "Come back soon, child. I want to get home before dark."

But even if the boys were contacted, and they were able to siphon off some gas and brought it here, it would take at least an hour. By that time it would be completely dark. Why was I so thoughtless? God, now we had the dark to contend with!

"Engineer!" He turned around looking irate, but didn't respond.

"Do you have a flashlight?"

"No!"

He was trembling with anger. I, on the contrary, had become calmer.

"What about a pressure lamp?"

"Yes, sir! Yes."

"Will you go and get it?"

"Sure thing! Whatever you say!" He put the pot on the ground and, without taking his eyes off me, went back toward the building. I turned on the radio and tried to situate myself in the middle of the road. I had to get in touch with the boys somehow.

I bent the whip antenna down. "Ehsan, Ehsan! Ehsan, Ehsan! Ehsan, Ehsan!" There was no answer. I wondered what I should do. It was almost nightfall and the old man and woman were alone in this desolation...

"Any other command, instruction?"

"Just pick up the pot and get going!"

He raised the lamp and asked, "What should I do with this?"

He was right; he had to use two hands to hold the pot. I looked at myself: the receiver was in one hand, the weapon in the other.

"Give it to me!"

He handed me the lamp slowly. I passed the handle of the lamp onto the antenna. Now it was hanging by the radio, and the cap to its kerosene supply was wet. It might start dripping onto my clothing but there was no sign of it now. I hung the weapon from my neck the way we did on patrol, keeping my hand on the trigger. I looked at the Engineer who was sitting with his hand on the pot, waiting for me. I wondered what was in store for us on this journey.

"Move!"

He lifted the pot and started walking. I waited until he was a safe distance away and then started moving. Half the route would be retracing the one we traveled by van, but after that we would have to take a shortcut through the alleys.

The old man walked at a slow and measured pace, although his brown and battered shoes twisted as he stepped on the stones and broken bricks that littered the ground. Who was this man? I should have delved into the matter before beginning the action. If the radar—or, in his words, the Doomsday Machine—didn't exist and if he was the only fifth columnist in the city watching from that elevated vantage point; then how was today's adventure going to turn out for the boys?

"Ehsan, Ehsan! Ehsan, Ehsan! Ehsan, Ehsan!"

Every few steps the old man would turn and steal a glance at me. The weight of the radio was wearing me down, and on top of that I was weak with hunger. In the Engineer's pot there was a nice juicy chicken sleeping like a baby in a bed of rice. I was so concerned about the Engineer that I didn't even think to grab some food for myself. It was vital that the mystery of the Engineer be solved during this outing. There would be time enough to get my food after I delivered Geety hers.

"Ehsan, Ehsan! Ehsan, Ehsan! Ehsan, Ehsan!"

Why didn't they answer? They were, surely, trying to save the battery and had the radio off. After the mourning ceremony, Asadollah and Mohammad would have to get in that trench and wait out the barrage of shells exploding around them. What were they doing now? Mohammad, shy and taciturn by nature, was most likely sitting by himself reading the Qoran. Asadollah, exhausted from filling and stacking sandbags, was probably asleep. He also may have been busy grappling with his own artillery.

The minarets of the mosque and the bombed bell tower of the church appeared around the second bend.

"Ehsan, Ehsan! Ehsan, Ehsan! Ehsan, Ehsan!"

The Engineer turned around for a second, and I saw a smirk on his face. What was so funny? Just wait till we clear the mosque and the church—I'll show you funny!

A long, undisciplined line of old men and women had formed in front of the mosque. Women on one side, men on the other. We approached them slowly.

The Engineer had placed the pot on his head and was walking in a way that reminded me of the village women carrying water jugs along the lanes. The only difference was that he had both hands on the pot.

A large cauldron was on the steps of the mosque, and there was the imam himself with his white beard doling out food into pots and containers. The crowd of about thirty people included five or six women. One woman had wrapped her child in her chador to protect the little one from the bite of the fall wind. The sun had dimmed in the sky.

I peered at the imam's ladle. They were having green-bean stew for dinner, which elated me. Today I served our people eggs.

"This side!" I reminded the Engineer, who had veered off on his own toward the mosque. After I spoke he moved back to the original course. As we both walked by the mosque, everybody in line looked at us in astonishment. One woman whispered to the woman with the child and pointed to us. In this get-up and the weapon and the Engineer with the pot on his head we must have looked very funny.

"What's for dinner, sir?"

An old man at the end of the line, his back bent, answered the Engineer, "Green beans, thanks!"

The Engineer turned around and laughed. "They've only got green beans, sir. Our dinner is really something special; this is the first time we've had chicken."

I nodded in agreement and then pointed ahead. The Engineer, quiet and baffled again, continued walking. I waved hello to the imam, who was wiping the perspiration from his forehead with his sleeve.

"Greetings, brother! Have you eaten?"

I nodded and touched my hand to my heart to say thanks. They had chosen a good time to distribute the food. Afterwards they would return to their homes, which were relatively safer than the open spaces and the alleyways of this part of the city.

The church was dead quiet. Father Hovanes and his colleague were very lucky to be away tonight, otherwise they would be saying the last rites.

"Ehsan, Ehsan! Ehsan, Ehsan! Ehsan, Ehsan!"

"Should I call them, sir?" said the Engineer and then stopped.

"What would you say, huh?"

"Ask them why they're not answering."

"So?"

"There's a reason!"

He sat on the ground and put the pot on the curb beside the dry drainage ditch. How did he know that they weren't answering? The best thing maybe would be to let him talk on.

"Sir! Would you allow me to say something?"

He was being over-polite, again!

"Yes, I give you permission to say something. Shoot!"

"Okay. I will overlook the condition for now. You changed the numbers on the dial."

He was right. I had changed them by the van, so the Engineer wouldn't see them. How could I have forgotten? How did he know that changing the frequency would cause them not to hear me?

I had to put part of my plan into effect. Just then I looked at the watch and thought: he so observant about the change of frequency! I trained the weapon on him and said, "Mr. Engineer, get up slowly and put your hands on the wall of that tower and spread your legs!"

I looked around; no one was there. The Engineer pointed to himself and asked, "Me? Stand by the wall, sir?"

"Yes, by that wall! It'll only take a minute!"

He glanced at the weapon and, realizing he had no choice, placed his hands on the tower and stood with his legs spread. I stepped forward, and acquainting the small of his back with the muzzle of the gun, began to search him with my left hand: around his waist, under his arms, and then his legs. With each motion the lamp made a clanging sound as it brushed against the radio.

"What's the meaning of this, sir?"

"It's nothing, sir!"

"What's that supposed to mean, sir?"

"Nothing means 'not,' which rhymes with 'what,' as in 'What is the meaning of 'what'! You understand? Now, turn around slowly and pick up your pot!"

He may not have heard me. From his pocket came an old sheet of paper, creased and wrinkled with something written in English. I opened it. Along the fold were two black lines, which were dotted and illegible. I took a few steps back. He had nothing else on him—even loose change! I refolded the paper and put it in my back pocket.

"So, turn around!"

"Sir, I'm not coming with you!"

I lifted the gun again and said, "So you're going to move!"

He still was leaning against the wall. If he had turned, he would have seen me smiling…. How long could he stand leaning on the tower? This was the best thing to do; I only had to wait calmly until his arms got tired.

"Fine, go ahead and shoot, sir! Put me out of my misery!"

I knew I shouldn't answer him; silence was more annoying than talk. I picked up a broken twig and looked at Asadollah's watch. The hands were still racing after one another; the clock in the tower remained silent, and the main city clock…

"Why did you bring me with you?"

"No reason! I felt like it. Is there a problem?"

"No," he said, "you're the one with the gun. You can…," and his hand slid slowly down the wall and dropped to his sides.

"Huh? What happened? Did you get tired? Pick up the pot and let's go!"

He turned and looked at the food and then lay down flat on the ground. "I'm tired. Got to get some rest."

There was nothing to do but wait. I took the paper from my pocket. It was headed in English "My father." The rest was written in script.

"Why are you reading this?"

He got up halfway, waiting for me to react. I was silent again.

"Where did you find that? Did you take it from my room, sir?"

"No! It was in your back pocket."

He sat up and linked his arms around his folded legs. With his head down he said dejectedly, "So, you know everything!"

I nodded in affirmation, but the only thing I knew was that it was addressed to someone's father.

"They left before I retired. I sold everything and gave them all the money. Then they wrote this idiotic letter on behalf of the mother! You be the judge! Isn't it obscene?"

I nodded, compounding my ignorance.

"…Obscene, is it not? Woman! You're no sixteen-year-old kid…!"

"Mr. Engineer. Get up. We have work to do…"

Before I could finish the sentence he had risen and picked up the pot. He started to walk and I followed him. It had gotten dark.

"I said to myself I had to get revenge, sir! Given what's written in that letter, didn't I have a right to?"

"Yes, you did. Now give me a match so I can light the lamp."

"A match? But I have no matches!"

"So what are we going to light the lamp with?"

"Sir, I...I...but you didn't tell me to bring my matches."

18

We had passed the crossroads. It was pitch dark everywhere except where light from the eternal flames at the refinery made it possible to see shadows. Now the deeper we went into the alleys, the darker it became. I was hungry—famished. If that chicken had not been meant for Geety and her daughter, I would have wolfed it down bones and all.

I had been a fool, letting my suspicion of the Engineer keep me from getting so much as one bite for myself. The thought of having that one luscious piece made my mouth water.

The Engineer had put the pot on his head and as he walked over the shattered bricks tried to keep his balance. If he had worn boots like me, it would have been easier.

There was no door or window anywhere without cracks or gaping holes. The slightest wind would make them buzz and whistle as it passed through them.

"If you had warned me, I could have at least fed the cats before we left!"

The cats! I hoped to God, Naneh and Javad's father had remembered not to allow them to get near the chicken. But this was one thing that I didn't have the strength to worry about.

"Stop! You've talked so much it made me forget to contact the boys."

The Engineer stood in the darkness. I took off the radio pack and dialed the frequency.

"Ehsan, Ehsan—Musa! Ehsan, Ehsan—Musa! Ehsan, Ehsan—Musa!"

This was the last time I would try to raise them. I had to conserve the battery for the operation. I had almost switched the radio off, when...

"Musa, Musa—Ameer!!"

It was Ameer's voice answering instead of Asadollah at the base. The Engineer brightened and looked at me.

"Ameer, Ameer—Musa!"

"Musa, I'm here. Did you need to speak to Ehsan?"

"Yes. Parveez's boat! Understood? Parveez's boat is out of petrol! Understood?"

"Yes, understood!"

"Now it's with one of Parveez's cash customers. Customer seven numbers."

"I don't' read you! Where, did you say?'"

I didn't want to mention the name of the seven-story building. How could I let him know without saying it directly? I never thought I would need a code name for the Engineer's building.

"Listen, Ameer! Cactus pot! 'What is the meaning of what?' Understood?"

The Engineer spat on the ground in disgust.

"No, not understood."

He had a right not to understand. During the past two days there had been no opportunity to explain things to him.

"Okay, no problem. Where is Ehsan, now?"

"Nothing more, Musa?"

It was clear that his patience had run out. According to military regulations, there had to be radio silence before each mission.

"No. Just be ready so that Ehsan can contact you! Understood?"

I said, "Understood. Over!" and put the receiver back into place.

"Move!"

We continued along the route at the same pace. This was the first time in the whole war that I wanted the flames from the refinery to get bigger so I could see the man better.

We approached the market and I thought of the woman greens-seller, solidifying slowly in the ice cream freezer beside the other bodies.

I wondered about her family. Had someone told them? Or, supposing she had a daughter, how would her husband explain it to the child? If he had any sense, he wouldn't tell her tonight. But how would he explain the absence of her mother? He'd probably tell her that the mother had gone to a relative's house. Just like me; I could never show Javad's mother the picture of her son....

Every once in a while the Engineer shifted the handle-less pot—at first from his head to hands and then from under his left arm to under his right, never saying a word.

Although it was pitch black, I could make out the remains of the yoghurt-sellers' market. I quickly found what I was looking for. Beside the wall there was the grooved piece of rebar, which, if it weren't spattered with blood, would look like all the other pieces that came down when the roof caved in.

No one had touched the debris of the market. No doubt, when people came round tomorrow, one look at all the shattered yoghurt pots would be enough to tell them what had happened.

"Engineer!"

"Yes?"

"Tell me something."

"What?"

"I don't know. Tell me whatever comes to mind. Like...like about that English foreman. Tell me about the time he raised your salary."

After leaving the market we entered an alley that was even narrower than the others, and we had to turn sideways. "Yes, sir, he did, but I don't like to..."

He stopped. What didn't he like? To talk about it or...?

I looked at the watch. The hands were not visible, so I turned it toward the flames, trying to catch some light, but that didn't work either. I had to know the time. Ehsan still hadn't radioed me.

"Mr. Engineer!"

"At your service!"

"Tell me about your chess game! You said we were the pawns? Are they playing with us, moving us around the board anywhere they want? Is that it?"

"I have no answer."

"Like when I tell you to move, for example? The way I tell you to turn into this alley or the next."

"Affirmative, but you have no more power than that."

Doomsday Machine always has the first move, the advantage

"However you want to figure it! Now tell me: am I a white or a black pawn?"

After pausing, he turned and said, "We humans always play black."

Now there was a kind of whizzing sound coming from his mouth, which soon became a hesitant chuckling, and finally grew into hearty laughter. In the blackness of that night, surrounded by all those ruined buildings and with the scene of that massacre fresh in our minds, his laughter seemed God-awful. It touched a nerve.

He continued. "Be so kind as to think for a minute! The One on top has been happy to visit Armageddon on your friends across the waterway, but any time He feels like it, He can unleash the kind of horror He did in that bazaar on the rest of the people."

"What? Somebody on top is doing what?"

"Well, you be the judge, my good sir! If He hadn't wanted it, do you think we would have had this war and all its miseries? Do you think it would have taken place at all? Doesn't He say it's fated? My dear sir, your real adversary is God; you're not battling those poor Iraqis! They are pawns just like you."

When he reached the head of the alley, his shadow, topped by a cooking pot, disappeared around the bend. He had begun philosophizing again—that was all I needed! Fatigue, hunger, and a thousand other concerns weren't enough?

I turned slowly into the alley; it was even darker than the street we had just left. I stopped for a moment to let my eyes get used to the darkness so I could find the Engineer. But…he was gone.

"Engineer!" There was no answer. I shouted louder, "Engineer! Engineer!"

I reached for the weapon. He had escaped. I pricked up my ears, which were still ringing with the sound of the last RPG I had heard. I turned to the left. My eyes, ears, and the barrel of the weapon were all focused on any sign of the Engineer. The slightest movement or sound would make my finger—now on the trigger—twitch.

The brick houses on the left side of the alley had caved in completely as if hit by a bomb. No shell could have done this; it must have been from aerial bombardment. I turned and, taking one step at a time, moved to the right side of the alley...

"Musa, Musa—Ehsan!"

The sound of the radio echoed down the alley. It was Asadollah's voice. I didn't have a chance to answer and turned the radio off. As usual, Asadollah would try to reestablish contact two more times, then there would be radio silence for another fifteen minutes; finally they would try to raise me again. In the meantime I had to find the Engineer somehow. It was too bad that Asadollah's watch didn't have a luminescent dial.

I got to the wall and clung to it, training all my senses and the muzzle of the gun in one direction. No—I ... I had to think.

He had entered the alley perhaps five or six seconds ahead of me, which hadn't given him enough time to escape unless he had found a way of passing through one of the bombed-out houses into the next alley. One thing was certain; he would have to step on something and make some noise.

A grating sound! I strained my ears to follow it. It was coming from the third house. I stepped forward with my right foot. The sound of the lamp banging on the radio was getting on my nerves. I took the backpack off and put it on the ground. What a relief! I walked toward the sound.

Why did he run away? Perhaps he had just been humoring me to this point. But when I searched him there was no weapon. Could he have stashed one here ahead of time? I had to keep my wits about me.

From the time we had begun walking, the weapon had been loaded with the safety off. There was not enough light to tell what the color of the door of the house was, but clearly it had received a large dose of shrapnel.

I stopped, wondering what I should do now. Go in? No, wait for the slightest motion or sound. Stay there until he made a mistake or there was motion in his hiding place.

It was strange how much I resembled the Doomsday Machine now! Waiting for the slightest movement to instinctively turn in the direction of my prey and pounce! Or maybe I was like Parveez's frog and the Engineer was that fly...?

Every second seemed like an hour. Despite the cold aut air, sweat streamed down the length of my body. I had to th

There was a difference between the Doomsday Machine and me; while it could spend hours, perhaps days, waiting for us to fire, I had only a few precious seconds.

I had to be back soon. Though it was too late for the mourning ceremony, it was vital for me to be ready for nine o'clock. I shouldn't have spent so much time on the Engineer...

I had a plan, though. Having reached the radio with a couple of giant steps, I flipped the switch and situated the set to eliminate static. I pointed the receiver in the direction of the Engineer's most likely escape route, then, doing my best to muffle the sound of my boots on the stones and bricks, I walked in the opposite direction.

The best place to hide was beside the metal light pole that had snapped in two. I crouched behind it and held the weapon to my chest, ready to fire, and waited for the boys to reestablish contact. I had to count on this.

The grating sound didn't recur. Had he been watching me the whole time? Or had he escaped through one of the ruined houses, causing me to wear myself out for nothing?

"Musa, Musa—Ehsan!"

This was the second attempt! There would be only one more!

"Musa, Musa—Ehsan!"

This was Asadollah's third and final try, but still there was no sign of the Engineer. I poked my head up from the light pole. Nothing! How I wished Asadollah would call me again. The Engineer had to be convinced that I had abandoned the radio and had gone down the alley after him.

He stuck his head out of the wall of the fourth house.

"Musa, Musa—Ehsan! Musa, answer please!"

I quickly ducked down behind the light pole. I was sure he hadn't seen me, but I could hear him shuffling away from the sound of the radio, thinking that the further he went from it, the safer he would be. All the while he was actually coming closer to me; I could feel him behind me. As he passed by the pole, I groped my way to the other side. Now I was behind him. He was bent low, feeling his way around the pole. My hand trembled against the weapon. With all the force I could muster, I had to make him freeze. I took a deep breath and pointed the weapon at him.

"STOP, Engineer!"

He froze and sat down.

"It's up to you! Move and I'll fill you full of holes. I had my doubts about you from the first. Now tell me why you ran away?"

"I was fed up with you, sir! Now, by all that you hold sacred, let me go and see to my cats!"

His tone was self-pitying. Every time he got caught, this was his attitude. I walked over and circled him. He was now completely under my control.

"You didn't say why you ran away."

"I want to go see my cats. They're hungry!"

"That's no answer!"

The sound of the radio echoed again.

"Musa, Musa—Ehsan!"

They must have had a reason to call me so many times, but the most important thing now was to interrogate the Engineer. Something brushed up against my leg; it was the Engineer's cat! Then it jumped into his arms, and he began to pet it. It had been following us and I didn't even notice!

"You still haven't answered my question."

"What more can I say? That letter said it all—that I mean nothing to them. For thirty years I worked like a dog, and then they say to me: You never loved us! I know that all this disaffection is their esteemed mother's doing. Did you read the last line? Did you see what it said? So how can you ask why I hadn't left? Whom would I stay with? "

The last line? My English was on the level of "My father"— just the basics. There was no time to wrestle with the rest, but I couldn't let him know that I didn't understand the letter. So I merely nodded.

"This was their last letter. They wrote hatefully that when I died, they would only observe one minute of silence out of respect for me. You see? Only one minute! I paid for ten years of schooling abroad for the two of them and then I even sent that seven-headed monster of a mother of theirs out of the country, while I remained alone day and night—and now this letter...! I had grown accustomed to being alone, until you came and robbed me of my solitude!"

"Why were you observing us from the roof with the binoculars? Huh? Hadn't I told you to look for the radar?"

"My dear sir, you with all of your experience were not able to find it. I also scoured the date grove, but I got bored and to amuse myself started looking in other directions: at the refinery, the waterway, then your van..."

I thought to myself, not my van, Parveez's.

"...Well, you attracted my attention. Then that military vehicle! I even waved to you and you waved back!"

Who was this man really? What he said seemed to make sense, but giving this inexperienced man my binoculars was sheer madness! It should have been the other way round.

"Get up, let's go! We have to deliver the food quickly and get back."

He opened his arms and the cat jumped down and stood by him.

"Go and get the pot; in the meantime I will contact the boys—but listen!" Here, I took his arm and said, "If you start playing cat and mouse with me again, I'll prove to be a very mean dog! Understand?"

He probably couldn't tell how savage my expression was, but my tone said it all. He walked toward the house with the broken wall and I headed for the radio.

I put on the backpack and paused for a second, considering whether to jettison the lamp, fed up with the noise it made banging against the radio, which sounded exactly like a camel bell; but I decided to keep it and pressed the button on the receiver.

"Ehsan, Ehsan—Musa! "Ehsan, Ehsan—Musa!" This was the first time I had made contact. I breathed a sigh of relief, no longer feeling isolated.

"Ehsan! Tell the big boss that Parveez's boat is stuck on the milk run; it needs aqua vitae!

"Musa! Ameer passed on your message. We solved the problem here with tinned rations. The big boss says there's no time now!" His voice stopped suddenly. He had taken a big risk. Time for what? If the enemy had been listening...

"When are you coming? Jafar is waiting for you."

Jafar wanted to start the mourning ceremony and was waiting for me to fill out the group, so they could begin the chest-beating!

"Send my greetings to Jafar. Tell him this from me: Begin without me, O tribal witchdoctor!"

He stood there with the pot on his head, looking dejected. I still hadn't reached a definite conclusion about him. The business with his wife and children had nothing to do with me...The cat was standing up with its forepaws on the Engineer's pants and its back paws on the ground! The smell of chicken was driving it crazy. He probably would have given the animal a thigh if hadn't been Geety's food.

"Standby! I will contact you later."

"Understood. But the big boss says it would be better to stay put. You are ready, right?"

The boys thought that I was in my position up on the roof, waiting for the start of the operation. There was no other reason for them to explain why I wasn't going to the chest-beating.

"Yes, I'm ready. Just standby!"

I put the receiver back and jerked the gun barrel to tell him to move. With what had happened, I decided to give up on the shortcut through the ruins and went straight down the alley to the next alley, then turned left until I reached the entrance to Geety's quarter.

This time there were three of us: the Engineer with the pot on his head in front, the cat zigzagging in the middle, and me with the weapon bringing up the rear...

19

He pointed to the door and muttered, "My good sir, I ...I won't knock on the door."

Both halves of the Dutch door were shut. In the open area light from the fire at the refinery flickered across our faces. As soon as we stopped, the cat rested his forepaws on the Engineer's pants. It loved him so much, like a child wanting to be held in his mother's arms.

"My hands are full. I can't."

The Engineer said nothing. He walked to the wall and put the pot in an alcove to the left of the entrance, hoping to keep the food safe from the cat.

I hoped to God that Javad's father was as careful with the cauldron.

Then the cat jumped into the Engineer's lap.

This left me with no choice. I stood at the entrance and swallowed hard, horrified by the thought of seeing that woman again. This was probably the reason why I had brought the Engineer in the first place. But now he was sitting safely on the sidelines. The two other times I had been there, the door had at least been ajar.

Bracing myself, I raised the metal knocker and then hesitated. I muttered a defiant *In the Name of God* and allowed the knocker to bang hard against the underplate.

There was a loud thud that made the cat's ears rear back, but no sound from inside. Don't tell me they sleep somewhere else at night. I raised the knocker again...

"Who's there?"

Unconsciously I let the knocker go and stepped back a few paces from the door. The light of a lamp in the hallway shone in the pane of glass above the door. There was also the shadow of a woman. I had to brace myself for the encounter. The door creaked half open and the woman holding the lamp in front of her face appeared. The lower part of her body was hidden behind the closed half of the door.

"Huh? Who is it? YOU!"

She looked around and saw the Engineer.

"Who's this? Where's your van?"

"Dead!"

The Engineer got up, sending the cat flying. He lifted the pot from the alcove and handed it to Geety. She hesitated and then looked more carefully at his face.

"So, what do we have now?"

She took the pot with one hand, raised the lamp with the other, and peered inside. She made a face as if she had seen something strange and put the pot back in the alcove. After sampling a bit of the rice with her finger, she made a look of disgust, spat it out, and wiped her pursed lips with the back of her hand.

"It's full 'a dirt! Happy now—you brought me food!"

I walked forward warily and tilted the pot toward me. It was filthy and peppered with pebbles.

"Would you give this to your mother to eat?" she asked and overturned the pot, spilling on the ground first the rice and then the chicken we had so painstakingly brought this far. The chicken was no more than a thigh; the cat—now happily ensconced again in its master's lap—had done what cats do!

"ENGINEER!" I barked, "Come over here, now!"

He shot up immediately, revealing, in the light of the woman's lamp, a large grease stain on his right pant leg. I pointed to his pocket, and ordered, "Take it out!"

He reached in and retrieved the rest of the meat. "I wanted it for the cat!"

"So this was why you ran away? How did the rice get that way?"

"I tripped and the food fell to the ground. Look what happened to my leg!"

He raised his pants. There was a black-and-blue mark on his left leg.

"To hell with you! You should've broken your damned leg!"

"That talk's not going to get us anywhere. What're we going to have for dinner?" asked the woman.

Without thinking, I said, "Standby!" which was what we used on the radio. She was quiet, either understanding what it meant or mulling it over.

"Take the lamp from the woman and use it to light the other one," I said.

I unhooked the lamp from the antenna and shook it again to make sure it had kerosene. Had I called Geety 'Madam' again?

Thank God she wasn't paying attention.

She raised her lamp and stared at the Engineer's face, then slowly handed it to him. He put both of them on the ground.

The woman leaned against wall; she appeared uneasy and kept shifting her weight until finally settling on the bench.

I had to do something. If I could reach the boys, they could get to the van in time, start it, and bring some food with them.

"Ehsan, Ehsan—Musa! Ehsan, Ehsan—Musa!"

As she watched the Engineer light the lamp, Geety's hand rummaged in the area of her chest and finally emerged from her collar with some dirt that she flicked away with her fingers. I turned away; she seemed to have no idea that there were two men present.

"Ehsan, Ehsan—Musa! Ehsan, Ehsan—Musa!"

"Musa! It's Ehsan, over!"

"Listen! That 'seven' business that I told you about—tell Qasem that he must get us aqua vitae any way he can."

There wasn't a sound anywhere. As I turned I heard Geety's grumbling, "The stupid fool doesn't even have what it takes to light a lamp. I'll bring some matches."

"Sir, I swear, it's because of the wind!"

"Okay, fine," I said and pressed the button on the receiver. "Listen, Ehsan! I'm in no position to explain now, but definitely try to send a vehicle. Javad's parents are also stuck; they haven't gone home yet. Understood?"

"Understood. Standby while I tell Qasem!"

I sat by the curb. The one-legged chicken on the ground, where the cat was going at it tooth and claw. It opened its mouth as wide as it could and dug savagely into the bird—consolation for being famished. I was so hungry that I felt like pushing the cat aside and swallowing the thing whole.

Would the headaches ever end? I did my best to deliver the food, but this madman had managed to spoil everything!

"Musa, Musa—Ehsan!"

"Musa here. Go ahead, Ehsan!"

"Mr. Qasem is tied up. If Javad's father is with you, that's much safer for them than their own place. Let them stay there. In the meantime observe regulations! Understood! Out!"

Regulations called for radio silence before an operation. But how could I enforce them in the middle of this mess? I had to think of something.

"Hi!" It was the daughter followed by Geety screeching, "Get inside!"

The girl quickly crawled back into the house. Geety put the lamps on the ground and lit a match. Then she lit the wick of one of the lamps, but, before she could light the other one, the match went out, apparently burning her finger because she tossed it aside angrily. With another match she lit the second lamp, making the alley look festive. Along the way, groping around blindly, I had been so careful not to make any noise. But now I threw all caution to the wind. I had to think straight, however.

But there was no solution. Qasem and the boys would never believe that I had abandoned my post and followed this maniac to come here. It was probably better that they would never get to the van in time.

I could just hear them: Where did he go? Why? And finally they would have at me in person: Really? With *that* man? A pot? A cat? Where? There? The night of the operation? With only two days left to find the radar, you wasted time on such lunacy!

Now what should I do about dinner? The time! What was the time?

I turned the watch face to the lamps, which had been placed a short distance from each other. Now I could make out the hands; it was 8:42—less than an hour before the operation was to start and less than twenty minutes before the mourning ceremony. Obviously my attending the ceremony was out of the question, but I had to get back to the building any way I could. What about dinner for these two?

If I ran, I probably could have reached it in time. Then what? Should I go up on the roof, while the Engineer returned with a pot filled with chicken and rice? No: the Engineer, with his cat, was completely unreliable and, besides, he would be walking back with the operation under way. What would happen to him as the bombs started falling? He would have no warning or shelter. No, that couldn't happen...

The Engineer was right; the wind had put the lamp out. This was all we needed. Each gust acted like a twister snatching bits of grit from the road, raking them over my head and face. My eyes narrowed to two thin slits. The flames in the lamps slimmed to thin flickering.

No, there was no other way. Having come this far, I had to try this one last thing. I should never have gotten into the van in the first place, should never have taken on Parveez's duties—however much against my will. Now there was no choice; I had to risk it and let the Engineer in on what I was thinking.

He was still toying with the cat—never stopped, it seemed. The woman was deep in thought on the bench, mining a nostril with her finger.

"Engineer!"

Without a word he came toward me with the cat on his shoulder.

"For heaven's sake, would you put that thing down for one minute?"

"You bet, sir! Little kitty, down my little sweetie! The man is armed!"

The cat turned feisty and arched its back, then slid on all four paws to the ground. I took a step toward the Engineer, closing the gap between us. The wind started to howl again. I turned my back on the woman, not wanting her to hear a word we were saying.

"Engineer! Just listen! And whatever you do, don't look at Geety!"

"Why not?"

"Fuck why not!" I erupted. "Just listen! Tonight, no matter what, we have to bring this woman and her daughter to the building."

"Which building?"

"Which building? Why, your Excellency's palatial abode!"

"MY BUILDING?" he screamed.

Geety jumped up. Things were getting out of hand. That couldn't happen before I finished talking this over. I put my hand on his shoulder moving him a few more steps away from the woman.

"Don't waste your breath," I told him. "Every thing that has gone wrong tonight has been your fault! Understood!" I had slipped into radio talk again.

Like a mouse caught in a trap, the Engineer pleaded at me with his eyes.

"How's that, sir?"

"Because you gave the food to the cat. What do you want me to do? Let these two go to bed hungry, just so your cat can belch happily in the morning?"

"No, sir, but there's another way around this."

"What other way? If there is, tell me!"

Suddenly the girl said, "Hey! Did you bring us food? I'm starving."

"They gave our dinner to the cats and dogs," said the woman, erasing the smile from her daughter's face."

I had to say something here. "No, child! There is food, but you'll have to come and get it yourself."

"What for?"

"Because I said so! The van is shot and I have something I need to do in an hour. The only way out of this is for your mother to come with us and get some food and then return home."

"Why are you speaking to my daughter? Huh?"

I made a chopping motion with my hand and said, "The van is still suffering from your noon-time handiwork."

"Musa! Come in, Musa!" said the Engineer, using code.

"Coming."

"No, immediately, sir—I need you right now!"

I thought: is this time for it, man? Geety remained glued in place. "Coming now. Think it over!" I then walked over to the Engineer, who also stepped toward me.

"Don't argue with this Geety. Sir! It's dangerous!"

"I found that out this afternoon. Is that all?"

"You mean she did it to you, too? Pulled your pants down?"

"What are you talking about? She smashed the van to pieces!"

"You were lucky, sir, lucky. Gorgeous Geety is notorious. People who would argue with her—she pulled their pants down right there in the middle of the street for everybody to see!"

I looked at her, amazed. "In the street, in front of everyone? She'd pull down a man's pants?"

As if this was the stupidest thing he had ever heard, he made a face and said, "The man's pants? His pants? No, sir. The pajamas of the neighboring women!"

"Are you serious?"

"Come, sir! Let's get out of here. This woman is worse than a wild animal!"

I unconsciously reached for my belt to make sure it was secure. There was definitely enough time to escape from her. No, maybe the Engineer was trying to pull something! Was I being played for a fool again? Placing my faith in this cat-lover?

The sound of the door closing interrupted my doubts.

"We'd better go, sir!"

I walked to the door and slammed the knocker down against it, annoyed that the woman had taken the initiative from me. "Outside!" I bellowed.

There was no sound except the howling of the wind. The Engineer had the cat in his arms, waiting for us to leave. I banged on the door with the knocker repeatedly, but the sound of the wind muffled the sound.

Suddenly the door opened. I stepped back, and the woman emerged without the lamp, "What the hell's wrong with you? BEAT IT!"

"Get your container! You'll have to bring dinner yourself!"

"We don't want your damned dinner. Besides I'm not going anywhere this time of night."

From the pitch dark of the hallway I head the daughter whine,
"But I'm starving! Mama! Starving!" She started to sob, and
her cries sent a sharp shiver up my spine that made me forget the
sting of the wind. What was this poor kid's crime? The mother
was no mother, nor was this a proper place for the child.

"At it again, girl? This crying will be the death of you!"

I was determined to put an end to the argument. "Your
daughter's hungry. Come on, get ready and let's go!"

The woman emerged from behind the door with a thick iron
bar. "What's it to you that my daughter is hungry? What the
hell do you want from us? Blood? I don't want any food. Get
out of here or I'll shove this between your legs and split you
down the middle! Hear me?"

I felt a scorching pain rush from my head to my toes. Yesterday she cursed my mother and now she was threatening me. I
should have whipped out the weapon and planted it in her chest
to spoil her appetite for threats. But the girl was sobbing,
"Mama! Tell them to bring us food! I'm starving."

I sighed. The Engineer yelled, "Sir! I told you so; let's get
going!"

I turned to the woman. This was my last try. With all the
anger I could muster, I clenched my teeth and, pointing at her,
barked, "LISTEN! Listen well! There's only one hour left before this place turns into hell! HELL! Do you understand what
that means? The enemy is supposed to shell the city in an hour.
You two have to find a safe place to hide until morning. This
dump is already on its last legs; just The sound of an explosion
would be enough to bring it down on your heads!"

She sneered, seeming to think I was kidding. "You'll have to
come up with something better than that, son; this is what *they*
are always saying."

"But tonight's different. Now, are you coming or not?"

"You men are all the same. Tell the truth, now! What have
you and this shithead cooked up for my daughter?"

I couldn't take it any longer.

"Shut the hell up, you crazy slut! For two days you've been
saying whatever comes into that foul mouth of yours. Enough!
Are you coming or do I ..."

I took the weapon from around my neck and unlatched the safety. Now she understood how serious I was about bringing them along. But this was pure idiocy! I shouldn't have tried to force her if she didn't want to go. But I knew that as soon as the operation started and each moment it lasted, the image of this place wouldn't leave my mind, and that innocent child and perhaps even that creature...the seconds passed slowly.

"I swear to the revered one, Ali himself, if you're lying, I'll rip you to shreds with my bare hands and eat your guts!"

"Fine! Rip away! But just get going!"

20

Without exchanging another word, she went inside. I turned to the Engineer, who looked away as soon as our eyes met. The way he was standing showed how upset he was.

I tried to ignore the horrible sound of the wind as it whipped through the windows and doors. I picked up a lamp and looked at the watch. It was 9:12 and the chest-beating had started. The boys would have formed a circle of seven or eight people, while Jafar recited for them. Who would be the first to lead the ceremony? Would it be—as it usually was—Mohammad Khalafi with that Arabic accent of his? Or would it be Qasem himself whose pipes were made for singing dirges. And where was I now? Besieged by wind and dust, listening to the ravings of Madam Geety.

Light from the lamp filled the hallway. Then Geety and her Daughtr, wearing a dark blanket, emerge. So she was on the level, getting ready to go. If Asadollah heard about this, it'd give him enough to laugh about for the next two weeks.

"Mahtob! Don't fidget! Let me button this for you. There's a cold wind and you'll get sick!"

The strange thing was that when she spoke to the girl, she seemed almost human!

It was hate and we had to get going. The girl was wearing a long knitted cap, which looked red in the glow of the lamp. The woman picked up the metal bar from behind the door and rested it on her shoulder, then with the same hand lifted the lamp.

"Get moving!"

The Engineer put pieces of chicken in the pot

followed by the cat. Finally he struggled to lift the entire thing, as though balancing a large stone. Inside the pot the cat busied itself with what remained of the chicken.

The Engineer began to walk balancing the pot, which left me with the lamp! I didn't hesitate to take it. With the weapon draped around my neck again I fell in behind the Engineer; behind us was the light from the second lamp.

The Engineer was finding it difficult to walk. It was clear that he would have to rest every few steps with his new burden. I would have to be patient with him. The gale was a nuisance, especially to my eyes. Without my overcoat, I felt its numbing chill go right through me.

Holdin' the girl with her right hand, Geety walked behind me. I felt this arrangement would allow them to walk more easily than the Engineer.

The Engineer had realized his mistake. He stopped for a moment waiting for me pass with the lamp and then fell in behind me. We passed through the gate of the quarter and entered the street opposite it. One after another the ruined outer walls of several houses left a chain of rubble along the sidewalk. We followed a short cut through the houses and reached the next street without difficulty.

"Careful! We're cutting through this house here," I warned. We walked over the debris to enter the inner courtyard. The flame in the lamp put up a good fight against the gusting wind. In the left corner of the courtyard there was a small, dried-up garden and a tree of unknown variety with several branches. We traveled the length of the yard and then stepped over the collapsed roof of a room.

The way was very uneven and I wondered whether Geety and her child could manage it. But there was no other option; we had to save time. The light from the second lamp moved slowly in my direction. The mourning would now be in full swing with everyone gathered around chanting, "*O Shia, beat your heads. With cries and lamentation. With cries and lamentation.*" And then: THUD, THUD, THUD! The boys would be pounding their chests with their fists.

The Engineer stood beside me. His pot was empty and the cat was leaning its forepaws against his trousers. What had he done with the chicken? The second lamp was nowhere to be seen. I raised my lamp.

"Where are they?"

Not waiting for an answer, I walked back. Why had they stopped? I retraced my path through the debris from the caved-in roof.

"Mama, there's a jinn!"

"Wait! Don't come forward!"

I froze. Who was she calling a jinn?

Then I head crying. Mahtob was sitting and wailing. Geety had placed the iron bar on the ground and was consoling the girl in her arms. We had absolutely no time to wait for the girl to stop and cry whenever she wanted.

I called out impatiently, "Okay, come on now! Why are you sitting there?"

The girl pointed at me and said, "Mama! I'm scared. The jinn's going to get big. Big! BIG!"

I was fed up with waiting for them. Enough time had been wasted already. Without considering the rugged terrain, I began to run. The girl began to shriek, which only added to the clamor of the windstorm.

"Don't come! Don't! MAMA!"

After two or three steps, I stopped again.

"Crazy shit! Ape! STOP RIGHT THERE! Mahtob is terri-fied! The closer you come, the worse it gets! BASTARD!"

Now it was my father's turn! The girl had her head down; she was only mewing now.

"What's your problem? What happened? Who's the jinn?"

"The guy behind you frightened her."

I turned to see no one except the Engineer. If she meant him, then why hadn't she been that scared before? Geety noticed my confusion. She let go of the girl and stood up explaining, "ASS! Get away from the lamp! It's the shadow on the wall!"

The concrete wall was peppered from end to end with shrap-nel. Projected onto it by the light of the lamp was the upper part of my body like some weird monster with its lower half removed. The black shape of the Engineer's head was bobbing in one corner of this bizarre tableau.

I asked, "You mean that my shadow is the jinn?" and then I moved out of the light causing the shadow to disappear. The dust, the grit, the wind, and the thousand other things weren't enough; jinn fever had to be added to the evils of the night.

"Put your lamp down!"

Geety's words drew my attention to the wall. My own lamp had sketched an even stranger picture there than hers, one that ran the entire length of the rectangle. The shadow of my arms had disappeared. I immediately put the lamp on the ground and went behind it. The shadows disappeared, except for the small one made by the Engineer's head, which, because it was stationary, would not cause any headaches.

Geety was caressing her daughter and wiping the tears from her face with her hand. Why did I have to be so stupid tonight? If I hadn't told them what was about to happen, at this hour—just like hundreds of hours in the past—they would be waiting for the enemy fireworks to begin. Why was it any of their business that...

How many hours had passed? I wondered.

There was no doubt that, by now, the corpse was as frozen solid as the other bodies. It made no difference now whether it had been warm ten, twenty days before. How many days would the frozen corpse wait before arrangements could be made to transport it in the ice cream truck? Transporting the bodies of the military dead ought to be easier—just name, rank and serial number. But would rank make any difference in the morgue? For example, if someone mistakenly called the corpse of a major "lieutenant," would that be an insult?

"Sir, let's go!" The Engineer grabbed my arm.

"I can't leave them."

Geety and her daughter were both sitting on the ground. The Engineer's presence made the girl shriek. The shadow cast by the stooping old man—come to think of it—*did* look like a jinn!

ed him behind the lamp and asked the woman, "Are
or not? I have work to do."

your work to do! She's terrified. What should I do?
afraid of shadows ever since she was a baby."

So the only thing to do would be to eliminate the shadows. But how? I extinguished the Engineer's lamp.

"Take the woman's lamp! But hold it in front of you!"

"But I'm carrying the pot and it's heavy!"

I took it from him. He had kept the grimy chicken—obviously with his army of cats in mind.

I broke the chicken up with my hands and spilled the pieces on the ground. The grease made my fingers sticky.

"Let's go!"

"Tell this monster not to come near us!"

Instead of saying a word, the Engineer did the best thing possible; he walked a few steps forward and put the lamp on a rock, but all the while glaring at me, and this said it all. As he passed the lamp from one hand to the other, his magnified shadow appeared on the walls for a moment. Everything went fine. The girl did not see the shadows because the woman was holding her in her arms.

"Let's go, Mother." I said. "We're not safe from the thugs here!" They started to walk and I fell in behind them.

It was too dark to see the smoke from the refinery or the clouds, for that matter. We reached the main street; the way from this point on would be smoother and straighter. I didn't have the stomach to revisit the bazaar, but every length of rebar that I saw became a knife-wielder waiting on the corner for his next victim. We should have taken another shortcut through the ruins of the houses lining the road.

The cat turned up again. After I had thrown the chicken pieces on the ground, I thought it would have gone away. How did it find us again?

As the Engineer marched along, it fell into step with him. The two were truly made for each other.

I absentmindedly touched my pocket, feeling the lump made by the Engineer's letter. Someone had really pulled the wool over his eyes! What gave him the idea that I could read English? Probably because of all the time he spent with the British!

"Didn't I tell you to stay away from my daughter?"

"I stopped on account of the cat, Madam!" said the Engineer.

She said, "Madam, your mother…" and her 'mother-this' and 'mother-that' faded in the wind.

"Mr. Engineer, don't argue! Just keep going!"

Geety snorted, "Who's the engineer? This punk? No doubt he crawled out of his mama's hole an engineer? Good thing I know every last one in that family; otherwise, he'd be claiming to be the vizier of the Great Khan of China. Did you think I wouldn't recognize you? Where are those stuck-up young mademoiselles of yours? Dumped you and left, huh?"

The Engineer was mortified but kept on walking. I felt sorry for him. Why was Geety being so brutal to him?

"I know everybody in this neighborhood. Hey, Basiji, want me to tell you who owns this house?"

I told myself not to respond. We didn't have the time for a catalog of who owned the houses and shops along the street. By the way, I thought, what had she done with her club? It was no-where to be seen.

As she led her daughter along, she began instructing us in local morality. "Was it this house? No, no, this one! Not when he pretended to be so devout in public, nor when he went after women in private. Son-of-bitch! I fixed him so he'd never think that he was so clever again! Know what I did to him? Right there in front of everybody, he couldn't show his face around here, cause I..."

She what? O, yes, she pulled down his pants right in front of everybody!

Was this the best way to handle it? Were there other things that the Engineer didn't have time to tell me?

"Ehsan, Ehsan—Musa! Ehsan, Ehsan—Musa! Ehsan, Eh-san—Musa!"

I had to escape from Geety's tattling, even if it meant break-ing radio silence!

I put my left ear to the receiver. The unlit lamp was back in its old place suspended from the antenna.

"Musa! Ehsan, here!"

"Ehsan! Is Jafar's task finished?"

"No! Understood?"

"Listen! If possible send to me...!"

"Send...? Send Jafar?"

"Right, send Jafar!"

Geety and her daughter were still walking by the side of the
road. All the while, Geety was blabbing about this person and
that.

"...I'll set you up with food. I'll take you to the marriage
registry..."

Every sound was garbled in the wind; Geety's voice faded in
and out. There was no better way. By taking the shortcut
through the ruins, we halved the distance to the Engineer's
building.

"Musa—Ehsan!"

I pressed the receiver to my left ear even harder. The howling of the wind and Geety's muffled curses echoed in my right
ear; while in my left ear there were the sounds of fists being
brought down hard on chests and Jafar's voice singing the dirge.
The ceremony had not reached the solo-chant stage. Jafar recited:

> *O Shia, 'tis the time to cry;*
> *The Day when God's the Judge is nigh!*

Then it cut out.

"Told me he'd buy me shoes, clothes, if I only slept with him.
And he'd brag: 'Look at the gorgeous piece of...I've caught!'"

"*...The resting place of our comrades is here! The field of
battle of the lads is here! Tell those with parched lips! The
source of rain to be had is here!*"

I tried to bring my right hand down on my own chest in time
to what I imagined was the boys' chest-thumping. The storm
was turning the whole place upside down, and now the woman's
voice was impossible to hear. A dry tree limbs snapped and fell
to the ground behind us. Only able to make out shadows now,
we groped along by instinct, following the Engineer with his
lamp.

Mohammad could keep the radio only on SEND for a maximum of seven seconds; otherwise, the transistors would burn
out.

Despite the storm, the woman didn't let up—unfortunately
her mouth was always on SEND. My only salvation was that I
had made the right guess about the chest-beating.

Suddenly she stomped on a metal door and shouted, "...FAGGOT...! Come on! Come on! Here's a swift kick from your Gorgeous Geety..."

If she continued in this way, in one hour she'd inflict as much damage as it took enemy shelling a month to do.

It was lucky, I thought, that we weren't going by my father's house; otherwise, Geety would smash in his door...!!

"...*Your martyr's blood shall flow in the field.*"

We reached the main road and the crossroads. On both sides the area was wide and spread-out, but the row of houses along the avenue was hidden behind the withered trees. This was probably why the woman was quiet now, leading her daughter along the way.

"...*foxhole to foxhole, face to face! House to house, here to there! The story I tell with exacting care!*"

The sound cut out in the middle again. They were definitely holding the ceremony in an enclosed space; the chanting, when it came, was loud and clear. The boys would have formed a circle that slowly revolved around the central chanter, and fists would rise and then come down.

"...*Now you of the Kufan plain! Wanting my death in greatest pain! I warn you, noble patrician: beware the shame of harming Hossein!*"

The Engineer was shaking my shoulder. I removed the receiver from my ear. The girl was squatting on the ground again, but I couldn't make out what she was saying.

"Huh? What happened?"

"Listen!"

She was crying. "Mama, the jinns are back! I hear voices!"

The woman was still, listening. Annoyed, I said to the Engineer, "More games? Must we, man? Come on, we have to go!"

He placed the pot and lamp on the ground and said, "No, sir! Not this time! There's a sound coming from over there. Listen carefully!"

He put his hands behind his ears. What could possibly be heard above the roar of the gale? Maybe the 'talk' was the wind whistling through the cracks in the walls.

But in the glow of the lamp, the Engineer's eyes were getting wider and wider, and the way the woman was acting made me curious. All three of them had their eyes peeled in one direction—toward the clock tower and the refinery.

I put the receiver back in its holder, then cupped my hands behind my ears exactly as the Engineer had done. All my senses were trained on what was ahead of us, but the only things I could hear were the clang of the tin roofs and the awful whine of the wind. No, there was nothing to be heard, I thought.

They had let their imaginations get the better of them, which was reasonable in this terrible darkness. But the Engineer—still with his hands behind his ears—was motioning with his head at something in front of us. I strained my ears again, concentrating solely on the sound. This was it; I had to put a stop to the foolishness. But, no...there may have been something! Was I letting my own imagination run wild?

From some unknown distance in the midst of that punishing wind, there *was* a sound—like a group of people reciting poetry in an alien language.

21

The girl had taken refuge in her mother's lap, while the Engineer was staring straight into my eyes, waiting for me to react.

It was really strange! I must have traveled up and down these quiet alleys in the dark scores of times, but I had never thought about jinns and fairies. Each cell of my brain felt like it was on fire.

Was I wrong? Was I being misled by the way the three of them were so focused? Three? No, it was four; the furry cat also had his ears trained on the sound! Now what should I do?

"Ehsan, Ehsan—Musa!"

It was no use; Mohammad was not listening. They were only broadcasting the sound of Jafar's recitation: "*...If the true faith of Mohammad lives through the flood of our blood, tell them to ready their swords! Hossein stands before them ready to die.*"

I had no choice but to prod them into moving. "Follow me! Put out that lamp too!" I snapped and, with my finger on the trigger, waved the end of the weapon at them. Geety, for the first time, obeyed without a peep and lifted her daughter from the ground and held her in her arms. I took the lead. The Engineer put the unlit lamp in the pot.

"Stay by the wall!"

"Do you mean there's a jinn?"

Here was another first; the woman was addressing me in calm voice. The Engineer answered her sarcastically: "You bet! It's a whole wedding party of jinns! They're waiting for you to make an appearance!"

"You shut your trap, baboon scum!"

...We moved toward the area around the clock tower. The closer we came, the louder the sound of people singing became.

It seemed to be some melody, followed by singing in a language I couldn't understand, which was followed by more music. The words were unlike any other I had ever heard.

Despite the storm raging around us, the radio was glued to my back, which was soaked with sweat. The path along the wall was more uneven, and the Engineer stumbled a few times. The two others were leaning on one another for support and moved along more easily. I readied myself for battle, not knowing what was in store for us. The only thing I knew was that time was running out and that the source of the music—whatever it was—had to be found.

"Musa, Musa—Ehsan!"

I held the weapon in both hands.

"Musa, Musa—Ehsan!"

The group reluctantly stopped behind me. I lowered the weapon and, before lifting the receiver, tweaked the tuning knob of the radio.

"Musa, Musa—Ehsan!"

"Ehsan. Musa, here!"

"Why don't you respond? Mr. Qasem has asked about your situation. Are you ready? How are Javad's mom and the rest?"

The boys imagined that I had taken refuge on the roof. What could I tell them?

"Listen, Ehsan! Just stay on the line only—until I contact you. Understood?"

"Understood, Musa! Over!"

I wound the coiled wire around my neck so that the receiver now rested on my chin. This would make it easier to talk in case something unexpected happened. Then I motioned them forward with the gun barrel.

The white, stripe-like tower was now clearly visible in the grit and dust. The music seemed to be coming from the left side along with the sound of spirits!

I quietly motioned with my hand for the Engineer to come forward. He caught up with me and we walked in lockstep.

"Take this lamp off the antenna!"

He unhooked the handle. If there really was something we didn't expect, the clanging of the lamp against the radio would give us away. He put the second lamp in the pot.

"What language is that?" I asked.

"I don't know, sir. It's not English or French."

It was surely not Arabic. The enemy would not be making such a racket right in the heart of the city.

Jinns were the last things we needed.

We were now in the middle of the crossroads. I motioned for the others to stop while I continued, taking one step at a time. I should have checked out the three other streets beforehand.

The melody was now quite clear, and there was a choir singing along with it. I reached the edge of the tower and, hugging the wall, slowly poked my face out halfway. Flickering light and music were coming from the window.

The priests? I wondered. But they had gone hours ago.

I crouched down. As quietly as possible, I tried to cross the road to reach the church wall. My pulse was racing. I had to reach the window with the light in it. Perspiration from my hands had moistened the weapon. This, mixed with the dust blowing in the wind, made the thing slide around in my fingers.

I was afraid that dust had gotten into the chamber and the weapon might jam when I tried to fire it. What about the cartridges? Were they all right?

I was now crouching under the window. I took a deep breath and stood up. The flickering light that poured from the small broken window made it possible to see the particles of dust furiously blowing by in the wind. Now there was only the sound of a man's mournful voice singing something incomprehensible, followed by music echoing in the church.

A blinding flash of light lit up the entire street for a moment. Was one of the storehouses on fire again? No! So where was the light coming from, a light powerful enough to pierce the wind storm and illuminate everything?

The window was too high up for me to peep through it. I had to find another way but could think of nothing else to do but open the doors of the building.

They couldn't be fifth column. Why would they announce their presence with such bright lights and fanfare? Jinns? Ridiculous! Jinns, by and large, were too smart to stay in a city under bombardment! No, there was no choice but to enter the church!

I crouched down again and started to creep beside the wall. I had to return to the crossroads and enter the grounds by vaulting the low, church wall.

There was a black shape back where I had tried to peek through the window. I turned the weapon toward it. It was the Engineer. I gestured for him to be quiet. He sat down. Behind him I made out the shadow of the woman and the girl. It was strange that, now we'd traced the source of the sound, there wasn't a peep out of the child.

I leaped toward the doorway of the church. I had to slip through the door, which might be dangerous with the heavy radio on my back. But what if I needed to contact the boys?

I breathed a sigh of relief. Luckily the door was partially open, but still I had to be careful. I glanced in the Engineer's direction and saw the shadow of the woman's iron pipe sticking out from behind her head.

A drop of sweat fell on my cheek. I wiped my forehead with the back of my hand. I had to get in the church quickly. They were still singing. My cheeks felt wet again, but this time—if I wasn't mistaken—it was rain, the rain that they had been predicting! It seemed that the clouds were also in on this joke of an expedition. With all the dust and filth in the wind, the rain brought a breath of fresh air! Would it start pouring?

Another flash! Yes, it _was_ lightning! I placed the toe of my boot against the outer doors and pushed. Despite their weight, the doors, with their two decorative crosses, parted easily. Now the dark, inner courtyard of the church lay before me. Another burst of lightning lit up the area, but where was the roar of the thunder? These flashes made everything visible for a second, and I worried that in the same second they would reveal my own outline to others.

Several more drops of sweat, or rain, fell from my forehead! The empty church building topped by a cross made a weird ensemble. A flickering glow like that coming from the window shone from the skylights.

I had to get this over with now. With my shirt I wiped the sweat from my palms. Ready? _In-the-name-of-God_! I said and walked toward the wall on the left side. Deafened by the roar of the wind and the music, I was forced to rely on my eyes to protect me. But the only time I could see the whole area was the instant the lightning flashed, temporarily blinding me anyway.

I reached the heavy wooden, inner door of the chapel. Was it bolted or was the knob locked? No, I had to keep the weapon in my right hand while I tried to turn the knob with my left. Absolutely no noise! With each millimeter the door cracked open, more light came out from within the chapel.

The first person that caught my eye was sitting at the piano; the second was singing along with him in the candlelight. It was them! In the same priest clothes! Hovanes and the other one, whose name I had forgotten.

They were so lost in the song, they didn't see me enter. But they'd gone, hadn't they? What made them return—with that cigarette-smoking driver—no sign of him! What did they do with their stuff?

Parveez! If he were here now, he'd probably be saying, "Didn't I tell you they were fifth column? Wearing priest clothes!"

But this was no time for such shenanigans. Here I was, soaked in sweat from all those scares, and these two were having a party! For what?

"ENOUGH!" I shouted, stopping them dead. The last note Hovanes had struck on the piano rang in the air for a few moments and died.

"Have any idea how wrong what you two are doing is? Having a celebration in the midst of all this misery?"

Hovanes rose, but the older priest just looked down and remained still.

"Hello, sir! It is you, isn't it? You scared us."

"To hell with that! Didn't you leave? Don't tell me that you had nothing better to do than come downtown and hold a concert!" To mollify me Hovanes walked toward me with open arms.

"Don't be so upset. This is my fault. When the storm began I begged him to let me play a few pieces on the piano to help me remember my childhood, when I was part of the choir. It was just to amuse us. You understand, don't you? Unfortunately I didn't realize that it was forbidden. In any case you'll forgive us!"

"I asked you whether you had left. Why did you come back?"

"Calm down, my dear friend! We are not aware of proper military regulations. There is no launch from the dock tonight, and we had no proper shelter. So, at my insistence, that same military vehicle brought us back here so we could spend the last night in the church."

"So the church has now become your grandma's house where you'll be welcome any time you want?" I was so annoyed, I was about to explode. I had never expected this to happen to me, but it had. I had to get these two out of my hair any way I could.

"Listen to every word I say! Tonight you have no right to remain in this church! Understood?" I had unconsciously slipped back into radio talk.

"Why, my dear friend? If it's about the piano or this candle, that's no problem," said Hovanes and he moved toward the candle.

"What are you doing? Don't put it out!"

I managed to stop him before he blew it out. I had to think. The first thing on the agenda was the operation, and under the present circumstances the best thing would be to contact the boys.

I said, "Wait right here! Don't move a muscle!" Then I unwound the wire from around my neck.

"Ehsan, Ehsan—Musa!"

"Musa—Ehsan, over!"

"Listen!..."

I stopped. What was I to say? As usual I had forgotten to put the code book in my pocket; so I couldn't ask about the start of operations without the others knowing.

"Okay, now you two have to return to the mouth of the waterway and wait there until morning, saying your prayers and benedictions."

"But, your Excellency, it was arranged to have the military truck bring us at dawn. Do you have access yourself to another vehicle?"

"My van is out of gas."

I sensed that they thought the gas was just a pretext. I was helpless. Now all I needed was these two! If Asadollah knew, what would he say? "Hey boys, guess what happened? Lookout boy here spent the night of the operation in the church praying with the priests!..."

"And, naturally, neither of you has had supper?"

They glanced at each other. Then the old priest spoke for the first time. "We are used to fasting. Of course, if this mandatory fast is acceptable to God"—and he stopped speaking with a meaningful look on his face.

Waiting for us outside were flashes of light, followed after a short interval by the fierce sounds of the rainstorm. Time was definitely not on my side. I noticed that the painting of the Last Supper was crooked. In the candlelight, none of the figures could be seen, not even Jesus or Judas. You'd think that they could have straightened it in the interim—at least out of respect for religion.

"Do you have any matches?" I asked.

"Yes, there are some in my case."

"Fine. Now without asking any questions, put out the candle, get your brief cases and fall in behind me. But no noise!" Before I could get to the door, one of them said, "But, my dear friend, seeing that this is our last night, we thought we take the opportunity to perform the Lord's Prayer."

"No problem, but you'll have to do it when we get where we're going, and, if it's not answered, we can all recite the Prayer of Last Resort together! Now MOVE!"

I went through the door and in the open air became aware of the rain again. Although it was coming down steadily in fine drops, I didn't find that the rain gave me the thrill I had expected. But even that was to be expected; every time I had looked forward to something desperately for a long time, it never turned out the way I had imagined it would. The two priests fell in behind me and began speaking in a language I didn't understand.

The first person from the original band I saw was the Engineer, hiding behind the tower and peeking out occasionally.

"Engineer!" I called out to him, "Come out; there's nothing to fear!"

He emerged from behind the wall and asked, "Who are these people, sir?"

The next thing that came out of the darkness was the little girl's voice. "Mama, there they are. There are the jinns!" She started to cry.

"Don't cry, my dearest. They're just men dressed in long black robes. They're not going to hurt us."

Hovanes was walking behind the other priest, whose name— hard as I tried—I couldn't remember. In any case, you had to call a priest "Father," so there was no need to know his name.

Now our entire band was huddled together in the rain. The Engineer and I were in the middle; Geety and her daughter near the wall; and the two priests holding their brief cases were staring uncertainly at the little girl.

"Why are you crying, my child?" asked one of the priests.

"Shut your trap, you creep! One look at that ugly shape of yours, even from far away, was enough to scare the daylights out of her! The thing speaks Farsi. Imagine!"

At that instant the old priest became speechless. I walked over to him and, with my back to the woman and her daughter so they couldn't hear me, I said, "Father! I can't explain now but a word of warning: it would be best not to go at it with this woman." I continued, whispering into his ear, "The honorable lady, when she gets into an argument with somebody, has a habit of pulling down his pants right there in the middle of the road."

The priest looked at me in disbelief and, no longer whispering, I went on, "So now you know. It's better that we get going before it starts raining harder. Engineer, you lead the way. You, pick up your daughter. And you, fathers, fall in behind them!"

The Engineer, carrying the pot and two lamps, began walking followed by the furry cat, then Geety and her daughter. I pointed the way with the end of the weapon and the two priests got the message loud and clear. My place was at the end of the chain and we seemed to keep an orderly distance from one another naturally—as if we were a trained unit marching to the front using the strictest concealment procedures to limit the number of casualties in case of enemy ambush. In this commando unit, Geety and her daughter were safely separated from the Engineer; and the two priests from Geety and her daughter, while I kept my distance from the whole group. We left the quiet and spacious confines of the church compound and entered a narrow street.

The rain had picked up; it was quite heavy now. The Engineer tried to avoid it by hugging the walls, and the others followed suit.

The Engineer put the pot on his head using it as a rain hat. Both the weapon and my clothes were soaked through and through. The wind did not let up, and the thunder and lightning added to the mess. My scalp began to itch like mad, which I was sure, was due to two things: my more than normally filthy hair and the damp.

Water was overflowing from the blocked-up drainage ditches onto the road. The woman's plastic sandals made a squishing sound as she waded through it.

Looking at the walls around us, I noticed that most of the gutters were empty. The reason was obvious. The roofs of the houses had taken so many hits that the rain was pouring through the holes made by the shrapnel onto the interiors below. If there were any good pieces of furniture in them, in a few days they would all be rotting with mildew. I thought about our own house. No, it still hadn't been hit. If the Iraqis, knowingly or not, took aim at it, then...?

"Musa, Musa—Ehsan! Musa, Musa—Ehsan!"

I raised the receiver and pressed the send button. "Ehsan! Musa, here!"

"Listen, Musa! Pass the receiver to Javad's father!"

Our party was still on the move, but the boys in the unit thought that I was now safely indoors, in dry clothes, sitting with Javad's parents, and waiting for the program to start.

"Ehsan! Why do you need Javad's father?"

"Musa! Grandpa needs to speak with him."

I had to make them believe everything was okay. If they were to learn the truth...? If Asadollah got wind of it...?

"Ehsan, Javad's father is asleep!"

"Understood! What about his mother?"

"Also just went to sleep. You want me to wake up those two old people?"

Mohammad delayed answering; he was obviously conferring with Qasem. "No, no need. It's only that Mr. Qasem wants to apologize. In the meantime make sure you see to their comfort!"

It worked. "Okay. Understood."

"Excuse me, can I ask where we're going?" It was Hovanes. No sooner had I escaped one interrogation than another began.

"Not now! Think of yourself under arrest until tomorrow for violating regulations by making all that noise."

"Does that mean we are really under arrest?"

The street, the sidewalks, and the ditches lay under a single sheet of water. Suddenly a filthy, black rat dashed out of a crack in one of the breached walls and, with everyone watching, went in another direction. This time it was Geety's turn to shriek. The Engineer rushed after his cat, but the creature had made such a feast of the chicken that it had no desire even to look at a half-drowned rat.

The appearance of the rat put an end to Hovanes' awkward questions. My boots were full of water, and the biting cold had penetrated my bones. I envied the barefoot cat. What was the difference between us in this rain? There were no boots on its paws, but it looked as thought it was walking with its paunch dangling in the water—probably because it had eaten too much. This made me wonder how much of the chicken it actually had digested.

A cat's eyesight must be different from a frog's. Even though the poor cat, like the frog, must lie in wait for its prey and see what fate has in store for it? What was the difference between these two? The cat was an eater of carrion, which was clear from the time the Engineer gave the creature the food meant for the two women; but the frog devoured its prey live just like the Doomsday Machine...!

When we reached the last bend in the road, the younger priest took the older one's brief case. The old man had started panting and was holding up the hem of his cassock with both hands so it wouldn't dangle in the water rushing by his feet. What was the point when we were all soaked to the skin?

The woman and her daughter were clinging to each other so tightly that I doubted whether the cold could get between them.

"We're here. This is the building!"

"Beg your pardon, sir, but is that the place where you'll hold us prisoner? With the girl and Madam?"

Still balancing the pot on his head, the Engineer had found a new head of steam and quickened his pace. Even as it was being lashed by the rain, the building cast a frightening shadow that was as awesome as ever.

As if realizing what the priest had just said, Geety suddenly snapped, "Watch your mouth! Your mother's the madam!"

"Madam, have I insulted you?" he asked.

"Again, Madam! He said it again!"

The old priest said nothing more. Thank God there were at least two civil people in the group.

A flickering light came from the doorway of the building. I breathed a deep sigh of relief, realizing the march had finally come to an end.

22

My body had begun to tremble.

"I don't know, sweetheart; he just said that he was going to get some gas. Now that you mention it, I'm starting to get uneasy myself."

"There's nothing to worry about, Naneh. He's probably waiting for the rain to stop before he comes back. Don't let it upset you."

I stared at the fire. Pieces of wood from the shattered doors and window frames crackled in the flames. Like poison gas, the chemical fumes made by the half-charred paint on them spread through the compound, making it hard to breathe.

I told myself not to show any reaction. Everyone had gotten a blanket but me. The circle around the campfire was complete: the two out-of-luck priests; the woman and her daughter who had been uprooted from their home at gunpoint; and Javad's mother. Each of them—except for the Engineer—were like peevish children refusing to come out of their own private little worlds.

What did you do in the end? I asked myself. For a simple supper, I had gathered them all under one broken-down roof—to do what? If one of those wicked shells were to find its way through the adjoining walls and land smack dab in that fire, it would spill so much blood that...!

And maybe tomorrow, when everybody sees what has happened, they'll hold me responsible. Maybe...and maybe Judas only wanted to treat Jesus and the Disciples to supper, and it was just his hard luck that what happened afterwards happened. And ever since that day, till the end of time, the poor bastard would be linked with the word "betrayer." Betrayer! Betrayer! Betrayer!

Driven wild again by the fragrance of the food in the pot, the furry cat was pacing by the fire, waiting for another chance to mooch more chicken. Or maybe it was just busy drying itself like the rest of us.

Javad's father, I thought, shouldn't have abandoned the old woman like that. He hadn't gone to the unit, or else Qasem wouldn't have asked for him over the radio. He should have been back by now—so why hadn't he made contact? He must have gone to the mess—yes, that was it!

The mess was the nearest place he could have gone.

Plumes of steam rose from my wet clothes. As soon as they reached the area under the stairs the two priests changed their soaked robes for two identical dry ones. I wondered how many years worth of the same sackcloth they had.

Geety was sitting quietly and, with her tattooed hands, was putting pieces of bread and chicken into her daughter's open mouth. They were both under the same blanket. Each priest also had his own army blanket. With a worried look on her face, Javad's mother was waiting for me to react, maybe in the hope that it would lessen her own fears. I was feeling rotten.

I tried several times to free my right leg from underneath me, but a numbness brought on by cold had made my body feel many times heavier than it normally was. What was Javad's father doing out there in the rain? Why couldn't the man have stayed put?

In the bottom of my heart I had hoped that at the time of the operation the old man would take charge of the band of stragglers I had gathered. He would probably be back by then.

I was waiting to dry out a bit more before I prayed the sundown and evening prayers. I'd thought of that when I was in Geety's quarter but had no desire to spend what may be my last night on earth praying in such a wicked place.

Rainwater cascaded down the sides of the building. Without gutters to channel the flow, it traveled swiftly through the cracks in the bricks. There was no doubt about it; the bricks were soaked through and through, which raised the fear that the rickety roof might collapse.

Still seated, I managed to spin around and grab more pieces of wood and throw them onto the fire. They were greenish, but it wasn't clear whether they were from a window frame or a door. I wondered how many times the inhabitants of the place opened and closed these doors and windows with their own hands before the war, only to have them burned as kindling now. The greenish paint blistered, then slowly ran the spectrum of colors until finally turning coffee-colored and burning in the flames.

My body was trembling again and now there was that sluggish feeling! I watched the girl eat. Her mouth didn't open very wide, as if her jaws had been wired with something dentists use. She was hardly able to swallow the small bits of food. Geety was mumbling something under her breath—no doubt saying how much she cherished her!

The priests ate little, while I had nothing at all, my appetite being zero. And how much did Javad's mother have to insist before I would swallow just one bite of bread? There was a bitter taste at the back of my mouth and this shivery feeling...

"Beg your pardon, but where can we lie down?" Through my half-closed eyes I barely made out Hovanes. If one of the boys had asked this, I would have said, "Wherever the hell you like!"

So, where should I tell them to sleep? When the shelling began, the place that was the safest from shrapnel would be under the stairs, but that belonged to Javad's mother, Geety, and the girl. By tearing pieces from Javad's mother's long cloak they could easily make a curtain that would keep the women hidden from view while they slept.

Where else could I suggest to them? I glanced around the area. Near the door was the worst possible place. What about the wall furthest from the door, which abutted the small houses along the side alley? I continued to survey the place but could find nothing better.

"You see that corner? Grab your brief cases and the blankets and set up a place for yourselves there."

"Where are you going to sleep tonight?"

"Maybe the graveyard."

He didn't expect this answer and probably thought I being sarcastic, but I wasn't. Given the fever and the chills, I had no patience for such conversations. He went back to his old companion. My eyes were so tired, I couldn't keep them focused. Was all this only exhaustion?

"Naneh, I've got something to do up there on the roof. Find a place under the stairs for yourself and this..."

I had to be on my guard; otherwise, Geety would start cursing my kin again.

"...woman and girl and stretch out till we see what God has planned for us."

Naneh had reached the limit of her patience and apparently had been waiting for an excuse to erupt.

To her absent husband she said, "Old fool! Didn't you say that your rheumatism comes back in the cold weather?..." and to me, "Can't you go after him? I'm afraid he's been hit."

Which is how it ended for Javad; I had to keep my cool. "Don't be afraid! Nothing's going to happen tonight. With this weather, they won't let the shells out of the guns to keep them dry." I added to myself: So long as we don't start firing!

"You haven't eaten! Have something, at least!" she begged me.

The cat was pretending to attack a bone. I couldn't figure out how it was able to leap up and pounce with such a full gut!

"I swear to God, Naneh, I don't feel like eating. After I come back down, I'll eat all of this."

I pushed away the large piece of bread she had broken off for me. I felt strange. The sight of the lid glued to the pot with dried grease made me sick. At the same time I was feeling severely weak, and this weakness had nothing to do with being hungry.

I got up slowly. That was enough sitting. Now it was time to wash and say my prayers, but my feet wouldn't budge. The priests had spread a blanket out under their legs and were whispering to each other. It was perfectly obvious that they were baffled by what was happening. And I was perfectly within my rights not to explain anything to them.

Rather than lift my feet, I dragged them along; this was definitely due to tiredness. When I reached the door I noticed that the thunder and lightning had stopped, but the torrential rains continued. It was as if God was trying all at once to make up for several months of drought!

I looked over at the van. There was only the vehicle's dark outline, droning monotonously under the downpour. O! Thank God! Then I remembered the helmet! When the action started, I would need it; right now, it was lying on the dashboard of the van. And, thank God also, I hadn't put the thing upside down—otherwise it would be full of water.

But how was I supposed to cross the distance between the van and me?

The thought of getting soaked again made me sick. There was no choice but to make a mad dash for it. I looked wistfully at the scene inside the building: the roaring fire and the blankets. If I put one of the blankets on my head, I probably wouldn't get so wet; but there were no extras, and getting a blanket wet meant that it couldn't be used—at least not until it dried.

My bootlaces were open, but, throwing all caution to the wind, I leaped outside and started running with all the speed I could command. There was the same sloshing sound under foot and my pant legs were getting soaked again, and the raindrops pelted my faced. None of this made any difference; I needed that helmet.

As I approached the van, I tried to keep my eyes open so I could see the helmet. But when I looked through the smashed windshield, the helmet's dark outline was not there. A few steps away, I was now certain my eyes had not been playing tricks on me—the helmet was nowhere to be seen. Javad's father might have taken it, but he never wore a helmet!

I reached for the handle on the passenger side and pulled. It didn't open, which was not surprising—it was always like this. I stuck my head inside the window. There on the flooded floor of the van was the helmet lying like a discarded tortoise shell.

The squall scourged the part of my body protruding from the van. I had to pick the helmet up quickly. I put my hand into the water and pulled the thing out by the brim. My finger brushed against the strap and in my mind the thick leather felt slimy and swollen with water.

Now there was nothing to do but go back. The slosh-slosh of my boots clashed with the other sounds in the flooded compound. Soaked to the skin, I crawled into the hallway. Now what should I do?

I instinctively headed for the welcoming flames of the open fire and squatted down, drying the inside of the helmet in the cone of heat. After the rain when the action started, the thing would come in handy.

God! Why had I gone out? To wash for prayer, of course!

The sight of the van made me forget everything. The van! On loan from Parveez! If he had been here, he would never have abandoned it under the rain like that. The rain had washed all the mud camouflage from it. Parveez would have found shelter for the vehicle even before he got situated himself. But now the van was in the same state as its owner—battered and full of shrapnel! Where was my motorcycle? Ameer would definitely have put it under the jetty. I was late for my prayers.

"Naneh, I'm going upstairs."

"Wait, darling, I need you for something."

She planted her hands on the ground trying to get up, but I motioned for her to stay put and went over to her. When I was next to her, she said, "You made me a promise. Remember, darling?"

My mind wasn't working. I tried hard to remember, not wanting to disappoint her.

"You don't remember?"

I forced myself to smile, but her face fell.

"What's the matter, darling? You don't look well." She felt my forehead with her hand and said, "You're burning up, sweetheart! What a fever! For God's sake, go and lie down!"

With the forced smile on my face slightly fainter, I said, "No, Naneh, really, I'm okay. You didn't say what you wanted."

"Your promise. You promised to bring Javad's picture for me. You remember?"

"Sure, Naneh. I said. Definitely! But not now! Not in this rain. Okay?" I dragged my feet over to the stairs. I hesitated, afraid the steps were so steep that I would fall down by the time I reached the second or third one. I had to get to the Engineer's room somehow.

Then Geety shouted up, "They're trying to reach you on this thing!" and pointed to the radio.

There were at least ten steps between the radio and me, and each one was torture. But there was no choice. Why hadn't I heard the radio?

"Coming," I said and, once again, dragged my boots along the ground. Now I could hear it, "Musa, Musa—Ehsan! Musa, Musa—Ehsan!"

Everyone's attention was riveted on the radio. Even the two priests were sitting up. I held the receiver in both hands. I guessed they wanted to tell me that Javad's father had arrived.

"Ehsan! Musa, here!"

"Musa," said Qasem, "After your swim, dry off! Understood?"

"Understood!"

"Over and out!"

It was Asadollah's voice, reminding me of the joke he made about blowing up the Bridge to the Afterlife with one of the unexploded shells that had landed in the graveyard. The receiver was back in its place on the radio, which was by the fire. Now in a terrible state, I made my way back to the stairs, but there was someone near me. It was the young Hovanes.

"Brother, if there is anything I can do to help, please don't hesitate!"

"No, there isn't anything you can do. Just go back to your corner and stay put till morning!"

"Why can't I help?"

I pointed toward the roof and said, "Because I have to go up there. To fight! Understood?!"

He was visibly taken aback. My foot slithered onto the first step and I continued to sidle up the stairs.

"Now, go and lie down!"

I reached the second and third step. Mohammad's last transmission erased all doubts in my mind about postponing tonight's operation. The message was short and sweet: Dry off after your swim!

Which meant that it would start when the rain was over.

23

represents walking up to salvation

He wishes he said his prayers before his death

Now I was on the second floor, far from the poisonous stares of my companions. No longer walking, I was crawling up the stairs on all fours. Naneh's words made me realize just how sick I must be. I hadn't felt feverish before, but now the heat hovered before my eyes like a cloud of blistering steam. I wished I had said my prayers on time, when I was in Geety's quarter.

I stood before the Engineer's room. I couldn't let him see me groveling this way, so I used all my strength to stand up, clawing the wall with my hand. As I did so, my boots made a sloshing sound. They still had water in them!

Only the bed was visible from outside. I had to enter. Dim light from a sooty lamp helped me see where I was going. Whenever I visited the Engineer's room, there was always something new to see. Now there was a thin wire stretched from one corner of the room to the other, and the Engineer's wet clothes were hanging from it. The Engineer himself was sitting cross-legged by a metal trunk, busy folding some clothes that were strewn on the floor.

"Hi! Where's the water jug?" I asked.

Not even bothering to turn around, he continued to fold a red shirt and pointed to a dark corner by the window. I managed to drag myself to the corner and lifted the jug. The plastic container was as light as a feather. I held the handle tighter and shook it. I looked at the Engineer and very quietly said, "But it's empty."

"That shouldn't present a problem, sir! There's no one who can top you in giving orders. Why don't you just issue me an order to go and bring you some water?"

It was a relief for me to see he wasn't holding a grudge. I walked to the window and cupping my hand, I tried to capture some rainwater. The drops first beaded playfully on my skin but finally succumbed and gathered in my hand. Gratified, I brought my hand back in and with the water on my left wrist washed both hands. The first step in my ablution was over, but if the rain stopped, I would be forced to go down the sloping stairs again.

The cactus! The potted cactus! The earth in it was saturated and was even overflowing. During the past several days, the torrential rains had given the cactus and its caretaker their fill of water. I envied the cactus, existing cheerfully without any responsibilities...

All that was left of my ablutions was to wash my head and feet. My wet hair presented a problem. I returned to the Engineer's plastic urn.

"Mr. Engineer!"

He deliberately ignored me. "I'm looking for a dry rag." He tossed a piece of an old sheet at me, something that could be used a towel. I didn't have the strength to catch it in the air and it fell to the floor. I bent down to pick it up and dried my hair with it.

I began, "...*God is great! God is great! God is great!*"

Then I put my forehead to the ground. I wanted nothing more than to get out of the things I was wearing and replace them with a warm set of wool clothes.

I prayed to God: Help me do my duty tonight. That's all I want from you. Just look out for Asadollah and Mohammad! I swear I won't be a bother any more!

I finished the prostration. What should I do before the thing started? I clawed my way over to the bed and propping my back against it, then sat with my legs stretched out. Every small movement made me visibly catch my breath. Without having to look at him, I knew that the Engineer was watching me like an eagle. I couldn't give it any thought; rest was the only thing that mattered before the start of the operations. Rest! Rest to replenish the last reserves of energy...

"Sir! Sir!"

Someone was shaking me. I opened my eyes and in the haze made out the Engineer's bent form in front of me.

"Change your clothes! Come, I'll help you."

My eyes shut again. How soothing was the dark world that opened up before me! How intoxicating! But I couldn't succumb to sleep.

"I'll undress myself."

I forced my eyelids open. There was a white shirt with a large collar and dark pants—not enough light to tell what color they were. I undid the top button of the shirt and then the second. My mind was still working. But I didn't feel like changing my clothes in front of the Engineer.

"Engineer, Mr. Engineer!"

He heard me, though my voice had lost some of its authority.

"Sir! You must be in terrible shape!"

"No, just tired. There's nothing wrong. Only...only do one thing for me, will you? Bring the weapon and the radio up for me!"

"You're that sick? Okay, I'll go and get them, but you have robbed me of my peace and quiet, forcing all these uninvited guests on me. It's not right..."

I nodded, agreeing with what he said.

"My dear sir! Especially that she-devil Geety! I can't stand her!"

"Okay, okay, we'll discuss it later."

He hesitated, then all at once stormed out. I looked around and, seeing only the fluffy cat, wondered where the others were. I took my shirt off. My body began to shake. I put on the Engineer's shirt slowly; the sleeves were too long for me... The pants were also too big. I had no choice but to hold them up with my wet military belt.

My uniform fell in a soggy heap beside my legs. I had to get up and put the old shirt and pants over the Engineer's clothesline. With one hand I grabbed the wet clothes and with the other took hold of the edge of the bed, and, using all the strength left in my weary muscles, managed to stand up. But all at once I fell backward onto the bed making the mattress springs go up and down before they came to a sudden halt—like it or not—they submitted to the weight of my body.

I was of two minds. I had no business being on the bed. The old man was right; I had obliterated the peaceful little world he had made for himself, and now I had even invaded his private resting place. Only for a couple of minutes, though; that's all!

I put my legs up. Now my entire body was on the bed. I got hold of the blanket with my feet, brought it forward, and spread it out with my hands to cover my face. In dry clothes, on a soft, warm bed, under the shade of the blanket and enveloped in the silence provided by the constant rain...were these all the things that I wanted from the world at that point? Unfortunately the sound of the Engineer coming up the stairs told me it was time to leave his bed.

To stay warm I rolled over and gathered myself into a ball. Ouch! Was something digging into my back? I should have known: a chess piece! He never got tired of this clutter. What was it? A short piece? A pawn? A knight? There was no point on the end. What color was it? You couldn't tell by feel.

I had to extract the piece from my clenched fist without looking!... I was sweating and shivering awfully. White or black? What had the Engineer said? We always played black!...Black moved second. Second....Which color was in my hand now?

I had become superstitious. If the piece was black, the Doomsday Machine would win. If it was white, we would win.

As soon as the rain stopped, the action would begin. Considering the lousy shape I was in, I had to think of something. I'd radio him. Ameer! The only way out was to have Ameer come and take my place. What a shame; after all this waiting, to have it end in nothing! So when the battle began, Asadollah and Mohammad would be in the trench with shells raining down on them; Ameer would have the binoculars; and I would be cooped up in a corner going through hell!

And all of it was my own stupid fault. How was it any of my business to gather all these people under one roof? Suppose a shell—contrary to what I had planned—were to penetrate one of the walls and blow all the miserable souls now sleeping downstairs to bits? Then would I say that they should have remained where they were?

How was the Doomsday Machine faring in the rain now? They definitely would have covered the thing with a waterproof tarpaulin. It was obviously a very sensitive piece of equipment.

Maybe God wanted it to be ruined so that the next day they would send it to the rear. But that wouldn't do any good. As the Engineer said, they would just replace it with another one. Just like the refinery, which with all its mechanisms, was becoming more useless everyday.

How long had the Engineer slaved to keep it in working order? Forty years! More than twice my age! And what did he have to show for it in the end? Several cats and one letter! Now I have only compounded his misery by being here. Before I came on the scene, all that Parveez did was to kid him a little.

Parveez! Parveez! Look what's happened to us! We're both in the same boat: sick and flat on our backs in bed. Are you going to make it, with all that shrapnel in you? Whatever happens, though, tonight's the night that will determine the fate of the electronic monster.

How much time had I wasted! If I had been more careful scanning the date grove in the last two days, then maybe there might have been no need to take such a big risk.

I still hadn't looked at the chess piece! So what? It was probably white anyway.... But what if it weren't? I was becoming as skeptical as the Engineer. Wearing his clothes and sleeping in his bed—were these enough to make an engineer out of me?

How could I let the ones downstairs know that they should keep on their toes when the time came? You couldn't expect anything from the priests, except to go and build a holocaust memorial for us.

But what about Geety? Suppose she stupidly decided to head out with her kid in tow as soon as the rain stopped? What should I do then? The only person who could stop her would be Javad's mother.

And what about her? She had her heart set on that picture of Javad. The matter had been forgotten ages ago. Why bring it up now, all of a sudden? How could I show her a picture of him after the explosion? With his two arms severed at the elbows and his face full of blood, even his own mother wouldn't recognize him. No, there was no way I was going to do something as foolish as that! Let her last image of Javad be his bright, smiling face. Whenever she asks about the picture, I'll just say that I had forgotten. This would just have to be another lie added to the heap in my life!

Now it's time to bring out the chess piece and see whether fortune came up black or white! The change of clothes had done me no good; my entire body was soaked. Before, it had been from the rain; now my very essence was leaching from me. Don't think! Relax! Take the piece out! All that's necessary is to take my fist out from under the blanket and open it before my eyes. There is enough light from the lamp to tell whether it is white or black. A little more! It's coming ...

I opened my eyes. The piece was caught between my fingers. There was no time to waste; I had to vanquish my doubts. And I did. One by one, my fingers slowly started to open. I could clearly see the dark color; but I still didn't trust my eyes, which I had forced to stay open. I held my palm up to capture more of the light. Black and blind! A miserable pawn, resting in my clutches, powerless.

What was the difference between the pawn and me? I wondered. Where did the difference lie, really? Both of us had been placed on our own special chessboards. The Doomsday Machine lay in wait to devour us all—just like the little flies that would become its prey with the slightest movement! Where was it written that you and your little friend had to go and embrace such a threat? Didn't the order from the War Room state that after each round of artillery, the unit had to change its position? So why not act according to orders?...

The piece was going in and out of focus before my eyes. I slowly released it from my fingers, then tightened them.

"Sir! Sir, wake up!" It was a familiar voice coming from the depths of my mind.

"Sir, wake up! They want you on the radio."

I forced my eyes open. Spasms rippled through my body as I still lay in the Engineer's bed.

"God! You're shaking something awful! I didn't want to wake you, but your friends have been trying to raise you for half an hour now! This thing has been yammering so much, it's given me a headache. Believe me!"

He extended the receiver toward me. I was barely able to extract my arm from under the blanket and take it from him. I didn't even have the strength to speak.

"Ehsan, Ehsan, Ehsan!"

The answer came almost before I let up on the switch, "Musa! Ehsan here! Where have you been? There's exactly half a foot to go. Understood?"

A jolt of electricity seemed to go through me. My wits were starting to return somewhat. The sound of rain had stopped. Half a foot—meaning half an hour and the thing would start.

"Understood! But where is Ameer?"

"Mr. Qasem said: Half a foot! That's all. Goodbye!"

That meant absolute radio silence until the operation began. But I was ill. I had to get word to Qasem somehow.

"Ehsan, Ehsan—Musa!"

The Engineer was standing there watching me.

"Ehsan, Ehsan—Musa! Ehsan, Ehsan—Musa!"

The interval gave Mohammad enough time to switch the radio off. The worst thing you could do before an operation would be to alert the enemy. But I had to violate the rule; there was no other choice.

"You are in horrible shape, constantly raving in your sleep."

I let go of the receiver and turned toward the window.

"The rain! When did it stop raining?"

"Ten, fifteen minutes ago. Why?"

"The time! What time is it?"

I was still wearing Asadollah's watch. It was difficult to read it in the light of the lamp. 3:42 in the morning. It would be 4:12 in half an hour.

I managed to get up halfway and sit on the edge of the bed. The cold floor made my feet tingle.

No, I didn't have the strength to get up. I had to think. The first thing would be to explain things to the others downstairs. When the operations started, they might not be able to grasp what was happening. They might even want to get out of the building. And what about Javad's father?

"Javad's father—has he returned?"

"Not yet. I spread your clothes out on the line."

My shirt and pants were still on the line. The basic problem remained, though. I had to do something. The seconds were ticking away, and the most important part of my body as far as the operation was concerned—meaning my vision—was dim and unfocused. It might have been possible for me, using every last ounce of strength to overcome the physical weakness, but there was no remedy for my eyes. If Javad's father were to come in time, I could probably ask him to take the binoculars and report the flashes he spotted to me. The old man's leaving ruined that plan. Could he make it in time? But, then, what if he didn't?

There was no getting around the risk, I told myself.

"Mr. Engineer! Do me a favor, will you?"

"What?"

"Those two priests downstairs—could you call the younger one for me? His name is Hovanes."

He hesitated.

"What's wrong?"

"Nothing, sir. I have the right to rest—haven't slept a wink since last night."

"Okay. I'll be going up on the roof in a few minutes. After you do it, go get some rest yourself. You can be sure if I weren't sick, I'd do it myself."

He nodded and left. I took the opportunity to stretch out again. This was the only solution; instead of Ameer, I would get Hovanes to act as my eyes. As soon as contact was reestablished, I would have Ameer take his place. It would have been better if he had come from the shore base.

There was the sound of two people coming up the stairs. Thank God! My ears were still working normally. But how could I get rid of this fever? I had to get up again. This time I wrapped myself in the blanket and sat up.

The Engineer came in with the priest behind him. The furry cat brought up the rear and went under the bed.

The Engineer said, "Behold, Excellency, here he is!" then stepped aside.

"You weren't sleeping?" I asked the priest.

"No, not sleeping. Please, do you need me for anything?"

I was up against the greatest challenge now. How could I ask a priest to help a Basiji in the fighting?

The Engineer reached under the bed and grabbed the cat, taking it in his arms. What an easy life that cat had! He had forgotten all about people and was content with a few cats. I knew what he was waiting for—for my discussion with the priest to be over would I would go on the roof.

The silence went on for an unusually long time. I had to break it. "Father! Do you know why I brought you two from the church to this place?"

"I have my suspicions."

"What, for example? Don't be afraid, speak up!"

"Well, I suppose that something big is going to happen tonight for you and your comrades. What that will be, I cannot say exactly. And you have gathered us here because you want to keep watch over strangers in the city on such a night."

I didn't have time to discuss it with him, or, more important, the strength.

"Whatever the reason, the important thing is that I expect you to cooperate with me."

"Cooperate? Cooperate in what?"

"Listen carefully! You've been here two days, and tomorrow at dawn you'll leave the city. During that time, how many times have you heard explosions?"

"I haven't counted; but I'll never forget the shell that destroyed the church. I'm going to report it to the central dioceses and probably raise the matter in a letter to the Red Cross."

I forced a smile to keep him from seeing the sneer on my face. "And the Red Cross will do what?"

"I don't know. Just doing my duty."

With a movement of my index finger I invited him to come closer. Now we were face-to-face.

"It seems like you are in a bad way. You should rest!"

"You bet! I'm in a terrible way. But I have to tell you something first. Tonight there's something very important I have to do. Very important. There's a certain machine on that side of the waterway that keeps our artillery from destroying the enemy batteries that have been shelling the city. Tonight a number of the boys have decided that this machine is going to meet with a disaster. But...but a problem has come up that only you can solve."

"Only me? What is it?"

"You see the shape I'm in. Tonight I have to act as spotter for the boys, but this illness, which couldn't have come at a worse time, has ruined everything—which is where you come in. Somebody has to keep his eyes open and report to me where the enemy fire is coming from."

He got the point perfectly. His head went back and seemed to be considering it. But then he said, "Are you kidding? I don't know how to fight; I just came to collect church property."

"No, I'm not kidding. We'll go up there on the roof together. The only thing I want you to do is locate the enemy fire when the shelling starts."

He turned to the Engineer, hoping perhaps he might help. But the Engineer kept toying with the cat, which was the best thing he could do at the time.

"That's not a problem, but I *am* a priest. How can you expect a priest to take a direct role in the fighting? That is impossible."

Although I was wrapped from head to toe in the blanket, I was still shivering; but the worst part was that he had turned me down. The priest was probably closer to me in every respect than the Engineer: both of us being devout, with a belief in human resurrection. But now when he had to act, he stepped aside. Now everything between us was over. So I should have said my piece: Listen! I don't want anyone to be upset with me on what may be the last night we spend together, but right now, under that very rain, several children are waiting for their mother to come home. I don't know what story their father has made up for them, or how many of them will be able to sleep after they hear it. This morning their mother was just as alive as you and me! But, then, a shell identical to the one that hit your church, and that you're going to complain about to God knows who, landed right next to the place where she sells greens. Know where she is now? Right now her body is in the freezer of an ice cream company, getting rock hard.

But I didn't say anything; instead, I started coughing uncontollably. But the anger in my face spoke volumes. Stunned, Hovanes brought his hand to his collar and, clasping a golden cross, said, "I swore by this holy cross that I would only work for peace."

"I have nothing more to say to you. You can go."

Hovanes got up and went to the stairs, but after a few steps he turned and said, "There is one thing I can do for you, however. I can pray for the well-being of you and your comrades."

"Pray, then! But, want to know what I think about that kind of praying? It's like if some able-bodied man were to go around begging. When you get to Esfahan, just don't forget one thing."

"What's that?"

"As I told you before—the holocaust memorial for the people of this city. That's something you can do, right?"

I was burning up with fever and might have been delirious. Hovanes went downstairs, while the Engineer still played with the cat.

Asadollah's watch read 4:01. Eleven minutes to go. With the rain over, they definitely would have removed the tarp from the Doomsday Machine, and in eleven minutes its delicate sensors would go into action.

I had never felt this helpless. A pawn had fallen on the floor beside the bed. I stepped on it and the round base rocked back and forth under my foot.

No choice but to accept defeat, I thought. Could there have been anything more ludicrous: asking a priest to get into the war? I lost. I had to accept it!

But you're not well, I told myself. The fever is gutting your body. No one is going to blame you. All you have to do is get on the radio and explain the situation to Qasem. No! That would be just another excuse. If you don't feel like having your name pinned to the failure of the operation, say you did it to protect Javad's father! Everybody's favorite. Just say that he left without permission and didn't come back. If we had started shelling something might have happened to him. That would work. And would be a way to save face.

The Engineer shook me saying, "What happened? Did you black out or something, sir? Lie down!"

"One little thing!"

"Why not?"

"What did you do with my binoculars?"

"They're in the niche upstairs. Want me to bring them?"

I tried to rise while, at the same time, keeping the blanket wrapped around me.

"Do you have some spare shoes for me?"

He grabbed a pair of faded brown shoes without laces and the back folded down and put them in front of my feet.

"You going somewhere?"

"I've got to go upstairs; but you can also do something!"

"I want to sleep."

"I know, but this is the last thing."

"Okay. What, sir?"

"I can't go downstairs and get my helmet. I'm going up on the roof. Can you do me a favor and bring the helmet upstairs? I'll take the weapon myself."

I slipped my right foot into the shoe. The stiff leather chafed against my foot. I shuffled toward the weapon. Unable to bend down, I sat and picked up the weapon.

"Go, already!"

"If I bring it, will that be the end of your Excellency's requests?"

I didn't answer. He had to be kept in the dark about the plan.

"Once you're downstairs, tell Javad's mother that the boys radioed that the Hajji is with them. He said he'd come in the morning. Tell her to pray for us."

"How do you know that this woman's husband is with them? You want me to lie, is that it?"

"Don't get all holier than thou, like that friend of yours. The old man definitely found some place to hole up to wait out rain. We just don't know where. I'll be waiting for you upstairs."

I dragged myself up the stairway. At least four stories with eight, half-finished stairs. The ascent was like rock-climbing with the rocks at a ninety-degree angle. I tossed the blanket to the floor and hung the weapon around my neck. Then I wrapped myself in the blanket again. The spasms that wracked my body made my teeth chatter. Saying *In-the-Name-of-God*, I latched onto the first step and forced my entire body up. By hunching over, I prevented the blanket from slipping off.

After the first stair came the second!

The Engineer said, "Sir, don't let my blanket get dirty!" Then he went in the opposite direction down the stairs, unaware of the trap that was set for him.

24

Because of the rain the refinery fire had died down, and I could see a single star sparkling between the clouds in the night sky. The only parts of my body not covered by the blanket were my two inept eyes.

Although I was crawling my way up the stairs on all fours, I found it hard to catch my breath. The first thing I did when I reached the top was to extract the binoculars from their niche.

The calm that came about after the rain was exactly what our plan had called for. If there had been the slightest breeze, the enemy would be less likely to blame the "near misses" we were manufacturing on the Doomsday Machine. I had to find a good position for myself, a place where I could keep the boys in view and, at the same time, see the whole date grove. The best place was where the Engineer was standing when I visited the gun emplacement.

I crawled over to it. Using the blanket, I periodically tried to wipe the sweat from my head and neck; but each time the seam split open, exposing me to the cold. The rapid staccato of my teeth rang in my ears like machine gun fire.

So, what was next according to the plan?

The first objective was to spot a proper target for our shells. It had to be important enough to provoke the Iraqis into firing back in self-defense.

Which of their positions should I choose? One of their mortar units at the end of the grove? Or the asphalt road? No, neither was that provocative.

I brought the binoculars inside the blanket, then put them to my eyes. The first glimpse made me dizzy and I adjusted the eyepieces. But I shouldn't have, because the settings had been right for the person who was going to take on the duties of spotting that night—25mm to the right and 25mm to the left.

I looked to the right with the binoculars. The bend in the waterway and the large, common trenches were hidden in the reeds.

Right there, or not? I asked myself.

Training the binoculars to the left, I realized that there was no better target along the waterway.

"Sir, here's the radio and the helmet and another thing that you had forgotten to mention. Now can you give me my blanket back?"

He meant my olive bag and dumped all of the things he had retrieved beside my feet. I grabbed the bag; it was soaking wet. I didn't have the heart to open it. The map and notebook would definitely be soaked. But this was not the main concern at the moment; except for the radio and binoculars, there was nothing was more necessary now than a spotter.

"Cold?"

"No, sir, I'm not cold; it's just that I want to sleep."

Several moments passed in silence. The most difficult thing about asking a favor was finding the right words to broach the subject. I looked at the watch. Not more than a minute remained before it was time to make contact.

"If you need the blanket, I'll leave it with you. I have an extra one downstairs."

"Mr. Engineer! I need you to do something for me."

He put his hands on his hips and said, "What's that?"

He was my only hope; I couldn't let him escape. There had to be some way to trick him into cooperating.

"Remember when you found a place up here to stand where you could see the boys? What I want from you now is to show me exactly where that was."

"Right there! He said, "That's it, right there!" and showed me with his hand. From that angle the buildings and the tangle of trees formed a single shadow; when the boys began to fire, it would be easy to locate the trench.

"Could you find two pieces of wood or two bricks for me and put them on the stone wall in a way that they are lined up with the boys' artillery?"

"Is that all, Excellency?   You didn't specify what kind of wood: teak or ebony?"

Time was flying. The Engineer looked around and dislodged two loose bricks from the wall.

"So much for the bricks. Okay to put them here?"

Where he put them was not right, from my vantage point. They had to be directly in my line of sight in relation to the artillery.

"A little to the right. Yes! Perfect!"

The wait was almost over. I swallowed and there was a foul taste in my mouth. Did that mean we'd be successful?

"Should I go?"

"One second!" I said and lifted the receiver.

"Ehsan! Musa, here!"

"The last half-foot is over! Understood? We're ready!"

It was Mohammad's voice. He would soon be joining Asadollah in the trench, waiting for my firing instructions. Now, how to make the Engineer understand that he would have to be my eyes?

"Sir, I'm going down to rest."

"I need you here for a few more minutes. As soon as they fire, I want you to line up these two bricks for me as precisely as possible!"

The two bricks would give me a clear idea of the position of the shells the enemy fired in response to our artillery. I opened the bag. As I suspected, the notebook and map were completely soaked. Huddled under the blanket I shined the small flashlight onto the map. Beside the waterway, the common trenches, designation: "Hossein-4"?

"Ehsan, Ehsan—Musa!"

"Ehsan! See map designation: Hossein-4! Understood?"

"Understood. Over!"

I put the receiver down. In a few minutes Asadollah would set the range-finder on the artillery piece and start shelling the Iraqi bunkers.

"Engineer! Put this helmet on!"

"What for?"

"Tonight I need your help."

"To fight?"

He was very quick. "More to play chess. Call it whatever you like; just sit up there with the binoculars and, report whenever the enemy fires to me."

He said, "I'm going to bed" and headed for the stairs. There was no choice but to threaten him.

"You don't like it when I use the language of the gun, do you? As long as this operation is going on, no one in the city except for those boys down there in that dugout will be in danger. I give you my word on that."

"Sir, your war has nothing to do with me. It's been ages since I've had anything to do with people. I don't give a good Goddamn about anybody. I'm only friends with cats."

"Fine—for your cats then! Have you ever seen what shrapnel does to an animal? None of your cats have been hit till now?"

The image of the dog with the wounded paw near the War Room was still fresh in my mind. Mentioning his cats must have struck a nerve. The Engineer sat down on the roof.

"Of course! The best-looking of them—I buried them myself in the garden of the house next door. You can't imagine how much I cried."

This one was a godsend: the thought of his cats. My intuition was still working!

"But I can't kill anybody."

"Musa, Musa—Ehsan! Musa, Musa—Ehsan!"

"Ehsan! Musa here!"

"We're ready. Should we *God-is-great*?"

"No! Stand by for a moment!"

I let go of the switch and said, "Don't tell me you're like that priest, trying to get into heaven free of charge, without any effort?"

"No, I'm not even trying for hell. You are shivering something awful."

Even though I was still holding the receiver, my hand was shaking horribly.

"So what are you going to do? Decide! If nothing happens tonight, there's no telling how many people in this city will be killed, or, for that matter, how many of these cats. I'm begging you! If you say no, you'll spoil everything."

"But I still have a bone to pick with you. You shouldn't have brought that harridan Geety around here. Am I right or not?"

"Yes, you're right. I robbed you of all your peace and quiet too. But it's all going to end tonight. I'll never show my face around these parts again, I swear."

He paused for a long time, then stared into my eyes. I was pleading, begging!

He stood up and began the cat-and-mouse game all over again.

"For the sake of the cats, then—not for people. But under certain conditions."

"Ehsan, ready?"

"Yes, Musa! We are ready."

The Engineer suddenly snatched the receiver from my hand. If I wasn't in such bad shape...

"What are you doing, Mr. Gentleman? I said I have a condition."

"Okay, fine. Whatever it is. God willing, after the operation is over—accepted sight unseen!"

"No way, Excellency! You have to do it here and now!"

Logic dictated that the best way around this would be to learn his condition, but in this crazy situation...?

"Fine, be so kind as to express it, only hand me the receiver! If the thing gets wet, it won't work anymore."

He picked it up off the ground, but instead of handing it to me he dangled the receiver in the air in front of me.

"My condition is this!"

"Well, out with it! What?"

"No, be polite! Treat me with respect from now on! Only with the utmost respect!"

Then the radio sounded: "Musa! We're ready."

"Respect! This is the inalienable right of an old man, even if you hadn't been my companion in this."

"Okay, fine!"

"Good, the second condition!"

"Accepted, sight unseen!"

"This is the second time, Excellency, 'sight unseen'? Here is an entirely obvious example of disrespect!"

"Faster, Master! Say whatever it is you want! They're all waiting below."

"Okay, okay."

He stood holding the receiver in his hand with his other hand on his hip. The coiled wire hung down from his back like a tail.

Was this the way I looked when I held the receiver? I wondered.

"I have three questions. If you answer..."

I didn't hear the rest. The idiotic games had begun again! The crazy jerk had no idea how serious the situation was! I wished I could radio the enemy and give them the coordinates of the building!

He shook me with his hand...and asked, "Why don't you answer, sir? I said there are conditions."

I had no choice but to control myself. The balance of power in our little test of wills had shifted in his favor.

"Okay, but only for the sake of God, not your cats; let's discuss this later. I don't have another minute to spare—I swear to God."

He looked at me mysteriously again. Without thinking, I began to count: a thousand and one, a thousand and two, a thousand and three, a thousand and four...Before I reached a thousand and five, he began to speak.

"Fine. On account of my cats, I'll make an exception in your favor! Start your operation. But, remember, you have to answer my questions."

Like his furry cat, I stood on my hind legs, snatched the receiver from him as though it were a piece of chicken, and looked at him.

He stared back at me mischievously. "Now, the first question!"

"Fine, but before you ask, the helmet goes on your head!"

He put the helmet on and sat with his back to me, facing the bricks and our artillery unit. I forced myself to look calm, but that quickly passed. Then I stared blankly at the trees and houses in the darkness. Pressing SEND, I said to myself, God forgive you!

"Ehsan, are you ready?"

"Yes, Musa! We're ready."

"Then, *You did not throw what you threw, but Allah did!*"

"Musa! *God is great!*"

"Mr. Engineer! Keep your eyes peeled!"

He looked through the binoculars. With the helmet on his head he was the very image of the old soldier. The momentary flash of the artillery split the infinity of the night sky like the beam from a projector. A few seconds later, there was the dull thud of a shell exploding.

"Now look in that direction, toward the bend in the water-way!"

I pointed to the place where the shell would have landed.

"Okay! But why did you do that?"

Now that he was considered one of us, he needed to know about the operation in detail.

"It's simple. We have to pressure their forces along the coast so much that they will be provoked into contacting their command for back-up. The Iraqi command will use the Doomsday Machine to find our artillery unit, then order it to be destroyed."

"I don't understand!"

"You will in time. Just don't lose sight of where the shell lands."

The light from the explosion was not as bright as I'd expected.

"It was over there!"

"Be quiet!"

The sound of the blast was muffled, which meant that the shell landed short, in the marshy area along the shore. Because of the rainfall, I didn't expect that we would face a rapid reaction from the machine.

"Move those two bricks a little to the right and focus all your attention on the enemy's response. The next shell will have to go a little higher; they'll need to make at least a fifty-meter adjustment."

"Ehsan, Ehsan—Musa!"

"Ehsan, here!"

"Ehsan! Seventy up and twenty to the left. Understood?"

"Understood. We'll be ready soon."

The Engineer arranged both bricks and then went back to his place.

"Sir, before I forget: Javad's mother was asleep and I didn't wake her."

"Excellent. Whatever you do is fine."

Right now Asadollah was taking another shell from its casing. First, they would wipe the excess powder from the shell, then they would correct the alignment of the artillery. Meanwhile, Ameer would be stretched out on the roof of the shore base without the slightest role in the whole thing. As was normal, when we didn't want the enemy to learn that anything was out of the ordinary, there would be no contact until the last minute.

Qasem and the boys on the dock would be sitting two-by-two at the ready in the bunkers along the water's edge. Even the Major and his buddies in the War Room would be monitoring our radio communications. Tonight everyone was waiting to see the results of our missile game with the radar.

"Musa, we're ready!"

"Good, now it's my turn." Was he starting again?

"Understood. Standby."

"Turn for what?"

"Turn for my questions. Are you ready?"

The radio repeated, "Musa! We're ready!"

I looked at the Engineer, pleading with him. He shook his head. There was no other way; I had to answer his questions. I nodded. "Ehsan, understood. Standby!"

And now it was the Engineer's turn.

"Fine, your questions, if you please!"

"First question! Right? First question, but remember that you only have the right to give one answer per question—and the correct answer at that. Three questions, three correct answers. If your answer is wrong, I will have to—however unwillingly—be excused from cooperating with you."

"But that wasn't what we had agreed."

"Did not your Excellency himself say that any condition I had would be accepted sight unseen?"

What did I have to do? What could I do?

"Okay, fine."

"Now then, the first question! Pay close attention! Ready?"

I didn't answer. "Then you're ready. I won't say it more than once. My good sir: Who was the first person in this world to lay the foundation of politics and political gamesmanship?"

The radio sounded again: "Musa! Where are you? We're ready."

I had to stall for time. I repeated the question, then said, "Mr. Engineer, get ready! The second shell is on its way."

He nodded to confirm that he understood. If I had been in better shape, I definitely would have been able to read the anxiety in his features at these moments.

I wondered what sin the old man had committed that merited a headache like me. And what sin had I committed that got me saddled with him?

"Ehsan! *God is great!*"

"*God is great!*"

I had arranged the way I was sitting so as to have one eye on the boys' artillery position and the other on the Iraqis. As soon as the ray of light from the blast split the night sky again, I unconsciously began to count: one thousand and one, one thousand and two, one thousand and three...one thousand and twelve. The sound of the shell landing stopped the count. Twelve seconds; multiplied by 333, plus 4,400 meters, the distance between us and our artillery battery. And this was the second blast.

"Explain to me what you are doing at least."

I put my index finger to my lips first and then to my ears. He quickly realized what I meant. Quiet, quiet!

Enveloped in total darkness, the date grove on the other side of the waterway seemed very mysterious. Usually the waters were bright with the red tracers that the two sides shot at one another. The heavy rains had forced everybody to abandon hostilities for a time.

The city that lay beneath my feet, though, awaited its fate, as it did on any other night—dreading the moment when a shell would hit and the explosion would tear doors from walls. Suddenly the shell, the second one, from our battery lit up the grove. The Engineer let out a yelp.

"There it is, sir! Did you see it?"

He found this game very entertaining! But I didn't feel like responding. The shell exploded among the trenches. By now the personnel in them would have called for supporting fire and the radar would have been contacted for help. The second shell must have provoked their forces, which were unaware that it was just a way of trapping the Doomsday Machine.

Once again, doubt was gnawing at me. Did the Doomsday Machine actually exist? Other than the enemy's near-perfect aim, there was really no reason to believe that they had installed such a system.

"Did you see it or not, sir? Are you with me?"

"Quiet, Mr. Engineer! Quiet!"

He didn't realize our need for absolute silence in this dangerous game.

The old man, now quiet, peered through the binoculars. The thick clouds left no opening for starlight in the sky. The shell had hit the sensitive spot that we had hoped to find. The dreadful explosion would have jolted the forces in the trenches out of their rainy-night slumber.

The Engineer jumped up from where he was sitting and felt his legs with his hands. "Wet! It's not damp where you're sitting?

Why would I feel the damp beneath my legs? I was wrapped in the thick folds of his blanket, keeping the water on the roof from getting to my body. The poor man! If he only knew what was happening to his precious blanket!

The normal interval between the explosion of the shell and the time when the spotter made contact was coming to an end. Everything had to proceed as usual. If the enemy was monitoring our transmissions, there could be nothing out of the ordinary in the way we communicated to attract his attention.

"Ehsan, Ehsan—Musa!"

And again the Engineer... "My dear sir! Now will you answer my question?"

"Huh? Which one? Say it again!"

"Never! Impossible! You have to respect our agreement: one question—one answer."

Who was the first in the world to play politics? Adam? No, the pathetic creature wasn't capable of anything. Cain and Abel? No, Eve came before them. Maybe it was Satan!

"Your time is up."

"What time is up?"

"The time for answering, my dear sir! Not counting the time you were working, which I didn't, twenty seconds have elapsed. So, give me your answer!"

What should I answer? Better to pin it on...on Adam!

"Was it Adam?"

"Wrong! Your first answer is incorrect! Let's go on to the second question!"

"So what's the right answer?"

Why are you wasting your time with this? I asked myself. Why even go into such things with a war going on?

"The answer? Why it's God Himself!"

"...! What the hell does that mean?"

"Look, sir! I'll explain it real fast so you can get back to work. When God created Adam, the Angels became jealous and went to the Almighty asking Him why He had done it. And what did God say? He told them not to meddle in things they didn't understand! Then He called Adam over and secretly whispered the Exalted Name to him. Later, He held a general audience and said, 'O coddled angels! Do any of you know the Exalted Name? If so, tell Me.' The benighted creatures had to say, 'No. What is the Exalted Name?' Then God turned to Adam and said, 'Well, my new creation! God's favorite little guy! Tell them the Exalted Name!' Adam told them the Name and all the Angels left the Throne-room with their heads hanging in shame. Well, do you think that if the Almighty had not played politics, sneakily telling your noble ancestor the Exalted Name, do you think that Adam could have prospered the way he did? Never!"

"So?"

"Well, that proves that the first person in the world to play politics was God Himself!" He nodded his head, satisfied with his answer.

You've got work to do, boy, I reminded myself. I pushed the send button on the radio. "Ehsan, Ehsan—Musa!"

"Musa! Ehsan, here!"

I saw no reason to change the particulars of the last target. The same place, at the same trenches—to stir up the enemy, this was the best place to hit.

"Ehsan! Ten meters to the right! Understood?"

"Musa! Understood. Stand by!"

After we finished the conversation, the Engineer sat down again at his position, still rubbing his legs.

"Okay, at least do me the kindness of saying why we had to put those two bricks up there?"

"Those two bricks? When their radar system goes into operation, targeting the boys down there, I'll use the bricks to make a sight line in relation to the position of the artillery unit. This way I can measure how far from the boys' position the enemy's shells explode. Understand?"

The stunned look on his face told me that the old man was confused.

"Leave the bricks to me! You just keep your eyes on the enemy."

"Musa, we're ready!"

This would be the third shell.

"Ehsan! *God is great!*"

"*O Mehdi!*"

My eyes were drawn to the unbroken line of palm trees on the other side. Slumbering somewhere inside that dark ribbon was an awful monster that these shells would force to come back to life.

Damned frog! Weren't you the one looking for a bite to eat? Well, come and get it! We blinked, so why don't you shoot out that long sticky tongue of yours? Slimy bastard, come and swallow us!

...Then I heard the sound of firing. The shell raced on in its path across the sky and now in free fall, hurtling toward the enemy trenches with certain death, got closer by the moment to its target. But tonight the destruction of a particular point in that darkness on that side would be of no help to us.

Flames from the violent blast tore at the blackness in the palm grove a few meters to the right of the previous one. I had forgotten about my fever, but my body was trembling just the same from a murderous anxiety. This wait for the enemy to fire back at us was driving me crazy.

Did I have to pray that they begin shelling us? I asked myself. What a weird thing to ask! So what should I do?

During these moments while I was sitting far from the trench, Asadollah and Mohammad waited, and with each firing the cold gun barrel would get warmer and warmer, like a stovepipe.

Mohammad would certainly have his eyes closed, repeating the familiar phrase *By remembering Allah is there not assurance to hearts* and repeating and repeating...

"Sir, the second question!"

He rested the binoculars on the wall. I pointed my finger at the two bricks.

"Take the binoculars off the wall! Your eyes should be on the grove. Now speak!"

He immediately removed the binoculars and rested them on his knees.

"The second question is this! You have twenty seconds to answer! Listen carefully. What was the reason why Adam was expelled from paradise?"

"Why are you so obsessed by these things now?"

"None of your business! Answer!" he nearly shouted my head off.

"Well, the answer is simple. Those two, when they ate the fruit or wheat that God had forbidden them; and that lack of obedience—or whatever—caused, or was the basis for, our troubles here on earth."

Nothing wrong with that answer. Now, Mr. Engineer, put your cards on the table; let's see what you have!

But he had no intention of backing down. "No, wrong! Totally wrong!"

"No, Mr. Engineer! Everybody knows this."

"Dear sir! You have all been deceived. All of you! Look! Of all the trees in paradise, if God had not singled that particular one out, would Adam and Eve ever have taken any interest in it at all? In a paradise with an area of seven heavens by seven heavens, it is more than likely that all of Adam and Eve's descendents could still be living happily and not have even encountered that tree."

"So who's to blame?"

"It's not about blame. The agent or basis of it was God."

"What does that mean?"

"Look, sir! It was God who created the two of them Himself. He fitted them with a certain nature, making them greedy. So why single out that tree?"

"Okay, why?"

"Bravo! Bravo! It's obvious. He was looking for a way of getting them out of the way, so it wouldn't bother His conscience. Then He could say: See! It was all their fault. I warned them not to eat from that tree! You know? If Adam, after eating the forbidden fruit, had visited the Tree of Eternity, then all hell would have broken loose. So, given this, is there any difference between Adam and God? Is there, my noble lord? You didn't answer the second question. Don't forget."

Didn't I have enough to torment me? Now I had to solve the eternal problem of Adam and Eve? And while I was doing that, what would become of the war?

Why didn't they fire at us? The people, the doors, the walls—even the asphalt on the roads, unlike the previous days, all of them were yearning for the enemy to start shelling. Fire! FIRE ALREADY!

"Didn't you hear, sir?"

"No, what should I hear?"

"I'm going to bend over backwards for you. The third question, if answered correctly, perhaps, just maybe, will give you a way out."

Was he mocking me? What did the old man want from me?

"Ask the question?"

There was no escape. I didn't have the luxury of arguing with him, even by his own twisted logic.

"Ask!"

"Fine. Keeping in mind everything I said, why would you want to participate in an impossible fight that is only going to end in your death? Even a person like me without the slightest knowledge of the military, can see that you have lost, that you had been defeated even before you started—a loser, just like Adam and all the Adams that came after him and all that will come after. So why should I take part in your idiotic war? Especially since I don't believe in it?"

Every cell in my brain was screeching NO. People were dying and he was parading the million-year-old debate about human creation before me. But what could I do? Without him, continuing would be impossible.

If those two holocaust-memorial-building priests would only lend me their eyes for half an hour...

Asadollah...Asadollah!

And this was the point that my new plan gradually took shape.

"My twenty seconds up?"

"There's still a lot of time, sir! A lot of time, but you've already lost everything."

"Can you make a friendly exception?"

"Why?"

"Since...since I'm sick!"

"Okay. What? I'm ready."

"Ready?"

"I said so, but remember that this is your last chance."

"You're right, but I can't say it out loud."

"Why not?"

"God might hear, of course!"

"What?"

"It's top secret. Come closer so I can whisper into your ear. He might hear otherwise."

The astonished Engineer brought his head closer.

"Musa, Musa—Ehsan!"

"Ehsan, ready."

"It seems you forgot to give them the corrected coordinates," the Engineer reminded me.

"In a minute."

I threw down the receiver, unconcerned now whether the mouthpiece got wet. I needed both hands. I cupped them around my mouth and whispered into his ear, "Mr. Engineer, I lied to you about the objective of our operation. We actually want to do something else."

"You lied?"

"Not so loud. God mustn't hear."

"What do you want to do?"

"You're right; those two boys in the trench will definitely be martyred. On the surface the operation will look like a failure, but the real objective is in the other world!"

"The other world?"

The radio started groaning again: "Musa, Musa—Ehsan!"

"Standby a moment!"

Though I knew what they were going through in that trench, I had no other choice. I cupped my hands around his ear again.

"The real purpose of the operation is..." I paused for extra credibility.

"What?"

"is to martyr Asadollah and Mohammad so that they can enter the next world and then, acting according to the established plan, blow up the Bridge to the Afterlife and take revenge on God!"

The Engineer stepped back and stared at me.

"You're lying!"

So he had enough sense not to take seriously the stupidities that passed for humor with Asadollah and me. But he continued: "If that's true, where are they going to get the explosives?"

I remembered the graveyard and the unexploded ordnance in it.

If your Excellency were to pay a visit to the cemetery, you would see how many of the grave slabs have been punched full of holes by dud shells. The Bridge was also made to be very slim and delicate, so that not just anyone can get across it. According to our calculations, a 120mm shell would be enough make it go up in smoke. Now isn't this enough reason for you to help in the operation?"

"Why didn't you tell me this before?"

"Military secrets, my dear friend! Military secrets! But the way you were speaking before made me realize that you were one of us. Just think of what will happen when that bridge explodes...!

He stood up and started pacing.

What have you done? I asked myself. He'll never swallow it. But this too shall pass; he'll go downstairs, leaving you to face this mess alone. Did I know what I was saying? I guess it's a lost cause anyway; he's already gone about his business!

But all of a sudden he let out a yell and sat down. He shook me so hard that the bones in my shoulders ached.

"Yes, my dear comrade! Damn right! God had it all figured out except this one thing! Blowing up the Bridge will wreck the whole machinery of eternity. What a plan! Pure genius! This I like. Revenge would be a good thing, considering everything He's put us through."

If Asadollah only knew about this..., I thought.

"Okay, now where do we go from here, Mr. Engineer?"

"I'm with you till the last, but...let me see. What if you play a trick on them? For example, suppose we let them know that the shells are coming?"

I cupped my hands around his ear and said, "And you call yourself intelligent! To cover our tracks, of course! Men have been programmed mentally to be afraid of dying, and this is His way of keeping us from acting. But those boys down there are not afraid to die, and this is how they discovered the weak link in the logic of eternity. All they have to do is become martyrs, set foot in the next world and everything will be over!"

This kid stuff was all I could think of on the spur of the moment. I forced a smile but had to struggle to keep it from becoming a sneer. The Engineer looked back at me, his face glowing with joy.

"Outstanding! Outstanding! I am with you until the end."

"Sit down, then, and not a word out of you until it's over. Okay?"

He sat. I was reminded of the Major with the stars on his shoulders. Qasem once said that those epaulette things were not stars; they called them "brass buttons."

The dark band of the palm grove began to dance before my eyes. Use your reason, your good sense more, I told myself.

I wished my eyes were like the radio and I could replace their batteries. Too bad I had to humor the Engineer so much; otherwise...

Then I realized—the common trenches! Maybe there wasn't anybody left in them to contact their back lines. Maybe...maybe the shrapnel from our shells cut the telephone wires that ran through the desert and they couldn't reach their command post. God forbid!

"Ehsan, one more shell: the same spot!"

"Understood."

The radio was silent. The moment I saw the enemy fire, I would have to notify Ehsan so that there would be time for them to crawl under their tiny dugout. But no matter how strong that shelter was, it had no chance of withstanding a shell with a delay fuse.

Would the ring on the enemy shell casing be set on "immediate" or "delay"? A shell with a delay fuse would not go off on contact; it would penetrate the roof of the dugout and after a short pause—no more than part of a second—it would explode. If Asadollah and Mohammad were in the dugout at that moment...? I couldn't think about it now.

"Musa! The bouquet is ready!"

"*O Mehdi!*"

The Engineer looked up so he could see the blast better between the houses.

"Mr. Engineer! Don't look over there. Keep your eyes on the grove! The place where the enemy is going to fire!"

He did what he was told, like an obedient child. I wiped my forehead with the back of my hand. It was soaking wet.

Why didn't I feel myself sweating? I wondered.

The fires in the ammunition dumps kicked up again. No matter how hard it rained, it wasn't enough to put them out.

Why hadn't Javad's father come yet?

25

"Hey, punk, where do you hide your tea?"

It was her. I had a vague image of her standing in the doorway with what looked like a kettle in her hand. What was she doing up here?

The Engineer jumped up and quickly came over to me. Although a shell would soon be on its way, he was so frightened of her that he turned his back on the enemy.

"Why'd you go there?"

The Engineer crouched down next to me and tried to speak so she wouldn't hear.

"See, sir? The she-devil called me a punk! For the love of God, tell me what was the point of bringing her here?"

Geety looked around and watchfully walked forward a few steps. Then, hands on hips, she suddenly started hollering, "You don't think I can hear you! That fancy-pants lady of yours—she's the she-devil! Where is she domiciled these days? Don't tell me, you old fool, that you sent her on pilgrimage so she can wash her sins away with holy water?"

The Engineer was badly shaken. I looked at Geety's hands. Thank God she didn't have her club with her. There was no immediate threat. We heard the sound made by our shell exploding on other side of the waterway.

"Go tell her where the tea is, for God's sake!"

The Engineer got up and stood facing Geety.

"You have no right to insult my esteemed wife. Just for that, I won't tell you where the tea is."

"You're making a big mistake—we're your guests and against our will at that! If my daughter catches cold, I'll grab you by the legs and dump you on your head from right up here on the roof. Hurry up and tell me where the tea is before the fire goes out!"

I had to end this. Taking the blanket off my head, I said, "Tell her where the tea is, for God's sake!"

"No, sir. Never! She has to apologize first! If not, that's the end of the tea!" He turned his back on both of us, and, sitting on the wall, he put the binoculars to his eyes.

"Should I hit him with this kettle and split his head open? You lousy bastard! Who do you think you are that I should apologize to you?"

The Engineer continued to peer through the binoculars at our artillery.

"Go away, woman! Don't make me say something that will have you bawling your head off! Get out of here!"

"What do you know—it talks! Be my guest. Is there something you want to tell me? I've heard it all, don't worry."

The Engineer placed the binoculars on the wall and turned around.

"You asked for it. Where's that darling boy of yours? Did you send his lordship to Europe for his education? Does he ever write his dear, revered mother? Does he? Answer me! Cat got your tongue?"

I looked at Geety. She was paralyzed as if someone had electrocuted her except she was biting her lips. Where was her son?

The kettle flew past the Engineer's head and continued in free fall down into the street. All at once the lump in Geety's throat burst and she went off like a rocket.

"SON OF A BITCH! You old jackal! You're making a big, fucking mistake bringing my son's name into this! Cocksuckers like you are the reason why it happened!"

She looked up toward the sky and said, "Lord! Why don't you take me now and put me out of my misery? Why do you torment me? How long do I have put up with it?"

Unable to control herself, she put her hands over her face. A nervous spasm took hold of her body. Fortunately she seemed to be leaving; but, no, she leaned her head against the wall of the entrance to the stairway and said, "Is there any escape from cocksuckers like you? God, where can I hide? Didn't I tell you that I was going somewhere there was no filth called 'men'? Almighty God, I don't have to tell you that if it weren't for the girl, I would have ended it all long ago. How much more of this crap do I have to take?"

The Engineer looked down saying nothing in response. I didn't know which of us should have been sorrier: Geety who started it; the Engineer; or me, the person who brought them all together tonight.

Suddenly it came; the sound that I'd been waiting for all night—the loud and drawn-out launch accompanied by the whine of an oncoming shell. I reached for the receiver to tell Asadollah and Mohammad, but it was too late.

The Engineer instinctively turned to look toward our artillery battery. This was the moment when the shell would have hit. I wanted to close my eyes to keep from seeing the explosion. The bickering between these two took my mind off the job during the most critical time. If the shell were to land in the trench and cut the boys to pieces...?

I looked along the sight line formed by the two bricks between the buildings to the trench where it ended. There was a long indentation made by the explosion, along with a shower of red-hot shrapnel.

The woman's sobbing became louder. The Engineer looked at me in surprise. Fortunately or unfortunately our calculations turned out to be right—there *was* a Doomsday Machine. The enemy's first shell hit precisely where it had to. The only possible reason why they had waited for us to fire three times before firing back was the rain.

The question of whether the Doomsday Machine existed was now answered, replaced by other, more urgent problems. Could we make the thing go astray? And, more important: What became of the boys in the trench?

The plan called for Mohammad to make contact after the explosion, when it was quietest. Otherwise, in the event that the artillery unit was destroyed, Qasem was to radio us from the jetty and introduce himself as Ehsan.

"What should I do, sir?"

Furious with myself for being so thoughtless, I took it out on the Engineer. "Just shut up! Both of you! Enough!"

I would never have missed the enemy's fire, if I hadn't been distracted by their stupid argument. Instead of going astray by a few meters, what if the shell landed in the middle of the trench at the feet of those two boys? Then the others on the jetty would have every right to ask: What the hell were you thinking? Weren't you supposed to let Asadollah and Mohammad know the second you spotted the flash? And even if they said nothing, how would I handle my own guilty conscience?

O Lord, it's all in your hands now. Don't let Asadollah and Mohammad die just because some worthless believer like me was thoughtless.

There was nothing I could do but wait. Wait! The fever prevented me from passing the time the way I normally would—pacing from one end of the roof to the other.

Geety's sobs turned into a full wail. While there was still time, I had to...

"Why don't you go downstairs?"

"I'm not going. This whole thing is your fault. If you hadn't brought us here tonight, this bastard wouldn't have shot off his mouth. I hope to God that some day you feel the pain raging in my heart and it's your turn to cry your eyes out. If there's a God in heaven, your life's blood will be drained the way mine has been!"

I was trapped, as I listened with one ear for Qasem's voice on the radio; but for the first time I dreaded hearing it because it meant that the boys were dead.

"Mother! I beg you; go downstairs! Your daughter is all alone."

"No. Javad's mother is with her."

"Do you mean she's awake?"

"The poor old soul didn't sleep a wink. She's been praying while she waits for her husband to come back."

So why had the Engineer said she was sleeping? Nothing this new spotter did made any sense to me.

"That's even better, mother! Go downstairs and say a prayer for us. Go, mother! I'll see that the Engineer gets what's coming to him!"

Geety removed her hands from in front of her face and stood drained of emotion, staring blankly at the old man and me.

"LEAVE! I can't referee between the two of you while there's a war going on!"

Grasping the wall for support, Geety began to go down the stairs.

"Mother!"

She turned.

"When you get down there, just pray for us. That's all!"

Her face almost disappeared in the darkness of the stairway, but, before it did, she turned and I was aware of her stopping on one of the steps so that the top of her head was still showing. She was looking at us.

If you only knew how much we need those prayers tonight, I said to myself.

The radio remained silent and the Engineer breathed a sigh of relief.

"Did you see what a load of nonsense she tried to foist on me?"

I motioned with my finger for him to be quiet.

Just pray! Pray!

The Engineer shrugged, and then remembered the game we had been playing.

"Wait a minute! If it is true what you say, why are you waiting for them to kill you?"

Was this ever going to end? Why doesn't the man leave me alone?

"Mr. Engineer, with your keen intelligence and all that knowledge at your fingertips, I'm surprised at you! Don't you know that only martyrs get their wishes granted and can operate in the afterlife?"

His eyes flashed again. "You're right, sir! That's right!"

By now the boys' corpses were probably soaked in blood and others were on their way to see about them. If the shell had exploded directly in the trench, then a couple of thousand pieces of light-alloy shrapnel, any one of which could sever a limb, riddled their bodies. Their bright, red blood would coat the bottom of the trench.

The radio crackled.

It was his voice! I could exhale. No, I wasn't mistaken; that
was Mohammad himself. I had to keep my emotions in check
and hide my delight.

"Ehsan! Musa, over!"

"Asadollah has a message for you."

My heart started beating faster. What message could he have
for me?

"Asadollah says, once again Parveez proved to be the better
man! At least he got the food here, but not always on time;
while your Excellency has forced us to dine on tinned rations!"

"Tell him that he doesn't even rate those!"

I got the double meaning of the message. First, it was a crack
about not delivering the food to the shore base; second, it was for
not letting them know on time when the enemy had fired. If the
ground around the trench had not been soaked from the rain,
their heads and faces would have been covered in a thick layer of
dirt. The thought of Asadollah's head, face and beard covered in
grime made me laugh.

"Musa! We are ready."

They were following the plan to the letter.

"Understood. *God is great!*"

"*God is great!*"

The enemy soldiers must have radioed their command for
help from the Doomsday Machine. It would locate our battery
and forward the information to their artillery. I closed my eyes
trying to imagine the Iraqis' situation.

"Mr. Engineer, don't bother with our artillery. Just open your
eyes and find out where the enemy's firing from!"

"Okay; but I don't understand what's going on."

"Just keep your eyes over there, and I'll explain it to you.
They located our battery and shelled it. Now they think it's destroyed and won't fire at it again."

As soon as our battery fired again, the Engineer automatically
looked in the direction of our trench.

"Keep looking in the other direction! The enemy is letting
their command know that they're still under fire. Their command will contact the Doomsday Machine asking what happened
because they're still under fire. Then they'll send another shell
our way."

"Sir, you are all mad! You're trying to let the Iraqis know where you are so that they'll wipe you out?"

"I told you that, if you wanted, I'd add your name to the list of those on their way to hell."

"Okay, sir. I understand. I understand the whole plan. Let me whisper something into your ear?"

Having no choice, I brought my ear closer. I had started shaking again. He cupped his hand around my ear.

"What you said about the martyrs is right. When those two get to the other side as martyrs, the Recording Angels will have to list them among those going to heaven. Once they blow up the Bridge, the Angels will be helpless because after Adam's death, they can't change two boys' files, which will throw a monkey wrench into the machinery of eternity. Meaning this will be a real coup! And—who knows—hell may go cold. Then they could join the progressive forces there, manufacture some weapons, and fall on the unsuspecting hedonists in heaven and take over the place. Sure, why wouldn't it work? This would be revenge, indeed! It would utterly foul up the bookkeeping of end-time. Unbelievable! Really marvelous!"

He rummaged under the blanket and gave me a strong hand-shake. He touched me with his fingers, making my wet skin feel prickly.

"But, sir, you haven't considered everything. There's still part of the plan that seems shaky."

"What part, Mr. Engineer?"

"Listen! Satan may get wind of the operation and go to God saying, 'Forgive me, Lord, for saying this but didn't I tell you from day one not to trust this two-legged creature? I was the only one who did not bow down to him. These fun-loving angels all lowered their heads, not out of respect for your commandment but because they were afraid of giving up a guilt-free heaven and their own pleasures. Now look what's happened! These two martyrs have found out the Exalted Name. How Adam was able to get it to them I don't know. Gabriel, after all, stipulated that only Adam could know it. And he couldn't even tell his wife, Eve, or that other woman, Lilith. Because these two boys are martyrs, I can't use my tricks and spells on them.

So, let's join forces before it's too late, stop them before they take over the whole world, overthrow them.'"

"What the hell are you talking about, friend?" I could feel the advantage slipping from my fingers, but I had to put up with this nonsense for at least two more hours.

"Nothing. I thought it would be a good idea to think about it, that's all."

"I like it. An excellent idea! Outstanding! Do you know what the Angels said to Satan after he refused to prostrate himself before your forefather? These same goody-goody, equal opportunists said to the poor sap, 'Are you crazy, man? Giving up a sweet, forever deal like this, just over a simple nod of the head...?'"

The Engineer asked, "By the way, supposing your plan works, what are you going to do with God?" and raised his hand over his head.

"We'll have a conversation with Him," he continued. "We'll just put Him in jail—no, we'll say to Him, 'Go away! You've accomplished everything you wanted; that's more than enough, and we still don't know why the universe was created in the first place or why it's going to end.' We'll just suggest that He go and create another universe for Himself. No doubt He's fed up with creation—we'll talk to Him; we'll be democratic, completely logical. There's not doubt He's fed up, hanging around all these eons and just waiting for an excuse to leave, waiting for someone to come and blow up the Bridge and say, 'It's all over. Your Heaven and Hell are now in our hands. Now kindly take your exalted Presence and leave.'" The Engineer stared, waiting for my reaction.

"But suppose He doesn't agree, what'll we do? Where can we imprison Him? No, no He definitely has to go. But what'll if the Angels and the Devil come back to stab us in the back?"

Once again, the blast from one of our shells tore open the dark band of trees in the grove. Then everything faded to black again. I had to shut him up. Parveez, God bless you, wherever you are!

"Fine, but that's enough. After the coup, we'll see that those Angels get what they deserve. For now, you should just be trying to spot their artillery!"

"Ehsan, Ehsan—Musa!"

"Ehsan, over!"

"Nice shot! Now, another orange a bit to the left."

"Understood."

You poor bastards in those trenches! Contact your command! Get on the radio and shout for help! Make them put pressure on the trained personnel manning that radar! They're going to see the same coordinates for our artillery battery on their screens and relay them to their guns again.

"But Satan was a *real* man, a man's man."

"There it is!" we both screamed at once. It was the enemy firing from behind the grove just a little to the left of the last shot. There was no time to count. I grabbed the radio and said, "All hell's broken loose! *We mourn for the Master of the World!*"

This was the signal, a line from a Bushehri dirge. Now Asadollah and Mohammad would be strapping on their helmets and completing the dirge with even greater determination. During the seconds the shell was coming at them, no power but God could help them.

"Engineer! Pray for them!"

"I don't know how."

"Don't talk nonsense! Pray!"

I looked along the sight line. It was just as dark in the area between the two buildings as it was in the grove. The shell was on its way. My eyes opened wider as the flames from the sudden blast traveled down the sight line and spread out over them. I felt strangely close to the rays of light. Why? Did I yearn to be there?

The radio came on: "Musa, Musa—Ehsan!"

"Musa, here!"

"Musa! We are ready."

It was only seconds after the explosion. How did they get out of their snug little dugout so quickly? They must have contacted me from inside.

"If you're ready, then *God is great!*"

"*God is great!*"

I shouldn't have let myself be distracted by our own shell.

"Sir, she made me angry; otherwise, I wouldn't have reminded her of what happened with her son."

"Just look over there! OVER THERE!"

"No, sir! It's eating at me. She made no bones about how indecent she had been. She didn't figure that one day when she wasn't careful, somebody, out of spite, would go and tell her boy what his mother's had been doing for a living."

"You mean he hadn't known? He found out afterwards?"

"Yes, her highness was making a living as a seamstress and her son was quite the student, when one day a man—for God knows what reason—took the boy aside and told him all about his mother."

...and again the enemy trenches were peppered with shrapnel and again they radioed their command asking why they hadn't silenced our battery.

"A few days later, the boy had gone, disappeared."

"Look in that direction! So you mean, after he found out, he never came back? Where is he now?"

"As far as I know, he became a drug addict. The poor thing; he was only fourteen."

Everything about this man was suspicious...

"How do you know that some man told the boy?"

"I just know—that's all! God, what questions you ask!"

Now I was peering at the point above the grove where the last shell was fired.

I wondered what I would do if I were that boy and someone said something so brutal to me.

"For the love of God, Engineer, stop! You're getting on my nerves with this kind of talk. Let me do my job."

"Okay, but it's her own fault!"

"Enough!" I shouted.

"There, sir, they've fired!"

As soon as I spotted the blast from their artillery, I grabbed the receiver with both hands. *They say when mother gave birth to me!* I stopped, realizing I had made a mistake. Instead of any of the poems we used for code, a line from one of my elementary schoolbooks sprang to mind. I immediately corrected myself, *"Now you of the Kufan plain! Wanting my death in greatest pain! I warn you, noble patrician: beware the shame of harming Hossein!"*

I let go of the radio and heard the sound of the explosion. Several seconds later, a missile whistled over head. Asadollah and Mohammad would have certainly noticed my confusion.

Once again, I positioned myself in line with the two bricks. Rays of light from the explosion came from the same exact spot, meaning that the Doomsday Machine had relayed the same co-ordinates to their batteries.

And again there were the same nerves and anxiety. Only a few meters in one direction and the shell would have landed right in the trench!

"Musa, Musa—Ehsan!"

It was Mohammad again. I had to keep the emotion from my voice. "Ehsan! That hit the spot. Another in the same place!"

"Asadollah is still making fun of you. He says you should take better care of the pot and ladle you borrowed from that bosom buddy of yours!"

"Tell him that his empty stomach is making music to my ears!"

"He heard."

"Instead of all this talk, why don't you send over another or-ange?"

I put the receiver down and found the astonished Engineer staring at me.

"Are you out of your mind? How can you make fun of each other at such a dangerous time?"

"We're just kidding around the way we normally do. We don't want the Iraqis to sense that there's anything out of the ordinary at the moment. It is all according to plan."

"_God is great!_"

"_God is great!_"

After this short exchange, another period of radio silence be-gan. The poor Engineer! Except for one hour during the Second World War and a puny raise for his years of devoted service at the refinery, what had he gotten out of life? And, God knows, he probably told people about that one adventure several thousand times, inflating it with each retelling.

...The sound of yet another one of our shells was on its way. How long did we have to keep doing this before the enemy started doubting the Doomsday Machine?

"What's the difference between me and that woman? Huh? The difference?"

"Don't start! Let me concentrate on the job!"

"No, sir! You know all about it. Why do you pretend otherwise?"

"What do I know? How should I know?"

"From the letter you took out of my pocket. By the church tower. Don't deny it!"

The Iraqis in the trenches sat waiting for our next shell.

Contact your command! Start hollering! Tell them that the machine is no good. Don't tell me they don't know how to operate the thing? 'What are you grumbling about?' their command was probably asking. 'The Iranians just fired another shell into our trench—that's what we're grumbling about!' they'll say.

My whole body began to tremble again. The strange part of it was that I could forget about being sick for a time. This was probably the only benefit of all the excitement and headaches.

"Engineer! Keep your eyes on the place the enemy fires from!"

"You are the one who knows all the ins and outs of my life!"

"Because of the letter, you're saying?"

He nodded his head and I smiled.

"But I don't know any English."

"Don't lie, sir! How did you know that it was from my children?"

"Simple. 'My Father' was written on top—that much English I can read!"

"You mean you hadn't read it?"

"Never! I can't. Now leave me alone. By everything you hold sacred, swear you'll just keep your eyes peeled in that direction."

He seemed to shudder with relief and then took the binoculars firmly in his hands and peered through them.

What are the Iraqis waiting for? I wondered.

"Ehsan, Ehsan—Musa!"

"Ehsan, over!"

"Ehsan! Fifty to the right; ten meters forward. This time, two oranges!"

I was aware that, to be on the safe side, the boys had a limited number of shells they brought to the emplacement; but we needed to put more pressure on the Iraqis in the trenches. This would make them even angrier when they asked their command for countering fire.

This time the light came from the right flank. The Engineer was still looking to the left. Did this mean that they had switched batteries?

I radioed, *"Unload your burden; a home is very nice, if it's close to paradise!"* and then let go of the receiver. Asadollah and Mohammad would now jump into the dugout, which was a trench only a meter away from the gun. But did the enemy have their sights on our gun? Everything would be cleared up in a few seconds.

By remembering Allah is there not assurance to hearts! By remembering Allah is there not assurance to hearts!"

"Engineer! Pray that this new shell is meant for our battery!"

"Sir, you can't be feeling well. You ought to get some rest! Before, you wanted me to pray for your comrades; now you want me to pray that the Iraqis blow them up! You're delirious!"

As I peered down the sight line, it seemed as if the two bricks were playing tricks, changing shapes—sometimes they were cubes, other times rectangles. Though it had been a while since the blanket had slipped from my head, I felt nothing.

God, please keep that shell from exploding in their trench.

I heard the sound of a shell hurtling through the air. Hurry up and explode! Faster, dammit!

When it did hit beside the trench, the blast seemed more fiery and larger than before as it lit up the entire area. Just like an incendiary bomb, the flames mushroomed into the air. There was nothing to do but wait for Mohammad to make contact and tell me their situation.

"Musa, Musa—Ehsan! We peeled two oranges."

"O Mehdi!"

"O Mehdi!"

Deliriously happy, I thrust my fist into the air and shouted, "Thank you, God!"

"What happened, sir? You must be in terrible shape. Have pity on yourself; it's only flesh and blood."

"The best thing in the world happened! Couldn't be better!"

"This is still a mystery to me!"

"They're starting to doubt the accuracy of their artillery. The machine still keeps giving them the same coordinates; they fire, but they can't take out our battery. So they conclude...?"

"What?"

"Guess!"

"Can't—my head is killing me, sir."

"Okay, I'll tell you myself! They think that the problem must be with their artillery. So they gave our coordinates to another one of their batteries. It's impossible for them to think that everything is okay, when we keep shelling them from the same position."

"Your shells have gone off."

I was so delighted that I had forgotten about our own fire. It was a good thing that I had called for two shells. I closed my eyes. More explosions from us—two of them—even though they had used a new battery to fire back! How would their command react?

"Where's my letter?"

"Which letter? The letter from your children?"

Where was that letter? In the pocket of the pants hanging on the clothesline back in his room! I wondered whether there was anything left to read after it had gotten soaked like that.

But the main danger was still there. The incendiary shells they were now using could pose a terrible problem. Shrapnel from a regular shell traveled in straight lines; but one of those shells could unleash flames that followed the contours of a trench and even go inside it and, combined with the explosive charge they carried, ignite everything in the area.

I stared at the terrible blackness above the grove, near the point where the new battery fired. I had to wait for the next shell.

"Now suppose..."

A new flash coming out of the darkness interrupted the Engineer. I had to contact them.

"If the true faith of Mohammad lives through the flood of our blood, tell them to ready their swords! Hossein stands before them ready to die."

I waited for the interminable seconds to go by. My joy had not lasted long. Short-lived happiness! If they had corrected the trajectory on this new shell and it went straight into our trench, then...?

"Why are you reciting that?"

A friend of mine, Jafar—he recites dirges. He's like a tribal shaman. I think that if it weren't for the war, that's what he'd be doing for a living! I'm practicing so I can take his place."

"Oh!"

Did he actually believe me? My eyes were fixed again on the sight line formed by the bricks. The flames from the explosion shot up about fifteen meters from the ground.

"It had a timed fuse!"

"What's a timed fuse?"

"The Iraqis have changed their tactics. They are using shells that explode in the air. Didn't you see it blow up above the ground?"

The Engineer scratched his cheek.

"Fine, what happens next?"

"This shell exploded several meters above our battery. These shells are more dangerous than the ones they had been using."

There was no threat to the boys from shrapnel coming at them from the side. The danger would come from above. So the Iraqis knew what they were doing, after all.

They may have guessed right about our tactics. Or maybe not; they probably figured on a certain amount of error from the Doomsday Machine and were trying to adjust for it.

"Musa, Musa—Ehsan!"

My heart started up again, but I had to keep the emotion out of my voice.

"Ehsan, over!"

"Why don't you give us new coordinates? If it's too much for you, we'll just shut the operation down. But Asadollah says we still have these ten or twenty peeled oranges to send them! How about it?"

"Ehsan! Okay. This time send them three oranges and you set the coordinates!"

"Understood, Musa!"

The Engineer shook the blanket and me at the same time.

"Generalissimo! I've just had a first-rate idea for this operation. Are you listening?"

He was so pleased with himself that his voice was quivering. "What idea?" I asked, not wanting to know the answer.

"Allow me to suggest to your enlightened Excellency that, instead of these excruciating waiting periods and all the needless formalities, why don't you just get on the radio and tell the Iraqis the exact position of your battery—give them the old twenty-to-the-left and twenty-to-the-right, so they can plant one smack dab in the emplacement and get it over with, once and for all? That way your comrades can reach the other side sooner."

I stared at him wide-eyed, wanting to say: Are you nuts? But silence was the best remedy. I had to focus on the job.

The entire length of the waterway was quiet; there wasn't even any gunfire. I was sure our troops were in their trenches, waiting for the results of the operation. But what about the enemy? Were they waiting to see who would win the duel between our two sides?

We heard the sound of three oranges.   Comrade heroes, I wanted to say to them, three more shells have been sent your way by registered mail just so you will contact your command and ask them to fire back! So what are you waiting for? Now it's your turn—send three our way!   You probably have wounded and dead, so the conclusion is obvious: that advanced radar of yours cannot stop one measly little battery. All the hype about the new system was just bullshit.

The light from three explosions going off one after another appeared on that side of the waterway.

"Sir, I counted three oranges."

"Mr. Engineer, you're talking radio talk?"

"Did you really want me to help out, or were you making fun of me? What kind of a war is this?"

These explosions would test the Iraqis' patience.

"Well look who's here! Bravo! It's our own Hajj Aqa! Where were you? We were getting worried!"

Javad's father was resting on his haunches outside the doorway. He waved his hand, acknowledging the Engineer's greeting.

I had completely forgotten about him. Probably because I knew that, while the enemy was focused on taking out our battery, they wouldn't start shelling other parts of the city. The big fireworks display would most likely come later on, after they had destroyed it.

Javad's father tried to get up but couldn't. The way he was gasping for breath ruined the good mood on the roof.

"Stay down! Don't try to get up!"

"No, no," he wheezed, "I brought some gas."

He brought gas? Alarmed I asked him, "You didn't put it downstairs, did you?"

Huffing and puffing, he said, "Yeah. I thought I would pour it into the truck later."

"They fired, sir!"

If it hadn't been for the Engineer, I would have missed at least two or three shells. I quickly got on the radio but couldn't remember the proper dirge. The radio was on send, but my mind wouldn't operate. Just one line, I pleaded. God, help me remember the dirge! One sentence!

Suddenly I remembered something in Arabic from the Qoran, *"You did not throw what you threw, but Allah did!"*

I switched off the radio and exhaled. While there was time, I had to get those below out of danger. They were probably resting, unaware that there was a barrel of gasoline next to them. If the Iraqis fired and a piece of shrapnel hit the barrel...?

"Hajji, go downstairs quickly and take the barrel to the house next door. Put it in their washroom."

"Let me catch my breath first."

"No, do it now, quickly!"

I glanced over at our artillery. Another shell! If I were in the enemy's shoes, I would have used shells with timed fuses again. Another explosion mushroomed into the air a little to the right of the two bricks, lighting up the sky.

"Give me the binoculars!"

The Engineer quickly handed them to me. I tried to fix the exact point where it exploded in my mind. I put the binoculars to my eyes and counted the number of hash marks to our battery. Then I put them down.

"Do you understand what just happened, Engineer?"

"No! I haven't a clue."

"The enemy raised the elevation of its gun a hundred meters. That means they are willing to tolerate that much of an error." Then the sweet bird of the radio sounded.

"Musa, Musa—Ehsan!"

Again, I had to keep the emotion out of my voice.

"Should we send some more to the same place?"

"Yes, this time, two oranges!"

"Understood."

The Hajji had left. I hoped he wasn't angry with me, but his wife would be happy to see him.

"Musa. We're ready."

"God is great!"

"God is great!"

The place was flooded with light, as if two projectors had gone on one after the other, then it got dark again. I was filled with the same old dread and the wait that took my breath away began again.

These two shells should make the Iraqis fed up. Lord! I recited the *You did not throw* verse over them. Vengeance is Yours, O Lord; avenge in any way You see fit that mother in the ice cream freezer and her two children sleeping alone on this wintry night. Don't allow that machine to take control of us! We have done everything in our power against it. Lord, You know better than anyone that all these boys could just as well have left this city and like so many others—who pretend to be Your servants—could have sat safely in some corner praying. So please grant this operation Your blessings!

"What are you mumbling?"

"Nothing! Nothing!"

"I hope you're not shivering from the cold?"

"Yes, it's the cold."

I pulled the blanket over my head. Was there any need to show him how much I owed the Lord?

Suddenly my eyes became saucers. There were five more blasts from enemy artillery—this time from another location. I congratulated myself; only an experienced spotter—however sick and feverish—could have made out the exact number of shells in all that chaos.

I switched on the radio and said, *"And the unbelievers plotted, but Allah also plotted and is the Best of Plotters."*

My stock of dirge lines had run out, and now I was resorting to the Qoran. This time they had unleashed everything they had even before giving our shells a chance to land.

"Look over there, sir! Something has caught fire!"

Flames were shooting up exactly where our shells had landed. The grove? But with all the rushes and reeds soaked from the rain, how was that possible? The flames suddenly exploded.

"A car! We hit a car!"

I looked back at our own artillery. Again, I had allowed myself to be distracted. The light coming from the two explosions was muted by the haze of dirt and debris raised by previous blasts. There was so much dust in the air that I couldn't tell how far apart the explosions had been.

"Engineer! Engineer! Did you see the first explosion?"

"No!"

"What are you doing, then? All you can do is distract me from the mission?"

Several faint rays of light could be seen in the haze. But the enemy had not fired another shell.

"Ehsan, Ehsan—Reza! Ehsan, Ehsan—Reza! Ehsan, Ehsan—Reza!"

Though I didn't have the heart to, I responded, "Reza, Reza—Musa!"

"Musa, standby! Understand? Just standby! Ehsan, Ehsan—Reza!"

Qasem's tone was sharp, almost savage. A second later there was the sound of static, as if someone for no reason had left the radio on SEND.

"...Reza, Reza—Ehsan!" said Asadollah in a weak voice. Why had Mohammad given the receiver to Asadollah?

"Reza! Help! Help!"

And then it broke off. The Engineer was also listening intently. The dust and dirt kept us from seeing the exact point where the enemy shell had gone off.

"Ehsan, we're coming now," said Qasem and stopped transmitting. The boys had definitely taken some shrapnel.

"Why was your friend's voice so weak?"

Lost in thought, I was in no mood to answer the Engineer. But, I said, "I don't know. I can't figure it out. I have to contact them."

"Ehsan, Ehsan—Musa! Ehsan, Ehsan—Musa! Ehsan, Ehsan—Musa!"

But they weren't answering. Whatever happened, I had to contact Qasem.

"Reza, Reza—Musa! Reza, Reza—Musa!"

They had also turned off their radio. I got up with difficulty and stood at the edge of the roof. There was no trace of the recent air of optimism. I shut my eyes; this was the best way for me to concentrate.

"Excellency! What kind of plan is this? Your comrades haven't been martyred; they're firing again!"

I forced both eyes open. So they were still firing. I tried with all my might to peer through the darkness; but the dust hadn't cleared yet.

I felt something bump against my chest. The Engineer was holding the binoculars before me. There was a faint smile on his lips. I immediately put them to my eyes, wishing the darkness would go away. Damn this dust and haze!

Several small flames were visible. But were my eyes playing tricks on me? The flames were nothing like muzzle blasts. So what was going on? One of the flames leapt up. It was clear—though I had no desire to admit it—that one explosion had united all the flames.

"The Iraqis fired!"

I lowered the binoculars. The Engineer was wrong. Something was on fire within the halo of dust and debris around our emplacement. I hoped to God I was wrong!

Then there was the low-pitched sound of a muffled explosion. The flames were still flickering.

"Sir! Look at the Iraqis! How much they're firing!"

I turned instinctively and saw two muzzle blasts. I sensed firing also coming from the left. At least four other shells! Both enemy batteries were firing at once. They had definitely spotted the explosions at out emplacement. I wondered how the boys were. What had spooked Qasem?

"They've fired again, sir!"

This time from another side.

I started counting: one, two, three, ... The blasts from shell after shell was accompanied by the thunderous booms of the previous firings and the whining of projectiles going by, and the explosions in our own emplacement...

I was still counting: twenty-five, -six,...thirty!

"Engineer! Those were their Katyushas! They fired thirty missiles!

"Where?"

Then there was the screech of a rocket. The first, some distance from the building, the second...

"Engineer, hit the deck!"

Without knowing it, I was now spread-eagle on the roof with the blanket over my head. There was the horrible sound of the second missile and of the third exploding and of shrapnel ripping through the doors and walls of the buildings below. They aimed all the missiles right at us.

By remembering Allah is there not assurance to hearts! *By remembering Allah is there not assurance to hearts!*

The missiles coming one after another acted like bombs dropping from low-flying planes.

The blanket kept me from seeing the real world, so I could only hear the explosions, which in itself was a kind of comfort.

But what about the Engineer? He was face down on the clammy roof, and in his mind marshalling all the polite swearwords he knew, curses that were too refined for Geety to use.

"Engineer!"

"I'm doomed because of you! Doomed..."

Then everything descended into another world. The blanket slipped from my head and I saw the stars through the debris thrown up by the explosions...

26

They're still banging the drums. Wham! Wham! Wham!
Sounds like the large pan drums Bushehri musicians use. But
there was no tambourine. Someone is drumming outside!
THWACK! Who is it? Why is it dark everywhere? Everyone's
lost in the gloom. I can't breathe! There's something blocking
my mouth. Shove it aside! You'll suffocate. Hurry for God's
sake! Faster!... Whew! I'm free!

When the blanket fell from my face, I couldn't believe it.
There was Asadollah propped up against the small wall of the
emplacement staring at me with eyes wide open. Was he joking
around again? Mohammad! Mohammad! Answer me! Why
don't you answer me? Why are you silent? Why don't you answer?

The furry cat was licking Mohammad's boots.

"Don't! Don't lick them!"

The two of them, their eyes were all white.

No! O GOD! Am I seeing this right?

Those same pieces of rebar! Split open the top of their skulls
and went through their bodies, and blood was flowing from their
noses and mouths. I leaned on the wall and stood up. What was
a rainbow doing in the pitch-black sky in the midst of all this
smoke? So the refinery was still burning. No, it wasn't a rainbow; it was a bridge! An arching bridge decked out in colored
lights. All the grooved rebar rained down from the bridge in the
sky.

Ouch, my ears! What a sound! The whistling sound they
made was worse than the whoosh of the Katyushas.

A piece of rebar flew past my face and ricocheted off the
metal artillery support and then spun in the air and, like the gatekeeper's stick, hit me in the thigh.

Yes, this was the same rebar they were going to use to connect the concrete blocks along the jetty...

The woman with the floral print chador leaned over the trench.

"That was wrong. Look what you did to him."

And someone pulled the woman's chador aside. As she disappeared from the trench, his voice remained, "Get moving. This is none of your business!"

No! It was all over for the boys. I should have gone.

Am I escaping? No! I'm going to bring help.

Liar! You're running away! You're afraid. Coward! That's the reason why you didn't bring the woman to the freezer. You're always afraid. Always!

No! I'm going to bring help. I have to get out of the trench.

I poked my head out of the trench. My thigh still hurt where the rebar hit it. But the bars were still raining down. The sky was full of pieces of grooved rebar landing all over the city. Every piece was glinting. The rebar was everywhere: metal rods, upright, grooved. But what a shame; none of the bars had a blast cone, so I couldn't trace where they came from.

Better run! Gotta run! RUN!

The radio was on my back and the lamp went clang, clang as it bumped against it. All of the rebar missiles in the air swerved and came toward me.

Better run! Must escape! Qasem, where are you? Ameer, where are you?

I took the weapon from around my neck. The rebar was getting closer every second.

Must fire at them. But the weapon won't fire.

The cartridges fell unspent from the barrel and were rolling around on the ground.

The sounds of praying were coming from a trench filled with women in floral print chadors. When they bent down, the whole trench went black and only the sound of their prayers came and their wails.

Get to your feet! The rebar's about to hit you!

But it was no use—they were coming only for me. Run! Run! They're coming. There's a sound. The sound of jinns? No, the sound of priests.

This time I must be sure. Heading 1440. Twenty to the right; forty to the left. They're coming. The rebar is coming at you. RUN, YOU FOOL!

Asadollah's eyes were open.

Now the bars are piercing the top of my head: then my throat: then choking. Is there a lot of pain! Not much! As soon as it enters, your nerves stop working; so you don't feel yourself suffocating.

But maybe not! During those moments you're conscious, you see everything. Blood flows from your mouth. You want to scream, but you can't. You beg. using your eyes, for someone to help you. But everyone makes a face, recoiling until maybe somebody says, "Let him go! Put him out of his misery!"

I'm still alive. Take the bar out of my head. Maybe there'll be a miracle! A miracle! So where is God? What does He think He's doing?

And the rebar keep pouring down.

You must lie flat! Get down! The only way to escape. Close your eyes and lie flat. Clasp your hands on the back of your neck! The bar will pierce your hands first: then your neck, then it'll rivet you to the ground.

By the way, the woman selling the greens—her hands weren't clasped behind her head!

Why is the ground so wet?

That's not water! I open my eyes.

It's white. The ground is all white. Salt? No, the earth is soaked in yoghurt. I'm treading yoghurt. A white marsh. And the bars, one by one, sink all around me and disappear. I am sinking. I must keep my arms and legs moving to stay afloat! O my God! There's a layer of red! A seam of blood under river of yoghurt. My arms are bloody to the elbows. I've always killed from far away, never killed anybody up close. Why are my hands bloody? I'm sinking. Help me! HELP! I need help!

Parveez is standing over me with serum, a sheet and scores of bloody tubes; and he's smiling.

"Tomorrow's ice cream day! ICE CREAM!"

Then I sink. I'm under water, but the bars keep coming after me one after another. No! No! They aren't bars anymore. White dixie cups! Yes, those are the ones: Mehr ice cream cups!

Good-tasting and fortified! After I had taken delivery of the ice cream, I tossed the cups one by one into the air and watched as they spun in the air and landed in the middle of the waterway, frost clinging to their outsides; and, when they were carried away in the current, the water of the Shatt cleaned them off. But they are still raining down. Who's hurling them now?

OH NO! Parveez's sharks are coming with hooks in their mouths!

I swear to God, I wasn't the one who caught you. It wasn't me! It was Parveez. Parveez threw you into that black oil drum.

But the sharks only swim by. Why are they ignoring me? They are attacking the dixie cups. One of the sharks opens his mouth right in front of my eyes. It doesn't bite me but rips into the dixie cup. The shark's mouth is ringed with white cream. But its mouth is filled with blood! All the sharks begin twisting and writhing. They are being dragged to the surface and pieces of grooved rebar are being driven into their heads and faces....No! It's Parveez's hammer!

"I'm here! Parveez! I'm here!"

Now I am being dragged up against my will. No! There's a shark hook in my mouth too! They are also hauling me in. All of the sharks are out of the water—only their tails stay in. They are suffocating.

"That's not right. Don't hit them!"

I'm also half out of the water, along with the radio, the lamp, and the weapon. They will certainly hit me too with the same rebar.

"No! Look! I can breathe out of water. Don't hit me!"

The rods of rebar enter the water one after another.

You'd better reach that side. Move! Try! The rebar is going to smash through your skull. GO! DON'T STOP!

I reach for the bank. My body is very heavy. The weapon! The radio! The radio is still working. Buzzz! Buzzz! Buzzz!

I pull myself up on the concrete bank and stretch out. It's quiet everywhere and pitch black. My eyes have to get used to the darkness. I don't have the strength. I am very cold. Very. I'm freezing.

They are still beside me. Cartons of Mehr ice cream cups. Frozen! And the woman green-seller, like me, lying on a bloody stretcher and looking at me with eyes bulging from their sockets. I have to turn away.

God! I'm freezing. But I'm still alive!

I'd better muster all my strength so somebody outside this freezer will hear my cries.

Better open my eyes! WIDER! And find out where the freezer door is. THERE! Over there!

No! Why is it light there? Why do they keep the lights lit on that wall?

Yeah. There it is—the same tableau, the picture of Mary with her baby. No, it isn't Mary. The priest said it isn't Mary.

HELP ME!

They can help me. They are the ones, the holy men, who can come to my aid. I fed them, so they owe me. But both are looking away. There's Geety! Yes! It's Geety with Mahtob resting in her arms.

Madam Geety! No! Mustn't say "Madam"! Now she's going to swear at you.

Geety! For God's sake, help me! For God...

27

"Hi!"

I forced my eyelids open a crack and saw the outline of a face flickering faintly and contorting.

I had to exert myself more to get my eyes open. Force them! More! MORE! A white curtain? No, wipe your eyes!...Whomp! The sound of an explosion!

I stretched out on my back. This place, this fire! Still glowing red, but no sign of flames. There was a shadow pacing beside me.

Better open my eyes wider.

It was him! The Engineer! Hands on hips!

Why was he pacing that way? As if banging something! Where was his drum? Wham! Wham! The little girl was squatting down, leaning over my face.

"Let him rest, girl!"

It was the Engineer's voice. As he stood there he looked at her, and the girl remained quiet with her eyes fixed on me.

"Shut up, you bastard! Even now, he's frightening my daughter! Where are you, girl? Come and lie down. COME!" Geety's hollering made the Engineer resume his pacing.

My back ached.

I had to shift my position somehow to relieve the pain, but the blanket lay like a heavy weight pressing my chest to the ground. Force yourself. You can do it!

Every part of my body felt like pins and needles. I began to turn over onto my right shoulder. As I did this, the blanket fell off, acquainting my sweat-soaked body with the cold outside air. I began shivering uncontrollably as if the breeze had become a conductor's baton, and in that absolute quiet with one movement set the entire orchestra of my body into motion. My teeth began to rattle so hard, they made my bones vibrate; the sound reminded me of machine gun fire: rat-a-tat-tat- rat-a-tat-tat-rat-a-tat-tat.

There wasn't any way to stop my teeth from chattering. They seemed to have a mind of their own. I had no strength in my hands; otherwise; I would have used them to pry my jaw open. I had to find a way of keeping my mind off the pain.

Where was I?

Near the fire. So that had to be on the ground floor. But as far as I could remember, I had been on the roof. How did I get down here?

I vaguely made out the shadows of the two priests by the wall. With as little movement as possible I tried to get a peek under the stairs, but it was too dark to see anything. If Javad's mother and Geety were there, where was Javad's father?

My forehead was cold. I tried with all my might to open my eyes again, but there was something preventing me from seeing. A cold, damp handkerchief, which, with this fever that was eating away at my strength, was like having the keys to heaven! In the darkness I couldn't tell how soiled the handkerchief was. I had the feeling that the fever was making steam rise from it. But who was doing this for me? Whoever it was, the person was sitting behind me.

Definitely Javad's mother.

The sounds of artillery fire and explosions kept coming. What about the boys? What could I have done in the meantime? If it weren't for this fever, I could have at least joined them in the artillery trench.

Someone put the handkerchief on my head again.

"Are you cool yet?"

It was unbelievable—the voice belonged to the little girl. I turned quickly. She was in front of me now.

"Who told you to do this?"

My voice was feeble.

"My Mom said you were going to die. So I said to her that you probably wanted to die so you could be rid of us. Right?"

She wrung out the handkerchief in a clay bowl next to her and put it on my forehead again. It felt so cold! The moment she put it on, how soothing it was!

What about the boys? I wondered what had happened to them.

"So...why...didn't you let me...die?"

"I figured that maybe you were like me and didn't feel like dying. Do you feel like it?"

The Engineer was still standing over me with his hands on his hips. He moved his head as if to ask me how I was feeling. I answered by blinking and nodding my head. He put his hand under his chin.

...The blast was so powerful that it pinned the Engineer to the ground. Shrapnel peppered the outside of the building. I didn't have the energy to react; but lying flat on one's back was the best way of surviving such a vicious onslaught.

Outside, someone was shouting, "Is everybody okay?" It was Javad's father. But what was he doing outside?

The Engineer said, "Yeah, sir! But don't bother with that pile of junk! This is no time for it."

His voice hoarse, Javad's father answered, "No! It's flooded everywhere. I'm trying to get the thing started so we can at least get the boy to the infirmary."

He disappeared into the darkness again. The Engineer knelt beside me with his knees to one side. I had to understand how I got down the seven flights of stairs.

"How...did I get...here?"

His eyes remained fixed on some unknown object, as if I hadn't said anything to him.

"Engineer! Mr. Engineer!"

"To hell with Mr. Engineer! Screw Mr. Engineer! When God made you ill and put you on your back, it was the greatest blessing He could have bestowed on this city; otherwise, you'd still be playing those radio games. Don't you understand what you did, sir?"

I was shocked. How brave he had become!

"Who got them to bombard the city like this? Those gentlemen sat around and thought they could fight with the Doomsday Machine. Well, this is the result!" Wagging his index finger, he added in a threatening tone, "From the moment they hit your artillery till now, they've been mortaring us with shells one after another as if they were candy. Just before daybreak they lobbed about ten to twenty over and then several more when morning came. Now they won't let up. What have you done, sir? Why did you get me mixed up in this? What a stupid old fool I was! Dummy, how could you let yourself be taken in by this brat still-wet-behind-the-ears? And it was so easy! I mean, really! Last night I really made a fool of myself."

The boys! The boys! Asadollah! Mohammad! Whose fault is it if they were martyred? Mine, certainly. Why did I have to be so stubborn and order them to fire? Wasn't it Qasem's fault?

Why did we have to go to war with that machine in the first place, when we didn't know if it existed or not? Why couldn't I have been more like the Major: just get my orders and follow them to the letter?

"Has the Iraqi Ministry of Agriculture sent that Medal of Honor yet? So many of the shells you ordered went astray that their farmers won't have to plow the fields or use any chemical fertilizer on them, sir spotter!"

What a face Asadollah made, when he made that joke. What was it? There's no news of him now. But, instead of him, now the Engineer is bellyaching! He's probably right. The shelling denied him his peace and quiet and, on top of that, there are all these uninvited guests to contend with. But what should I have done? What could I have done?

"...Sir, all of these fancy gestures that they've taught you are just diversions. Why did you wake up that monster?"

"Stop shouting!" was the only thing I could say to him.

"Stop shouting? Stop shouting? Mister, you're the one who came here and in the space of two days managed to ruin seventy years of tranquil existence—and I should stop shouting? I want an explanation from you, sir! 'Wait!' 'Wait' is all you can say!"

He rose halfway and, pointing at me, took the young Hovanes by the hand. Hovanes at first hesitated and then got up. The girl stopped putting the wet handkerchief on my head, and, stunned by what was happening, placed her hand in front of her face. Why was he driving me crazy?

Hovanes and the Engineer were standing beside me now. The Engineer said, "Be my guest, Excellency! Be so kind as to tell this young gentleman your opinion!"

Still hesitant, Hovanes said nothing.

"Excellency, why are you unsure? Kindly give us your candid and unvarnished view! I have explained everything to you. I beg you as a member of the clergy, state your opinion of the gentlemen's suicidal actions!"

It was quite obvious that Hovanes found himself in a bind and didn't want to look me in the eye.

"Don't ask me to do something so difficult. You spoke with the Father. I merely expressed my opinion."

The Engineer became more obstinate, as if he had a better lever to force Hovanes to talk, and continued, "That's all I want—your opinion, Excellency! The issue here is to make this young man see the error of his ways. Isn't that what you priests do for a living? Well, here is a person who had been misled and needs your guidance. He doesn't realize the suffering he had brought on himself and this city."

The whine of a missile made the Engineer stop for a few moments. When he spoke he could be so slick! The missile landed relatively far from the building.

Hovanes' hesitation was visible. He was obviously in a very bad place. Finally, he came to a decision.

"My dear boy! I can only state my view. When your friend asked us to help carry you downstairs, he gave us a complete picture of what you were doing. The reality is that..."

He stopped and the Engineer said impatiently, "Go on, Father! Bestow your guidance on this wayward youth, this young man who is beset by devils. He is in dire need of your preaching."

Despite my weakened condition, I was able to spot the devilish look in the Engineer's sunken eyes. He was obviously very pleased to have found an ally in his tussle with me.

"No, it's not that he is surround by devils. My view is that it would have been better to let events take their natural course in the struggle with this Doomsday apparatus," said the priest and then pointed around.

"Are you listening? We, of course, are going to leave this place in the morning, but you have to consider what happens when you stir up a hornet's nest. The truth of it is that your plan has not met with success and only—as your friend says—has upset everything. Of course, as soon as we heard about the plight of your comrades in the trench, the Father and I started praying for them."

The Engineer was practically beaming now.

"I couldn't have put it better myself. You see? It is merely you who have no religion! These two have, sir! They came to pack up the church property and haul it away. Geety and I have no way out."

"Shut your trap, punk! I've told you time and again not to mention my name with that filthy mouth of yours!"

Geety's outburst silenced the Engineer, forcing him to look down under the stairs. While I—I was marshalling all my strength to speak up. I had to take advantage of the situation. I couldn't show weakness, even though I had no logical explanation for the failure of our plan.

The Engineer pulled Hovanes by the hand away from me, but then he returned and, placing his ridiculous face close to mine, continued, "Better use this illness as an excuse, so we can get you to the rear. This is a golden opportunity. Don't waste it! Stop playing the pawn in this game. What do you think, uncle?"

He laughed. Hovanes' expression told me he was still deep in thought.

"Please forgive me! You're not in the best of health. I've been disturbing you and you need the rest." He tried to sit down where he had been resting, but the Engineer had beat him to it. My being drained and sick, on the one hand, and the failure of our plan to fool the Doomsday Machine, on the other, had clearly given the Engineer the upper hand. He made no secret of the fact that he was getting his revenge. I had to think of something.

I closed my eyes. Was it true that I was only a pawn in this war? Had we no other option but to fold our arms, waiting for the Doomsday Machine to impose its will on us? Was the Engineer right when he said that we merely had to sit and, like the Major, carry out orders?

The Doomsday Machine had been just like a frog, and we had acted like flies. It watched our every move, then shot out its tongue to snare us. My worst fear was that my friends were clinging to that tongue.

"Why are you crying?"

It was the little girl. Her eyes were fixed on my face. She was probably right. Both my eyes were watery, but I didn't know whether it was from worrying about the boys or from the fever.

"How come you're crying? Your mom's not around to beat you, is she?"

"I wish she were!" the words flew from my mouth.

"So are you crying 'cause she's not here?" she asked and once again put the cold handkerchief on my forehead. And that cold compress was my only comfort in the midst of this mess.

"Does your mom also say things like 'I wish you were never born? God! Will you die so I can be rid of you!'?"

My mother! Where was Mother now? If she were awake at this time of night, she would be reciting the Throne Verse to keep me safe. I wished she were here! She would definitely have fixed me a piping bowl of soup and spooned it into my mouth or she would be washing my legs in cold water to bring down the fever. I wanted so much to have her cradle my head in her lap and stroke my hair until I fell asleep.

"You've started crying again!"

I wiped the tears from my eyes with the back of my hand. I couldn't help myself at all. You're a man, I told myself; it's wrong for you to cry—especially in front of a little girl. Enough!

"When I ask my mom why I should die. What have I done? Know what she says?"

"No! What?"

"If it weren't for you, I would have killed myself and escaped from this world. Why does mom want to die so much?"

What could I say? It was probably a blessing that she didn't know.

"Nah, your mom is just joking. She loves you very much."

"First, when I was younger, she used to hit me. Now she just fights with me, and then she hits herself. Would you tell her not to hit herself? Promise?"

"Okay, I'll tell her."

Happy, she replaced the handkerchief on my forehead with a damper one.

Who was in worse shape tonight, this girl or me? She was dragged into this mess unwillingly, while I embraced it. Both of us were trapped in a whirlwind that, no matter how much we tried, we couldn't escape. If Javad's father could get the truck started before going to the infirmary, I would definitely pay a visit to the artillery trench.

"Little brat, where have you gotten to? Come here this minute! What are you doing over there? Come here and lie down! If you make me get up, I swear to the Almighty One, I'll beat you black-and-blue."

The girl got up from where she was sitting.

"You'll tell her, right?"

"Right. Definitely!"

She left the handkerchief beside the clay bowl, which was filled with a little water. There was little choice. Despite my weakness, I managed to lift the handkerchief and put it into the bowl; but I didn't have the strength to wring it out and had to put it on my forehead the way it was. My aim wasn't that good, so the cloth landed on my eyes. Steam rose from my eyelids, which made me wonder how high my temperature was.

There was still the sound of shelling, but the explosions were coming from the other side of the city. What time was it?

Why hadn't ended that night? Whatever happened, I had to get some sleep...

"Get up. Let's go!"

Was the Engineer calling me again! Why couldn't he let me sleep?

The handkerchief was no longer over my eyes. The Engineer wasn't there. Whoever it was, I couldn't make out his face in the darkness.

"Hurry up! We're taking you to the infirmary!"

It wasn't the voice of Javad's father. The fire showed in profile and now I recognized him! It was Qasem!

I tried with all my might to get up halfway, but I was too weak. I fell back down onto my back.

"Come on! I'll help you myself."

"What happened to the boys, Qasem? Huh? What happened?"

He lifted me up by the shoulders and said, "Now isn't the time to talk about it. I'll tell you later."

Something bad must have happened; it wasn't like Qasem to duck a question.

"No, tell me what happened?"

He looked around slowly. The Engineer, the two priests, and even Geety were looking at him.

"You really want to know?"

"Yeah."

"Remember: you asked for it...right! Both of them were martyred!"

I wished he had lied. The words came so easily! How?

Pretending that they hadn't heard what he said, everyone sat down.

"Well, now get up! Let's get going!"

But I had had it. There were a thousand questions! A thousand questions without answers! Was the Engineer right, after all? What about the priests? Geety had a right to wish she were dead? I wish I hadn't asked.

The Engineer got up and stepped forward. He was hesitant but finally said, "Sir, the two of them were martyred?"

Qasem nodded his head and the Engineer chewed the edge of his lip. Qasem went on, "That's war. It's not a cake-walk, after all."

I felt like saying something, but the Engineer was quicker, "Mister War! Mister War! It's easy enough to say, but if it hadn't been for your pride and the airs you military people put on, those two poor souls would be alive now. As I told your friend over here, you were the reason why that radar went into action. You are the cause for all these kids' games."

Qasem turned to me and, with that special brand of sarcasm of his, said to himself, "My! My! Congrats! So the whole world knows about the radar operation! Nice going!" Then he replied directly to the grief-stricken Engineer, "I know a little bit about you from Parveez, sir. Luckily nothing bad has happened to you, has it?"

Hovanes rose from where he was sitting and took a few steps forward. As soon as the Engineer noticed him, he immediately went off on a different tack.

"Okay, granted I'm an infidel and an atheist! But what about this man? A man of the cloth, meaning a Christian priest. He can't figure out what you are doing either."

Qasem then became aware of the priest and said, "Hello, father! Forgive me, but what are you doing here, of all places?"

"We came to gather up church belongings. Tonight we had the pleasure of being your friend's guest in this building."

"So what is this man saying? You have no idea what we're about?"

"No. It is not as our host has explained. I have just now become aware of matters that are still not clear to me."

"What matters, for example?"

"I know that there is a war going on here, and, as a priest, I have no right to get involved; but your operation is very strange."

"So you know about it too!" he said, glaring at me.

"Certainly."

"And your question is…?"

He said, "Well, for example…", but then hesitated. Qasem noticed.

"Wouldn't it be better for you to follow the path of God and, to the extent that you can, extinguish the horrid fires of this war, instead of fanning them?"

Qasem laughed. I wondered how he could do this, what with Asadollah and Mohammad fresh in their graves.

"And you, Mr. Engineer?"

"I also have an objection. God Himself, in whose name you fight, has pre-determined the outcome, and whatever you and I do in the meantime won't make the slightest bit of difference. Suppose you do manage to destroy the radar—they will just replace it with a more powerful one. What is the purpose of provoking the Iraqis, sir?"

There was the sound of someone trying to start the truck again and again. It was definitely Javad's father. And again there was the occasional shell being fired and the explosions when it landed. During the entire discussion, I hadn't heard the sounds of shelling at all.

"So, tonight you've been having a rip-roaring seminar on philosophy here? No wonder our lookout's mind was not on his job."

The Engineer became quite irritated and barked, "No, my dear sir! He's merely a pawn in this chess game. The same as you and I. All of us are pawns, sir!"

Qasem stared at me again, with a smile on his face.

The sound of the starter came again from outside; this time the motor turned over.

"Fine, but we must go and take our friend here to the infirmary. God's path doesn't lie in his death here, does it?"

Putting my weight on his shoulder, he got me to my feet. There was something odd in the way Qasem was acting. His laughter, his silences...I should have gone earlier but not to the infirmary, to see to the boys.

Javad's father entered and said, "All the sparkplugs were soaked. I hope to God they don't get wet again while we're driving."

He went over to where his wife was sleeping and began to wake her up. The Engineer supported my other shoulder, and I hopped out to the compound. It was still dark, and the flames from the refinery fire had sprung to life again. If a downpour like that was unable to put out the fire, I wondered, what could the largest fire department do?

I sat down in the truck, still thinking about the boys. Did it happen at the emplacement? Had they said anything before they were martyred?

Qasem was surveying the damage done to the outside of the truck. "If Parveez comes back and sees what misery you put his truck through, he'll be after you with his skimmer for days!"

"Qasem, this is no time for jokes! The boys are dead!"

I had managed to keep myself under control up to this point, but I couldn't hold it in any longer. Never in my life had I been so miserable. It was my fault. I started bawling and put my head on Qasem's chest. In between sobs, I managed to say, "It's all my fault. I was too proud to admit I was sick. Ameer should have done the job. I wish I had been in that trench instead of the boys. The Engineer was right when he said all of us were pawns. Where did all that effort get us? The boys were certainly just torn to pieces. What kind of a chess game had we played tonight?"

Qasem showed no reaction.

"We never have control over our own fate. We are always victims. We'll all end up like the Engineer."

Qasem put his hand under my chin and drew closer until we were standing face to face. "Your fever is so high, you're raving. Who's been martyred? Asadollah? Was he supposed to be martyred?"

Qasem was not his normal self. He was joking and laughing too much. He was ducking questions...Whenever anybody had been martyred in the past, he would keep to himself for a couple of days.

"Know what your problem is? You think too much and always say what's on your mind. If you promise to keep your mouth shut, I'll tell you."

"Okay."

"Okay! Just OOOkay? No! Thanks to you, every geezer and grandma left in the city knows about our battle plans! I don't know how to thank you!"

"Fine! I'll take an oath."

"You don't want to do that, 'cause you know you'll be forced to break it. But I'll tell you anyway. Yesterday evening we added another step to the plan—detonating a few unexploded shells in a spot far from the emplacement. After that, Asadollah was to call for help on the radio. That was it."

I didn't know how to react: happy because the boys were alive, or upset because they didn't let me in on the plan.

"Now don't get upset! First, there was no time to tell you, and, second, your frantic calls on the radio made the thing seem more realistic. Besides, everybody knew that you wouldn't be able to keep your mouth shut."

The reason why they did it was absolutely not important to me.

"So the Doomsday Machine was fooled?"

"What the hell's the Doomsday Machine?"

"The radar!"

"Listen, I don't care if you understand or not. But we're going to have to repeat the action for a few more days and your

Excellency is going to play dumb—GET IT? While you are having your rest, Ameer is going to do your job. Now, tell me, what is this about being a pawn in a chess game?"

"Nothing!"

"What do you mean, nothing? Out with it! I want to know."

My voice still weepy, I said, "The Engineer says we're all just pawns! Miserable little things always playing black."

"You don't need to go on; I get the rest. Would you like to hear the answer?"

I nodded.

"You really want to hear it?"

"Yeah, me and my friends—you got us into this mess, so you have to explain!"

"Why do I have to explain?"

"Because you're the one who designed the plan."

Qasem paused for a time, a very long time. "Though not every problem in this world can be solved merely by saying two plus two equals four, I'll tell you what I think, just the same. First, the thing about humans being pawns, without any free will of their own. Now, pay attention. When a pawn—whether white or black—leaves the board and then is redeployed for the next game, it doesn't carry with it any experience from the previous game. It just moves the same one square forward or to the right or left—or, at most, two squares, repeating this over and over again. But every person who enters this world, benefits from the experience of all the human beings who lived before— from the discoveries, medicines, the clothing we wear and thousands and thousands of other things that, had it not been for previous generations, going on living would be completely without meaning. We are really like the players who move the pieces in the game, who if we are wise—and, unfortunately, most times we aren't—benefit from experience."

"Of course, there is another way to look at the issue you have raised, my towering lookout. Even if we are pawns—which we are not—you should know only this: the most effective piece on the chessboard is the queen. The queen has absolute authority in the game. Now, if those eight pawns—or, as the Engineer says, those miserable victims of destiny—combine forces so that one of them makes it to the other end of the board, he becomes a queen. At that point, the play changes totally."

"I don't follow."

"Very well! It doesn't matter."

"...Really, it doesn't matter?"

"No, I was just kidding. Son! It's actually the opposite! It's important that you know. Do you know what the issue is? I'll try to explain it in another way. Consider the idea that God made the world like a building with seven stories; but He didn't make it so that we humans would just lounge around in the building. Rather, the plan was that we would build an eighth story on our own. Understand? We mustn't waste our time staying on one particular story; we have to keep climbing higher and higher..."

"Why did God pull a fast one? What was the point of whispering the Exalted Name only to Adam?"

With that faint smile of his, something between mockery and affection, Qasem patted me on the head and said, "These things are all allegorical. God didn't whisper into anybody's ear or anything like it. He gave us the Exalted Name only so we would borrow some of His will from Him. It's just like the land, which borrows the light of the sun—the more of your own capability and power you exert on it, the more you make use of the sunlight. In this way, humans are the successors to God in the world of existence. But instead of acting, we mortals justify our own laziness with cheap philosophy—things like "predetermination," "pawns of fate,"—when, in fact, destiny is like a wall that is about to collapse. We exercise our wills to avoid being under it; the wall will definitely come down, but there is no reason that we have to be under it when a bomb goes off."

"I still don't follow."

"And it's still not important. Just think of it this way; tonight we stood shoulder to shoulder trying to defeat that invisible radar, which is like the enemy's queen. As a practical experience that was enough for you. You got it, son?"

I was a little calmer, and this was more important than anything. Bawling like that had completely shattered my self-confidence. I had gotten bits and pieces of what Qasem had said, though I still didn't know how to play chess, something I should have done. But now that I was back to my old self, I had some unfinished business to do.

"Mr. Qasem! Could we go back inside for a moment? There's something I have to do."

He helped me to my feet. I leaned my hand against the wall. Noticing this, Hovanes and the Father came toward me. I held out my arms to them.

"I wanted to say goodbye to you—for the second time, I guess."

The old priest squeezed my hand affectionately and began to say strange words under his breath again. Hovanes explained, "The Father is praying for your well-being." Then he said, "I shall never forget the events of tonight. There are a number of priests in South America that think as you do."

"Just one thing!"

"Yes, my friend!"

"You don't have to build a holocaust memorial for us anymore. We're better off without it." They both laughed.

Geety was sitting with the child's head cradled in her lap. The Engineer was carrying the radio, weapon, and binoculars out to Qasem, but then he turned and walked back to me.

He said, "Okay, it looks like this is really the time to say goodbye!" and then hugged me. As he let me go, I felt my eyes welling with tears.

"You were a real pain to me, but you brought a little change to this miserable existence. Even so, you lied to me about your comrades' mission."

"No, I told you the truth."

"You told the truth?"

"Yeah. Don't you hear the sounds of explosions?"

"So?"

"Those are the sounds of the Bridge blowing up! Those two went to the other side to destroy it. But at the last moment the plan was changed; it was decided not to involve God at all. We figured that, if God were to leave this world, there would be a fight about who would take His place and that would end up making thousands of gods. The present infiltration to blow up the Bridge is enough of a warning. From now on they'll be looking at us humans from up there in a different way—maybe even show us a little respect! Don't you think so, my dear Engineer?"

He looked me up and down doubtfully.

"Don't worry! Tomorrow night they'll be a couple more paying customers...!"

I immediately held my tongue; it had only been a few minutes since I spoke to Qasem about talking too much.

"What about tomorrow?"

"Nothing! Just that from tomorrow on, Javad's father will be bringing you your food. By the way, you never said what is the meaning of 'what'."

"'What' means HEARTACHE!   Means AGONY!   Means SCREWED UP!"

We both laughed. The Engineer noticed Geety.

"Geety! The boy is leaving. Don't you want to say good-bye?"

She laid the little girl's head on the ground and walked toward me. The Engineer stood there uncertainly.

"You go over there! GO!"

The Engineer walked away dejectedly. After making sure he was gone, Geety said, "Javad's mother invited me and the child to come stay with her in the grove. She says with Javad's father gone, she's all alone."

I breathed a sigh of relief. It was as if a large burden had been lifted from my shoulders.

"I don't know whether to go with the child or not."

"Definitely go! Definitely! And if there's anything you need, just let me know and I'll get it for you."

"No. Many thanks. I have just one question."

"What's that?"

"I'm ashamed to ask!" She began toying with the burnt bricks. She was suddenly strangely bashful and with her head down she asked, "Up there...why did you call me 'mother'?"

I hesitated. Why did I say that? Why? I didn't even know myself. "Because...I missed my own mother. That's all!"

"Thank you! I hope to God you never change."

Javad's mother was still asleep. "Javad's father gave her a sleeping pill for the pains in her leg," Qasem explained. "He'll return for her tomorrow. Stand up so we can get you to the infirmary. They'll shoot you full of antibiotics and you'll be right as rain again."

We left the building. I looked back; it was still dark but I could see the light coming from the flames. Despite all the fatigue, I managed to step lively and enjoyed the walk. The seven-story building in front of me now seemed seedy. I felt like a mountain climber who has just reached the top. The radar had been defeated, and I was now sitting in Parveez's food truck—this time not as the driver. My days ladling out food from a cauldron were over, and I felt like sleeping for years and waking up to find that all this had been a dream.

Javad's father put the truck in gear and we were off, with Qasem following us on Ameer's motorcycle. The van rocked back and forth like a cradle. Despite the thick clouds and smoke, the stars could be seen twinkling in the sky. I automatically blinked back at them and then placed my arm against the door to use it as a pillow.

The grooved rebar, the ice cream clouded with frost, Geety, the Engineer, the destruction of the Bridge to the Afterlife, the pawns that became queens, the two priests, the holocaust memorial, the artillery shells, and everything and everyone...slowly, slowly...began to fade and nearly disappear before my eyes...

Oh no: there was Parveez's voice again! Don't tell me that the pigeon-keeper has come back to mock me, "The Major's jeep! In your dreams, shithead! See where it got you? They bent the rules to let you be the driver's helper on a chow wagon! Turd! Tomorrow's ice cream day! ICE CREAM...!"

Postscript

It was, perhaps, ten years later that what had happened that night was cleared up once and for all. They located a document that only the boys in the dugout could have appreciated and understood completely. It was just like thousands of other documents found among the ruins of enemy strongholds during the eight-year war and translated from Arabic.

TOP SECRET

11-5-1980

To: Seventh Army Command.
From: Battalion 3 Cymbeline Radar System, Type 111 Stationed in the Sibah Region, Shatt al-Arab.
Re: Results of testing the aforementioned radar.

This is to inform High Command that the results of field tests of the European-made Cymbeline Radar System are as follows:

1. The System performs so accurately in desert and mountainous regions that locating all artillery batteries and mortars positioned in the Muhammarah protective desert area is possible.

2. In the urban region of Abadan, however, the System encountered errors to an astonishing distance of about 300 meters, which the advisors were not able to rectify. It is possible that the existence of buildings in urban areas had a completely negative effect on radar function.

Conclusion:

Considering the large sums required for such highly advanced military equipment, it is recommended that, absent the expression of convincing explanations from the manufacturer and the elimination of faults, the purchase and use of said systems be avoided.

Battalion 3 Radar System Commander,
Colonel Maher Hamood

Cc: To the attention of all Radar Battalions 1-6 for necessary action.

About the Author

Habib Ahmadzadeh is a veteran of the Iran-Iraq War, whose military career began when he served as a teenage Basiji and ended after he attained the rank of Captain in the regular army. He has studied theatre arts and is an accomplished scenarist. Ahmadzadeh is also the author of a prize-winning collection of short stories called *The War Involved City Stories* (Dastan-ha-ye Shahr-e Jangi), one of which became the basis for the film "Night Bus" (Autobus-e Shabaneh; directed in 2007 by the well-known film and television artist Kiumars Poorahmad). Ahmadzadeh also provided the research for "Conversation with the Shadow" (*Goft-o Goo ba Sayeh*), directed in 2006 by Khosrow Sinai, a study of one of Iran's greatest writers Sadeq Hedayat (d. 1951). Part biography, part literary criticism, the film is an original contribution to the voluminous literature on Hedayat's most important work of fiction *The Blind Owl* (Buf-e Kur).

About the Translator

Paul Sprachman is Vice Director of the Center for Middle Eastern Studies at Rutgers University. He has worked and studied in Afghanistan and Iran. He is the translator of a number of works from Persian including Jalal Al-e Ahmad's *Plagued by the West, A Man of Many Worlds: The Diaries and Memoirs of Dr. Ghasem Ghani*, and *Journey to Heading 270 Degrees*, by Ahmad Dehqan. He is also the author of *Suppressed Persian: An Anthology of Forbidden Literature*, and *Language and Culture in Persian*.

Cover Art

The painter Gizella Varga Sinai (b. 1944 in Hungary) is responsible for the art on the cover. She writes: "This painting is an image from my childhood memories. My childhood and Christmas! These are the dreams of my father and mother, who had hopes of a better life in Hungary after World War II. These hopes have been with me all my life. Now there is war again. Near my home there are the sounds of explosions; the windows rattle; flames shoot into the air and people flee.... And I—my heart throbbing—wonder: Will my little angels return home from school safely and sound?" [Back cover of the second Persian edition, Tehran: Sureh-ye Mehr, 2006]